CASANEGRA

CASANEGRA

A Tennyson Hardwick Story

BLAIR UNDERWOOD

WITH TANANARIVE DUE AND STEVEN BARNES

ATRIA BOOKS

New York London Toronto Sydney

ATRIA BOOKS
1230 Avenue of the Americas
New York, NY 10020

Library of Congress Cataloging-in-Publication Data
Underwood, Blair.
  Casanegra : a Tennyson Hardwick story / Blair Underwood, Tananarive Due
and Steven Barnes. —1st Atria Books hardcover ed.
     p. cm.
  1. Actors—Fiction. 2. Private investigators—Fiction. 3. Hollywood (Los
Angeles, Calif.)—Fiction. I. Due, Tananarive, 1966–   II. Barnes, Steven.
III. Title.

  PS3621.N383C37 2007
  813'.6—dc22

                                                              2006101281

ISBN-13: 978-0-7432-8731-9 (alk. paper)
ISBN-10:   0-7432-8731-2 (alk. paper)

First Atria Books hardcover edition July 2007

Designed by Joel Avirom, Jason Snyder, and Meghan Day Healey

10 9 8 7 6 5 4 3 2 1

ATRIA BOOKS is a trademark of Simon & Schuster, Inc.

Manufactured in the United States of America

For information about special discounts for bulk purchases,
please contact Simon & Schuster Special Sales at
1-800-456-6798 or business@simonandschuster.com.

For Sidney

Who are you, really?
And what were you before?

—Rick, *Casablanca*

CASANEGRA

ONE

HERE'S WHAT YOU NEED TO KNOW: I hate lines. That's the only reason I stopped by Roscoe's that day. I would explain this to the guys from Robbery-Homicide, not that LAPD ever believes a word I say. But it's the truth.

Any other day, if I had swung by Roscoe's Chicken N' Waffles on Gower and Sunset, there would have been customers waiting in the plastic chairs lining the sidewalk, hoping for a table inside, out of the sun's reach. Me, I would have driven straight by. I love Roscoe's, but what did I just say? I hate lines. Lines are an occupational hazard for actors looking for work, so I *seriously* hate lines on my days off. Maybe it was because it was ten-forty-five on a Monday morning—too late for breakfast and too early for lunch—but the sidewalk outside Roscoe's was empty, so I pulled over to grab some food.

Chance. Happenstance. Karma. Whatever you call it, I walked in by accident.

As anybody in this town knows, some people give off a magnetic field. A few lucky ones have it naturally; and some, like me, have worked on it over time. A certain walk, the right clothes, a strategic combination of aloofness and familiarity. When I walk into a room, strangers' eyes fix on me like a calculus problem they can't solve: *I know you from somewhere. You must be somebody, what's-his-name on TV, or Whozit, from that movie that just came out.* Being noticed has always been an important part of my work—hell, half the people in L.A. moved here hoping to refine the art of being noticed, with no cost too high. By now, it's second nature. Customers looked up from their plates and lowered their voices when I walked into Roscoe's.

Later, half a dozen people would describe me down to the shoes I was wearing: white suede Bruno Magli loafers. Bone-colored light ribbed sweater. White linen pants. Gucci shades. Any cop knows that if you ask six people for a description, you get six different stories. Not this time. One seventy-six-year-old grandmother at a table in the back had the nerve to tell the cops, "I don't think he was wearing anything under those tight white pants." I'm not lying. And she was right. They noticed me, down to religious preference.

But as I walked through the door of Roscoe's, I tripped over someone else's magnetic field. The air in that place was crackling, electrified. It made the hair on my neck and arms stand up. Remember that scene in *Pulp Fiction* when those two small-timers tried to hold up a diner, not knowing the customers included Samuel L. Jackson and John Travolta, stone-cold killers there for a quick breakfast after blowing away three dumb-ass kids? Well, either somebody was about to hold up Roscoe's at gunpoint, or someone close to royalty was eating there. Had to be one or the other.

"Hey, Ten," Gabe said, nodding at me from behind the cash register.

"Everything cool, man?"

"Cool as a Monday's gonna be." Gabe looked busy, counting the dollar bills from his cash drawer with meaty fingers. Gabe was a short, fleshy brother with worried eyes and a low BS quotient. He wouldn't tolerate a holdup without showing something in his face, even if someone had a gun jammed in his back. I tilted my head to scan the tables to see whose magnetic field was trumping mine.

I didn't see Serena at first.

Although there were only six customers in the place and she was sitting alone at the corner table, she fooled my eyes and I looked right past her. All I'd seen was a petite, busty brown-skinned girl with a braided crimson weave and a baggy white track suit, like countless ghetto goddesses I pass every day. If someone had asked me at the time, I wouldn't have recalled her as all that attractive, much less someone I knew. It was her *voice* that gave her away, that raspy, spiced honey that would be unforgettable even if it wasn't one of the best-known voices in the world.

"Oh, so you ain't talkin' today?" she said, a smile peeling from her lips.

There isn't a man alive who could have blinked an eye, taken a breath, or remembered his middle name for at least two seconds after seeing that smile aimed his way. The girl froze me where I stood, my ass hovering six inches above my chair.

Serena Johnston. *Damn.* The girl was a chameleon. Some women need an hour in front of a makeup mirror to make the kind of transformation Serena could make in a blink, just in the slant of her chin and something riveting in her eyes. All of a sudden, she'd gone from nobody I needed to know to a creature like the ones described in longing song lyrics by the great, dead soul singers—all the woman any man could ever need. Her face filled my head with memories of every other inch of her.

The world might know her as Afrodite—the superstar rapper whose first two movies had both scaled the $100 million peak, making her a straight-up movie star, too—but she'd always be Serena to me. Five years ago, the last time I'd seen her, films were just a dream she was chasing the way a freezing man might fan a glowing ember. I knew she'd get it going sooner or later, but nobody could have expected her to rise so fast. I couldn't even take it personally that she hadn't returned either of my phone messages—one to congratulate her on her first blockbuster, the second to give my condolences after the rapper Shareef, a friend of hers, was killed the night of his Staples Center concert soon after the last time I saw her. I knew Serena had known Shareef almost all her life, and he'd started her career, so that must have torn a hole in her heart. She didn't call back either time. A woman that hot was too busy for niceties.

Besides, I figured she was too much like me. The past was the past.

And now here she was. Here *we* were.

Stupid me. I thought it was my lucky day.

I went to Serena's table and leaned over to kiss her cheek, soft as satin. I caught a whiff of sandalwood and jasmine, last night's fragrance. So, the fan rags were right: She wore Christian's Number One. Girlfriend had come a long way. My clothes and watch were worth four hundred dollars more than my bank balance, and this woman could afford damn near two thousand Gs for a bottle of perfume. It's a wonder I could even see Serena beyond the massive chasm that separated our prospects. Being that close to magic made me ache.

"My father raised me not to speak to ladies unless I was spoken to," I said.

A ray of girlishness transformed her smile, and I felt a tug from somewhere new. "No ladies at this table, T."

"So, where's your crew, Big-Time? No assistant? No entourage?"

"T, I'm a big girl. I don't need no babysitter to eat waffles. If you were anybody else, I'd give you a peck and say hey, and then I'd tell you I'm not in the mood for company, so give me a call sometime. But instead, I'm hoping you'll shut up and sit down. Damn, you smell good. But that's not Opium."

"Not anymore," I said. I'd given up all my old fragrances five years ago. All I wore now was Aqua di Gio, leaving the exotic Oriental spices behind. I couldn't wear Opium, Gucci Envy, any of them. There's something about cologne: It can make you a different man. Whenever I went back to my old fragrances, I itched for old habits.

Serena rested her chin on both fists, studying me like I mattered. "How you doin'?" Her eyes said she wanted me to say I was doing fine. Great. Never been better.

"Fine, darlin'. Great. Never better."

"Don't lie to me, T. For real."

Right then, I wanted to tell her about the past month. I could feel the story clawing from my stomach, trying to break free. A bad taste flooded my mouth, and I took the liberty of sipping from her water glass. Serena had never minded sharing. "Everybody goes through changes now and then. You know how it is. You?"

"Fine. Great. Never better."

Two liars, then. Serena's eyes didn't look like they belonged to a woman who owned her own powerhouse production company and had more brokers on her speed-dial than a girl from the Baldwin Hills "Jungle" had any right to fantasize about. I might as well have been staring into my own problems. If I could have, I would have yanked Serena away from whatever was bothering her and taken her to my favorite Maui spot, an out-of-the-way beach where the sun-crisped tourists don't treat locals like their personal valets. Just for a few days. We wouldn't have to say a word. The otherworldly sunsets would have cleansed us beyond anything language could provide.

I'm not the wishing type, but I wish I could have done that for Serena.

"I've got a steady gig," I told her. "Deodorant commercials."

"I thought that was you. What else you got going on?"

"One gig pays the rent, for now. My agent isn't worth shit. You ever heard this joke? An actor comes home and his house has burned to the ground. His wife is bruised up, her dress torn. She sobs, 'Your agent came to the house, he raped me, he killed our children, and he burned up everything we own.' The actor says: 'My *agent* came to the house? What did he say?'"

I'd hoped to win another smile from Serena. I got a smile *and* a laugh.

"I feel you. That's harsh," she said.

"If I can get my agent to call me back two weeks later, hey, it's all good. I must be sentimental, or maybe I'm just too lazy to shop around."

That was only half the story. Blaming your agent is a citywide pastime in Hollywood. If I hadn't scored the Dry Xtreme gig, Len would have given up on me. Before the commercials, I hadn't made him any money in eighteen months. Len could have cut me loose in the nineties, but he never had. We had been together for ten years, longer than his marriage. Len used to think I was going places. On rare occasions, he still believed it.

"You're a lot of things, T, but you ain't lazy. *Or* sentimental."

A lilac business card materialized on the table in front of me. CASANEGRA PRODUCTIONS, read the black embossed script, which I could see was modeled after the script on the *Casablanca* movie poster. Classy. I also recognized the name on the card: Devon Biggs. He was from Serena's old neighborhood, a friend she and Shareef had known since elementary school. Apparently, Biggs was the gatekeeper to her empire.

"Call him *today*. Tell him I told you to call," Serena said.

"Nah, girl. I was just playing. I'm doing fine."

It didn't feel right. Don't get me wrong: I gave up the luxury of pride long ago. But both times I'd met Devon Biggs, back when I was hanging with Serena, he'd looked at me with a combination of pity and scorn that set my teeth on edge. I'd chew my leg off before I called that smug SOB.

"Don't hurt my feelings, T. I've got two or three things popping I could use you for. Speaking parts, too. *Good* parts, and I need someone who can fight. You have to audition, but this is the short line—and I know you hate lines. Talk to Dev."

A snap of her finger, and she could change my life. Maybe it was a combination of my usual insomnia the night before, an empty stomach, and the pile of unpaid bills stuffed in my kitchen drawer, but I wanted to hug Serena like a sister right then. I don't know why the hell I didn't.

There I go, wishing again.

I was down to one of my last cards, since I'd been leaving them all over town. In my hand was the card I was saving for my chance encounter with Steven Spielberg outside of Mel's Drive-In or Spago, but instead I gave it to Serena. Nothing special—just my name, head shot, cell number, and PO box. TENNYSON HARDWICK—ACTOR AT LARGE.

Serena smiled when she saw it. If I'd had more to spare, I would have given her a dozen to coax out that smile again.

"You look like you've got your own stories, Mighty Afrodite."

I knew Serena would never take the bait, but for some reason I gave it a try. Serena lived far behind her eyes, and always had. Sure enough, she only shrugged as if she hadn't heard me.

I was hungry as hell by the time the waitress came to ask what I wanted, but I noticed that Serena's plate was empty and her check was already waiting, so I only ordered coffee. I didn't want Serena to think I expected her to sit while I ate my meal, and I didn't want to be sitting alone at the table when she got up and walked back into her life. I didn't have room for any more empty spaces, not that day.

"How's your dad?" Serena said once the waitress was gone.

I felt my face harden into steel. I wasn't going to talk about my father, especially on an empty stomach. "Same old same old. What's up with your sister?"

I got steel in return. "Same shit, different decade."

Small talk had never been our forte, I remembered.

"Do you know how to use those espresso machines, T?"

"Why? You got some restaurants you're hiring for, too?"

Serena gave me the finger. The gesture would have been coarse from anyone else, but I appreciated how slender her finger was, how smooth the skin, how delicate the pearl coloring on her nail; it seemed more like a bawdy promise. Serena took that same finger and dabbed from a pool of syrup on her plate, then gently kissed the pad clean.

"Because, T, I was thinking . . . somebody I work with gave me one of those machines—a housewarming gift. And it's been sitting up on my kitchen counter for six months because people I came with can't even pronounce 'espresso.' And if you're not too in love with that cup of coffee you just ordered, maybe you could skip it and make yourself a cup at my place. Like a virgin voyage."

It took my mind a second to register that she had just invited me to her place. I expected her to break out into a laugh, to own up to the joke.

She didn't. She was waiting for my answer.

As if a sane man could utter any answer except one.

Gabe could barely contain his smirk as I held the door open for Serena. She walked out into the midmorning sunshine, brightening the day. "You take care, Ten," Gabe said with a wink.

"It's not what you think, man."

But at that moment, I wasn't sure what it was. And I didn't care.

Outside, Serena and I almost ran headfirst into a man who looked like he might have been a linebacker in his younger days; broad from the neck down. Serena's not an inch more than five-foot-two, and in his shadow, she looked like an acorn that had dropped from a tree. The man's smallish eyes were locked on Serena's face. Whether he meant to or not, he was blocking our path.

"*Hey*," the man said, dumbstruck except for the single word.

"I get that a lot," Serena said. "It's not me. We just look alike."

The man raised his pointing finger, his head drooping down so low to the side that it almost rested on his shoulder. "Oh, uh-uh," he said, not fooled. "*Afrodite*. Hey, it's Afrodite!" He was shouting, raising the alarm like it was his civic duty.

Back when I knew Serena, she was still dusting off the asphalt of Crenshaw and Jefferson, taking diction and acting classes in a quest for refinement so Hollywood would see her as more than a famous face with a lucrative demographic. In The Jungle, if someone had stepped up on her like this fool, Afrodite would have cussed him out, then kneed his groin if he didn't take the hint. But not this day. I felt Serena shrink against me as if she thought she could vanish inside the crook of my arm.

Yeah, something was wrong.

"Hey, playa, give us some room," I said. The man had a good four inches on me, but no one would have known that by my eyes. "My lady says you made a mistake."

The man was ten years my senior, probably in his midforties, but he was still thick and solid. I'd much rather negotiate with a two-hundred-thirty-pound man than fight. Wouldn't anybody? But I'd already made up my mind that if he didn't take two steps back to let us by, I was going to break his instep. Something about Serena's trusting weight against me made me feel like taking chances.

A light went out in the man's eyes. I could see that he was a big man who sometimes forgot his size, and he hadn't meant anything by it. He backed up. "My bad. She sure looks like her, though. You got a twin, baby-girl."

I took Serena's hand as she led me down Sunset, where her downy white Escalade was parked at a meter. I knew it from the rear plate: CASANEG. I felt her tiny fingers tremor against mine.

"It's not like the old days, Serena. You need a minder."

"I got one. He's off today."

"Then you need two. You can't be out alone."

As she zapped off her car alarm and the taillights flashed a greeting, Serena looked up at me with irritation and something else that made my stomach queasy. A shadow cut her face in half, and a single brown-green eye, glimmering in the sun, was searching me in a way she never had. "You looking for that job, too?"

"I'm not working today."

"Who said you were, Tennyson?" Hearing her voice wrapped around my Christian name made me remember that my mother had named me for a poet.

A wall of heat rose with her as she stepped onto her Escalade's running board to bring us to eye level. There was only one thing to do: Right there on the street in front of ten other witnesses, I kissed Serena Johnston as though I had the right.

TWO

SERENA COASTED OFF MULHOLLAND past the steep, winding display of Hollywood Hills palaces, stopping at the gate that guarded her own. The ebony placard on a black marble column announced that we had reached the true CASANEGRA.

Like most people raised in the shadow of ostentatious wealth, Serena had always had expensive tastes. I knew this was the house she had hoped would be big enough to make amends for everything that had been missing during the days when she and her mother and sister had slept in the backseat of their Impala. Before I could see a single window through the isolated property's well-groomed stands of jacaranda trees, I knew Casanegra would be a wonder, even to me, and I'm not easily impressed.

Silence had haunted much of our drive, so I wouldn't have learned the story behind Casanegra if Serena hadn't told me back before it was real. Serena never knew her father growing up—lucky girl, in my book—so she built a fantasy around what she thought he was like. One of the few things her mother told her about him was that he had a thing for old-school film classics. *Casablanca. Citizen Kane. On the Waterfront.* It's easy to idolize the parent who isn't around, which I know from experience—my mother died before I was old enough to know her—so Serena started watching those movies, as if she figured they would give her and her old man something to talk about one day. *When my movies were playing, I couldn't hear the noise around me.* Along the way, she fell in love with the actresses. She never figured she would be rapping for long—*I'm just going through the door that's open, T.* She was all about Katharine Hepburn, Dorothy Dandridge, and Diahann Carroll. Visions of legacy danced in her head.

If the Casanegra estate was any proof, Serena's legacy was well underway. The hilltop three-story Spanish-style house was a creamy beige-yellow with a tile roof the color of a wet clay road, like a postcard from the mountains of Granada. I wasn't going to ask how much she paid, but I guessed the eight-million range; still a bargain compared to Beverly Hills. When she unlocked the front double doors, Serena smiled for the first time since Roscoe's. Our soles pattered on the mansion's floors as though we were touring a museum after closing time.

"It was built in 1929. Some movie producer owned it, I forget his name, and he used to throw the bomb parties. Charlie Chaplin would come. Douglas Fairbanks. Mae West. They've all been here." She lowered her voice as if to avoid disturbing the sleep of the guests' spirits. "Twelve thousand square feet, twenty rooms. Six bedrooms, eight bathrooms, and a home theater. God as my witness, I don't think I've spent more than five minutes in most of the rooms, especially upstairs. I live in my office and my studio. But there's a room upstairs where you can still see the mark where they say Bugsy Siegel put someone's head through the wall. And somebody's kid drowned in the pool in the 1940s. Studios hushed it up."

Serena paused in the upstairs hall, dusting her fingers gently across the wall. She chuckled, shaking her head.

"What?"

"I was just thinking, T . . . I paid cash for this house, but I don't own it. Nobody can own anything that'll still be standing fifty years after you're dead."

That was it, I realized. I couldn't fault Casanegra's sheer space, the sheen on the dark-stained hardwood, and the lushness of her potted eight-foot palm trees. But the house was all eggshell white walls, floor-length windows, and yawning floors. There were framed movie posters—most of them classic, except French-language posters for her two movies, *Gardez-le Réel* (*Keep it Real*) and *Monsieur Rien* (*Mister Nothing*)—but there wasn't much in sight to tell me that Serena Johnston lived here. My house was the same way.

My stomach growled loud enough for her to hear. It practically echoed. Serena tugged the back of my sweater. "You know what? All the rooms up here look alike. Let's go to the kitchen. You figure out that espresso machine, and I'll fix you a plate. I had a party Saturday, so there's enough jerk chicken wings and blackened catfish to eat all night long."

"You always had a way with words, darlin'."

I was glad to take a detour to the safe stainless steel and black granite of her spacious chef's kitchen, and not only because I was starving. Sooner or later, her bedroom would have appeared on the upstairs tour, and I wasn't ready to go there. I'm not shy in the bedroom. But my memory kept gnawing over how Serena melted against me when we bumped into that stranger on Sunset, that shiver in her hand, and I knew that once our clothes started coming off, I could forget about conversation. That was how it had always been. I thought about lying, saying I had a girlfriend to keep her at a distance long enough to coax something out of her. But I'd have an easier time convincing her I could levitate. We might not know each other anymore, but she knew me far too well for that. I hadn't had a true girlfriend since high school.

Maybe not even then.

The espresso machine perched on the corner of her counter was a beauty, a top-of-the-line Krups pump, but whoever gave it to Serena must have been crazy. Fifteen hundred bucks, and she'd never touched the thing. Espresso can be tricky to make, especially with a pump instead of a steam machine, and not everybody wants a Starbucks in their kitchen. Obviously, the people in Serena's circles had money to burn.

I went to work grinding beans and filtering water while she dug inside the refrigerator closest to me—there were two, both with massive silver doors—and piled a plate with food. It was a strange feeling, standing there with our elbows brushing in the kitchen. I felt like I belonged there, a new sensation for me. And a dangerous one. Maybe her bedroom might have been safer after all.

"My father just had a stroke," I said, once the brown foam was flowing. No need to mention his heart attack three years ago. It was all the same story.

Serena gasped. "That's awful. Is he all right?"

"He's alive." No, Dad wasn't all right, but I'd only brought it up so we could trade tragedies. I'd told her mine, and now maybe she would tell me hers. I was considering moving Dad in with me, taking him out of the zoo where he'd been caged the past month, but I didn't want to get into that.

"Oh, God. I know that must be hard," she said.

"It's interesting."

"'May you live in interesting times.' Isn't that a Chinese saying, or something?"

"A curse, actually. You look like you're living in some interesting times, too."

"More every day." I waited for her mask to fix itself back in place, but she was having trouble with it this time. Too much of her hurt was shining through. "It shouldn't surprise me, but it does. There's always somebody trying to pull you down."

"If you let them. That's one choice—but there's another."

She looked up at me suddenly, her eyes almost accusatory. *Who told you my business?* Then she turned back to the microwave, where she was about to heat my jerk chicken wings back to life. By purest accident, I'd said something of significance.

"You got a boyfriend giving you trouble, Serena?"

Her eyes narrowed to slits. "Shoot, I ain't lettin' no man stay around long enough to give me trouble. That hasn't changed, T."

I was glad I'd never been in love with her, or that would have stung. It almost smarted on principle alone, on behalf of every brother I'd never met. Serena's music wasn't kind to the male of the species. A line from one of her songs popped into my head: *Were your words just words, or maybe a game? / Is w-w-w-dot-Dog your domain name?*

"Something's changed, though."

"Nothing you can help me with."

Instead of probing for another dead-end, I sighed. "I'm moving Dad in with me this week." I'd never said the words aloud. Suddenly, my decision was made.

That seemed to shock her more than the stroke. This time, she cupped my elbow in the soft of her palm. She let out a soft humming sound. A grieved breath.

"We don't get to do what we want," I said. "We do what we have to do."

Yes, Serena's eyes said, wide with private enlightenment. She looked up at me as if I was a winged seraph visiting her in human form.

She never said what her trouble was, but I think she had made her decision, too.

The first time Serena Johnston saw me nude, I couldn't get it up.

Tennyson Hardwick. Ten for short—OK, more like eight-and-a-half, but close enough. My name was a prophecy, as if my parents knew my future from birth.

Part of it was my face—the Face emerged from baby-fat when I was ten years old, smooth and sharp in all the right places. Despite a few scrapes and bruises, the Face only improved with age, like peaking wine. The Face stopped strangers in their tracks and made grown women felonious. When I was thirteen, my junior high school drama teacher seduced me in her pool after school; so all things considered, I have to count Ms. Jackson as my favorite teacher. When zit-infested classmates bemoaned their invisibility to the female gender, they were speaking an alien tongue.

Once I realized the power of the Face, my demeanor did the rest. No one ever thought of me as a child again, least of all me. I can wonder how my life would have been different without Ms. Jackson, but since I don't have a time machine yet, there's no point in trying to take myself back. Sex had never been a problem for me, even before I knew I wanted it.

Except that night in the suite of the Four Seasons Hotel with rapper Afrodite, when she was ready to see what there was beyond my face. To see if Ten Hardwick lived up to his porn-perfect name. And at that moment, my qualifications lay lifeless across my thigh.

I was twenty-seven and speechless. All I could do was blink and stammer. "Sometimes I bug out before a show," she said. "Performance pressure."

I blinked some more, and a three-alarm fire scorched my face. If I had been anybody else and she had been anybody else, I could have laughed and played it off, enlisting the tongue tricks I first practiced with Ms. Jackson. But I was *Ten Hardwick*, and this was *Afrodite*. Sweat appeared on my upper lip. All sanity had left the world. It was a genuine existential crisis, reinforced by all of my father's predictions about how I'd never turn out to be shit. *If I can't . . . CAN'T . . .*

When she reached for my limpness, my stammering became an apology. But Serena grabbed me, a gentle clasp. "Hey, baby, just sit still," she said. Then, she bent over me and practiced a few tongue tricks of her own. Problem solved.

They say you never forget your first. In a way, Serena Johnston was mine.

Serena's master bedroom at Casanegra was bigger than the Four Seasons suite, with a balcony overlooking the city and a California King bed big enough for a family. Her walls were bare except for one of her concert posters. More striking emptiness. More of her absence. But she didn't walk me out to the balcony or show off what was sure to be a luxurious master bath. Instead, she climbed out of her clothes, and I followed her lead. Except for that first time, we were always most comfortable when we were naked together, the way most people feel when they put their clothes back on.

I couldn't see any signs of the past five years on Serena's delicious little body. She was petite but thick-muscled, with strong arms and shoulders, and a luscious C-cup to give shade to a waistline that spread out into smooth, ample hips. Her ass was solid enough to knock someone unconscious. She'd had a bikini wax, the Brazilian kind, so she was as bare as a woman could get. The sight of her was pure privilege.

"*Damn*," she said, stealing the word from my mind. "You look good, T."

No repeat history this time. I'd been ready for her as soon as we started climbing the stairs. I was so hard, I plowed into the soft of her belly when I pulled her close to me. I kissed her, massaging her arms from the shoulders down to the wrists. Our tongues wrestled before I sucked her, syrup-sweet, into my mouth. She surrendered.

"You remember what I want," I said.

With a smile, Serena sat at the edge of her bed. Like a dancer, she raised her bare leg, delicately angling her soft, tiny foot toward me. I lowered myself to my knees, kneading her heel and sole. Heaven. Serena's feet felt as if she'd never walked a day barefoot. Her toes beckoned me, wiggling. Holding my prize with both hands, I slipped her toes into my mouth and nestled my tongue between them, sucking. Even Serena's foot was sweet. I'm a foot man. I can suck on pretty toes from dawn until dusk.

"Ooh, you're still freaky, T."

First, the appetizer. Next, dessert.

"Spread your legs," I said.

Every woman tastes different, and men are lying if they say every flavor is good. But Serena had always been like candy, a combination of sweet and tart. Spiced honey, like her voice. Her thighs seemed to guard her honey jar at first, but after my tongue's first few flicks, I felt those hard muscles relax. Her knees gave a tremor, but not like the tremor outside Roscoe's. This was the good kind.

My ears brushed her thighs as my tongue bathed her, licking wide at first, then with precise darts to nudge open the warm folds of her skin. I flurried until I felt the first bath of her juices. Serena's fingernails became claws across my shoulders.

"Oh, shit, shit, *shit* . . ." she hissed.

Guys, let me school you on head: Do not treat a clitoris like someone would treat your penis. It's the most sensitive place on a woman—probably on the human body, period—and it doesn't need yanking or bullying. It's a snail in a shell that needs a little coaxing to swell and stick its head out. There is no end to its shudders, given the right tending. I've turned women on until they can't walk right, as if they're carrying a grapefruit between their legs. Unlocking a woman's passion is like cracking a safe. When I feel that responsiveness budding—when her hips begin to buck and my chin is drenched—I don't let it go. I go back to the same spots, again and again. There's an invisible alphabet down there, and all I have to do is spell her name with the tip of my tongue. S-E-R-E-N-A.

Serena's thigh muscles locked across my ears when she let out her first shriek, muffling the sound. *That's one,* I thought. If I couldn't get half a dozen screams out of Serena before we got down to business, I was doing something wrong.

"Wait," she said. "It's my turn."

Except for that first time, Serena had never gone down on me. I figured she was one of those women who will give head only when obligated, but I was wrong. After I lay beside her, she nuzzled my orbs with her tongue, taking her time as she savored one and then the other, weighing me in her mouth. Then, the moist tip of her tongue teased its way upward, following the trail of a swollen vein. Sparks shot through me, and my back arched. Her lips came next, fleshy and wet, the entrance to a cavern. I gritted my teeth as I pushed against the softness at the back of her throat. My thoughts swam. Her mouth pulled slowly back, her tongue wrapping me in a slow circle as she retreated. Then, she drew me inside her throat again, locking me tight in her mouth's urgent caress. The glow under my navel surged, coiled and ready.

I don't make noise in bed—I pride myself on it, unless it's for show—but Serena's mouth made me groan, sigh, and groan again. Each new stroke was a surprise, with exact repetition where it mattered and enough variation to keep my tide rising. Maybe she was spelling out my name, too. Maybe she was growling my name, and her throat's subsonic trembling transmitted a message directly to my spine, bypassing my thinking centers altogether.

Gently, I rested my hand on top of her mussed hair. "You better stop," I said.

She gave me a lusty grin. "You sure?" she said, her lips bobbing against me like a dog unwilling to let go of a meaty bone.

"I want to be inside you," I said.

Standard dialogue in my script, but this time the words surfaced on their own. I *did* want to be inside her. The realization startled me. I hadn't felt this hungry for a woman in a long time. I could hardly remember when, unless I thought all the way back to Ms. Jackson's swimming pool, but that memory had a bad smell to it. Not this time. This felt clean.

Serena's hairless skin was so slick, gliding inside her was like discovering an extension of my own flesh, a new limb. Most women feel tight because I'm so thick, but Serena was a different level altogether, cleaving to me with so much pressure that I forgot to breathe. I locked my arms above her, steadying myself, sure to angle my pelvis against her so I was rubbing her naked clitoris, too—but gently, leaving room for it to breathe between strokes. Leaving room for it to grow.

I stared at Serena's face. Her eyes had fallen shut, and all the worry had washed away. Her chin was pointing skyward, anticipating the next current of pleasure. I didn't want to disappoint her, so I pulled back four inches and burrowed into her again. She opened deeper for me this time, welcoming me, and our pelvises locked. I cupped her waist in my palm, positioning our bodies so I would poke the spot deep inside her that would unlock the prize every woman's body kept hidden. *The* spot.

I hit it. Serena cried out, and her body rained gratitude, quivering.

The room was cool, but I was sweating. Perspiration dripped from my nose, washing her breast. I bent my head to suck the moisture away, and her nipple was as big and solid as a marble against my tongue. Serena wrapped her legs around me, her fingernails gliding across my ass, tickling first, then digging harder. She probed with her index finger, playing with the perspiration dripping between my cheeks.

"Yes, Ten . . . Fuck me."

And I did, as long as I could stave off release in her body's merciless embrace. But I wasn't counting her screams, measuring her breaths, or reciting my favorite lines from old television shows. My thoughts were gone. The room was all heat, sweat, motion, and pleasure. I wanted to seep into her skin and get lost in there.

Was this how people felt when they were making love?

"Shit, Ten. Yes, that's it. That's *it.*"

A hurricane roared through me, hot pleasure burning away flesh, bone, thought itself. Then, it was done, almost a foggy memory already. Slowly, sound and sight and sensation returned. Serena nestled on my arm for a time, and maybe we dozed. But the next thing I knew, her eyes were wide open, staring at me as she played with the hair on my chest. Her worry was back.

The light outside was bright. The day had hardly begun.

"I have a lot to do, baby," she whispered. "You know how it is. I'll call you a cab to get you back to your car."

I'll admit it, I was disappointed. I don't know what I expected—or if I expected anything—but I didn't want to go so soon. Still, I knew arguing would be a waste of breath. I've made a home on the other side of that argument, and there's no such thing as winning. Once that door is closed, it's closed.

"Why don't you come back Friday night?" she said.

I didn't want to be as relieved as I was. I didn't *want* to want anything. My head was floating away from me, and I didn't like the feeling.

"We'll see."

"Please? Don't you make me beg."

I nodded. "OK. Friday night. But only if I can cook you dinner."

"I've missed your cooking, T."

I'd almost forgotten that I used to cook for Serena. One of my extras.

So, that was all. I put on my clothes, she called me a cab, and we kissed good-bye at her door, in front of the elaborate fountain and circular driveway on her hilltop estate that had cost more money than I could dream about.

I was in such a good mood, even the cabbie noticed it. He was a hairy, thickset man with a mustache and a Greek name, Micolas. "Life is good, no?" the cabbie said to me in his rearview mirror, hoping to share vicariously in my fortune.

I couldn't help smiling. I had a business card promising some work in my back pocket, a dinner date for Friday night, and a memory worth keeping. "Yeah. Life is good."

I didn't tell him the real reason I was celebrating. I'd just had sex with Serena Johnston, *Afrodite*, and she hadn't paid me for it. Not a cent. She hadn't even slipped me a twenty for cab fare. I was just a man, and she was just a woman. Time was, I would have walked away with an easy ten grand in my pocket after an encounter like that with Serena. My usual fee, on Tennyson Hardwick's infamous sliding scale. Before I quit the game, of course.

Ten grand would take me a long way. Ten grand would pad my bank account, pay some of my father's doctor bills, and stand me upright.

But ten grand was nothing compared to coasting down Mulholland Drive with the prospect of work with my clothes on, and a dinner date on Friday. I left Serena's with a feeling ten grand couldn't buy.

The way I spent the rest of my afternoon would become significant later, so I'll spell it out for the record.

After I left Serena's, I went to a cattle-call audition at Raleigh Studios on Melrose, across the street from the gated kingdom of Paramount. I stood in line for two hours shooting the shit with the brothers with theater degrees, including one I thought I remembered from my classes at the Lee Strasberg Institute. They were complaining about how all the good roles are going to rappers. That audition was a waste of my time, but when my bank account gets low, I try out for roles I'd ordinarily consider beneath me. I guess it shows; I never get callbacks for the most pathetic parts. Three blank stares from the casting table, and a curt "Thank you" halfway through the reading. I hate that shit.

Even though my body and clothes still smelled like Serena, the hours I had spent with her—and the lingering sizzle left by her fingers across my skin—felt like an episode of my own personal *Twilight Zone*, a day from someone else's life. When I got to my silver BMW 325 convertible, which I'd paid cash for back when I could afford to, I put in my first call to Devon Biggs at Casanegra Productions. His chipper assistant took a message and sounded sincere about having him get right back to me, asking for my home *and* mobile numbers. Could Serena have already mentioned my name? That got me smiling again. I could already tell I was going to like the short line.

To celebrate my friendly treatment by an assistant—in this town, you learn to celebrate even the teensiest victories—I decided to splurge and spend ten bucks to see a movie and buy a small popcorn at the Playhouse, a second-run movie theater not too far from where I live in the Hollywood Hills. I saw an old Sonny Chiba martial arts movie, *Sister Streetfighter*, which is really a rip-off, because the Man barely appears in it, and doesn't do his patented psycho–Bruce Lee bit at all. I hang out at the theater almost every weekend, and the guys know me. Later, they would all vouch that I was there between six and eight-thirty. I wish I'd stayed for the double feature, but I didn't. Instead I went home. Alone.

The Friday-night snake of traffic on the one-lane canyon road leading to my house was coiled tighter than usual, so it took me thirty minutes to make a ten-minute drive. By the time I got to 5450 Gleason Street, I was ready to hibernate for the night.

My neighborhood is one of those in the hills with narrow streets, houses stacked on top of each other, and five steps from the curb to the front door. But I love my house. *Love* it. I might not be hooked up like Denzel or Serena, but I have a bomb crib.

The house was designed in a New Mexico adobe-style, with a pale clay façade and very few front windows, a fortress. But that's as far as any consistency goes. The house was originally a sixteen-hundred-square-foot bungalow, but the previous owner added on floors and wings whenever her stocks split, building a five-thousand-square-foot architectural hybrid. Maybe that's what I like best about the house; it's unpredictable, and it isn't always pretty. There's even a small hidden room, just because. It doesn't get any better than *that*.

Being pauper-poor doesn't sting nearly so badly when you can walk through the doors of a home you're not ashamed to claim. My crib is assessed at between $2 and $2.5 million, depending on the day. That's not saying much by Southern California standards, and paying the taxes is a struggle by itself, but Tennyson Hardwick lives well.

Still, that's not the reason I love it so much. A house's soul doesn't rest in how it looks or how much it cost, but in how it makes you feel. Just like Luther (rest his soul) said in his song, *A house is not a home.* But mine is. Maybe it's the first home I've ever had.

That's why it pissed me off so much that my father had never come to visit me—sight unseen, he decided the house was the result of "ill-gotten gains." Yes, that's really how he talks. Hell, maybe he was right. But although some people may consider it ill-gotten that I started out as a house-sitter and never paid a cent to buy it, 5450 Gleason Street had been mine free and clear for four years.

The mailbox was overflowing, but I didn't bother checking it. Nothing but junk. I lived without a permanent address for so long that I never took up the habit of receiving mail at the house. Anyone who needed to find me could use the PO Box listed on my card, the same one I'd had for a decade. I like the idea that most people don't know where to find me.

My short walkway is flanked by cactuses, which, like me, don't invite touching and don't need a lot of fussing and tending.

Anyone who's determined can look up the old real estate records, but I don't divulge the name of the previous owner. I have my faults, but lack of discretion isn't one of them. Let's call her Alice. I met Alice a long time ago, toward the end of her career and the beginning of mine, soon after I met Serena. Alice was an actress; not the kind whose name and face got her good tables or invitations to preen on red carpets, but she worked steady for thirty-five years and survived Hollywood, which makes her a hero in my book. Like her house, she made it through all the earthquakes. Alice was older when she sought me out because she had an ego and her pride to maintain, and most men can't see that a woman's eyes are her most beautiful feature. At sixty, Alice's hypnotic eyes fluttered like she was twenty-five, with thick lashes and a playful gleam. She was still a knockout, her Bikram yoga-toned body stubbornly refusing to sag and wither in the places you might expect. But when I think of Alice, I remember her eyes.

The front doorway is barely six feet high, custom-built to suit Alice's tiny five-foot frame, but I haven't changed it even though the top of my head brushes it when I walk through. And if I had to guess how much of everything in the house is Alice's and how much is mine, it's probably seventy-thirty Alice. Maybe eighty-twenty. She's everywhere.

Sometimes I feel like I'm still house-sitting for her while she's off on another adventure to Rome or Cairo, and her weathered voice will surprise me on the other end of a telephone one day: *"Well, dear heart, I don't know how you expect me to drink this cheap Chianti without your perfectly beautiful face to help me wash it down. It's so thoughtless of you not to have surprised me at my hotel by now. But I trust you're keeping an eye on the place and sleeping in my bed alone. I'll be heartbroken if I come back and I find you've soiled my sheets with a stranger. You know I'm old-fashioned that way, sugar."* I can still hear Alice in my head.

I hadn't seen Alice in two years when a certified letter told me that pneumonia had silenced that husky voice, leaving me her house and everything in it. Alice doesn't live here anymore, but at the same time she always will. Most actresses have pictures of themselves prominently displayed everywhere, but Alice never did. I had to hunt to find any pictures of her, and the only one I found was from her run in *Raisin in the Sun* on Broadway in the 1960s, the performance she told me she was most proud of. She was more handsome than pretty; stocky, with smooth skin, a strong jaw, and those unchanged eyes. I keep that picture on my bedroom nightstand, and a curious visitor might ask me one day if the fiery woman in the picture is my mother. That was a common misconception when we traveled together, and it always made Alice peal with bad-girl laughter.

The rest of the house is crammed ceiling to floor with kitsch and show-business memorabilia, every inch covered with the footprints of successful careers. Alice was a race woman, so she rescued mammy dolls and old-school advertisements featuring fat-lipped coons whenever she found them in antique stores—"That's a part of our history, too, honey," she always said—but most of her shrine was to the people who followed her path beneath the stage lights. In the foyer, she hung her most precious possessions: signed movie posters from *A Raisin in the Sun, Guess Who's Coming to Dinner,* and *In the Heat of the Night.* Alice was a huge Poitier fan—but then again, who wasn't?

In the living room, there's a three-sheet of Lena Horne from *The Bronze Venus,* a five-sheet of Dorothy Dandridge in *Carmen Jones,* and a cool poster for a movie I've never seen, *The Decks Ran Red,* with Dandridge and James Mason. "The true story of one girl on a crime ship!" it screams, over the image of a white sailor pawing at a beautiful woman. The woman looks pretty white, but I figure the studio execs were just keeping their race cards close to their narrow little chests.

I would need a catalogue to keep track of the posters, dolls, figurines, photographs, and movie programs that make up the treasure stashed inside 5450 Gleason. I keep promising myself I'll start compiling one on a rainy afternoon.

That night, when I walked into my house, I thought, *Serena would love my crib.*

I never have visitors in my house, but suddenly I wanted to bring one.

At ten o'clock, after I ate the last of the paella I'd made over the weekend, I sat in the family room sipping a Corona. The platinum-gold lights of the San Fernando Valley streamed through my picture window while Sarah Vaughn sang on a crackling LP from Alice's collection. I remember wondering what Serena Johnston was doing that very moment. I used to wonder the same thing about Alice across the sea.

Something floating in the wall-wide tropical tank beneath a *Harlem Rides the Range* poster caught my eye. I walked over to the tank, and in the bluish light saw two corpses: a neon and a tetra, bobbing in the filter bubbles. *Damn*, I thought, fishing them out with the little wire net. When I was house-sitting for Alice, I'd been great with the fish. Now that they were mine, they died off like summer sitcoms.

Burial at sea, then a return to my paella, which had cooled off and lost its flavor.

I couldn't have picked a worse night to be alone.

THREE

HOPE REHABILITATION Center in West Covina wasn't a hospital, with occasional curing to break up the monotony of misery; and it wasn't a hospice, where the business of dying is up-front. Hope was a collection of beds in closet-sized rooms for people who weren't likely to get better, whether they knew it or not. Whether they were *capable* of knowing or not. And that's where Dad had been sent after his stroke, to undergo physical therapy and lie in bed for endless hours to think about how much he hated what was left of his life.

On Tuesday, the day after Serena reappeared, I went to see Dad. The visits had started out daily, but by now they were stretching to every third day. Dad's roster of retired LAPD buddies who dropped by to see him had shrunk fast after the first two weeks, so I knew I was the only visitor he was likely to get. Even with the bonus that Dad couldn't mouth off at me—at least not yet—those visits were rough. I loaded up on Excedrin just to walk through Hope's automatic doors.

I once worked for an A-list actress with two Pomeranians, and she used to send me with them to the vet whenever they got a sniffle or snagged a nail. Let's just say that the staff at Wilshire Veterinary gave more of a collective shit about the welfare of Fluffy the cat or Tweetie the canary than I'd been able to detect from most of the staff at Hope Rehabilitation Center. They're not bad people; just overworked, underpaid, and unwilling to invest themselves in a bunch of old people who would be dead by Christmas. I know there are better facilities out there, but this wasn't one of them.

There are two systems you want to avoid at all costs: lock-up and long-term medical care. All in all, I'd rather be in jail.

"Good morning, beautiful," I said to Marcela, one of Dad's nurses, as I passed her in the hall. The statement was a lie start to finish—Marcela's mustache was almost as coarse as mine—but I figured a little flirting might keep Dad from being overmedicated or outright forgotten.

"He's doing great today," Marcela said, leering at me with coffee-stained teeth.

I took that for what it was worth. Dad's first roommate was "doing great" the day before he died, or so they told his daughter. The place is called Hope, after all.

I stopped in front of Dad's door, room 106, and bowed my head with my ritual silent prayer that I would wake up from this nightmare. Then, I went inside.

Richard Allen Hardwick was alone in his semiprivate room, having outlived two roommates in fifteen days. His walls were the color of old oatmeal, and his television set was perpetually set to *Judge Judy* or anybody else with a black robe and a gavel. His only joy anymore was in the dispensing of justice, even trite justice. The remote control never left his clawlike hand, and his King James Bible on the nightstand was always open to the Book of Proverbs. The only things that changed were whether he was asleep or awake, whether he smelled like piss or didn't, whether he looked at me or pretended I wasn't there. I think Dad resented my coming by as much as I resented being there.

But what could we do? We were all we had.

"How's the therapy going?"

Dad didn't blink, hanging on Judge Judy's every word. He *could* talk if he wanted to, because I heard him spit out a few vulgarities at an orderly two weeks after his stroke. But his words were slurred, and the sound of his voice horrified him. I can't say I blamed him, but the nurses told me his speech wouldn't improve if he didn't practice.

During my father's willful silence, I studied his face and tried to remember what he used to look like. At seventy-five, his hale cheeks were deflated. His once-strong brow sagged with wrinkles, and the whites of his eyes were vein-webbed and yellowish. Somewhere in that drooping face resided the man who had retired as one of LAPD's most decorated police captains—and he could have made chief somewhere else, if he'd been willing to leave LAPD politics behind. He had overseen more than three hundred men, had been responsible for more than seventeen square miles. Somewhere in that bed was the man who used to scare the hell out of me, and who might have kept me in line if he'd ever been at home.

Dad and I always had our problems—if someone had told him he'd have to raise his son alone, he'd rather I'd never come along, and we both knew it. Some people aren't meant to raise children. For the record, I was a smart-assed, impossible kid who wanted no part of Dad's disciplined way of life. But despite our differences, we might have been able to overlook them all if I hadn't been locked up in '99, booked at the *Hollywood* precinct no less, his old command.

It's a long story. Dad and I were running out of time to recover from that.

I watched TV with Dad a while, which was how I spent most of my visits. Sometimes it was almost painless. An hour, an hour and a half, and I could escape back to the world of people walking around on two legs—*the temporarily abled*, as Dad's physical therapist liked to call us. Once I walked out of the doors, I could forget that Hope's dour halls were killing my father. The stroke had only started the job.

But that day's visit was going to be different. I'd made my decision, even if it took me a half-hour to actually say it. I was hoping I'd change my mind.

"OK, Dad, this is how it's going to be," I said when the next Verizon commercial came on, and my voice surprised him so much that his eyeballs shot my way. "This week, I'm getting you discharged and you're coming to live with me at my place. Maybe tomorrow. On the days I can't be around, you'll have a nurse. I'm not going to hear any arguments. I won't have you living in this shithole. You deserve better, man."

His eyes went back to the TV. Dad liked to pretend his hearing was worse than it had been before the stroke, but he heard me. His index finger drummed the remote. When the next set of commercials came on, he reached for the pad beside his Bible.

He scrawled something with his left hand and tossed the pad my way. It took me a while to make out the words, since his writing was worse than his slur. Unfortunately for him, the stroke had messed up his right side, and he wasn't a lefty.

Can't afford, he'd said. A five-year-old's scribble.

"You let me figure out what I can afford."

Judge Judy ruled in favor of the plaintiff, and Dad changed the channel. Since he didn't write me any other notes, it was settled. I didn't know whether to be sad that he'd given in so easily or glad he was accepting my help.

I felt neither. Pissed was more like it. The situation made me mad as hell. "OK, Dad, I'm out of here. I've got some calls to make."

His eyes never left the TV. We're a Hallmark card, Dad and me.

Still, I felt better leaving Hope Rehab Center than I had on any other visit. It wasn't often that I got to do the right thing. It didn't feel good, but it fit.

Until I got to 5450 Gleason and saw two guys who couldn't be anything except plainclothes LAPD waiting outside my door, I thought I was having a decent day.

Here's the thing about cops: I grew up around them. When my father had a barbecue or wanted to go to the beach, all the guys who came with their wives and kids were cops. In junior high, to make my dad happy, I joined the Future Police Officers' Club. Hell, I got within two weeks of graduating from the police academy, but that's another story from an earlier life. Maybe I didn't really think I'd be driving around in a black-and-white one day—not on the good side of the mesh, anyway—but I know most cops are righteous. I'm not one of those people who secretly jabs cops the finger when one pulls up alongside me, and my foot doesn't jam on the brakes when I see California Highway Patrol. Even after that run-in in '99, when I could have been looking at a long stint behind bars on a bullshit beef, I'm not scared of cops.

And I *knew* the guys waiting there beside my cactus garden, or at least I knew their names. I'm good with names, a leftover skill from my former line of work. The tall, ruddy one was O'Keefe, who'd given such a heartfelt toast at Dad's retirement dinner that I'd felt a sting in my throat, wishing I'd known the guy he was talking about—the guy you could come to with any problem, who always made time for you. The Latino guy with the mustache was called Arnaz, another man I'd met at the dinner, whose name I remembered because of *I Love Lucy*—but believe me, with his stick-thin build and pockmarked face, he looked nothing like Desi. They were both detectives from Hollywood division, where my father had retired as captain after thirty-five years on the force. Practically family.

O'Keefe and Arnaz met me with mournful eyes. I hadn't run into either of these guys at Hope yet, so I figured they didn't have the stomach to see my father. Coming to see me instead was the coward's way out, but I didn't blame them.

"Hey, guys," I said. We all shook hands.

"Tennyson." O'Keefe's voice was hoarse, so he cleared his throat behind his fist. "How's Preach?" That was Dad's nickname. If my father hadn't followed his calling into law enforcement, he would have been a minister. Maybe he always had been.

"Just saw him. Still surly." I stopped short of mentioning that I planned to move Dad in with me, since I wasn't ready for even an unsteady stream of well-wishing cops knocking on my door. I decided to dress up my report with the promise of a happily-ever-after. "He seems to be getting better, though. Bit by bit."

Both of them thanked Mother Mary and the saints and mumbled excuses about why they hadn't made it to see him yet. I reached for my keys to unlock the door, and they stepped aside for me, ready to follow me in. Technically, I *invited* them inside, they could say. I made it easy for the SOBs.

"So . . . is Dad up for another commendation? Somebody naming a youth center after him?" I hoped no sarcasm bled into my voice. I'd already attended two functions on Dad's behalf, and nothing made me feel like a bigger fraud.

The look O'Keefe and Arnaz gave each other as we walked into my living room was my first hint that I'd screwed up. Cold, invisible talons squeezed my temples.

If you don't know already, here's Rule Number One: Never invite a cop inside. Even if they ask with a winning smile, never say, *Sure, officer, come on in.* Or *Sure, officer, take a look inside my glove compartment, knock yourself out.* Not unless they have a warrant. Unfair as it seems, you don't win points for thinking you have nothing to hide. You never know what they're searching for, and you might have something just like it. There is nothing more dangerous than a clear conscience.

I watched the way their eyes studied my family room, and they weren't admiring the décor or Dorothy Dandridge's heart-stopping face. They were *sniffing.* O'Keefe's eyes stayed rooted to the shirt I'd been wearing yesterday, left across my sofa. I could almost hear his brain's neurons firing, making connections.

"Hey, man, what's this about?"

"A body turned up on Sunset this morning," O'Keefe said in a bland voice. "We think it might be someone you know."

"It's probably on the news by now," Arnaz said. "You watch the news, Tennyson?"

"Not if I can help it. Who died?"

While they stood there in a calculated silence considering their strategy, I felt myself *know*. It was like crashing toward a waterfall in a flimsy raft, with nowhere to go but a long, long way down.

"A rapper." O'Keefe said *rapper* like most people would say *cockroach*. "You know a girl named Serena Johnston? She went by the name Afrodite."

Went by. Past tense.

I didn't say anything. Couldn't have if I wanted to. There aren't any good ways to hear about the death of someone you care about, someone you were intimate with so recently you could still smell her mix of sweat and jasmine on your skin, but this way was so wrong it was unholy. My ears rang.

"Yeah, so she's dead, Tennyson." Arnaz might have been trying to sound gentle, but he missed by a mile. He whipped out a notepad. "When did you see her last?"

"Serena's . . . *dead*?" I felt confused, light-headed. Maybe I'd heard wrong.

O'Keefe showed me a crime photo, and my heart cracked in two at the sight of it.

Serena lay open-eyed on a sidewalk, her head nestled by a crumpled Coke can, a black plastic bag pulled across her shoulders like a shawl. Her skin was leeched of color, ashen and gray. Her beautiful lips, so recently loving, cradled bloodied teeth. I had to look away.

I could hear her voice, so vivid she might have been standing behind me: *It shouldn't surprise me, but it does. There's always somebody trying to pull you down.*

"Not a pretty sight," O'Keefe said. "We found her in a plastic bag next to a Dumpster. Split skull. We're guessing blunt trauma to the back of the head." He pulled a small plastic baggie out of his coat pocket and dangled it in front of my nose. Inside, I saw my business card held captive. "This was all she had in her pocket."

"So you can see why we wanted to talk to you," Arnaz said. "Could you tell us when you saw her last?"

I was reeling, dizzy. Bad news and worse news, in the space of a minute. Serena was dead, and the police thought I was wrapped up in it somehow. I hadn't seen Serena in five years, but a room full of people had seen us together the day she died. I felt the ringing in my ears stop, and everything snapped into clarity. I was in trouble.

"I ran into her at Roscoe's Monday, before noon. We exchanged cards."

"Which Roscoe's?" Arnaz said, taking notes.

"Hollywood."

"On Sunset?" Arnaz said, as if he didn't pass Roscoe's on Gower and Sunset a dozen times a day. As if there was another Roscoe's in Hollywood. Instead of answering, I only stared.

O'Keefe gave me a crooked half-smile. "I've seen you in that commercial. You hanging with all the big rappers and movie stars now, Tennyson?"

In my mind, I told these two guys to fuck off and get the hell out of my house. But instead, I heard myself speaking in a dutiful monotone. "We were friends before she hit it big. We knew each other a long time ago."

"And that's it?" Arnaz said. "You ran into your old friend. 'Hey, here's my card.' Then what?"

"Then, nothing. She left, and I left." My first lie, but discretion is a hard habit to break. Remembering Serena's smile in her bedroom, then the horrible photo of her corpse and those bloody teeth, I felt sick to my stomach. "You guys need to go."

"Can we ask the nature of your relationship, Tennyson?" O'Keefe said.

The thin line between love and hate is no joke—Dad's only injuries on patrol were on domestic calls—so you don't want to be the boyfriend or husband of a murdered woman. There's no faster way to be anointed Number One Suspect.

I met O'Keefe's gaze squarely in the gray eyes beneath his hefty brow, trying to find the space where we were just two men talking, like we did at Dad's retirement dinner—two people who loved someone in common. *Hey man, back off. I know you have a job to do, but you just knocked the wind out of me. Give me some time.* "She had some acting work for me. She was a friend who'd made it. I was proud of her. We were supposed to have dinner Friday. I guess I'll never know the nature of our relationship."

It was more than I wanted to say, but the photo of Serena had knocked me off-balance, just as they'd intended. I don't shed tears in front of anyone unless it's for a part, but that day brought me the closest I'd come since I was ten. Only pure will kept my eyes dry. These were not people I could grieve with.

Yeah, so she's dead, Tennyson. Ho-hum. Another dead rapper out with the trash.

Dead is a blunt, ugly word. Dad's stroke was one kind of shock, but I'd been waiting for something to happen to him for years. Serena's death cut harder and deeper. The world lost some of its sheen that day. Even the air tasted different; bitter and sour and heavy, a toxin I wished I didn't have to bother breathing.

O'Keefe backed down, giving me his card in a flash of white. "Call me in the morning, first thing. We need you to come in and talk to us. Maybe you know more than you think you do." Being Preach Hardwick's son won me that much courtesy, at least.

"Every lead helps, Tennyson," Arnaz said, winking. *Just fucking with you, man.*

I nodded.

O'Keefe squeezed my shoulder so hard that it hurt. "We'll get the asshole who did this. Give our best to Preach."

I almost took back my lie right then. Almost told them what was none of their business about Serena and me. Like I said, I grew up around cops. They think lies are like roaches; they see one, and they're convinced they'll uncover a nest of them. Anything else you say is a waste of breath; I learned that from Dad. I wanted to tell the truth.

But Serena was dead. Worse than dead: Somebody had killed her.

All my words were gone.

FOUR

CALL IT PREMONITION, but I couldn't sleep that first night. My mind was running through reels of old footage between me and Serena: the Four Seasons, the MTV Music Awards on South Beach, the Black Film Festival in Acapulco. Serena liked the beach, and so did I; swimming in the ocean is never the same twice. I thought of Serena's nakedness, I won't deny it, but mostly I remembered her smile. Sadness kept me up the first half of that night.

The rest was bone-cold nerves. My heart was at a full gallop.

Life was full of coincidences, but cops don't believe in coincidence. If you're close enough to something wrong, cops figure you've got wrong stuck to the soles of your shoes, so chances are, you're guilty of something. They'll pin this one on you for the ones you've dodged in the past.

O'Keefe and Arnaz knew about '99, and they probably thought I should have done time back then. Thought I'd only gotten off because my father was the precinct captain, one of the department's favorite sons, and I can't deny it. Everyone knows that. As bad as the trumped-up charge against me had sounded then, murder was something else. A murder conviction would end my life, whether fast or slow. There was no logic behind it, no sense, no reason, but a feeling of certainty sat in my stomach and kept me awake until dawn: *They want me to be the one.*

Serena's death was high-profile, which meant there was pressure to make an arrest soon. If I kept them waiting, they would send a cruiser, and I wasn't about to ride in a police car back to Hollywood division. Never again. I had to control the chessboard, make the next move.

The real murderer had an advantage, I realized: He knew what to expect. I didn't even know what time Serena died. I didn't know shit. The killer had shoved me into the path of an oncoming truck. *Who are you, you bastard? Did you have it all planned out? Did you sit and think it through, hammering out every detail, making sure half a dozen people can say you were somewhere else when Serena died? Or did she just piss you off and make you lose your mind?*

I needed a lawyer. I should have started making calls as soon as the cops left.

But I didn't have lawyer money. A couple of high-profile female attorneys had sought my services in the past, but I couldn't call them about this. I couldn't call them, period. That was always my rule: *They* call *you.* Except for Serena, who was my first paying customer, I never contacted clients directly—only through Mother.

That was when the idea came to me, gentle and soothing as a hot oil massage: I could run. My passport was valid. The four hundred dollars I had in the bank wouldn't last long, but I had a few thousand dollars I could get in cash advances on various pieces of plastic. I could vanish to Amsterdam. Or Mexico City. Or Cape Town. I could find a way. I just had to stay gone long enough for the murder to work itself out. I wasn't under arrest. Running wasn't even a crime yet. What made me think I had to hang around and get caught up in this shit?

Then, I remembered Letitia Howard. In the fifth grade, she was the pig-tailed brown-noser who sat behind me. Since our last names both began with H, Letitia Howard always ended up in project groups with me. We were at polar ends of the productivity scale. When I started my stalling—*Why do we have to do this?*—she always snapped off a list of reasons that whipped me into a sulking silence. Because the teacher said so. Because that's the only way we're going to learn. Because we're supposed to. To this day, when I wrestle with questions of *Why,* I hear Letitia Howard's mosquitolike voice lecturing me. Why couldn't I run?

Because running will make you look guilty, and that might send Dad to Glory for once and for good. Because you promised you would never shame him again. Because you promised him a place to live.

Like I told Serena the last time I saw her—on what may have been the last day of her life—you don't get to do what you want. You do what you have to do.

✦✦✦

Back in '92, when Len's boss at William Morris first signed me, I expected to be a different story. I fooled a producer into thinking I knew something about balling, so I won a regular role as a basketball coach-slash-spiritual-guide on *Malibu Academy*, that 90210 knockoff about prep school kids. I was in nearly half the episodes, and the show lasted two seasons. I had it made. For a while, people recognized me on the street. Finally, my life fit in place the way I'd always thought it should.

Like most actors who stumble into a good thing early, I thought that show was just a start. Instead, it's been my high point. *Academy* was my longest stretch in front of a camera where I could actually emote rather than just playing Negro Number Three Wearing Tie. And Len never gave up on me.

Len was just an assistant promoted from the mailroom back then, but I always treated him with respect. Only a fool is rude to assistants in a town run by twenty-somethings. But I liked the guy, too. His boss was a cokehead who got mean when he was high, so we built a friendship commiserating about that. When Len jumped ship to CAA, then got himself a few partners and started a new agency, he invited me along. That's Len. Maybe every agent has a charity case, and I'm his.

Len and I had lunch every week back when he used to give me scripts for guest spots and made-for-cable knockoffs, and I was cocky enough to pass. I didn't want to play thugs, pimps, or informants on *Homicide*—with The Face, who would cast me as a street thug anyway?—and I thought I could hold out for something better. During the *Academy* days, when Len represented teen stars Dusty Michaels and Jenna Atchison, too, we traveled in a pack while photographers followed us to and from the Viper Room. Sometimes, I think Len keeps me around for nostalgia's sake. Those were good days.

I was supposed to have lunch with Len the day after the cops showed up at my front door and told me Serena Johnston was dead. Considering everything else that had just landed on my heart and soul, one lunch might not seem like a big deal. But as my bedroom filled with gray morning sunlight, I vowed that nothing was going to get in the way of my lunch with power agent Leonard Shemin.

That's why I always meditate in the mornings. There's an answer waiting, if you're willing to sit still long enough.

✦✦✦

Len, always punctual, beat me to the corner of Wilcox and DeLongpre Avenue, where I'd told him to meet me. He was easy to spot, since he was the only person in sight wearing a tailored suit—Hugo Boss, if I knew Len—on a street where the closest business was SOS Bail Bonds. Like most Hollywood agents, Len had been dressing like he owned a Fortune 500 company since he was still sleeping on his roommate's sofa bed, pushing a cart in the William Morris mailroom.

When Len saw me approaching, he outstretched his arms. *What the fuck?* "What are you doing to me, Tennyson?" Len said, once I was in earshot. "You drag me out here when I told you I'm at Lions Gate at two? They're all the way in Santa Monica. And where's the food on Wilcox? A taco stand?"

I grinned. Len was in a good mood, considering. If he'd really been pissed, I would have gotten a call from Carlos, his assistant, telling me Len couldn't make it. More and more, I talked to Carlos more than Len. I'd been dreading Carlos's cancellation call. It was a minor miracle the man was even standing there.

"Sorry, man," I said, giving Len a quick, heartfelt hug. Len is a couple of inches shorter than I am, a little thick-bodied, with Clark Kent glasses and curly blond hair spiked with gel. His manicure was probably fresher than mine. Agents and actors are the only straight guys who spend half their money on grooming. "There's no sushi on this block. But I brought you something to hold you over."

I opened the sack I was carrying from Pink's, where the scent of grease and processed meat floated free. Two hot dogs, two bags of fries. Len has low blood sugar. If you want to be on Len's good side, feed him. I learned that a long time ago.

"What the hell . . . ?" Len scowled, but dug into the bag anyway, snagging a fry. If he didn't lift and stretch and treadmill for ninety minutes every morning, Len would weigh three hundred pounds. The man likes to eat.

"Mustard's already on the dog, just the way you like it. Hey, man, is your law license still valid?" Like many of the former mailroom employees at William Morris, Len also had a law degree. Apparently, the courses in bullshit they teach in law school translated to the world of agents, too.

"What kind of question is that? Tennyson, why are we standing on the street?"

Instead of answering, I pointed half a block east. Hollywood division.

"What am I looking at?" Len said.

"The police station."

He looked pained. "I know that. Allow me to rephrase: *Why* am I looking at a police station?"

"I need to pass you off as my lawyer for a minute."

Len's known me a long time, like I said. He didn't see any jokes in my face. "Jesus H. . . ."

"It's a long story, but I was at the wrong place at the wrong time. Everything's straight, I promise. I just need a lawyer to sit with me while I'm questioned."

"Questioned about what?" he said with a rather owlish expression. "Should I be afraid to ask?"

"Yeah, probably," I sighed. I would have to admit aloud that Serena Johnston was dead. I had to slow down to dredge up the words. "You know the rapper Afrodite? She was—"

"*You* are being questioned in the Afrodite murder?"

I hate the sound of that word, *murder*. Especially when it follows the word *You*. Or *Afrodite*. Damn. "It's not as bad as it sounds, man."

Len fumbled inside the sack for his hot dog. He bit off a mouthful like it was a giant dose of Xanax. "Fucking unbelievable," he said, his voice muffled as he chewed. "I'm due at Lions Gate in an hour, and you have me out here to hold your hand while you get interrogated by the police? Tennyson, for God's sake, have you been arrested?"

"Not yet."

"Good. Understand, there are a million reasons this isn't going to happen."

"It'll take twenty minutes," I said. "It's just another meeting."

"Another meeting my ass. I've never practiced criminal law. All I know is what I see on *Law & Order*. You need a real lawyer."

"You're right, I do. But you're all I've got. I'm asking for twenty minutes."

I'd never begged Len for anything. Here was a man who dined with Hollywood royalty, whose Rolodex of home telephone numbers was fatter than the Yellow Pages, and I was stealing precious moments out of his day. I would have killed me, if I'd been standing in his place.

"Jesus H. Christmas," Len said. But he was thinking about it. He took two more bites of his dog, filling out his cheeks like a chipmunk's. "You promise me you had nothing to do with this?"

That pissed me off. I gave him a look. "Please."

"Then I don't understand how—"

"Shit happens, that's how. All you have to do is go in there with me and tell the friendly officers that your client has nothing to say. That's it. I know the guys who'll be questioning me, and we can handle them. No big deal."

"Jesus H. . . ."

"I need you to be a pricy-looking white man in a suit. Nothing else, Len."

I knew he would do it. Len was bored with his life of dining with Hollywood royalty. He'd rather go surfing and rock-climbing on weekends like he did back when he had free time. During the Maui Film Festival once, Len and I scored weed at a local park and passed it out like candy at after-parties. Len enjoyed a good adventure nearly as much as I did. He owed me. I had a favor coming.

"I take it you knew Afrodite," Len said, with a glance that said *Tell me straight.*

"Serena. Yes, I knew her."

"How?"

"The old days."

Enough said. Len knew how I'd maintained my lifestyle during the lean years.

"I was always afraid that would come back to haunt you, Tennyson." He sounded like a sad older brother, blaming himself. He was one of the few people who hadn't lectured me about my former job, but I'd always known how he felt. Sometimes I traveled with clients for weeks at a time. I'd missed a lot of auditions.

"Come on, man," I said. Arm around Len's shoulder, I led him toward the squat brick building at 1358 North Wilcox. "Cops don't like to be kept waiting."

Call me crazy, but I felt safe walking into that police station, Ten and Len, like the old days, about to take a meeting that might change my life. I couldn't even remember the last time Len came with me to a meeting. I would have given anything to be going with Len to Lions Gate, and he would have given anything to be taking me there instead. If a whiff got out that I was questioned in the murder of Afrodite, I'd be lucky to work at a Hollywood hot dog stand. And it *would* get out. Everything did.

Still, I felt more at ease than I had any right to with Len Shemin at my side, even if we both understood we'd been riding this particular train far beyond the end of the line.

✦✦✦

O'Keefe and Arnaz weren't around. The desk clerk, a buzz-cut youngster who looked about fifteen, told me I would be meeting with Lieutenant Rodrick Nelson instead. Lieutenant Nelson was from Robbery-Homicide. I figured Nelson was there at Hollywood division instead of behind his own desk at the Parker Administration Building because he was picking up the murder book. High-profile cases always go to RHD.

More resources. More manpower. The case had been kicked upstairs.

"Shit . . ." I muttered after we took our seat in the folding chairs to wait.

Len leaned close to me. "What? You know that guy?"

I shook my head. That was the problem. I didn't know him, and he didn't know me. He might not know my father. And even if he did, Dad had retired. I was alone, adrift in LAPD bureaucracy, and I'd never missed Dad more. And if Robbery-Homicide decided I was a suspect in this case, Dad wouldn't survive the news.

The reality of the moment stabbed me, and Len must have seen a change in my face. He leaned close, concerned. "Tennyson, listen, my ex brother-in-law's a trial lawyer. He hates me, but he'd know people. Let's call him and be sane. I don't know the first fucking thing about—"

"We're here. It's too late now."

"Jesus H. . . ." Len slumped in his chair, loosening his tie, tightening it again. He slicked back his hair, wiped his hand with his handkerchief, digging between his fingers. His complexion had gone from ruddy to gray as soon as we walked inside. My lawyer looked like he needed my doctor.

But I understood. LAPD was on the other side of the universe from any meetings Len knew about. In his world, you were offered cold water or a soft drink the moment you walked in, and everyone lived by a carefully practiced veneer of overpoliteness and chipper delight. We were at Hollywood division, but we weren't in Hollywood.

Len and I looked up when our light was blocked. A shadow stood over us.

Lieutenant Rodrick Nelson was casting the shadow. He was six-three, so solid that his dress shirt looked too tight. *Any* shirt would look too tight on him. He had a face like Richard Roundtree's. Sometimes it does you good to run into another brother, but I knew better this time. Black cops could be the worst ones. Black suspects are an embarrassment to them. And a lieutenant? He was on his way to captain, and he wasn't about to let my monkey ass fuck that up.

Lieutenant Nelson's clothes told me Brooks Brothers. The sheen of his shoes told me he had landed at LAPD via the United States Armed Forces. Probably joined ROTC in high school. I knew the type, and we had never gotten along.

"Good afternoon, Mr. Hardwick," Lieutenant Nelson said with a firm but friendly pump. "I'm glad you could spare a few minutes to talk to us. Hope it isn't too inconvenient." His politeness almost sounded sincere. Lieutenant Nelson nodded toward a back room where a door hung open, waiting for us.

Len cleared his throat. "I could use some water," he said.

Lieutenant Nelson smiled, but it wasn't a smile I trusted. No cop likes to see a lawyer show up at questioning. "No problem. Can I get your client anything?"

"All I want is my time, brother," I said. *Just cut the crap, man.*

Lieutenant Nelson's smile went south, becoming a sneer as he walked past me. "Oh, you'll get your time. This won't take long. Go sit down."

The conference room was empty except for a metallic table and a half-dozen folding chairs. And bone cold. While we waited for Lieutenant Nelson to return with Len's water, we sat there in Zenlike stillness. All I heard was Len clearing his throat. Len, widely regarded as a fearless asshole, was scared shitless. Under different circumstances, I would have thought it was funny. As it was, I was wishing I'd searched the Yellow Pages for the first criminal lawyer I could afford. *What happened to Serena must have made me lose my damn mind.*

Mostly, I hoped I wouldn't be forced to look at that photograph of Serena's lifeless face again. O'Keefe and Arnaz had been pricks to shove that picture in my face, and I should expect Lieutenant Nelson to be a higher-ranking prick. Feeling sad about Serena made me want to go back to bed. I was exhausted.

Nelson came with a Styrofoam cup filled with what I guessed was tap water. Len would be lucky if Nelson hadn't spat in it first, but he drank it like he was on fire.

Niceties behind him, Nelson slammed his palm down onto the tabletop with a thumping sound that made Len jump. When the lieutenant moved his palm away, I was staring at my business card in a plastic baggie in the center of the table.

"Mr. Hardwick, you told detectives O'Keefe and Arnaz that you only saw Serena Johnston at Roscoe's Monday morning. I thought we'd start with what happened between you and Serena at her house later in the day." He was looking at me like he knew something, eyes twitching because he could hardly contain his glee. That's a part of any decent cop's job skills, but he was so good, I believed it. Maybe my face had shown up on a security tape. Maybe the cabbie had said something. Or a gardener I hadn't seen. Lieutenant Nelson had gut-punched me without taking a step.

Len's sideways glance told me, *Yeah, I'd love to hear about that myself.* He hurled back his last shot of water, whiskey style.

I spoke up. "Look, I—"

"We have a problem, Lieutenant," Len finished for me. "Mr. Hardwick would love to help you find the person behind this heinous act. That's why he's here. But he knew Miss Johnston as a business associate, and he's an actor with a very busy schedule. While he has no information about the killing, he does have a set call—so he needs to make it very clear to you, very fast, that you're wasting your time. That's why *I'm* here." Rumor was, Len had once told Bob Weinstein to go fuck himself. *To his face.* Len never copped to it, but right then I believed the story.

Nelson gave Len a glance no one wants to see from a man wearing a gun. That glance said that if Lieutenant Rodrick Nelson had his way, on a desig-nated day each year, any man, woman, and child in the country could shoot a lawyer dead for a nickel.

Then, his eyes came to me and sat, simmering. "I know you were there," Lieutenant Nelson said. He tapped an unsharpened pencil on the desktop, eraser side first. Three times. Four. Five. "What I don't know is . . . why don't *you* want me to know?"

Suddenly, that sounded like a damned good question. I felt the same im-pulse I'd felt with O'Keefe and Arnaz to divulge things that were none of their business.

"Trust me, though, I'll find out," Nelson went on. "You hooked up with Serena for business, all right, but acting's a funny word for it. Don't piss this op-portunity away . . . *brother.* You'll be back to see me soon, and your lawyer won't be in lockup with you. Captain Hardwick's son or not, don't plan on any trips."

I wavered at the border of his trap, ready to tell him everything for the sake of getting on his good side. *It's not like you think, man. She didn't pay me this time. And she was alive and beautiful when I left her, not that broken girl in the picture.*

Len didn't give me the chance. "I'll refer you back to my earlier statement, Lietenant Nelson," he said, and I noticed that the gray had left my agent's face.

His skin was flushed with the power of *the game*. "If you have an arrest warrant, let's see it. If not, have a good day."

I might never get Len on the phone again, never mind another lunch. I would be lucky if his assistant would accept my calls now. But take it from me: Leonard Shemin is the best lawyer 10 percent can buy.

Len rushed off with hardly a good-bye, but my feet stopped just outside the front doors. I wanted to be anywhere else, but I couldn't move.

At the door at Hollywood division, there's the Walk of the Dead. That's what I called it when I was a kid. See, in Hollywood, there is no higher honor than to have one's name forever memorialized in the "Walk of Fame" on Hollywood Boulevard. So at Hollywood division, every officer killed in the line of duty gets a star on the sidewalk outside the station house. There are seven names; the first, Clyde Pritchett, died in 1936, and the most recent, Charles D. Heim, died in 1994. My father used to make me memorize the names of the fallen.

I learned it from Dad, maybe. The dead should be honored.

I made the decision right then: I was going to find out who killed Serena. A cynic could say that decision was made on the basis of feeling the first sparks of LAPD heat on my ass, and that's part of it. But the Walk of the Dead did it.

I knew Serena would get her tributes, that the legend-building was already underway. She would have a celebrity-infested funeral I probably couldn't get an invitation to. Her friends and family would remember what made her laugh, her fans would hear her soul through her music, and two DVDs would preserve the first glimpses of her wings as a caterpillar morphed into a butterfly before our eyes.

But after all was said and done, I knew most people would sum up Serena's life as JADR: Just Another Dead Rapper. Tupac, Jam Master Jay, Biggie Smalls, Shareef. And I was tired, like I said. I was tired of dead rappers, and I was tired of no one getting caught. This was going to be different.

That day, I knew two things: Number one, someone was going to jail for killing Serena Johnston. Number two, it sure as hell wasn't going to be me.

I swore it under my breath on the Walk of the Dead.

✦✦✦

Three news vans were parked across the street by the time I left the police station, and I didn't have to wonder why. I'd been avoiding television and radio since I heard about Serena, but even in a jaded town like Los Angeles, a celebrity murder is news. I slipped on my shades and pulled down my white Howard University baseball cap, in instant invisibility mode. Not that anyone would recognize me. But just in case.

A woman climbing out of a dented old rose-colored Toyota Camry caught my eye, even if I wasn't in the mood to notice women. This one made me look longer than usual because I was sure we had met. I have a nearly photographic memory for faces, and I'm almost as good with names. I knew her from somewhere.

The woman looked like a kid, about twenty-five. She was ginger-skinned and cute, with her hair cut short in a bold natural you don't usually see in Hollywood, where the weave rules; if she was a reporter, she wasn't in television. A slim reporter's notebook fell to the ground, and she cursed under her breath as she leaned over to pick it up, struggling to hold a sheaf of papers in place under her arm. As she bent down, two healthy half-moons sprang into view behind the back pockets of her faded jeans. Even on a day as bad as that one, her ass commanded proper admiration.

My game must have been way off. She caught me looking. And she didn't smile.

"Can I help you?" she said, ready with an attitude. Before I could answer, she lost control of her papers, and they flurried around her in the breeze. "*Damn.*"

"Looks like you've got that question backward, darlin'," I said, snatching a loose page that had cleaved to my thigh. "You're the one who needs help."

Attitude gone. She shook her head and gave me a sheepish smile that dimpled her cheeks. "Yeah—get that one behind you, too, please. Thanks."

I've studied people all my life, the closest thing I got to acting lessons before college. I examine their faces, their style, their gestures. Sometimes I can see things people have missed after a lifetime in their own skin. So, I knew what this woman was about. Her clothes were neat but not fashionable, she used minimal makeup, and she wore flats, not heels. She was a worker. Ambitious, trying to impress somebody, and she was in over her head.

And she had no idea how pretty she was. I knew all of that right away.

Suddenly, I knew her name, too. "April Forrest," I said.

She was the reporter from the *Los Angeles Times* who had covered my father's retirement dinner, and she had interviewed me, briefly, over my half-eaten Caesar's salad. I never saw the story she wrote. I've put some newspapers and certificates aside to make a scrapbook one day, but I'm not good at collecting the stories. With Dad, it feels too much like writing his obituary. I can already feel the questions I'm going to regret never asking him, but I still can't bring myself to ask most of them now.

The woman's look said, *Honey, I think I would remember knowing someone who looks as fine as you.* I took off the hat first, then the sunglasses. I watched my smile light up her face. "You're . . . Captain Hardwick's son," she said. "The guy from that TV show."

"Guilty."

Three years ago, and she remembered me, too. But her memory had nothing to do with my luminous personality or any profound remembrances I gave her about my father, believe me. She remembered The Face, that's all. That's what most people remember.

"Any chance a word from you would help me pull any strings here?" she said with a mischievous smile. Like me, she was already trying to work out her angle.

"Not likely."

"Well, good to see you, anyway. How's your dad?" Her eyes settled into mine when she asked about Dad, letting me know she wasn't just making conversation.

"Fine." My voice cracked as I lied, and I'm usually a much better liar.

"Oh." Her eyes dimmed. She heard the lie, just like Serena had. "I'm up to my ass in this Afrodite thing. Figures she'd get killed when I'm supposed to be on vacation."

From a bad subject to a worse one. My stomach hurt. I was ready to go back to bed, but April Forrest might be the only ally I had. A reporter could be useful.

"What kind of strings would you like pulled?" I said.

"Are you asking me that as a Hardwick?"

"Depends on what you need."

She sighed, fumbling through her papers. "What *don't* I need? Media relations is no help. I got a copy of the police report, but it's so sketchy, there's nothing—"

My heart thumped so hard, I felt weak. "May I see that?" I said.

April shrugged. She had to do some shuffling to get the order right, but she handed me four pages. A couple of the pages were off-center on the copy machine, cutting words in half at the margins, but suddenly I had the official incident report on the murder of Serena Johnston. I read as quickly as I could, trying to pick out details.

V, the report called her. Serena was Victim now.

Body found at 10:00 A.M. Tuesday—the day O'Keefe and Arnaz came to see me—by the manager of a camera shop at Sunset and Highland who thought somebody had moved his garbage out of the Dumpster. V was found wrapped in two garbage bags behind the Dumpster. Newer-model white Escalade found abandoned at Santa Monica and Highland at 9:00 A.M. DOB 1-10-72.

My fingerprints will be in her car, I thought. *And in her house.*

But by then, I was beyond panic. I already knew it was time to employ serious ass-saving measures. I read the report to see if it mentioned anything about me or my business card. Not at first glance. But no cops were going to put pertinent clues in a public document. The report was matter-of-fact and didn't say much about the police investigation itself, but I needed it.

"What would it take for me to get this copied right now?" I said.

"Look, can't you just get your own? I'm trying to—"

I pulled out the business card Lieutenant Nelson had pressed into my hand before I left. I waved it in front of April's face.

April's eyes followed the card as if it was tasty enough to smell. "What's that?"

"The name and number of the lead Robbery-Homicide investigator on Afrodite. There's a pager number on here, too."

"You're kidding. You have that, and you can't get a report?"

"Do we have a deal or not?" I held out my card, too.

April cast a pained glance at the coiffed television reporters readying their cameras. Intimidating competition. I felt her hunger. She wanted to scoop them.

"The best time to call him at his desk is after hours," I said. "Cops on a hot case work late. Try seven. He won't want to talk to you, but it's the best I can do. Absolutely do *not* mention my name."

"I don't even remember your first name. Wait—a poet, right? Keats?"

"My name won't help you, even the Hardwick. I can't be *any* clearer about that. My name stays out. Got it?"

She nodded, convinced. "Deal. Let's go find you a copy machine."

What did I have to lose? Lieutenant Nelson would slam the phone down in her ear as soon as she mentioned she was a reporter. Even if he didn't, there was no way he would name me as a suspect to a reporter. Not yet.

A single-story bungalow across the street called itself SOS Bail Bonds, and we jaywalked to the door. The interior was unkempt and looked like the end of a bad day, but at least the copy machine worked. Raul, the man at the desk, charged me a dollar.

"Give me your number," I said to April as the machine glared on her face. She began to raise a playful eyebrow, but I went on, all business. "If I hear anything else that can help you out, I'll let you know. You wrote a nice story about my father."

"Thanks. Sorry it got cut so short . . . and I really didn't think I captured—"

"It was great," I said. That didn't even feel like a lie. I knew it must be true.

I left Hollywood division with a police report and a reporter's telephone number. Not bad for someone who might have ended up spending the night in lockup.

It was two in the afternoon, and Serena had been dead more than thirty-six hours. If I was going to find a killer, I had to get started.

I searched my wallet for one last business card, the one Serena had given me.

It might not be a good day for the meeting I was promised, but I didn't have any leads, and I had to start somewhere. I decided to head straight for Beverly Hills. To Casanegra Productions.

More than ever, I wanted to see Devon Biggs.

FIVE

MOST PEOPLE THINK ABOUT RODEO DRIVE and shopping when they picture Beverly Hills. To me, it's all about the hotels. The Beverly Hills Hotel. Le Meridien. The Peninsula. The Regent Beverly Wilshire. If it has five stars and a king-sized mattress, I've been there. I know the stairwells and the line of sight in the hallways. I know the concierge and the maître d', and I've overtipped the bellhops so they'll be eager to tell me about anyone, or anything, out of the ordinary. A client once put me up at the Raffles L'Ermitage for nearly a month so I would be within walking distance of her desk at DreamWorks. At the Hotel Bel-Air, I had to wrestle a sawed-off shotgun away from my client's jilted ex in the elevator. All part of the job.

And, of course, there was Serena. The meaning of the term *old haunt* became clear to me as I drove past the Four Seasons on my way to Casanegra's offices. Seeing the place where I first beheld her nakedness, the scent of Serena suddenly filled my car. Trust me, there is nothing more haunting than a dead woman's cloying smell.

Grief is a selfish feeling—you want everyone around you to share it. But somehow, life was going on as usual for the tenants of the ten-story Art Deco office building at 8602 Wilshire—home to a law office, a health club, an accounting firm, several casting agencies, and Casanegra Productions. In the lobby, the deliverymen, lawyers, executives, and actors were all smiles, lax faces, and careless banter; going about their day's adventures. An epidemic of good moods only sharpened my bad one. I didn't feel like explaining my business to the security guard—I couldn't handle answering to anyone else with a badge and a uniform—so I slipped to the bank of elevators with a gaggle of giddy secretaries who were happy to have me join them. My smile masked feelings they wouldn't want a glimpse of. A broad-shouldered black janitor pushing a laundry cart toward the service elevator nodded to me as he passed, as if he wished we could trade places. I nodded back. My grandfather put three kids through college with a mop and squeegee. I might need the work soon myself.

The elevator was full when it left the lobby, but it emptied out floor after floor. By the time it climbed to its last stop, there was no one left but me.

The long, black marble receptionists' desk beneath the Casanegra Productions logo was unmanned, and I could hear the gentle trilling of unanswered telephone lines. In the waiting area, above a mounted heart-shaped wreath of chrysanthemums and red carnations, a forty-inch television monitor played one of Serena's music videos with the volume turned low. On the huge screen, dressed in flowing white, Serena twisted, danced, and teased, her eyes searing my soul. *You want some of this? Better bring it. / You want some of that? Bring it on . . .* I almost went back to the elevator. What the hell was I doing there?

Since no one was in sight, I headed for a black door with a silver M affixed to it I guessed was the men's room. I wanted to compose myself, but someone else had beaten me to the sink. A man stood with the water running full blast, his face cupped in his hands. Water dripped freely between his fingertips, soaking the sleeves of his dress shirt. He glanced up when he heard the door open, his eyes pulled down like a bloodhound's.

Devon Biggs straightened, surprised. Serena's childhood friend was a wheat-toast-colored brother, smaller than I remembered at five-foot-six, with wiry, almost feline limbs. His hairline had carved out a U shape above his forehead, which made him look ten years older than his true age of thirty-five. The whites of his eyes were blood-red. He looked like I felt.

"I didn't get much sleep last night either," I said, and handed him a paper towel.

"I'll be damned," he said, shaking water from his arms. "Tennyson Hardwick."

"That's me."

"The last message," he said, gazing at my image in the mirror rather than staring me in the eye. He wiped his face. "You know that, man?"

He wasn't making sense, but I cut him some slack. "What's that?"

"The last message she left me was to call Tennyson Hardwick. No shit."

The air in the bathroom became too thin to breathe.

As if Devon Biggs thought I needed proof—or maybe just so he could have someone else to share her with—he took me to his office and played his voice-mail. The call came at 2:34 P.M. Just like that, Serena came back to life.

"*Whassup, D? Listen, before you leave for Cannes, I need you to do me a solid. I saw Tennyson Hardwick today, he's looking good, and he could bring something special to* Deluxe. *No, I don't wanna hear it.*" She gave my number. "*I told him to call, but if he don't, I want you to have Imani call him, a'ight? We'll settle all that number shit when you get back from France. We've both come a long way, huh, Lil' D?*"

And the message ended. Serena's voice and spirit had filled the room, and now she was gone again—except for her face frozen in framed movie posters I was keeping my eyes away from. I was disappointed that I hadn't had as much pride as Serena had thought I would. Only pride would have kept me from calling Devon Biggs.

"It all comes tumbling down," Biggs said. "*Deluxe* was in development hell for five years, before we grabbed it in turnaround. Another eighteen months of development, and we nailed it. The script was tight. We'd signed a director, got Robin Williams on board. Studio gave a green light. *Forty* million dollars. And you know what? Those motherfuckers called over here yesterday before Serena's body was cold. No Serena, no movie. Listen to those phones. Serena set up deals all over town. Yeah, man, yesterday was gonna be your lucky day. Now, we're both . . ."

Devon Biggs didn't finish, but his blood-red eyes told me that my luck, or his job, were the last things on his mind. He shook his head, laughing bitterly as he reached into his desk drawer for a cigarette. He didn't try to hide his trembling fingers, so he wasn't worried about his pride either. When he lit up, I realized he wasn't smoking tobacco. He puffed twice and offered the joint to me, dope-smoking etiquette. I shook my head. One of us needed a clear mind.

"Cops were here yesterday," Biggs said. "Asking about you, matter of fact."

My stomach cinched, but I kept my face in check. "What did you tell them?"

"I played them the message. I said baby-girl was trying to put you in her movie, so it didn't seem smart for you to kill her. But I don't know you. That's what I told them." His eyes turned quizzical. "Is there something else I *should* have told them?"

"I wouldn't hurt Serena for the world," I said. "But why'd you try to smooth things over for me with the cops? That message sure sounded like you know me. Lying to the police on my behalf is a very friendly gesture."

His face hardened. "How Reenie spends her money is nobody's damn business. Besides, you're too soft to kill nobody."

That was the Devon Biggs I remembered, emerging from his fog. Under different circumstances, I would have been tempted to correct someone who called me soft. He could fill a book with the things he'd gotten wrong about me. A lot of people don't know my public face, and it serves my interests to keep it that way.

I followed his eyes to the wall behind me, where I saw a slightly blurry eight-by-ten photograph framed on the wall. I stepped closer to examine it. Three kids with ashy elbows posed with their arms around each other in front of Serena's old blue Impala. They were about eleven. Devon Biggs wore thick glasses and a black Michael Jackson-style jacket, Shareef was a grinning MC with his fist doubling as a microphone, and Serena was squeezed between them. If not for the context, I wouldn't have known who she was. Serena was stick-thin, and her face hadn't discovered itself yet, but she was dressed in an over-sized party gown, the belle of the ball. Three kids playing dress-up, smiling like they would live forever.

A rock seemed to lodge in my throat. I had to look away.

"Last man standing," Biggs said, his voice so low I could barely hear him. "First Shareef, now Reenie. My family's gone."

Shareef had been shot soon before Serena launched Casanegra Productions, if I remembered right. Five years ago, almost to the day. There was speculation about rap rivalries and gang affiliations, but no arrests—all the more reason LAPD would want a face to plaster on the news.

My mind raced. Serena might have confided a lot to Biggs, including our last encounter. *If he said something to the police, that definitely would explain why Lieutenant Nelson crawled so far up my ass.* I didn't trust Devon Biggs to be my friend, but he was the only place I had to start.

"I need to find who did this," I said. "That's why I'm here."

"You ever heard of a book called *The Hollywood Rules?*" Biggs said in the same monotone, like a sleepwalker. When I shook my head, he went on. "Advice book by industry insiders. Reenie carried it around like a Bible, read it until the pages were falling out. There's one line I memorized, the most important line in the book: 'You're going to make enough enemies just by being successful.' "

"Serena had enemies?"

Biggs gestured at the office—the shiny platinum records, Grammy Awards, and movie posters displayed around him; the spoils of success. The office centerpiece was a foot-high bronze *Black Music* magazine artist-of-the-year statuette displayed on its own marble pedestal; it looked almost like an Oscar, and probably weighed as much.

"Names?" I flipped open a notebook I'd picked up at a drugstore.

"Same name I told the cops after Shareef died. But what the hell would you do with a name?"

"There are a lot of homicides in L.A.," I said. "I only give a damn about one."

"You wanna play detective?" Biggs said. "Be careful what you wish, my man. You'll be fucking with people who don't like to be fucked with."

"I can take care of myself."

"I guess we'll see." He chuckled, although his face was anything but mirthful. "Write this name down in capital letters: Alphonse Terrell Gaines."

The name had a muted familiarity, out of reach. Then, I knew: "M.C. Glazer?"

Biggs nodded.

M.C. Glazer—named for the Teflon-coated armor-piercing bullets called "cop-killers"—was also the hip-hop world's suspect of choice in the murder of Shareef. M.C. Glazer's radio wars with Shareef had been notorious. And Afrodite had chimed in with her own salvos against her friend's rival now and then, claiming M.C. Glazer was a poser. I remember wincing when I heard a line from one of her first hits: *M.C. Glazer ain't no ladykilla. / He might penetrate, but he'll never fill ya.* I'd figured it was all hype to sell records, but apparently Devon Biggs didn't think so.

In retrospect, M.C. Glazer was the obvious choice. Almost.

"Why wait this long?" I said. "Serena hasn't recorded a CD in years. She'd moved on." I knew Afrodite's music, even if much of it wasn't my taste. When Serena became my client, I bought all of her CDs so we would have something to talk about.

"It's not just about the records," Biggs said. He blinked, and I saw moisture on his lashes. "Serena never let that ghetto shit go. I told her she had to be about business now. We planned all this back in junior high. Her, me, and Shareef. Hell, they were the reason I went to college, so I could manage the finance side. But she was still twisted about what was real and what was hype."

If it was possible, I felt even more grieved. Part of me was hoping—almost praying—that this wasn't another hip-hop murder. Serena deserved better than to go out as a cliché, even if it would guarantee her martyrdom.

And M.C. Glazer wouldn't be easy to get to. Biggs saw the dilemma in my face.

"Don't worry, Hardwick. Don't you watch *CSI?* The cops will figure it out, just like they did with Shareef. And Tupac. And Biggie." Biggs remembered his joint, inhaling a long toke like it was pure oxygen.

His point was a good one, and it pissed me off. Maybe it really was up to me.

Another glance at the treasures showcased on Biggs's walls reminded me that Serena had built a valuable empire. What was that old saying again? *Follow the . . .*

"Did Serena have a will?" I said.

Biggs still holding his breath. "Yes and no. Not on paper. I told her she had to be businesslike, but she was almost superstitious, like she thought she'd die faster if she wrote it down. I talked her into sitting in front of a video camera for a video will, which is better than nothing. But she wanted to do it privately, and she never let me see it." With a small cough, Biggs finally exhaled a stream of spicy smoke. His lungs must have been steel-reinforced.

"Where's that tape?"

"My safe. Sealed envelope. Probably be a court officer here next week when I break the seal. Reenie used to always say she would leave all her money to her church. I guess we'll see."

"Church?" I didn't remember Serena attending church when I knew her; but then again, it's not like she would have invited me to Sunday brunch at God's house.

"Oh, yeah—Reenie caught the Holy Ghost after Shareef got shot." He said his friend's name quietly, as if out of reverence. "Neither one of us ain't been right since."

I followed Biggs's gaze to the photograph of the three of them posing in front of the car as children. Serena stood between the two boys, her head resting on Shareef's shoulder. I almost couldn't make myself ask the next question.

"No offense, man, but I've got to ask: Where were you when Serena died?" I couldn't guess at what Biggs's motive might be—like he said, her death put him out of a job—but if I was investigating Serena's murder, I had to get used to asking.

Biggs's eyes rested on mine. "OK, Columbo: Cops said it happened about nine. I was here, working late. I took calls, and I can give you a list of the people I talked to. What about you, Hardwick?" His stare didn't flinch. "Were you at home chilling with your girl?"

The question carried more weight than it should have. "Wish I had been," I said. Maybe Serena could have been my girl, except that she was lying on a slab at the coroner's office. Probably with my DNA all over her. I was well and truly fucked.

Suddenly, Biggs coughed out a plume of smoke, half-laughing. "I feel you, man. What gets me, Five-O shows up here with a hard-on for a prettyboy like you. Don't even make it *look* like they're trying, do they?"

Devon Biggs wasn't the most observant brother in the world. If he had been, he might have noticed the way my lips snaked into a hard smile, might have wondered why my first and second knuckles were flat and scarred. He might have wondered just what I did that kept my stomach hard and ridged, my shoulders wide. But he didn't, and probably never realized how much I wanted to reach across his desk and slap the gold out of his teeth. Even if it was true that he'd tried to smooth my way with the homicide guys, Devon Biggs had gotten on my next-to-last nerve.

"Just tell me the best place to find M.C. Glazer," I said. My smile was ice.

Biggs studied me, his glassy eyes sharpening. "You're serious, ain't you?"

"Like you said, you'll see."

"You must not have a radio. Anybody with ears knows about M.C. Glazer's CD release party at Club Magique."

"When?"

He blew a ragged smoke ring at me. "Tonight, prettyboy."

Dad always says God gives you clear signs when you're on the right path. That day, I almost believed it.

Some things are meant to be done man-to-man, not on the telephone. I knew I was a coward the minute I flipped open my cell and began dialing the number for Hope Rehabilitation Center instead of driving out to see Dad.

There are people who take pleasure in spreading bad news, so it was possible Dad already knew about my trip to Hollywood division. But that wasn't the only reason I couldn't face him. And it wasn't even because it was already three in the afternoon, and I needed a solid plan on how to talk to one of the best-guarded icons in hip-hop without getting mired in east-west traffic on the 10.

No, it was worse: I was about to back out on my word. I had told him he had a way out of hell, and now I was about to say he should hang with the devil and the damned a little while longer—which, to his mind, would mean forever. I was backing out, just like he expected me to.

The nurse I regularly flirted with, Marcela, was happy to patch the call through to Dad's room and even hold the phone up to his ear. She promised to let me know if he wrote any messages for me on the pad. My investment in Marcela bore fruit that day.

"OK, Tennyson, I'm putting him on," she chirped.

Dead silence, except for a low buzzing sound on the line.

The first time I tried to speak, my throat only growled. Dad has always had that kind of impact on me. He was my best ally—a top-notch investigator back in the day, and he still had active contacts in LAPD—but I couldn't ask for his help.

"Hey, Dad," I said, once I'd coughed and found my voice again.

Silence. Not even in a growl in return.

I was alone in a car that was hot from sitting in the sun, parked at an expired meter in Beverly Hills where only passing strangers could see me. When the tears came, I let them flow freely for the first time since I had heard about Serena's death. If I had known I was going to choose that moment to cry, I would never have called my father. In all my life, I had never seen Richard Allen Hardwick shed a tear.

The phone's silence roared at me.

"Listen, man . . ." I said, shocked at how difficult it was to mold words from my boiling breath. "I know I, uh . . . promised I'd get you out of there. And I *will*. You have my word. But I can't do it until next week. Something's come up, and I have some work to do. The money really will help us out." Dad had always known when I was lying, and all the acting classes in Hollywood wouldn't change that. "I'm sorry, man. I really wanted to—"

I heard a sound and waited with a pounding heart. Maybe there would be some absolution. *Don't worry about it, Tennyson. I'll know you'll do what you can when you get back, son.*

But the next voice I heard was Marcela's, a whisper. "Tennyson? I'm sorry. He turned away from the phone." She sounded embarrassed. "Do you want me to . . . ?"

"No, that's all right, beautiful," I said. Speaking sweet words to a woman lifted some of the weight from my heart. "Let him be."

In a strange way, that conversation with Dad was liberating.

Going to prison for a murder I hadn't committed could hardly be worse.

M.C. GLAZER ROSE TO RAP STARDOM in the wake of Dr. Dre, Ice-T, Ice Cube, and Snoop. He and Tupac borrowed a few pages from each other's books, except that Glaze spent most of his teenage years behind bars instead of at a performing arts school, he never had 'Pac's poet's heart, and—most important—he lived to tell his tales. No one has ever taken a poll, but I would bet most rap fans would rather have lost Glazer that night in Vegas. He was at the MGM Grand sitting right behind 'Pac the night Tyson trashed a punching bag named Bruce Seldon in 109 seconds. He was on the outs with Suge Knight, too. A slight blink of fate might have put M.C. Glazer in the path of the bullet that stole Tupac. But we don't choose who lives and who dies. Dad would say that's God's call. Sometimes, I wonder if Dad's got it upside down.

It took me only a few minutes at an internet café on Vineland to bring the picture into better focus, and Devon Biggs's claims made more sense with each hit on the search engine. M.C. Glazer had been arrested for attempted murder when he was only fourteen, and he'd just been warming up. You name it, he'd been charged with it. Sexual battery. Assault with a deadly weapon. Trafficking. Statutory rape—that put my teeth on edge. When he was twenty-two and already a burgeoning superstar, he was arrested for having sex with a fourteen-year-old girl. The case went away when her family withdrew the charges, probably after they bought themselves a new house with the payoff they sold their daughter's soul for. The more I learned about M.C. Glazer, the less I liked him.

But rap fans had canonized him. Every trip through lockup's revolving door sold M.C. Glazer another mountain of CDs. After diversifying his exploding assets into a fashion line and turning himself into a megaproducer—hey, you know the story—M.C. Glazer hadn't been arrested in at least six years. But I'm not a big believer in miraculous recoveries. Money doesn't fix a person who's broken. Money just entices people to accept your eccentricities and makes your tracks easier to hide. Cool James had it right: Man made the money; money never made the man.

M.C. Glazer was worth talking to, and fast. I just had to figure out how.

I couldn't expect to walk into CopKilla Records and gain an audience the way I just had with a king stripped of his kingdom like Devon Biggs. And getting inside Club Magique on the night of an M.C. Glazer release party wouldn't be any easier than scoring a ticket to a White House garden party—not unless I was willing to go to my list of former clients, and I wouldn't do that. Even if I could convince the club's management to hire me as a bouncer, I'd never get the job by nightfall.

I would have to go Hollywood on this one.

When it comes to Making It in Hollywood—whether you're an actor, an agent, a writer, you-name-it—everyone in the business knows there's no such thing as The Way. Anyone who's selling The Way is a liar. If you don't have access to the big auditions or the premiere after-parties, you have to engineer your own way to meet people in power. It can happen in the restroom. Or an elevator. Or a parking lot. I knew a guy who sold a script delivering pizzas in Hollywood Hills. And an actress who got her first real break singing telegrams around Universal Studios. Hardly any two stories are alike.

If I wanted into this party, I had to find someone else with access. I didn't have time to research who M.C. Glazer's bodyguards were to see if I could find a buddy of a buddy. Bodyguards are low-profile by definition—the good ones, anyway.

But if it was a rap party, there would be hoochies. *Lots* of hoochies, many of them top-dollar. Now, let me give you some of Tennyson Hardwick's Hoochology 101: *Hoochie* is not a word I use lightly. I'm not talking about the sisters with dreams of video-dancer stardom, the college students and single mothers training their asses off to compete in the industry. I'm not even talking about the strippers doing what they think they need to so they can keep the lights on— although trust me, some strippers are straight-up hoochies, too. Dancers, strippers, and prostitutes may look like hoochies to the untrained eye, but those sisters are selling a fantasy.

But real-life hoochies have bought *into* the fantasy—they see themselves as a walking set of buttocks, breasts, and orifices—and their only aspiration is to use their bodies to con as many men as they can out of as much as they can get, before they pass their sell-by date. Some hoochies are paid with cash, and others are paid with dinner at Spago, diamonds, backup singing gigs on videos, or invitations to the bomb parties. You know what I'm talking about. It takes one to know one? Maybe so. But even when I was working seven nights a week, I never lost sight of the difference between fantasy and reality. One reason I quit was that I knew I was walking too close to that line.

I've met a lot of hoochies. And if there was a Hoochie Convention at Club Magique that night, the only person to talk to was the Convention Planner herself. I hadn't dialed that telephone number in five years, and the last time I'd called, I told the woman at the other end of the line that she would never hear from me again. But maybe she was a prophetess, because her slow, Serbian-accented rasp laid it all out: *You'll be back, Tennyson. You don't have anywhere else to go.*

And in the end, she was right.

After all this time, I was crawling home to Mother.

The pager number still worked. Mother's procedure was this: no direct calls. Given the nature of her business, she operates with buffers to keep under the radar. You dial Mother's pager number, and then you wait for her to call you back. I didn't want to use my cell, so I bought a throwaway Nokia Tracfone at a Best Buy in Culver City. More money than I could spare, but I needed to take precautions to keep from getting in more trouble. It was not a time to be sloppy.

Back in the day, Mother's organization returned a call within five minutes. This time, my new cell hadn't rung in twenty. I wondered if the number was so ancient that I had lost track of her. I also thought that might be for the best, considering.

I decided to drive back home to wait, since I wanted to pack a small bag with essentials for a couple of nights, in case I had to make a trip. I felt a surge of paranoia, just like Ray Liotta in *GoodFellas*, expecting cars to follow me, peering skyward every time I heard a ghettobird chopping the air overhead. I drove past my house a couple of times, and as far as I could tell, no one was watching it.

I threw together a sandwich on stale bread while I packed, and it helped. I had been too nervous about Len and the police to eat the hot dog I bought for myself at lunchtime, and I realized my blood sugar had flatlined.

I was wondering how long it would take to drive to Canada when my new cell rang. A woman's voice, but younger than Mother's. *"Da?"* she said. Serbian.

"I need to talk to Mother."

A brief pause. "Name?"

"Tell her it's Ten."

The voice clicked away, the line dead. Mother's operation never had been much for employee relations, always emphasizing customer service instead. I hadn't spoken to Mother yet, and the word *employee* was already in my mind. I sighed. *If you know what's good for you, you'd better hope Mother doesn't call.*

Then, of course, she did.

Her voice was girlish, no small feat for a woman who must be past seventy. *"Ten!* Very long time, no? I see you on my television. Very nice-smelling underarms, eh? But to us, you always smell nice. Your friends still ask for you. One last week, only." That was Mother—always closing.

"You're the only friend I called to talk to, Mother."

She *tsk-tsked*, muttering in Serbian. "This is a pity. Your voice is sad, Ten. Now I am sad, too."

"I'm sad because a friend of mine died."

"A friend I know?" Suddenly, Mother sounded wary.

"No, Mother. I met her before I knew you. A woman I cared about."

"And I knew nothing of this woman?"

"Nothing at all."

She breathed, full of relief. "Then why do you call?"

"I need a favor."

"You know I am not in business for favors." So much for sentimentality. There was a time I brought Mother a lot of money. During those days, she used to sip too much Smirnoff and tell me teary stories of her flight from Subotica into Hungary after her husband was killed during the Kosovo War. We almost *were* friends. Almost.

"Hear me out, Mother. Please." She was silent, so I went on. "There's a hip-hop party at Club Magique tonight. I'm sure you've heard. It's all over the radio."

She laughed, a wicked rumble. "Yes, I hear."

Her laughter gave me hope. At least she wasn't in one of her evil moods. "I need to get inside, but I'm not on the guest list. So I'm offering my services as a bodyguard. In case you can think of anyone who needs special attention."

"Your friends in need of special attention, they are not at Club Magique."

I wasn't irritated with Mother for pushing, but I was irritated with myself for the part of me that was realizing how much easier it would be to get out of town with a few thousand dollars for a night's work. "We can have this conversation my way, Mother, or we can say *pozdrav*." One of the Serbian words I had learned—*good-bye*. I'm fluent in Spanish, and I can get by in French. I also know enough Japanese and Serbian to raise eyebrows. A good memory is useful for more than memorizing lines. Languages are my hobby; they come easy to me.

She *tsk-tsked* again. "Such a choirboy now, eh? This is a tragedy. I know of no one in need of . . . special attention. The club takes good care." A throaty chuckle. "I know you are a very clever boy, but I worry about that lovely face. The bouncers, they are like mountains."

"It's a favor, Mother. I just need someone to get me in the door."

It took her a long time to answer. "And what does Mother get for this favor?"

"One of your girls needs protection, you know how to reach me. No charge."

I used to make her money, and now I was promising a different set of skills; one almost as high as the ones she'd marketed in the past. But not quite. And for whatever reason, Mother was happiest when her employees worked with their clothes off.

Again, she muttered to herself in Serbian. "No, no. This is not enough. You will come to see me. We talk face to face. I accept nothing less." Mother knew she would be more convincing in person. She thought I would be too weak to say no if she had an enticing client and a ridiculous fee waiting for me—and maybe she was right.

My mouth was dry, and something stirred in the deepest pit of my stomach that felt like a glimmer of arousal. The sensation alarmed me, but I had run out of choices. "I don't have time today. I'll come this week." *If I can keep my ass out of jail.*

"Tomorrow," she insisted.

I closed my eyes, cursing silently. "Tomorrow."

"*Tsk.* You say this like Mother would hurt you. How could I, silly boy, when you are so dear to me? You know this. And also, you should know something of this word you speak, *pozdrav:* You speak it to mean good-bye. But it is also a greeting—like you say, *hello.* So good-bye is not good-bye, eh?"

"It never is, Mother. Not with you."

Again, she laughed. She sounded like she had just won Lotto. "You will go to Club Magique at ten o'clock. There, you will meet Honey."

"How will I know her?"

"You will not, but this is no worry. She will know you."

Mother was wrong: I pegged Honey on sight. I couldn't have missed her if I'd been blindfolded.

Some people don't have any common sense. That's what I thought when I saw a young woman walking naked on the curb outside Club Magique, smoking a cigarette like she was in her own living room. Oh, she didn't *know* she was naked—after all, she was wearing stilettos and what looked like a minidress made entirely of chain mail. But as I got closer, I saw that the chains were really bandoliers—loaded with Glazers, no doubt. Her silicone breasts could not be caged, so her business was poking out all over. The rows of shiny copper bullets couldn't do much to cover this girl's double-Ds and their dark nipples pointing skyward, the V-shape of her closely trimmed pubic hair, or the dimpled ham hocks otherwise known as her ass. The girl was naked. On a public street.

Needless to say, she was drawing a crowd. A growing huddle of men trailed after her, hooting and pointing.

"Hey, sweet stuff, you wanna take a ride?" One dude hanging out of the driver's-side window of his black Lexus ran the light, nearly broadsiding a yellow Hummer. Two cops near the club's door were already peering in her direction, ready to investigate the commotion. Honey's pace slowed, uncertain. The crowd began to close around her, penning her in.

"Honey!" Ten feet behind her, I called her name like I was her daddy. Hell, I could have been; she didn't look a day over nineteen. She froze in midstep, pivoting around to look at me. Yep, she was the one.

It was a good thing Mother hired Honey a bodyguard. This sister needed one.

"I'm Ten." I whipped off my black leather jacket, flung it across her shoulders, and pulled it closed across her bosom in a single motion, hiding her tantalizing banks of skin. The crowd groaned and cussed, but I had gotten to her in time. The cops were pushing their way past the gawkers, but for once, there was nothing to see. Just a man with his arm around a girl in a black jacket and heels. No flesh, no blood. The cops hardly gave us a glance, their hands relaxing away from their holsters.

Honey had the nerve to poke out her lip at me. "Who the hell do you—"

I spoke close to her ear. "Sister, if you want to see the inside of anything except a police station tonight, you best learn you can't let all your shit hang out on the street, even in L.A."

Her head bobbed, making the bullets tinkle. "For your information, I'm not—"

"All I'm saying is, a lady's got to leave something for the imagination." To try to placate her before she was in full cuss-out mode, a beacon for the cops again, I extended a chivalrous arm toward the velvet rope. "Now, shall we?"

The gesture seemed to work. That, and she got a better look at my face under the streetlamp. Her lower lip retreated like a snail into its shell. "Mother sent you?"

"Yes, ma'am. Where's your ID? And it had better say you're twenty-one."

A conspiratorial twinkle. "Oh, mine says I'm twenty-three."

I hate lines, so I wasn't about to fool with the crush of radio listeners waving passes to get in the front door. I spotted the VIP entrance on the side, with the inevitable caravan of stretch limos depositing people trying to look important. I kept my eyes on the people who climbed out, watching for M.C. Glazer. But I knew Glazer wouldn't show up in a stretch. The biggest ones like their own cars, their own drivers. More likely, he'd show up in an Escalade or a Lexus SUV.

The bouncer at the door could have passed for Ving Rhames, except a head taller, with arms the size of my legs. I hoped we wouldn't get on each other's bad side. "Name?" he said, challenging me. No one who wasn't on his list—or whose face he didn't recognize on sight—was going to get by his solid three-hundred-pound frame.

"I'm with her." I showed him Honey's ID. The brother was sharp, looking from her face to the license and then back again. In his head, the math wasn't adding up. "She's part of the label's entertainment, brother," I said, and jostled my coat to open it. Honey's costume came into full view, his private peep show.

The brother grinned like he knew her. "Oh, a'ight, then. *Love* the bullets, girl."

"Glaze here yet?" I asked casually as he thrust out a meaty arm behind him to make a path for us into the cavernous, throbbing club. Club Magique was already knotted with people crowded near the door.

"Naw, bruh. You know Glaze ain't showin' up nowhere till after midnight." I glanced at my watch. Only eleven.

"He wants her in the booth," I said. Every club has a VIP area where patrons like M.C. Glazer can chill with their friends, ring up a bar tab, and play with a few select honeys without having to fight off fans. Club Magique's VIP booth was enclosed in glass, on the second level overlooking the dance floor. I knew it well.

"Ain't she a little long in the tooth for Glaze?" the bouncer said with an ironic chuckle. "Tell 'em Manny said ya'll can hang out up there."

Manny. Jackpot. I would be throwing that name around all night.

As we walked inside, M.C. Glazer's latest dance-floor anthem, "Ain't This Where the Party At?" roared from the sound system, its college-marching-band-style percussion booming in my ears. A dozen huge silkscreen replicas of Glazer's CD cover for *Plugged* billowed from the ceiling, with Glaze's eyes glowering from on high. Once we were indoors, Honey shrugged her shoulders to shed my coat like it was itching. It almost fell to the beer-sticky floor before I caught it. A four-hundred-dollar Kenneth Cole. Lambskin. But I bit my tongue. The girl was just foolish. *Easy, Ten. You need her.*

I'll say this for Honey: She knew how to do her job. Trailing behind Honey was the best camouflage imaginable. Everyone was looking in our direction, but no one noticed me. If I'd worn clown makeup, no one would have noticed my red nose. She worked that room like royalty, her head held high, proud chest in full strut. As she walked, the bullets tinkled and swayed with choreographed thrusts of her hips. A chorus of *Oh, shit!* and *Damn, girl!* greeted Honey like rose petals strewn in her path. I gave her space to work, walking a foot behind her. Anyone who got too close, or came up on her too fast with his hands in the wrong position, found me in his path, polite but firm, my body language suggesting that he find somewhere else to play.

The bodyguard game isn't about violence; it's about awareness, and presence. The guys who think the primary qualification is the willingness to break heads don't last very long. From time to time, yes, a bodyguard has to employ physical force, but in our litigious society force needs to be a last resort. "Looking comes free," I told Honey's admirers. "Touching will cost you."

A more daring brother sidled up to her and whispered in her ear—not too close, hands behind his back—and Honey made her deal with a discreet nod of her head and a whispered word. Honey was an earner. *Mother should list this girl on the New York Stock Exchange,* I thought.

Meanwhile, I scoped the place out. The bartenders were wispy and androgynous, nothing to worry about. I counted five bouncers inside, all huge and easy to spot in skintight black T-shirts. With three or four outside, that was about ten people who might stand in my way. And that wasn't counting Glaze's people, another matter entirely. I would have to play this one smart, or it would be a short interview. I slowed my breathing. The adrenaline was flowing, and if I didn't calm myself, my hands would start to shake. It had been a long time since I walked toward trouble with my eyes open.

I checked my watch. Eleven-thirty. From my headache, it could be dawn. The club's music crashed over my ears, and I felt like I was drowning in it. For all I knew, these hundreds of revelers were dancing on my grave.

"You ready to meet M.C. Glazer?" I said to Honey.

"Mother said to work the floor."

"You don't look like the type of girl who always does what Mother says. Big money's in the booth, darlin'."

"I'm thirsty," she pouted.

I sighed. It would be a long night if Honey was in a bad mood. I steered her to the corner of the closest bar counter, where I signaled a Latino bartender who couldn't have been less interested in Honey, but who was entranced by me. I winked at him, smiling. "Manny said to set the lady up with whatever she wants."

"What can I do for *you?*" he said once he'd fixed Honey's apple martini.

"Not a thing, friend. I'll come holla next time through."

"Promise, *papi?*"

The road not taken. Not negotiable. With Mother, male escorts willing to service male clients were set up for life. The business was ten to one, easy. Call it a blessing or a curse, but I can't even think on the downlow. No reason to be rude about it, though. Anyone who appreciates you is offering you a gift.

The VIP booth was large, but not empty. Spread out among the plush sofas and pillows were a couple of low-level rappers and a TV actor who had been famous in the eighties, all of whom I assumed were friends of Glaze's. With Manny's name to get us past the bouncer in the doorway and Honey's bullets to keep everyone smiling, we had no problem. Honey's apple martini improved her mood, so she began spontaneously swinging her hips and shimmying her shoulders when Glaze's war-cry hit "You Better Duck, Fool" boomed from the mounted speakers. Nobody in the room was mad at that, so I kept her drinks coming. Courtesy of Manny, of course.

Before I knew it, it was twelve-fifteen.

Right on time, M.C. Glazer was in the house.

Perched on the cushions at the edge of the glass booth, I had a perfect view of the club, so when Glaze and his posse arrived and made their way through the pulsing dance floor, it was the parting of the Red Sea. The throng melted, leaving a clear path down the center of the club. M.C. Glazer himself wasn't much to notice from above; just an average-sized man in a white skullcap, baggy jeans, and a bulletproof vest that covered his upper torso. Four hard dudes, three black and one white, walked in formation on either side of M.C. Glazer, all of them in red T-shirts with the CopKilla bullet insignia. Glazer's posse wasn't steroid-bulked like the club's bouncers, but they were far more dangerous. From the haircuts and the slants of their baseball caps, I guessed that each and every one of them was a cop.

When the door of the VIP lounge opened, only three of the guards I'd seen escorted M.C. Glazer inside. The fourth, I guessed, was keeping a watchful eye on the club below. I know people never look quite the way you expect up close, but I was still surprised that Glazer was only about five-eight, smaller than me despite his thick upper arms. A girl trailing behind him was dressed up for her years; despite her expert makeup and hair worn up to give an impression of age and height, I could see the lie in a glance. If Honey was nineteen, this girl couldn't have been more then eighteen. If that. But when you walk in on M.C. Glazer's arm, security tends to look the other way.

M.C. Glazer greeted his friends, but his eyes still scanned the room. And me. I never knew whether Glaze gestured somehow, but within a blink of his eye contact, one of his bodyguards stood between us.

"Who the fuck are you?" He reminded me of a black Telly Savalas, bald head and almost Arab nose with Ethiopian skin. He talked like a man carrying a gun who was accustomed to rapid answers.

I held his eyes and matched the pace of my breathing to his to create an emotional link. It makes people feel like they know you, without ever understanding why. "Hey, man. I'm working, just like you. I'm with Honey."

"Naw, man, he's a'ight," said the television actor. "He's with Honey."

"Who the fuck is Honey?"

That broke the ice. A room full of brothers cracked up because this bodyguard was so on point that he hadn't noticed the near-naked woman standing in front of him. I smiled, too, inviting the bodyguard to join the joke. He glanced at Honey, and he didn't smile. He didn't step completely out of the way, but slid to the side a bit, to see if Glazer wanted to engage with me, but Glazer was checking out Honey, too. I nodded a humble thanks to the guard. It's useful for your enemies to underestimate you.

"Oh, shit—it's all *bullets*," Glazer said, walking closer to Honey. She came to life under Glazer's eyes, straightening her spine, shifting her hips from one side to the other in a slow, entrancing rumba. Glaze grinned. "That's *tight*. Come here, girl. Hey, Renzo, take a picture of me and these bullets. Don't she look like a CD cover?"

Instinct made me want to shadow Honey's every step, but I was glad to get my mind back to the reason I was there. Honey would occupy the room's attention for a while. The girl who had come in with Glazer sat at the edge of the sofa, staring at Honey with equal parts envy and loathing. That girl was cute, with playful spiral ringlets of dark brown hair nestling her neckline and café con leche skin that reminded me of Little Havana, but she didn't have Honey's plastic surgeon. Her chest was nearly flat. She would have looked like a boy next to Honey, and she knew it.

While Glazer and his friends took turns posing with Honey ("Hey, man, email this one to me . . . This is my phone's new screensaver . . .")—I studied the two other bodyguards. One was at the door, and the other was at an angle from me, similarly perched at the window for a view of the club. The one at the window was a white guy, about thirty, with a face that had seen a few beat-downs. I nodded at him, and he nodded back.

The white guard was studying the dance floor, but the brother at the door was scrutinizing only me. I never saw him blink. He was closer to my age, about thirty-five. His hair was short, Marine-style, and he wore round gold-rimmed glasses that were out of style. Something told me he wasn't having a good day. His shoulders were squared. He looked locked down.

"Real shame about Afrodite," I said, out of the blue. I spoke directly to the brother staring me down, although it was loud enough for everyone to hear.

I think what happened next is what people mean when they say *Time stood still*. To me, it sounded like there was a thunderclap, but it was only a percussion crescendo from the club's massive speakers. The camera's flash went off in a near-dark room, so I was momentarily blinded. When my sight cleared, the first thing I saw was this brother's eyes on me, still not blinking. But his eyes had changed, so subtle I wouldn't have noticed if I hadn't been looking for it. I was willing to bet my life on it. It's almost as if I saw his pupils narrow from across the room.

For a time, no one said anything. I'd brought the party down.

The second girl wailed. "I *lovvvved* Afrodite."

"Shame when a hot piece of ass like that gets killed," the white guard said, his eyes still scanning the floor below. "What a waste."

"Fuck Afrodite," said the gravelly voice that could only belong to M.C. Glazer. He stood with his arm hooked around Honey's shoulder. His face froze in a smile, and the camera flashed again. "Someone should have put that bitch down a long time ago."

This time, I saw spots. They might have been from anger. The thundering bass no longer seemed so bone-rattling, almost far away. Maybe the deejay had decided to be merciful, or maybe it was something else; maybe my focus had telescoped because rational thought was giving way to raw emotion. *Not good.*

"What you mean, man?" I said, trying to sound casual.

"I've told you about this shit, Glaze," said Kojak, who was taking the photos.

The flash ignited again.

"What? A nigga gotta pretend we was tight just 'cause that ho's goin' in the ground? Shit—Jenk knows. She was a straight-up ho. For *real*. They was gonna put a *ho* in a movie with Robin Williams. That shit was too funny."

"You cold, man. You cold," said one of the rappers in the corner. He was a little guy in a USC jacket fringed with rolling-paper logos.

No one else spoke. Hardly breathed.

"That's what y'all niggas will never understand about me," M.C. Glazer said, as if he were at a podium. "I'm a poet. I ain't careless with my words. So if I stand here and tell you Afrodite was a ten-dollar ho, I ain't playin'. OK, she's dead, so I won't speak ill. Rest in peace, whatever. But you know you was a ho."

"*M.C. Glazer ain't no ladykilla* . . ." the USC rapper in the corner said, the words from Afrodite's song, and his actor friend laughed, joining in: "*Might penetrate, but he'll never fill ya* . . ." they whooped, teasing Glaze like school-boys.

Glaze laughed, too. "Oops, aw shit, that bitch is *gone*," Glaze began, his voice a chilling sing-song. "But Glazer's here to carry *onnn*. Fuck ya'll, then."

The man at the door wasn't smiling. *Jenk. Short for Jenkins?*

His eyes were still on me. "You a friend of Afrodite's?" Jenk said. I could barely hear him over the laughter, but I didn't need to. We could have been the only two men there. We were the only ones who understood what the conversation was really about.

"Yes," I said. "Serena was a friend."

When I called her *Serena*, his eyes changed again. Just for a second.

Gentle as my voice had been, my words brought another hush, the laughter dying. Energy crackled from one person to the next. Smart idea or not, I was inviting M.C. Glazer to fuck with me. I felt something going hot inside me, and the music faded almost completely. Blood surged to the thick muscles banding my chest. I had to fight to keep from balling my hands into fists. There was still a chance—just a chance—that this would end peacefully. Hope springs eternal.

"I never caught your name, bruh," said the guard beside me, one of those white boys who must have grown up near Crenshaw.

Slowly—very slowly—I turned my hip to the side and pulled open my wallet. Every motion I made captivated the room. No one was taking pictures anymore. I found my business cards. "Tennyson Hardwick."

The brother who'd been staring me down walked over to get a card, too. He studied it. "An actor? You worked with Serena?"

"A long time ago."

"What was she *like*?" said the too-young girl on the sofa.

M.C. Glazer didn't give me the chance to answer his plaything. He stepped toward me, his head cocked attentively. He played with the peach fuzz above his upper lip. "Lemme ask you something, man . . ."

"What's that?"

"How much does it cost these days to bury a ho? Y'all need some help with that? Because I believe in contributing to worthy causes."

Catcalls and laughter. *You're cold, man,* one of them said. With casual precision, Kojak and the white boy were on either side of me, as if they expected me to spring. They were used to subduing people after Glazer pissed them off.

A cool smile crawled across my lips, but my arms were trembling. I wanted to hurt that sonofabitch. I wanted him to know the pain I'd been feeling since I heard Serena was dead. Wanted it so much that my throat burned.

"Come on, she's dead. That's not nice," the girl said. Her voice was much younger than her face. Damn, she was young.

M.C. Glazer glanced at her over his shoulder. "Nobody . . . is talking . . . to your narrow little ass." Even with the emphasis on each word, he'd said it politely enough—he hadn't even raised his voice—but the girl's body coiled as if he was standing over her with a two-by-four. Her eyes went wide under all that mascara, like a raccoon's. She glued her lips shut. She was scared. *When that girl gets home, she's probably gonna get the ass-kicking Glaze thinks he can give me.*

"Thanks, man, Serena had plenty of money," I said without sarcasm, enlisting every thespian skill I had. "But since we're asking questions . . . I have one."

"Watch yourself," Kojak cautioned me.

M.C. Glazer stepped within a yard. There was nothing behind me but a picture window, two bodyguards on either side of me and a third waiting to jump in. Glaze folded his arms. "Don't ask nothin' you don't want the answer to."

I lowered my voice, nearly whispering. "Why'd you hate her so much?"

"I don't have time for hate," Glazer said, his jawbone rock-hard.

"You don't seem sad she's dead."

"If I had to take time to mourn every ho who got a beat-down, I wouldn't have enough hours in my day," Glazer said. "She brought it on herself."

"Why?" I said to Glaze. My voice was as soft as a priest's in a confessional. Kojak tugged on my arm, as if to encourage me to shut the hell up.

M.C. Glazer's eyes sparked. "You know who Aphrodite was? The *real* Aphrodite? She was a goddess. The Goddess of Love. See how that ho tried to twist it? Like a ho by any other name ain't still a ho?" I couldn't help the surprise in my face; I hadn't expected to hear Greek mythology and Shakespeare in the same breath from the likes of M.C. Glazer. His eyes slitted. "You think you're the only one who knows something? Fuck you. I'm a poet. In your whole lifetime, you will never have the capacity to learn the most basic shit I know off the top of my head. And listen close, brother: Later on, you may live long enough to ask yourself where this conversation went wrong. And I'll tell you now, so you won't have to wonder. You made the same mistake that dead ho made. It's the same damn mistake every triflin' nigga lying dead on the pavement makes: You *forgot*."

I didn't have the chance to ask him what I forgot, because he sucker-punched me in the groin. His boys grabbed my arms to hold me in place, but I saw Glaze's shoulder move, saw him bend, and I knew his mind. My arms were pinned, but I turned my thigh into the path of his fist. Glaze's fist landed on muscle instead of nerve clusters, but it must have given him a satisfying *thunk*, because he grinned like boxer Jack Johnson. Even a partial blow to that region is no fun. The room went black for a moment, and then came into focus again. I bent over and moaned, more for effect than out of pain, and even Glazer didn't seem to notice how much of his blow I'd avoided.

Glazer leaned over me. "You forgot who the fuck you wuz talkin' to."

The two cops held on tight, in case Glazer wasn't finished with me.

"Any more questions, asshole?" Glazer said.

I did have a few, in fact, but I decided to keep them to myself. Since I didn't move or speak, his guards let my arms go. Laughing, Glaze sauntered over to talk to his friends as if nothing had happened. The white guard grinned at me with piss-colored teeth, offering me a glass of champagne. "Get a drink and chill out," he said.

Jenk, the brother with the glasses, slid my card into his back pocket. He stared at me, then shifted his eyes meaningfully toward the door. Subtle advice. If I didn't get out there, I was about to get LAPD's Rodney King Special, and he knew it.

Two giant breasts bobbed in front of my eyes. "You OK?" Honey said.

"I'm fine. Go on back down to the floor now," I said, real quiet.

"But you said—"

I smiled, but through gritted teeth. "Just do it, darlin'."

The thought that I might be standing within a few yards of the man who was responsible for Serena's death was doing strange things to my mind, or I would have followed Honey downstairs. M.C. Glazer was right: Later, I would mull over where I'd gone wrong. Instead of sitting quietly to chill with Glaze and his crew, eavesdropping on their conversations, I'd provoked him. I can't tell you how much I would have paid for ten minutes alone with him, but I didn't have that luxury.

Oh, well, I thought. *No pain, no gain.* I just hoped I wouldn't get hit in the face.

"Here's a little bit I know about Greek mythology, too," I said in a sweeping stage announcer's voice everyone in the booth could hear, even over the music. "My father taught me the story of the first murder trial, at least according to the Greeks. The daughter of a god named Ares was raped . . ." As I said the word *raped*, I looked squarely at the jailbait on Glaze's arm, who seemed younger every time I noticed her. Seventeen? Sixteen? Her wide-eyed stare made her more childlike. I avoided Glaze's eyes, but I could feel his glare. "Now, Ares is the God of War, so he killed that fool—probably slow and with considerable relish. The other gods brought Ares to trial for murder, but when they heard the facts, they let him go. The way the Greeks saw it, the man he'd killed deserved to die for this terrible act against this woman. So the message history teaches us is this: Don't fuck with the God of War. Or his daughter."

I don't know where all of that came from, to be honest, but I felt like Laurence Fishburne rallying his warriors in the third *Matrix* movie, when all of Zion is ready to fight for its survival. I think I mesmerized them. For a moment, eight pairs of eyes looked at me as if I were brandishing Poseidon's trident and could make the earth itself shake. As if I was Ares himself. That was a good moment; a real actor's moment.

I felt the white guard beside me swing and slipped his punch with peripheral vision alone, simultaneously popping the heel of my right hand against his chin. Sidestepped into him as his head snapped around, spinning him so that he was between me and Glazer's other two men. I kept spinning until his back was to me, stomped the back of his thigh, and brought him down, ramming the base of his skull with my knee. He sprawled forward, as unconscious as a man can be, his limp body a line in the sand.

Two on one instead of three on one. Much better odds.

The guy at the window had been drinking a Coke from a slender glass with a stemmed cherry. That glass still sat on the windowsill, and before anyone could take their eyes from their fallen comrade, I swept it up and in a single fluid motion threw it into Kojak's eyes. He was going for his radio, and I wasn't interested in company.

He threw his hands up to protect his eyes, and never saw the front kick coming.

I have a problem finishing some things. I dropped out of the police academy, I never gave my acting career everything I could have, and Mother would probably say I let my greatest talent languish. I also never earned my black belt. What I do have is two brown belts—one in kenpo karate, one in judo—and five years of studying mixed martial arts at the Inosanto Academy in Los Angeles. I'm what they call a dojo bum, hopping from art to art, never nesting. I learned something along the way: I'm not the toughest, or the best, or the strongest, or the most dedicated.

But I'm faster than hell.

The ball of my foot took Kojak in the solar plexus, and the air exploded out of him in a rancid cloud. I could have sealed his fate right then and there, but I pivoted just in time to slip a punch that would have landed squarely on my left temple.

Next came Jenk, the one with the glasses. He moved like a boxer, so I raised my hands like Mike Tyson. I saw a light in his eyes as he realized I was playing his game. He feinted right, expecting me to slip again; he had the left waiting for me. Instead, I dropped to the ground and mule-kicked him in the groin. He fell back into a cocktail table with a cry. I sprang up and turned back toward Kojak, who was starting toward me, still wobbling from the solar plexus blow. I parried a pawing punch, stepped inside with a rising elbow that almost took his head off, and spun him into Jenk on the floor.

Total time, about five seconds.

Glazer was opening his mouth to say something when I crossed the five feet separating us with a single sliding quick-step, lifted him up by his armpits, and pinned him to the wall like he was a scarecrow, my elbow jammed across his throat in case he thought about moving. Out of the corner of my eye, I could see Jenk climbing from behind the overturned table, so I had ten seconds at best.

"Did you kill Serena?" I said.

The eyes of Alphonse Terrell Gaines were bottomless, showing nothing. Nothing I did would shake him. He'd spent most of his young adult life behind bars, where he'd brushed against people far deadlier than me, even with enough pain in my heart to make me want to break his neck.

"Yeah, I killed her," M.C. Glazer said, and my heart nearly stopped. "And I killed Shareef. And Tupac. And your mama, too."

I jabbed him in the groin with my knee. He didn't know the thigh-deflection trick, and screamed like a little girl. He couldn't have known my mother was dead—he was only being a smart-ass—but I got him as if he'd been the one who planted the cancer in her breast, just for speaking her name.

When Glaze screamed, strong hands pulled me from behind. Clubbing blows on my shoulders. I remember pivoting, hitting someone, getting hit, sliding down to the carpeted floor. Rage and pain and anger at my own asininity mingled as the room started to swirl and fade, then there was yelling—*mine? theirs?*—and I was rolling on the floor trying to protect my kidneys, arms crossed in front of my face as blurred vision revealed incoming shoe leather.

Red. Blackness coming soon.

Another yell, and the fresh pain stopped. I heard voices, but the ringing in my head trumped every other sound.

A sturdy, slender arm was around my waist, and I looked up into the famil-iar face of the bartender who had made a polite pass, and been gently rebuffed. Courtesy goes a long way. "I was checking you out from downstairs, and I saw something was up. Can you stand?" I was already on my feet.

Five beefy bouncers, larger than the off-duty cops by a factor of three, were standing between Glazer's boys and me, the object of their antipathy. Appar-ently, the bouncers were the only ones allowed to stomp ass in Club Magique. Professional pride is a wonderful thing.

"Show's over," the largest bouncer said. I stared at his lips moving, either still slightly in shock or genuinely surprised that one of the Mount Rushmore faces had spoken aloud. Club Magique's gargoyles gripped my arms and car-ried me out through the crowd, my feet barely touching the ground. They pushed me through the door and out onto the sidewalk in front of a line of wannabes hoping to get in before 3:00 A.M.

"Don't come back," said a bouncer I recognized. Manny.

I spat out blood. My mouth was filled with the coppery taste. "Don't worry."

As the door slammed shut, I remembered my four-hundred-dollar coat. Shit.

I ignored the staring faces and stretched my limbs one by one to see if anything was broken. My left ribs were sore as hell, but they were only bruised. I checked myself out in a mirror on the side of a Jeep parked at the curb. Bloody lower lip. Bruise over my right eye. *Shit.* But my teeth were intact, thank God.

Even with the bruises and lost jacket, I knew I was damned lucky. For now.

But Glaze's bodyguards knew who I was, since I'd been stupid enough to hand out business cards. My problems were just getting started.

SEVEN

YEAH, I KILLED HER.

M.C. Glazer's voice haunted me in bed that night. I wasn't having night-mares—you have to be able to sleep before you can dream—but I couldn't get his voice out of my head. And I was entertaining elaborate fantasies about the different ways I would have liked to throw him through Club Magique's plate-glass window. The fantasies were sweet. Believe me, I understand wanting to kill someone.

I knew he'd said it to piss me off, but what if he *had* killed Serena? Between not knowing and the painful throbbing of every muscle in my body, I felt like I was caught in a bad dream, slowly losing my sanity. I don't like drugs in gen-eral, but I found some Tylenol with Codeine I'd been prescribed after I had a wisdom tooth pulled, so I took two. Slowly, I felt my anxious mind emptying out, and most of my body's complaints quieted. Good. Rest. I would need it.

I had promised Mother I would visit her the next day, but I didn't have time for her games. I knew exactly where I needed to go, the one place I proba-bly should have gone first. I wasn't looking forward to it. I dreaded it like noth-ing else, in fact.

But any detective knows he has to visit the scene of the crime.

I stopped at the mouth of the alley near Highland and Sunset, practically across the street from Hollywood High. For a while, I couldn't make myself step be-yond the sidewalk into the shadows. It was one of those cool Los Angeles mornings, and I knew I would feel the bite as soon as I left the sanctuary of sunlight. My skin was going cold already.

This was no place to die, or to be found after the fact. A dog deserved better.

The narrow alley was sandwiched between two brick buildings—a camera shop on one side, an abandoned auto detailer on the other—dead-ending at an eight-foot chained fence leading to a small apartment complex with fading yellow paint. The complex wasn't the projects, but it was nowhere anyone would choose to live long.

Well-wishers had come and gone, and their offerings lay against the camera shop wall a few feet from the sidewalk; bouquets of flowers, stuffed animals, publicity photographs of Serena, and handwritten messages like AFRODITE FOREVER!!!! The gifts helped brighten the alley a little, but not much. My eyes clouded, so I looked away. I hadn't come to join the line of the grieving.

Otherwise, it was just an alley. Dirty. Smelly. A large green Dumpster emitted the familiar, sour smell of ripe garbage to mingle with the muted smell of old piss that slimed the walls. There were a few newspapers and fast-food wrappers strewn around, and an old tire from a semi truck propped against the auto shop wall, but I didn't bother examining them. The homicide investigators were long gone by now, so I hadn't come hoping to find physical evidence. Even the crushed Coke can I'd seen in the photo was gone, probably confiscated for fingerprints.

I just needed to stand there for a while. I would know what I was looking for when I found it. After a deep breath, I took a slow tour of the alley.

Why would Serena be in this alley that time of night? It made more sense that her body had been dumped. The lock on the fence at the other end was rusty and looked as if it hadn't been touched in fifteen years, so unless whoever killed Serena had a key, it wasn't likely that her body had been brought from the apartment side. Someone had come through the front of the alley—probably in a car—and dumped her from the street side.

Like a director blocks a scene, I tried to visualize the way it happened. The alley was too narrow for a car to bother trying to turn in, especially with the Dumpster in the way. I figured the murderer had backed in, unloaded the body from the rear, and then turned easily onto Sunset. That's what I would have done. All told, the stop might not have taken more than a minute, if that—and certainly no longer than two. A man or a woman could have moved the body without help. (As I considered the scenarios, she was no longer *Serena* to me. Her name would have been too painful to think or speak.)

I crouched to examine the cracked asphalt for tire tracks, as no doubt LAPD's forensics experts had done in the past forty-eight hours. There was no mud to leave telltale signs, or tracks of any kind. Clearly, this alley didn't see much traffic, and the sidewalk didn't get much more. I hadn't seen a pedestrian since I arrived. Most of the traffic whizzed by on Sunset, and there was plenty of metered parking stretching down the curb. The street was only moderately busy during daylight, so it might be dead at night. A camera shop would have been closed by nine, and the body would have been dumped later than that. No obvious witnesses.

I looked upward for streetlamps, and I didn't see any within view.

The killer picked this alley because it was so dark.

"You won't find the answer up there," a woman's voice said.

I nearly jumped out of my skin. For a split second, the voice had sounded like Serena's, as if I'd expected her guidance all along.

It was the reporter I'd met at the police station the day before, April Forrest. She had a reporter's pad ready, so we'd both had the same idea. "Sorry. Didn't mean to scare you," she said, smiling.

Maybe it was the grim loneliness of that alley, or the throbbing across my face as my muscles contemplated last night's beating, but I have never been so grateful for a smile. For a moment, I couldn't speak.

"Someone had a bad night," she observed.

Self-conscious, I touched my face, trying to hide my swelling eye. Knowing how bad I must look made the pain seem worse. "Long story."

"I love a good story."

I tried to smile, and probably failed. "Another time."

"Your choice. You're a grown-ass man," she said, shrugging. "Anyway, I'm glad I ran into you, Mr. Slick. You were holding out on me yesterday."

"Holding out how?"

"You never told me you were a suspect."

Whatever smile I'd managed died. I felt blood rush to my ears. I was too stunned to pretend I didn't know what she was talking about. "Who told you that?"

"Your friend Lieutenant Nelson was pretty helpful, actually. Thanks for the tip about when to call him, by the way. He was right at his desk, like you said."

Now, I was angry. "I told you not to mention my name."

"I didn't, and neither did he. But when I tried to press him about the obvious angle—you know, whether it was M.C. Glazer and a rap vendetta—he told me off the record that there was another suspect. Well, a *person of interest*." She flipped through her notebook. "Here it is: 'A minor actor Afrodite was involved with' is how he put it. I put two and two together. Your TV show?"

Insult to injury. I was annoyed at the *minor actor* reference, but I was horrified that Nelson was throwing his suspicions around to the press. This guy was trying to rattle me. "That sonofoabitch."

"I did some research on the guy before I called him. Lieutenant Nelson and I both went to Florida A&M, it turns out, and my dad was his mentor in the criminal justice department. It's a family thing, so he gave me inside tips. Go Rattlers, right?"

The alley seemed to spin. I was genuinely dizzy. I'd forgotten to eat breakfast.

"So, the suspect *is* you," she said. I'd given her all the confirmation she needed. She looked delighted with herself for figuring it out.

I held her shoulders, as gently as I could. "My father has a bad heart, he just had a stroke, and he's in a nursing home," I said. "If you write that in the newspaper—"

April's face changed, apologetic. "Oh, don't worry about that, Mr. Hardwick. For real. To me, off the record means off the record. Some of us still have ethics, believe it or not."

I bore into her eyes, not letting her go. "April, I did not kill Serena Johnston."

She studied me, her face noncommittal. "You might want to tell Lieutenant Nelson that."

"I already have. The police are desperate to close this, and I'm all they've got. I knew her before she was a movie star, and I was with her the day she died. I ran into her at Roscoe's and gave her my card, so it was in her pocket when they found her. But I did *not* kill her. I . . ." I almost said *I loved her.* "I really cared about her."

"So . . . you're here to try to find the real killer. Like O.J." April's brow furrowed, and the tip of her pink tongue flicked nervously at her upper lip.

I released her shoulders. Being grabbed by a murder suspect in an alley was enough to make anyone feel intimidated. I wanted an ally, not a reporter who doubted my sanity. "O.J. was found guilty in civil court, so I'll say it again: *I did*

not kill Serena Johnston. I'm here to find out who did. I want that person fried."
My voice shook.

Finally, I saw it in her face: She believed me. There was nothing in her de-meanor to show that she had ever believed I had killed Serena, from the instant she approached me. What was it she had said when she saw me? *You won't find the answer up there.* A killer wouldn't be looking for the answer.

"You know I didn't do it," I said as soon as I realized it.

"All I *know* in this life is that Jesus loves me," she said. "But do I think you're the killer type? I could be wrong, but you don't strike me that way, Mr. Hardwick."

Maybe her empathy did something to my eyes, but I noticed April Forrest's features for the first time then; full lips painted lightly with pink gloss, large eyes, a button nose, and deep dimples when she smiled. With a little rouge, she could look like an actress. And she didn't have to tell me what Lieutenant Nel-son said about me, but she had.

"My name is Tennyson. Call me Ten."

"What happened to your face since I last saw you, Ten?"

"I had a disagreement with M.C. Glazer's bodyguards last night. I was try-ing to get some answers about Serena."

She frowned with naked envy. "At Club Magique? I tried to get in, but—"

"All I learned is that he doesn't like to be accused of murder."

She nodded toward the alley entrance and the morning light. "Come here. I want to show you something. I missed it my first time out here. Maybe you did, too."

Without a word, she led me half a block east, toward the corner. She stopped in front of an MTA bus shelter. I glanced up at the route numbers on the sign, wondering when the 2 and 302 Metro Buses ran, if someone might have seen the killer leaving the body. April tugged on my sleeve. "You're looking the wrong way," she said.

I turned around, toward the bench and its shelter. My heart leaped.

The shelter's Plexiglas back wall was the victim of street stickering, covered with posters of M.C. Glazer's face from his *Plugged* album cover, the same one I'd seen at Club Magique. His eyes stared back at me, twentyfold.

"See what I'm saying?" April said. "Seems like a big coincidence. I don't think even Lieutenant Nelson picked up on it. I just noticed it. It's going in my story tomorrow."

I looked back toward the alleyway, calculating the distance we'd walked. We weren't even thirty yards away from where the body was found. I examined the shelter again and noticed the LED bulbs overhead, probably solar-powered. So, it was lighted. The lights weren't on yet, but they would be at night. The Glazer posters would have been in plain view, even more noticeable than during daylight.

"So . . . it could have been Glazer or someone on his behalf . . ." I said, gazing toward the traffic on Sunset, ". . . or someone with her body in the car saw an opportunity to point the finger in Glazer's direction. Maybe it wasn't even planned that way. But they're driving along, they see the posters . . ." My eyes went from the posters to the alleyway. ". . . and they've found their spot. They drive a little ways past the bus shelter, back up into the alley. *Voilà.*"

April was busy scribbling notes. "I see you know how to think like a killer."

"An actor is trained to think like anyone. Besides, the big mistake is to believe a killer doesn't think like the rest of us."

April looked up at me, one eyebrow raised. "Under the circumstances, you can keep your cryptic little adages to yourself."

I laughed then, for the first time in a while. She laughed, too. Then she gave a start, gazing at my face in the light. "*Damn.* You got tore up. I don't suppose you bothered to put anything on those cuts on your lip or above your eye."

"I've been busy."

She slipped her warm hand into mine, squeezing. "Come on. There's a convenience store across the street. You need somebody to be your mama today."

I don't remember having a mother, but if it was anything like April Forrest's gently clinging hand on a day when I felt more alone than ever, I couldn't argue. While we dodged traffic on Sunset to get to the Korean-run grocery and sundries store across the street, April told me what she'd learned during her own investigation. She talked nonstop, without taking a breath.

"The police have been canvasing the apartment building behind the alley for two days straight, and the residents there aren't interested in talking to any more strangers. I don't think anyone there saw anything, or if they did, they're not saying so. Auto shop's been closed for two months, and the camera store closes at five-thirty. Cops have also interviewed the proprietors across the street. I've already talked to Mr. Kim, who runs the grocery store. They're open all night, but he and his sons are pretty much the only ones who work there, and they didn't see anything either. Like it never happened."

The store was cramped with too many aisles and products, and smelled like sweet rotting produce and floor cleanser. April stopped talking only once we reached the COUGH/COLD/FIRST AID aisle, studying the disinfectants like she had a medical degree. She picked up a tube of Neosporin and some Band-Aids.

"Now it's your turn," she said, once we had settled into a line six people deep. "What did you learn at Club Magique?"

I sighed, in no hurry to revisit that memory. "Well, as you suspect, Glazer didn't like Serena. I don't know if it was a radio rivalry or something more personal, but he was crowing about her death. Being an asshole doesn't mean he killed her, though."

"Doesn't mean he didn't."

"Believe me, I like him less than you do. But I'm trying to keep an open mind."

"I am, too, Ten, or I wouldn't be standing here with you."

"Touché."

"But I really don't get why the police aren't more interested in M.C. Glazer. Lieutenant Nelson kind of shrugged him off."

"Maybe it's because M.C. Glazer is up to his ass in LAPD. Those guys on his payroll last night were all cops. LAPD got embarrassed by O.J., Rodney King, and the dirty cops working security for Suge Knight and Death Row Records. Nobody's eager for more bad news involving LAPD and rappers. Money buys blue friends."

"You have friends, too, don't you? Your father was a captain."

My throat tightened. Dad wasn't LAPD anymore; Dad was hanging on to the world by his fingernails. "Doesn't work that way," I said.

"Well, here's something juicy: Lieutenant Nelson said they have DNA. They're putting a rush on the results."

My stomach knotted. "Did he say what kind of samples?"

"Not specifically, but he mentioned her bedroom, so I got the feeling it was sexual. A condom, maybe?" She saw something in my face that made her decide to look away politely. "Listen . . . I don't know what was up with you and Afrodite—Serena—but if you were with her the day she died, you may be about to get cleared, or your life is about to get interesting."

May you live in interesting times. Serena had spoken those words the last time I saw her. The dizziness came back. I really needed to eat, not that food would help.

"Here she is again!" a stranger's voice exclaimed ahead of us, followed by laughter so carefree that it offended my ears. The shopkeeper was grinning at April.

Mr. Kim was balding, about sixty, with uneven teeth stained from too much coffee, but the kindness of his face made him striking. "This woman, she is like reporter in that movie . . . *All the President's Men!* She want whole story. Truth and nothing but the truth." Considering that he had obviously learned English late in life, his mastery of the language was impressive. Humor is difficult to translate.

"She talk about Afrodite," he said. He turned to me, gesturing toward his chest. "Big murder on Mr. Kim's street, you see."

"So I heard," I said.

His smile faded as he shook his head. "I like Afrodite. She good in that movie."

"Mr. Kim sees a lot of movies," April said to me.

"Mr. Kim see *every* movie. For two year since I come here, every Saturday, twelve o'clock, Mr. Kim is at movie. Popcorn. M&Ms. In movie, I learn English better. So I know Afrodite—I see *Keeping It Real.* She good-looking girl."

"Yes, she was," I said. Mr. Kim's good nature was a welcome diversion. He pulled me out of my own mind, which had been boiling into panic since April mentioned the DNA. It was easier to feel sad.

"Mr. Kim didn't see anything Monday night," April told me.

"I no see street from cash register," he said, pointing to the ads and posters in his windows. It was true. His view of the street was entirely blocked. "If only I see, you know? Maybe Afrodite no dead then."

"She was probably dead before she was brought here," I said.

He inhaled, his teeth hissing. Mr. Kim shook his head, finally ringing up the items April had bought for me. It was an old-fashioned cash register, with a pleasant-sounding bell. "I still no believe. No believe. I so excited, see, because Afrodite in my store. I say I go tell granddaughter."

Between his accent and his butchered English, I couldn't catch what he'd said despite the way my ears perked.

April straightened up, leaning forward. "Afrodite was in your store? When?"

He shook his head. "No, *she* not in store. I . . ." He paused, searching for his words for the first time. "I *think* Afrodite in store. I see with eyes. My eyes say, 'Hey, this Afrodite.' But she come Tuesday morning. Police say she dead already. She dead before. So, my eyes say wrong."

April translated. "You saw someone Tuesday you thought was Afrodite?"

"What time Tuesday morning?" I said.

"I say . . . nine o'clock, maybe. Later, police come and say Afrodite dead."

How the hell could Serena have visited this store at 9:00 A.M. Tuesday, nearly twelve hours after the police said she died? Was it possible? After all, I hadn't seen the corpse. Just possibly. Just maybe . . .

I was afraid of the hope glowing faintly beneath my breastbone, but I let the idea sit in my mind in case there was a way to make sense of it.

"Are you sure it wasn't Monday?" I said. She might have stopped here on her way to Roscoe's. If so, at least I might get a better idea of why she'd been brought here.

Could she still be alive? Tired of it all, and slipped away into anonymity, or ready to resurrect herself in the cruelest, most bizarre publicity stunt in history?

"No, *Tuesday*. Same day police come. Police come two hour later. But this girl, she wear hair same like Afrodite, clothes same like Afrodite. I say she twin."

The glow in my chest was irrepressible. Now, I understood the legions of Tupac and Elvis fans who couldn't let go. I wanted to erase Serena's death so badly that I could believe she might not be dead, especially with such an earnest witness. *She didn't look like herself in that photo. Maybe . . .*

I reached over to borrow April's notebook. She gave me a puzzled look.

"Describe the girl to me, Mr. Kim," I said.

"He reporter, too?" he asked April.

"Something like that," April said.

"She Afrodite. Look like her. Only different here." He touched his earlobe, gesturing down the length of it. "She wear earring all over ear. Up and down."

There are few genuinely revelatory moments in life, but as Mr. Kim ended his description, I had one of mine.

My exhilaration melted, and the knot in my stomach tightened into something like nausea. I'd only met Serena's sister once—at a premiere party at a nightclub on Wilshire—but she'd made an impression on me. Serena was a year older, but the sisters looked remarkably similar, especially considering that they shared only a mother in common. The Johnston family women had strong genes, apparently. And Serena's sister had littered her ears with piercings, perhaps a dozen in each one. I couldn't remember her name yet, but I could see her face as sharply as if I'd seen her Tuesday morning, just like Mr. Kim.

"Did she have earrings in just one ear, or both?" I asked him.

"Both ear."

Tyra Johnston. That was her name. I'd asked Serena about her sister when I saw her. *Same shit, different decade,* she'd said. They had never gotten along, I remembered. Damn. They had never gotten along, and Tyra might have been within a block of the spot where Serena's body was found two hours later.

I didn't like this idea nearly as much as I'd liked the M.C. Glazer scenario.

"What are you thinking?" April said.

"Serena has a half-sister. Right here in L.A."

"A sister? I've read through all her bios. She never mentioned a sister."

"They didn't like each other. But I've met her. She wears earrings like that."

Neither of us spoke for a while. April said good-bye to Mr. Kim, and after we walked back outside, she asked me to lean over so she could apply the cream to my wounds. For me, that was a first. I've always nursed myself. I enjoyed her care so much that I didn't mind people staring at us as they passed, or the stinging from her touch.

"Ten," April said softly, "I have a sister, too. And a brother. And if I told them I was hanging out with a murder suspect, they would freak out. So don't think this isn't against my better judgment."

"OK," I said. Candor isn't always comfortable, but I appreciate it.

"I think I trust you, but that doesn't matter in the end. It could be a mistake."

"True. Just like it could be a mistake for me to trust you."

Carefully, April applied a bandage above my eye. She pressed with her index finger, steady pressure to hold it in place. "My instinct says we can help each other."

"We already have." April's inside track with Lieutenant Nelson made her precious.

"I'm writing a story about Serena's death. That's the bottom line. If you tell me anything off the record, I'll respect that—but I'm going to report on anything I see."

"That's your job," I said.

"I'll tell you everything Lieutenant Nelson says that I think might help you clear yourself. But I want you to help me find Serena's sister today. You want to talk to her, and so do I. We need each other."

She was right. April Forrest could be a lifeline. There was no reason not to cooperate with her. But I wasn't sure I could help her. It had been five years since I'd seen Serena's sister, and I had never known where she lived. "Maybe she's still in the Crenshaw district, where Serena grew up. The Jungle. But I don't know her address."

"Do you know her name?"

"Sure do."

April smiled, surveying her dressing. One last pat. "Then I'll do the rest."

On Harvard Avenue near the Crenshaw district stands First AME, a megachurch boasting twenty thousand members. My father used to take me there when I was a kid. He's actually named for the man who founded the African Methodist Episcopal church in 1787, a former slave named Richard Allen, so Dad didn't play about church. I wasn't anybody's choirboy, but I liked the way Sundays gave me Dad's undivided attention—he ironed my clothes, pointed out where to find the Bible passages, taught me the songs his mother had sung to him, like "How Great Thou Art" and "Leaning on the Everlasting Arms." When he closed his eyes to talk to God, it was almost as if he left me to ascend to some great height, challenging me to follow.

I didn't know how to find God at church like Dad did. If God loved me like the preacher said, why had God cursed me to be motherless? But Dad's face was rapturous when he closed his eyes to talk to Jesus. Then, he always came back to me, and after church we had a big lunch at M&Ms—smothered chicken, oxtails, greens, candied yams, and sweet iced tea—the only time we ate out other than fast food. Sundays were our best times. Whenever I'm in the Crenshaw district, I think of church. I stopped going to church after I left Dad's house, but I always went with him to Easter and Christmas services. Were those days gone?

First AME is nestled in an enclave of grand old gated properties that once housed black Hollywood royalty. Hattie McDaniel, the first black woman to win an Oscar, in 1939—the actress who ordered Scarlett O'Hara around in *Gone With the Wind*—had her house there, and it still stands today alongside other fine homes in a residential island surrounded by what most people would call The 'Hood. Ten minutes southwest of First AME, you'll find yourself in Baldwin Village, a twisting warren of narrow streets and aging single-family homes and cracker-box apartment buildings. Ironically, nearby Baldwin Hills is one of the wealthiest black neighborhoods in the country.

Los Angeles is a city of polarities. Baldwin Village is also five miles from Beverly Hills, but that kind of wealth is a universe away to its residents. That's what statistics show. Let a statistician know where you're from and what your parents had, and that's the greatest predictor of what your life will be. You're from The Jungle? No father in the home? Get used to food stamps and government cheese.

April had used Intelius.com to ferret out Tyra Johnston's home address. Most white faces have vanished by the time you get to this part of town. The Jungle. Ask city planners, and they'll say the area was nicknamed "The Jungle" because of the eucalyptus trees planted to give it a tropical look. Believe that if you want, but I don't buy it. Dad told me stories of white cops sniggering that rooftops in the Crenshaw district should be painted with house numbers to help track "jungle bunnies" fleeing patrol cars.

Serena had gone to the moon. When I saw her sister's street, I realized exactly how far from home she had flown.

I had expected to find Tyra in one of the neatly manicured homes that still persist despite poverty, where longtime homeowners struggle to hang on to the memory of better times. I was wrong. The apartment building that matched the address in April's notebook made the drab complex we had just seen behind the alley look like a Maui condo. Everything about the building was weary; from paint so chipped that the naked cement blocks showed through to an elevator that didn't come when we called for it.

Tyra's apartment was listed as 3C, which meant we climbed two flights of stairs in the courtyard while wary residents watched our ascent and assumed we were cops or social workers. A boy who looked like he was fourteen sat atop an overturned water drum on the ground below, surveying his kingdom up and down the street, clearly at work rather than play. The bassline of loud reggaeton vibrated through a window as we climbed upstairs.

"*Lifestyles of the Sisters of the Rich and Famous,*" April said.

"I noticed."

I knocked on the door to 3C, preparing myself to see Serena again.

Tyra Johnston was about two inches taller than her big sister, which was easy to overlook because their faces were nearly identical. She was even wearing hair extensions nearly the same deep burgundy color Serena had been wearing. I could see why the shopkeeper confused them, but I wasn't fooled by Serena's face at the door. Tyra's life-hardened eyes couldn't have been more different from her sister's.

"I already told you motherfuckers everything I got to say," she said.

Charming.

Tyra was as colorful as I remembered from Serena's party. She had knocked a tray of finger foods out of a waiter's hand because she claimed he'd ignored her. When someone on the club's staff tried to calm her, she cussed him out. I had never seen Serena look as angry as when she yanked her sister aside and whispered fiercely in her ear. I'd hung close, just in case it turned into the fight it looked like it was going to be. It hadn't. Still, I was on Serena's arm at a lot of parties after that night, and I never saw her sister again.

"Tyra?" I said. "I don't know if you remember me, but we met a few years ago. I'm Tennyson Hardwick."

"Police?" she said, resigned. Like me, she was tired of talking to cops.

"No. I'm a friend of Serena's."

"And I'm a reporter for the L.A. Times," April said, nudging a shoulder past me to show Tyra her press badge. "We'd like to talk to you."

I had hoped April would let me gauge Tyra's mood before we mentioned she was a reporter. But Tyra's face lit up. "How much?"

"Excuse me?" April said.

"You're about to ask some nosy shit that ain't none of your business," Tyra said, arms crossed. "And I'm about to get paid."

April tried to suppress her sigh of irritation. "The Times doesn't pay for stories, Ms. Johnston."

Tyra's door was about to slam shut when I braced it open with my foot. I flashed Tyra a grin. "Under the circumstances, I feel moved to offer a personal donation," I said. I flipped open my wallet and emptied it, pulling out four twenties. "Well?"

Tyra snatched the money, and I felt the pinch. Damn. I should have offered her half as much, I realized. She might have gone for it, and I'd be forty dollars less broke.

"Where's the photographer at? Where's the video camera?" Tyra said.

"We can definitely get a photographer here. No problem," April said. She gave me a hesitant glance, then fumbled inside her purse for her cell phone. "We wanted to talk to you about what happened to Serena. It's so awful . . ." Her voice faded as she began dialing. She held up one finger to us, apologizing as someone picked up.

April had her story. I hoped I would find what I needed, too.

"I'm so sorry about Serena," I said. I cradled Tyra's hand with both of mine, watching her eyes carefully for her reaction. Grief? Regret? Guilt? Tyra rested the weight of her hand inside mine, but her eyes didn't change, as if she hadn't heard me.

"I thought more reporters would've come by now—but it's just cops. Like I have to explain my every movement. All in my business, asking questions."

"Most people don't know Serena had a sister," April said, hanging up her phone.

Tyra's face turned sour. "That's how she wanted it. You coming in?"

The inside of her apartment looked much better than the exterior. The living room was bigger than I would have thought, with enough space for a large faux black leather sofa wrapped around her wall and a plasma TV mounted across from it. Her matching black bookshelf was crammed with DVDs and dozens of paperback novels. The room's off-white carpet was plush and spotless. But, like Serena's house, the room struck me as bare.

"They're still tripping about that restraining order," Tyra said. "That was *four* years ago. We moved beyond it."

"Restraining order?" April said, her notebook ready.

"We got into some drama and slapped each other a few times. I shoulda got a restraining order against *her*. Like I'm gonna go all the way to Hollywood Hills to mess with her. Please. She's living like a queen in her castle and won't let nobody come near her. I don't gotta' prove myself to *nobody*—especially not her." Tyra's eyes might have looked angry except for all her hurt.

"April is a reporter," I reminded Tyra.

She cut her eyes at me. "So? I ain't ashamed of nothing I've done. I bet Serena can't say the same thing."

"Serena can't say anything," I said.

Tyra looked up at me with the strangest combination of emotions I've ever seen; if a director had asked me to produce it, I wouldn't have known where to start. Annoyance. Pity. Indifference. Sadness. They all splashed across her face like a school of neon tetras. "You're beat up. I remember you now," she said. "Just as fine as you can be! Serena could always get anybody she wanted."

"So . . ." April said. "You and Serena didn't get along?"

"Like I just said—and like I just told the police—we put that behind us."

"But you weren't close," I said.

"If we was close, I guess I'd be living in her house. I guess she'da helped me do something with *my* music. Serena went her way, I went mine. She can't tell me how to act the way she tries to tell everybody else. All she cares about is her image. You can write that down." Tyra hadn't said a single kind word about her sister, I noticed, yet she hardly ever referred to Serena in past tense. Was that her way of keeping Serena alive?

I gave April a look as she scribbled her notes, but she pretended not to see me. I hoped April would use discretion when she decided what to print in the newspaper, but Serena wasn't her friend. To April, Serena was just a story.

And Serena wasn't here to give her side.

"Can you think of anyone who wanted to kill her?" I said. I was itching to ask Tyra what the hell she'd been doing so close to that alley only hours before her sister's body was found, but I'd learned my lesson from M.C. Glazer. *Take it slow.*

Tyra shook her head, and she seemed to shiver. "The first thing I thought was, well, maybe she went back to turning tricks. Even though she had all that money, maybe she still needed to get her freak on."

My face went hot. "What do you mean?"

Tyra gave me a heavy-lidded smile. She seemed to relish my surprise. "Oh, you didn't know? That's right. She don't talk about that in Hollywood, huh?"

A ho by any other name is still a ho. She was like M.C. Glazer all over again.

Tyra folded her arms, ready to make a declaration. "Serena let every boy in junior high fuck her for free before Shareef taught her how to do it for money. Why pull trains in the locker room when high school boys pay ten dollars a pop?"

Her words were so ugly, they blotted out everything else in the room. I wanted to tell April it was time to go, but I couldn't. If this was true, it might be relevant to Serena's death. If it wasn't true, it told me a lot about Tyra. Either way, I had to hear.

"You're saying she was a prostitute?" April said. "When did that start, and how long did it continue?"

I didn't know what Tyra was talking about, but I didn't like the turn in con-versation; not with a reporter present. "Tyra, if you tell her it's off the record, she won't put it in the paper," I said.

"Let her print it," Tyra said, shrugging. "I don't care."

So, it was settled. For the next hour, as we sat on Tyra's faux black leather couch, I heard sordid, heartbreaking details from Serena's childhood that I wished I could have heard in a moment of private commiseration with Serena herself. Instead, I had to hear from a sister boiling with so much resentment that every disclosure sounded like an indictment. As I listened, I realized that the story was too awful to be anything but true.

Tyra and Serena were raised by a single mother roughly six blocks from where she now lived. Their mother, Regina Johnston, had training as a secretary, but bounced from job to job because of a battle with alcohol she sometimes over-came for months at a time. In the end she lost, was killed driving drunk after both girls were grown. The sisters considered her parenting such a poor exam-ple that they had vowed never to have children of their own. During the early part of their childhood, the girls were best friends. They were mature beyond their years from taking care of themselves when their mother refused to get out of bed, making threats to end her own life. They learned to rely on each other in a way Regina Johnston could not be relied upon.

Their mother was a regular Saturday-night clubgoer, and one day she brought home a man she'd met there. She called him Big Ray, and soon, fre-quent visits became a constant presence. He was living with them before long. As far as Tyra and Serena could tell, the main thing their mother had in common with Big Ray was that they both liked to drink, argue, and watch TV. But Big Ray always had money to spend on them for furniture, for clothes—and even a 1980 Impala he bought their mother for cash.

His only job was answering his pager and ducking out of the house. It was only when they saw him and their mother cutting up bricks of marijuana on the kitchen table one night that they realized he was a drug dealer. All their friends had said so, but the girls hadn't believed it. Within six months, he'd moved them into a three-bedroom house big enough for each girl to have her own room for the first time. Despite the constant arguing and a few broken glasses to accompany late-night shouting, life felt good. He spent freely on them when their mother asked, but he wasn't trying to be anyone's father.

On their new street, Serena and Tyra met the two boys: Shareef Pinkney and Devon Biggs. Tyra found the boys nerdy and too talkative—and she preferred jumping rope with the girls on the street—but Serena and the boys quickly became inseparable. They always played games of make-believe. Often, they sat inside the parked Impala and pretended they were taking long road trips together, with Serena at the wheel.

Serena's breasts had developed by the time she was twelve, and at the same time Tyra noticed a change in Big Ray. He had rarely talked to them before, except in passing. But now he slipped Serena gifts of Bubble Yum or Now N' Laters from the corner store. Tyra got nothing. Big Ray began sneaking into Serena's room. Tyra could tell by the way Serena started mouthing off at their mother that she felt a sense of power from the special visits. And she never lost her taste for it.

Then, the really bad times started.

At thirteen, Serena got pregnant. She kept her secret until it was almost too late for an abortion. But she did get one. Big Ray arranged it without her mother's knowledge. But Serena told when she woke up bleeding in the middle of the night and thought she was dying.

Regina Johnston refused to believe that Big Ray was the father. Her first reaction was to slap Serena hard enough to black her eye. But after seven days, Regina accepted the truth and threw him out—except that it wasn't her house. Big Ray showed up with some hard-looking men from his crew, all Black P Stone gangbangers, and tossed their belongings into the street while everyone watched. The only thing in Regina Johnston's name was the Impala. For nearly a month, with the trunk stuffed with clothes and dishes, the three of them lived in the car.

Serena stopped playing games of make-believe after that.

Soon, Tyra heard a rumor that her sister was having sex with any boy who would meet her after school in the boys' locker room, which a careless janitor was leaving unlocked. When Tyra went to investigate, she found three ninth-grade boys waiting—and she could hear her sister's voice echoing against the walls—so she knew it was true. Serena became notorious at Audubon Junior High for allowing boys to run trains on her. Because they looked so much alike, Tyra found herself in fights trying to defend her name. Tyra always expected

Serena to get pregnant again, but somehow she never did. Later, a doctor told Serena she might never conceive because she'd had her abortion so young.

By the time Serena was fourteen, she was stashing money in an empty Jiffy peanut butter jar under her bed. Serena swore Tyra to secrecy and then boasted that Shareef had "hooked her up" so they could all get rich. Shareef had orchestrated a network of high school boys from two different schools who would pay to have sex with her, and Devon converted his backyard shed to a makeshift lair with an old foldaway bed. Serena said she had already made a hundred dollars in *a week*. She, Shareef, and Devon divided the money into thirds.

They all knew what they were saving the money for: Shareef had a quick mind and a gift for poetry, so he could be a rapper like his heroes, Run-DMC. With the money they earned with their sex-for-pay game, Shareef selling nickel bags after school, and Devon's knack for sound equipment, they bought a second-hand Tascam mixer that was just good enough for Shareef to record his first CD by the time he was sixteen.

The sound was terrible, so their CD circulated only in the local house party scene, but one of the songs on Shareef's first CD was "Coming to Get Mine." Three years later, with a professional studio and a label's investment, that single helped his first real album reach sales of a million copies. And up until the day that first hit CD was released, Shareef, Devon, and Serena were still in the sex business. While he was a business student at USC, Devon sometimes introduced his "Nubian Princess" to rich white kids for two hundred dollars a night.

But Shareef kept his word to Serena. Once Shareef was earning money from his music, he hired Serena as a dancer. She didn't have dance training, but after a couple of years of touring, Shareef let her take the microphone and lay down her own rap tracks on his CD.

Afrodite was born.

"And she hasn't given a damn about anybody else ever since," Tyra finished.

I wanted to wash out my ears. I had just heard the story of a little girl so desperate for a father figure that she'd had sex with her mother's boyfriend, and Tyra had made it sound as if Serena had schemed to destroy their family. It was as if Tyra was still a little girl herself, blaming Serena for taking their toys away.

My stomach churned. Tyra could have been telling my own story.

April's bearded, disheveled photographer arrived. He suggested a prop for his photo, so Tyra went on talking while she held an unframed photo of her and

Serena as young children close to her face; identical twins in pigtails and tooth-less grins. But the adult Tyra's pose looked wrong. I've seen those photos in the newspaper after tragedies, with relatives' faces weighted with raw shock and sadness. As the photographer's bulb flashed, her eyes seemed to glint with something more like triumph.

Maybe Tyra was just happy to be the famous one for a change.

Or, maybe she had hated Serena enough to kill her.

While April huddled with her photographer near the doorway, I crossed my leg so that my knee rested gently against Tyra. I had seen her eyes eating me up. Once upon a time I had belonged to Serena, so to her I was a prize.

"How did you hear about Serena?" I asked her quietly.

She leaned closer, making sure I had a view of the soft cleavage exposed above her tight-fitting tank top. I hadn't noticed her chest until then. "Cops showed up knocking around noon, soon as I got home. One minute it's, 'Your sister's dead,' and the next thing, it's 'What's your alibi?' "

"What did you tell them?"

"I haven't seen Serena in four months, that's what. And if it happened Monday night, I was with my girlfriends at Mackey's. Happy hour's at six and the music starts at nine, so we were there till midnight. A shitload of people saw me there." While she spoke, she slipped a bold hand to my leg, above the knee. Her fingers fluttered. I almost flinched, but I caught myself. I wanted her to stay in a talkative mood.

"What about Tuesday morning? Where were you then?" I said.

At that, Tyra looked at me askance, but she didn't remove her hand. In-stead, she spread her palm and began rubbing a circle. "Why you asking?"

"Someone thought they saw you somewhere."

"Where?"

"A grocery store on Sunset."

Understanding washed over Tyra, and she almost smiled. Her hand went still. "Oh, OK, I get it. I had some work Tuesday morning for a couple hours." *Probably heavy lifting,* I thought. "What kind of work?"

"Music work, no thanks to Serena. There's a building on Sunset and Cherokee with a recording studio on the third floor. I went by for a couple hours to lay down some tracks, then I went home for lunch."

"Who paid for the studio time?"

The glint came to Tyra's eye again. "M.C. Glazer," she said.

April and I couldn't help looking at each other, surprised. I hadn't expected to hear Glazer's name from the mouth of Serena's sister. April sat cross-legged on the carpeted floor in front of Tyra, taking notes again. The photographer had just left.

"He liked it that me and Serena sound so much alike. He said he would put me in his video, too. He said we were like twins," Tyra went on. For the first time, we were getting somewhere.

"Was he doing that to humiliate Afrodite?" April said.

Tyra shrugged. "Hey, the pay was good. And like I said, he let me lay tracks."

"So you happened to be in a recording studio a couple of blocks from where your sister's body was found," I said. "On the same day."

Tyra looked at me blankly. "Fucked up, huh?"

"Do you think Glazer had anything to do with her death?" April said.

For the first time, Tyra seemed to realize she was in the presence of a reporter. She stood up abruptly, towering over April. "Don't put words in my mouth, bitch. And you better take out anything about M.C. Glazer. Period."

"Hey, sweetheart, calm down," I said, standing. I squeezed Tyra's upper arms in a promising embrace and spoke intimately into her ear. "She's cool, Tyra. She won't print it if you don't want her to. Besides, you can ask her to leave."

April's eyes sliced into me, but she didn't argue. I knew April wouldn't be happy, but I didn't want to get kicked out, too. I wasn't finished with Tyra Johnston.

Tyra pointed the front door out to April. "You got *that* right. So, go."

"You heard the lady," I told April. "Sorry. Call you later."

You better, April's eyes said. She sighed and gathered her things.

"I need to find somebody who can pay some real money for a story. That is some bullshit," Tyra said, watching as the door closed behind April. We were alone.

"Try the *National Enquirer,*" I said.

She smiled at me, her irritation forgotten. "Ooh. You're right. And *Star.* Thanks, sexy. So who beat you up?"

I decided to go fishing. "Jenk and his friends," I said.

I got a nibble. Tyra knew the name. "Works for Glaze?" When I nodded, she chuckled. "Well, if you've got beef with Jenk and them, you truly do have beef. You know all those guys are Five-O, right?"

"Where do you know Jenk from?"

"High school. He was in my class. He was tight with Shareef and Lil' D. He used to fuck Serena. Everybody else did."

"Were they still friendly?"

She shrugged. "After she got big, Serena wasn't friendly with nobody from back in the day except Shareef and D."

"What about Shareef? Was Jenk friendly with him?"

"I guess so. They played ball together at Dorsey High."

"Why would a friend of Shareef's work for M.C. Glazer? They were rivals."

"Don't take that hype serious. They were all just making money."

"Except that Shareef and Serena are both dead."

Tyra didn't have an answer for that, nor did she seem all that curious. Her eyes drifted, as if I'd lost her interest. She got so close to me that her breasts were brushing my chest. Her skin seemed to burn through her clothes.

"My turn to ask the questions," Tyra said. She pressed harder, crushing her chest to mine. "You and Serena used to fuck, huh?"

"For a while."

"She never told you she was a ho?"

"I never asked."

Tyra's hand traveled like a snail from my chest to my stomach, and the journey didn't stop at my belt. She slid her hand across my zipper and gave me a meaningful squeeze through the denim.

My head ached with Tyra's revelations. I was a murder suspect, and my spirit was heavy with the possibilities that either Tyra or an LAPD officer might be involved in Serena's death. But an attractive woman's hand was playing with my crotch, and any man will tell you that in a tug of war between big and little heads, the little head wins too damned often. Besides, standing this close to Tyra, I couldn't ignore what I saw of Serena in her face. Suddenly, my jeans pinched.

"*Damn*," Tyra said, impressed with the mound she felt growing beneath her fingers. Not letting go, guiding with great care, she led me back toward her sofa by my jeans. I let her pull me on top of her. Her hand still owned me.

I kissed her like I meant it, and her tongue was sweet. I didn't know how far I was willing to take this, but I knew I wanted to keep her in a friendly mood. For just a blink of an instant, the room melted, and I was with Serena. Her hand was cold when it burrowed inside my jeans. I quivered to my spine, remembering.

"What's Jenk's real name?" I whispered.

"Robert Jenkins," she said, stroking me with soft, plying fingers. "Now, shut your mouth and show me."

"Show you what?"

"Show me what you did with her."

I pulled back so I could see Tyra's eyes. I would have been surprised at how soft they were if I hadn't thought I heard it in her voice; suddenly, she didn't sound like a woman desperate to show up her sister by playing with one of her toys. It was almost as though Tyra thought I could help her find her way back to Serena.

I thought of the photograph she had posed with, two smiling sisters. The interrogation was over, I decided.

"You have so much poison in your heart," I said, thinking aloud.

She scowled, surprised, yanking her hand out of my jeans. "Excuse me?"

"Let it go. She's gone."

Tyra was strong for her size, and her push sent me to my feet, off-balance. Her face was knotted with rage. "Motherfucker, don't talk like you know me."

"Serena was afraid her past would drag her down. She couldn't take the chance you would say the wrong thing to the wrong people."

"*Get out!*" Tyra screamed. Her voice probably traveled three flights down.

"It doesn't mean she didn't love you."

I knew the slap was coming before it arrived, but I didn't move to avoid it. She hit me hard enough to rattle my teeth. Damn. That lip would be bleeding again.

I left Tyra Johnston's apartment without another word and without most of the answers I had come looking for. But I couldn't have stayed. As I climbed down the stairs, I heard the keening sound of Tyra's sobs through her closed door. A terrible sound. But I was relieved, for Tyra's sake.

Maybe Tyra had something to do with killing Serena, and maybe she didn't. I still didn't know. But no matter what, the woman in apartment 3C needed to cry.

EIGHT

STUCK ON THE 10 FREEWAY behind a truck spewing tarry smoke for twenty minutes, I finally called April. We were moving only inches at a time. In Los Angeles, sometimes the cars decide to camp out in their lanes without a reason, as if the memory of last night's accident still haunted the freeway.

"Well?" April answered without a hello.

"You heard most of it. Whether or not she's a suspect depends on her alibi. Maybe you should go to that club, Mackey's. Ask around."

I didn't really care about Tyra's alibi, given that she had been so close to where the body was found. She might not have killed Serena, but it was more than likely she had been an accessory after the fact.

"Want to meet me there?" April said. When I didn't answer right away, she sounded disappointed. "What's wrong? I thought we were a team."

April had been candid with me, so I chose candor, too. "I don't want everything I find out about Serena to end up in the *L.A. Times.*"

"You knew I was writing a story, Ten."

I hadn't planned to beg outright, but that was how the words came out. "Please don't print what Tyra said about Serena's past. About the prostitution. Please."

April sighed. "Ten . . . Nobody tells me how to write my stories. I'm sorry."

I felt personally betrayed, and surprised myself in the process, as if April's kindness toward me made her something more than a stranger. "Then this is where we part," I said. "If I find out anything I think you can use, I'll let you know. I hope you'll do the same."

I wasn't in the mood for a proper good-bye, so I hung up before she could protest.

The next number I dialed was for Casanegra Productions. Devon Biggs. But the assistant who answered told me that Mr. Biggs would be in meetings all day.

"Tell him Tennyson Hardwick wants to talk about his Nubian Princess," I said.

She called back not even ten minutes later. Surprise, surprise.

Mr. Biggs had an opening right away.

"Skank-ass *bitch*," Devon Biggs said behind his desk at Casanegra, his eyes wide and unblinking. He looked more stunned than angry.

"Thought you would want to know. There's a chance it'll be in the *Times*."

"Tyra's always talking shit. And for what?" He sounded grieved. "Whenever she called Reenie and said she needed money, Reenie was there. Reenie set her sister up in a nice place out in Santa Monica for a while—a house with a pool—and Tyra fucked that up. Drunk and loud, just like their damn mama. I can't count how much money Reenie pissed away trying to help Tyra get her shit together. And now she says *this*? It's sad, man. That was one sick fucking family."

"So it isn't true? About you, Shareef, and Serena?"

Biggs looked up at me, his eyes clear. "Hey, man, I never said it wasn't true."

I blinked. Tyra's story had sounded plausible at the time, but I had started to hope for a different past for Serena. A different childhood.

"Fuck you, Hardwick," Biggs said, reading my expression. "*You're* judging?"

Clear implication in that tone: He knew of my financial arrangement with Serena. My face went hot. "I'm not judging. I'm just . . ."

"Serena did the best she could with what she had. The girl was wild, and we kept her from getting jumped. We got her through it, and it took her where she wanted to go. '*The white man ain't left me nothin' but the underworld, and that is where I dance . . .* '" he said, leaning across his desk, and I recognized Larry Fishburne's line to Gregory Hines in Coppolla's *The Cotton Club*. "Where do *you* dance?"

"Was she still dancing?"

Biggs raised his eyebrows. "Maybe you haven't been paying attention, man, but Serena Johnston was worth thirty million dollars. She'd been off the streets for twelve years. The way I hear it, she got off paying dudes to fuck *her*. Although if you ask me, a dude like that is more a pussy than a man." He gave me a contemptuous smile.

I wouldn't let Biggs get under my skin. There was big money at stake, and he and Serena might have been romantically involved. Devon Biggs deserved a closer look.

"What about you two? Tyra said you had history."

"You picked the right word—*history*. We played some games when we were kids, but we were family." Biggs went on. "And I'll be straight, Hardwick: I loved Reenie, but she had mileage. That might turn some guys on, but not me. I guess you could say I knew where she'd been."

"What about the business side? Was everything still cool there? Like you said, it had been a long time since Serena needed a pimp."

Biggs's face turned hard. He didn't like that word. His hand tightened around the coffee mug on his desk. I made a mental note to be ready to duck.

"If you're really trying to find out who killed Serena, then we're on the same side, so I'm gonna let your ignorance slide," Biggs said. "But let me break it down: I came up with the business plan for Casanegra and took it to *her*. She didn't know shit about the money side, but she knew a good thing when she saw it. If she hadn't trusted me, she wouldn't have made me her CFO and personal attorney. Shareef got Serena started, but I made her rich. So you tell me: Were things cool?"

"Things change," I said, shrugging. "Maybe she outgrew you. Or, maybe you didn't like a ho telling you how to run your business."

Biggs leaped to his feet, leaning so far over his desk that he could have been standing directly in front of me. "You call her a ho one more time," Biggs said, his eyes so glassy they shimmered, "and I will throw you out of that window."

I got the idea that he might just try it, although he wouldn't get far. But I couldn't take offense. Frankly, I was glad to see a protective streak in Devon Biggs that had been so absent in Tyra. From the look on his face I might have been talking about *his* sister.

I held up my hands, surrendering. "My bad, man."

Biggs's face softened slightly. "Serena liked you. I don't know why, but she did. The day she died, she called me and asked me to hook you up. So I'm giving you the benefit of the doubt. But don't you ever walk in here again disrespecting Serena's name, or I'll remember some things about you and Reenie I forgot to mention to the cops."

I nodded. "Understood," I said. I didn't like to be vulnerable, but he had me.

Biggs sat again, straightening his sport coat. "If Tyra was working for M.C. Glazer, you need to be asking what's up with *that*."

I had told Biggs about Tyra's recording session for Glazer, although I'd been purposely vague about the location, and I hadn't mentioned how close she was to the body. If Biggs was trying to put up smokescreens, I wasn't going to give him any smoke. But Biggs had said exactly what was on my mind.

"Do you think Tyra would go as far as helping someone kill her sister?" I said.

"Tyra was killing Reenie softly every single day," Biggs said. "I wouldn't put anything past her. Tyra pulled a *knife* on Reenie a few years back."

"Was that when Serena got the restraining order?"

Biggs looked surprised I'd heard about it. "She said that, too?"

"She said they slapped each other a few times."

"That's bullshit," Biggs said. "They were eating dinner in the back room of El Compadre. Tyra goes nuts, punches Reenie in the face, and tries to slice her with a steak knife. That's Tyra's idea of gratitude. Tyra Johnston and M.C. Glazer are an unholy union. *Count* on it."

Biggs's phone rang for the first time since I'd been in his office, and he answered without excusing himself. "What now?" he said, spinning his black leather executive's chair away from me, erecting an invisible wall. "Fuck you, man. You know what your problem is? You have no respect. Afrodite ain't even buried yet. Maybe I need to send the police over there to ask where *you* were the night she died."

The man on the other end spoke so loudly that I could hear his voice, insectlike through the phone's speaker. "Gimme a break, Dev. That's bullshit and you know it."

"What's bullshit is you calling over here riding me this week. *This week.* You call me again, and I'll walk straight into hell before you see a dollar. Believe it."

He slammed down his phone so hard he almost knocked it off his desk. In that instant, I felt sorry for Devon Biggs. Death rarely brings out the best in people.

"Bookie?" I said after he hung up, a halfhearted joke.

"Worse—a producer," he said. "Stan Greene. Greedy motherfucker. He was trying to sue Serena, and now that she's dead, he thinks he's getting paid. The cops need to check him out, too. He and his lawyer are both straight-up Vegas mob. Greene used to talk shit when he directed videos for Shareef, bragging about doing this or that to people who tried to rip him off. I know you think I sound paranoid, but just remember what I said: *The Hollywood Rules.* How do you make enemies?"

"By being successful. I remember."

I had never heard of Stan Greene, but I wrote the name down, just in case. Biggs's claims would be easy enough to research. I knew the list of suspects would get longer, and it was a wearying idea. With DNA test results on the way, I was running out of time to chase after every lead.

Biggs looked at his watch. "OK, so now, thanks to you, I have to waste time and money calling the *L.A. Times* to let them know that if I see a story in the paper saying Serena was a prostitute, they will get sued until they can't walk straight."

"I'm doing what I can on my end. I asked the reporter not to print it."

Biggs looked at me, incredulous. "And you couldn't handle that bitch?"

I wasn't sure if he was referring to Tyra or April Forrest, but it was the first time I had heard Devon Biggs sound like a pimp. When I was in the seventh grade, my father heard me say the word *bitch*, and he knocked me out of my chair. I wasn't happy with April either, but that word is not in my vocabulary.

I didn't answer Biggs. I only got up to leave, until my sore lip reminded me of a piece that was still unsorted in my mind. One name kept coming up everywhere I went. "Hey, man . . . one last thing . . ."

Impatient, Biggs rested his telephone receiver on his shoulder. "What now?"

"I got jumped by some guys last night. Tyra said one of them might have known Serena back in high school. His name is Robert Jenkins. Goes by the name Jenk."

Biggs's face froze, like a photograph. He held the pose for a minute, then he shrank into his chair. If he had looked stunned when I mentioned Tyra's accusations, now he looked shell-shocked.

"I take it you know him," I said.

Biggs swallowed hard. His voice was a hush. "He's a lying cop. Dirty as they come. Gangbanger. Where'd you see him?"

I decided to dole out a few details. "Club Magique. He's a bodyguard for M.C. Glazer. I got the feeling he knew something about Serena."

Up until that moment, I'd never seen it happen: The color drained out of Biggs's face, wheat toast turning white. Suddenly, his upper lip was beading with sweat. "He's working for Glaze?"

"Him and a whole bunch of other Lap Dogs."

"What?"

A wan smile. "LAP Dogs. Private joke."

Biggs didn't say anything else. His face set so hard it looked chiseled.

"What about Serena and Shareef?" I said. "Did they know Jenk?"

Biggs nodded. He blinked rapidly, rubbing his forehead. Droplets clung above his lip, a mustache of sweat.

"Jenk was tight with Shareef for a while, but that all changed," he said.

"Why?"

"Because Jenk was hardcore and Shareef wasn't," Biggs said. "In high school, Shareef never had to join a gang because bangers left the ballplayers alone. But Jenk was Blood to the bone. After Shareef started making it in music, Jenk wanted him to live the gangster life, started calling him soft. But Shareef wasn't a fool. He didn't want to go down like Tupac, with all that gangster hype. See, if all the money wasn't in gangsta rap, Shareef would've been more like Will and LL Cool J, right? Party tracks. But Shareef tried to have it both ways. He talked gangsta on his CDs, but he could never get to M.C. Glazer's level—he didn't live the life."

"Was Serena sleeping with Jenk?"

"In high school? Maybe. Now? Hell, no," Biggs said, not hesitating.

"Why?"

"Reenie didn't like gangbangers. She and Shareef were all about business."

"Would Jenk have a reason to kill her?"

"Jenk wouldn't need a reason. Not if he got paid enough." Biggs still spoke softly, as if the room might be bugged, but suddenly words tumbled quickly from his lips. "But maybe it was personal. Jenk had a security company he tried to push on Shareef and Serena, and he'd sweat them to release his sorry-ass CD. He made them nervous when he was around, and he didn't like being brushed off. I thought about him after Shareef died, but I didn't have proof. Just a feeling. You saw Jenk with Glaze?"

I nodded.

"Well, that's tough luck for you, Hardwick," Biggs said.

"Why?"

"Why do you think? Because he's a cop. That's why they'd rather nail *you.*"

I knew exactly what he meant. Dad had confided that he knew an investigator on the Shareef murder who complained that he was thwarted by his bosses at every turn, whether it was because of racial politics or because of fear of department-wide embarrassment. He said gangs had infiltrated LAPD, and the whitewash went to the top. Biggie's murder investigation had gone nowhere because of the same damned problem, he said.

Dad, whose deepest contempt was reserved for bad cops, was sickened by the whole mess. *Misguided loyalties will kill our community*, Dad said. *I can't stand to see thugs with money invoke the name of Martin Luther King and walk. Dr. King didn't die so killers could roam free.*

Biggs sighed, making up his mind to tell me something.

"If Glazer is thick with dirty cops, they ain't just bodyguards," Biggs said. "You need cops for their badges. For their access. Get it? Glazer deals guns. That's not just an act for him. Drugs, too. Maybe Glazer and Jenk thought Shareef and Serena knew too much. Had too much dirt on him, like Tyra does on Reenie."

"Then they probably think you know too much, too."

Without blinking, Biggs pulled open his coat and unbuttoned his white dress shirt. Underneath, I saw a blue Kevlar bulletproof jacket. Suddenly, I understood the sweat above his lip; I'd worn Kevlar at the police academy, and it's hot.

"I already thought of that," Biggs said. "Did you?"

Devon Biggs gazed at me like a man who was already seeing a ghost.

"*POZDRAV* IT IS AFTER ALL," Mother said.

I'd heard worry in Mother's voice when she called me after I left Casanegra's offices. She was finally looking her age; she must be at least seventy-five. She was vain enough to wear a bright red wig, but in her pantsuit and reading glasses, she could be anyone's grandmother. I wasn't used to hearing Mother sound like an old woman.

"What happened?"

"Nothing, maybe," Mother said. "Maybe something. I don't know."

With Old World elegance, she motioned for me to sit. Mother always stands over her visitors during meetings, a subtle power maneuver. I took my seat on her Louis XVI sofa, in front of a coffee table covered in doilies. Mother worked from her home in Brentwood, where her neighbors on both sides drove Mercedes SUVs and had yards cluttered with children's toys. No one suspected there was a madam in their midst. Mother did most of her work on the phone, but she used to invite me to her house often. I always left with a lucrative job, a head full of vodka, and an earful of stories.

The living room was silently guarded by two white mastodons—Mother's standard-sized poodles, Dunja and Dragona. They sat on either side of the room with attentive eyes, their pink tongues lolling from their mouths in a way that made them look like they were smiling. Their downy fur was lavishly fluffed and groomed with bows, their nails hot pink, but those dogs were well-trained and vicious. Attack poodles: Mother's private joke. I didn't mess with those dogs.

I thought Mother and I were alone, until a blond-haired woman with a fashion model's height and build emerged from the back of the house wearing an unseasonably long leather coat. I readied a polite smile and nod—until I saw her face. I had to stand up to keep from falling out of my seat.

Mother was the only one of us still smiling. "Ah! A reunion."

Let's call her Jeanine. She averted her eyes, but she was too close to disappear and pretend she hadn't seen me. Her bottom lip curled beneath her teeth like a repentant child about to cry. I had no idea Jeanine was still working for Mother. I don't know which of us was more mortified.

I'm not the only actor who's discovered the financial rewards of sex-for-pay.

Jeanine was once the bombshell lead in a popular television series, where she had a reputation as a diva. She was cast opposite an unknown actor who later became an A-list star, but Jeanine's career stalled after the show ended. She hadn't invested her money in anything except travel and spas, and she'd been going broke.

One night, she saw me working for a client who was a friend of hers, and Jeanine asked me question after question. Here was an actress who'd been a pinup on my locker when I was in high school, and she was asking *me* for advice! I had a fat bank account and more frequent flyer miles than I could use, so I told her Mother was the answer. She worried about publicity, but I assured her that Mother's clients were discreet. I brought Jeanine to Mother's house for the introduction, and *Cestitam!* We all toasted while Jeanine laughed so hard she got red in the face, saying *I can't believe I'm doing this.*

Her first job paid forty thousand dollars for a single night's "entertainment" with a Japanese businessman addicted to American television. It wasn't her last.

I'd brought Jeanine to the wolf's door.

Eight years later, I wiped my expression clean, matching Mother's smile. Jeanine hadn't changed much physically, thanks to the work of a skilled plastic surgeon, but her eyes devastated me. The blue had lost its luster, replaced by a vacant glassiness. I didn't have to ask to know she hadn't done any acting lately. Her eyes broadcast that loud and clear.

"Hey, girl, you're a vision," I said, trying to sound happy to see her. I squeezed her shoulders and kissed each of her cheeks. Her skin reeked of cigarettes and coffee.

"I'd like to say the same." Jeanine stole a glance at me and pulled her coat tightly around herself, as if trying to hide. Her lip gave way to an unmistakable sneer as her eyes glimmered, mocking. "Moonlighting, Ten?"

I shrugged. "You could say that."

"Then I won't delay you. Mother doesn't like to be kept waiting."

I took Jeanine's hand before she could brush past me. She sighed impatiently, but held on. She still wouldn't look me directly in the eye. "You all right?" I asked.

"I'm going to Bahrain tomorrow," she said with a luminous smile. "A sheik."

That didn't answer my question, but it was the best I would get. "Then good for you," I said. "You deserve nothing less, beautiful."

A little girlish spark in her eyes, and she was gone. Jeanine couldn't get out of Mother's house fast enough; the door practically slammed behind her.

Mother seemed to enjoy my discomfort. Still smiling, she offered me a tray of finger-length Serbian cookies. I shook my head. Although I couldn't remember the last time I had eaten, I wasn't feeling social right then.

"No one would guess she is in her fifties," Mother said. "So dedicated! I owe you more for her than I have paid."

My empty stomach turned. "No thanks. I can't afford that money."

Six months after I brought Jeanine in, Mother gave me a check for twenty thousand dollars: A "finder's fee," she called it. I ran out and put a down payment on my convertible. Mother offered to partner with me if I brought her other famous faces. *Clients pay top dollar to spend the night with someone they see on TV,* she said.

I considered it at first, I'll admit—but the change in Jeanine changed my mind. In those first months after I introduced Jeanine to Mother, I watched Jeanine smother the part of her that believed she could be respected again.

Mother sipped from a mug, lips tightening as her smile faded. Just that quickly, Jeanine left her mind. "There is a problem, maybe, with one of my girls from Club Magique." Mother was so quiet, I almost hadn't heard her. Suddenly she was an old woman again.

I was glad to talk about anything but Jeanine. "Honey was doing fine the last time I saw her," I said.

"Not Honey. This girl is named Chela. You may know her as . . . M.C. Glazer's favorite new toy. A young one."

I studied Mother's jade-colored eyes, still bright despite the wrinkles around them, and I was almost sure I saw some shame. Or, maybe I just *hoped* I did. I'd worked with Mother for five years, and I'd never known her to send out underage prostitutes. Call me naive. I wanted to drop-kick that old lady across the room.

"Up pretty late on a school night, wasn't she?" I said.

Mother made a hissing sound, waving her hand at me. If there had been shame in her eyes before, there was only annoyance now. "*Tsk.* I don't tolerate lectures. You know this about me. My business is my own."

"Fine. Then what am I doing here?"

Mother sat beside me to rub my knee. I'm no stranger to Mother's touch. She once made a polite advance, soon after we first met, but I refused just as politely. The look on her face: wistful, but resigned. She never tried again.

"It is very good to see you, my dearest boy. I have missed the sight of you." Mother sighed and went on, her voice low and pained. "You say you will no longer work for me. You are too shy now. Or you have a girlfriend, perhaps?"

I shrugged. She knew my reasons: One of them had just walked out of the door. Five years ago, I was flipping through channels and came across one of Jeanine's reruns, when she had top billing. A soul-sick feeling told me I had to quit working for Mother. I was afraid of ending up like Jeanine—but more afraid I would be tempted to bring Mother another prize for her stable. Unlike Devon Biggs, the pimp game wasn't for me.

Neither was the rest. I won't lie and say I didn't miss the money—Mother could have put thirty thousand dollars in my hands by the end of the week—but I never missed the work. I was so busy trying to get parts and pay my bills that I could have gone six months without sex and hardly noticed, if I hadn't run into Serena.

"I accept this, Tennyson, although it makes me sad," Mother went on. "So much money lost, for both of us. You called me in a time of need, a time of trouble, and now I call you. Bring Chela to me."

I groaned inwardly. I was in a fight for my freedom, and Mother wanted to send me on a rescue mission. Worse, she wanted to send me back into the path of M.C. Glazer. I might end up in the hospital this time. Or worse.

"M.C. Glazer's bodyguards don't like me," I said.

"Yes . . . so I see," Mother said, regarding my bruised face with the same sour expression she might have reserved for a marred Picasso. Gently, she touched my swollen lower lip. "Which is why I worry for Chela. This is not a nice man."

"Did you figure that out before or after you handed Chela over to him?"

Mother's eyes gleamed with hurt. "You know I am careful. But he pays well—too well, maybe. I did not listen to my instincts."

I decided not to share my suspicions about M.C. Glazer and Serena, even though Mother deserved to be scared shitless. "What makes you think Chela's in trouble?"

"When she is working, Chela is to call me each morning. Eleven o'clock. This is an important rule, and each morning she calls as directed. But not today. Also, she does not answer her cell phone." I doubted that Mother's regular girls had a designated time to call. I was glad Mother had at least bothered to give Chela special rules.

"How old is she?"

Mother's face snapped away, as if the question bored her. "Older than I was when I was eating garbage in Kosovo."

"Tell me how old she is, or we've finished talking. The truth."

"Fifteen. She came to me a year ago, but I waited, Tennyson. Until now."

I noticed a pink duffel bag hanging by the door that looked like it belonged to a high school student, and I realized the kid actually *lived* here: Mother had taken Chela in and turned her out. I thought of Serena in a backyard shed, and suddenly I was pissed. But why should I be? Her job had always been the same. Mother found broken birds. I had been one of Mother's broken birds, too; no different from Jeanine. Maybe I still was.

"Like Chela, you are too old for fairy tales," Mother said. "She has no one, and she earns top money. You would envy her bank account. Where else will she go? Life leaves few choices for a girl alone in the world."

My mind was tired. I didn't want to hear any more. "Where is she?"

"Glazer has an oceanfront house in Laguna Beach. Chela has said he takes her there, away from everyone. Privacy, you see."

My heartbeat shot up a notch. If finding Chela meant I could see M.C. Glazer without his bodyguards, Mother's call was a blessing. A few years ago, M.C. Glazer had gotten in trouble again when a video on the internet turned up showing an underage girl in his bed. The video wasn't sexual, only someone taping a party at Glazer's house—but it showed too much of Glaze's life. He'd avoided criminal charges, as usual, but now he apparently was a bit more careful, keeping the girl isolated.

"As you see, of course, I cannot go to the police," Mother went on. "Bring Chela back to me safely, and I will pay five thousand dollars. I realize this is only a small portion of what you could earn otherwise . . ."

"If that five thousand is for bringing Chela back to you, I won't take money." I stood up, and the height advantage went back to me. "Tell me where the beach house is, and I'll go get Chela, Mother. I'll make sure she's safe. But when I find her, don't expect me to bring her back here."

Mother's expression suddenly reminded me that she had shot a man in the face during the war. It would be a terrible mistake to think her just a small-boned old woman drinking tea. Mother is a chameleon. Just as quickly, her lips curled up into a small smile, revealing pale teeth that could have been made of glass. She sipped from her mug.

"Chela will go where Chela will go," Mother said, untroubled.

She was right, and I knew it. It was hard to walk away from The Life. If she was still alive to make the choice, Chela would want to go straight home to Mother.

M.C. Glazer's beach house practically sat on a private beach, penned in by a vast cliff to the north and bluffs hiding it from view. I drove past the sandy road to the house twice before I realized I'd missed it, since it wasn't visible at a distance.

The house was so secluded that it seemed like an optical illusion; invisible at most angles, then suddenly right in front of you. Improbably, the two-story house looked like a dollhouse, made almost entirely of glass. It wasn't huge, probably not even as large as mine, but its location was breathtaking. The house was virtually hidden from sight inside a cove, so close to the beach that a determined storm could sweep it out to sea. I could hear the ocean crashing from the other side of the bluff, where the waves must be a surfer's paradise. They don't call Laguna Beach the "California Riviera" for nothing.

Even standing where I was, at least fifty yards from the blue-black water, I saw three fins carving a wake in the ocean not far from shore. Probably a school of dolphins, I realized. M.C. Glazer could go swimming with dolphins any time he chose. His front yard was a dazzling ocean and a beach stretching from here to eternity. I don't often envy people, but jealousy cut into me. How could such a beautiful place belong to such a sick soul? I couldn't guess how much it would cost to rent the house for a week, much less to own it, but I learned long ago that almost nothing is impossible for people with enough money. Private beaches. Private planes. It's all a backdrop to them, something to take for granted. M.C. Glazer was living on a level few men in human history even dreamed about, a true king. If I remembered my history right, trying to topple a king was a dangerous undertaking.

I stood beyond the sun-faded vertical picket fence cutting the property off from the private road and watched the house, looking for movement from any of the windows.

There were no sounds except the steady race of doomed waves to the rocks and the jeering of seagulls. The tranquility filled me with dread instead of peace. Everything around me urged me to turn around and go back to familiar ground. I didn't belong here. People became mesmerized by places like this. *No wonder he brings Chela here.*

I tried to recall Chela's face from Club Magique, but my usual talent for faces deserted me. All I saw was large eyes slathered in mascara and a slender, underdeveloped frame. Except for her youth, Chela had barely registered to me that night. I was risking my life to rescue a girl whose face I could hardly re-member. But there was always that *Maybe*, dangling right in front of me. Maybe I would learn something about who killed Serena. Serena was the only reason I was there.

I climbed over the fence and felt my shoes sink into the sand. No one was in sight. There weren't many lights on inside, so I wasn't sure anyone was home. If there was a car, it must be parked in the detached, vine-covered garage on the far side of the house. I hunched over, taking stealthy steps to keep clear of the staring windows. With late-afternoon sunlight reflecting against the glass, I would be lucky to spot someone inside before he saw me. I hoped he didn't have a dog.

There was a deck above me, and pale flesh caught my eye. A petite foot dangled over the balcony, and I had no doubt that it was Chela's. Either she was sunbathing on the deck, or she was lying there for a reason I didn't want to think about. But I could hear tinny strains of hip-hop music, a persistent beat: Chela was listening to music on headphones with the volume turned way too loud. She probably wasn't hurt, but even if I shouted out her name, she wouldn't hear me.

Just as well. Before I made a move, I wanted to know where M.C. Glazer was.

I only had to take three more steps, toward the front door. Through the ceiling-to-floor window, I saw him plain as day, sitting in what looked like a living room with a view of the ocean. He was easy to spot because the room was so spare: white leather sofa and loveseat, mounted plasma TV, and large speakers on either side. M.C. Glazer was sitting in the center of his sofa, his eyes glued to his television screen. He was animated as he talked on his cell phone, so I guessed he was watching the Lakers with a friend on the other end. I was close enough to see the Corona label on his bottle of beer. I could also see almost every corner of that empty room.

So much for privacy.

For a full five minutes, I stood frozen, breathing hard as I watched him watching his game. After three minutes, he hung up his phone. I reminded myself that it could still be too good to be true. Jenk and Kojak might be in the kitchen getting snacks. Or sitting on the toilet, like John Travolta in *Pulp Fiction*. Or maybe Glazer was strapped. That was likely, considering his reputation. My heart thrashed.

How the hell would I pull this off?

I was wearing a fanny pack with just the basics: rope, a small toolkit, a flashlight, and a pocketknife. No gun, unfortunately for me. My Nine was in its box, at home. I don't have a permit to carry, and haven't fired a piece since I left the police academy; to me, a gun is just part of the uniform my father used to wear. Besides, my plan was to stay *out* of prison for killing Serena, not to get arrested for a shooting a major rap star.

I wanted to slap Mother's face. Or my own. I was acting like somebody who wanted to die.

I gazed up at that dangling foot again. Chela had shifted slightly, almost out of sight. I played with the idea of throwing a pebble to get her attention. *And then what? She'll skip down to meet you and leave happily on your arm?* I couldn't count on that. Maybe she didn't want to leave. Chela seemed to have made herself comfortable.

No, I had to get to Glazer first.

I flipped open my new disposable phone, my only weapon. Mother had not only gifted me with an address, but divulged M.C. Glazer's personal cell phone number, the way she contacted him when she had girls she thought he would like. I could only think of one way to get him out of his house, and it felt so flimsy, I almost changed my mind.

Then, I dialed his number.

I heard the ring first in my ear, and then, two seconds later, muted through the window from inside. I saw Glazer look at the Caller ID on his phone, trying to decide whether to pick up. He didn't recognize the number. The phone rang again.

"Speak," M.C. Glazer's voice said, already pissed.

"Yeah, Mr. Gaines? Alphonse Gaines?"

".Who is this?"

"This is Roy from Westwood Auto Body. Sorry to disturb you, but we're calling to make sure you're satisfied with the car. We'd like to keep your business, sir."

"You've got two seconds to tell me what you're talking about. Clock's ticking."

"Aren't you the owner of the car Mr. Jenkins brought in with the scrape across the hood last Tuesday? My guys here damn near cried when they saw it. We just want to see if we matched the paint to your satisfaction."

"A scrape? On what car?"

I had no idea what cars M.C. Glazer owned. I felt a surge of certainty that his bodyguards were about to fly out of the house and hunt me down, but he couldn't hear it in my voice. My voice was a guy sitting calmly at a cubicle at Westwood Auto Body with a Diet Coke in his hand, making his last calls of the day. "You know what, Mr. Gaines? They just give me the names and numbers—"

"*Who* brought my car in?" Suddenly, M.C. Glazer was on his feet. "And who gave you this fucking number?"

"Mr. Robert Jenkins signed the paperwork, and your number's here on the invoice. Wow. I'm looking at the total. Holy moly. But he wanted us to get the job done right for you. He said it's your favorite car."

There was a long silence. "The Lex?" he said, and I held my breath.

He's bought it.

"Can you hold while I check back with the guys who worked on your car?" I said.

"Naw, I don't want to—"

"It'll just take a second. Hold on, sir." And I clicked off my phone.

M.C. Glazer moved faster than I thought he would, so fast that I had to sprint around the side of the house to keep up with him. He wasn't going to wait for

Westwood Auto Body to come back to the line. And he didn't try to contact Jenk, either by phone or by yelling for him. M.C. Glazer was headed for the back of the house—the garage. My story must have had more than a whisper of plausibility. Even someone with luck as bad as mine has to catch a break once in a while.

The back door flung open too soon, surprising me in midstride. I jumped backward, ducking behind the house, and M.C. Glazer walked past without seeing me, pointing a remote toward the garage. I considered everything I saw near me as a weapon, even the clay flowerpots. A garden hose. A bird bath too heavy to move. A child's sand bucket. Nothing. *Shit.*

Six steps took M.C. Glazer to his garage. As the door hurried upward, I saw a glimpse of chrome gleaming in the darkness. A Lexus convertible. Silver. No wonder he wanted to check on her.

"Jenk better *not* have fucked up my Lex . . ." M.C. Glazer was muttering.

Should I slip inside the house, or take M.C. Glazer out first? Wait to jump him from inside, or follow him into the garage? Possibilities swam in my head. I had to make up my mind fast, and I did. *Get in the house.* I glanced back at M.C. Glazer, who was leaning over the hood of the Lexus with a powerful flashlight. Then, I trotted up three coral steps to the back door and slipped inside.

I found myself in the L-shaped kitchen, with its Mexican floor tiles and granite counters. The sound of the jeering crowd from the Lakers game told me where the living room was. The kitchen was spotless except for piles of Chinese takeout cartons on the counter. I glanced around anxiously, looking for a weapon again. A row of knives gleamed at me from a cutlery set, but I ignored them. If the only way I could subdue M.C. Glazer was with a knife, then I was in more trouble than I thought.

The cold realization came: I didn't have a plan. I was a natural at improvisation on a stage, but this was different. A mistake now could cost me my life.

I had to hide myself and wait, so I stood in the deep corner alongside the door frame. The door would open inward, so I would be hidden. I had to subdue M.C. Glazer as soon as he walked in, or I might not have another chance. He knew his house better than I did; if he saw me, he could vanish, and I could be trapped.

I waited, breathing harder than I wanted to. The house had an open floor plan, so I could see the living room's winding staircase from where I stood; Chela couldn't miss me if she came downstairs. One minute passed. Two. The kitchen seemed hot, suddenly. Sweat stung my eyes, but I didn't dare move.

". . . five minutes ago," I heard M.C. Glazer say outside, on his phone again. Was he getting closer? "Westwood or something. Then how'd they get this number, man?"

His voice sounded muffled for a moment. Then, he was only a couple of feet from me, right outside the back door. "Yeah, I'm serious. I'm in Laguna watching the game, and this fool calls . . ." The doorknob turned.

The door swung open, farther back than I'd expected. The doorknob jabbed me, and I shrank back so it would open unobstructed. Holding my breath.

". . . I was thinking it's that Kutcher bitch on *Punk'd* or somebody fucking with—"

When the back door closed again, M.C. Glazer and I were face to face in his kitchen. He froze, his mouth open in the O of an unfinished sentence. Only his right hand moved, fishing toward the back of his jeans. I rammed the point of his jaw with the heel of my hand, hard enough to loosen teeth. Glazer's head snapped back. As the shock scrambled his brain's switchboard I slid behind him, snaking my arm around his throat, my wrist bone constricting his carotid arteries in the classic blood strangle Brazilians call *"mata leão,"* meaning *to kill the lion.* Performed properly, it renders a man unconscious in seconds. Glazer thrashed and bucked . . . and went limp.

His phone clattered beside him on the tile. *"Glaze? Glaze . . . ?"* I heard the voice on the other end of the phone growing alarmed.

I dropped M.C. Glazer and grabbed the phone, hardly thinking. "Yo, man, call you after the game," I said from my throat, hoping my imitation was credible enough for one sentence. I hung up the phone and waited. It didn't ring right away. I must have fooled him, I thought. *Either that, or Jenk is on his way here with backup.*

I wasn't winded, but I couldn't help panting. I felt dizzy. Superstar rapper M.C. Glazer was lying unconscious on his kitchen floor, drooling blood from a bitten lip, and I had no idea what I was doing there. This was not the way I lived my life.

His face was slack on the floor, but I heard his voice: *Yeah, I killed her.* Suddenly, it took all of my willpower not to stomp him until my anger dissolved in his blood. I wanted him to hurt, badly. I knelt and patted down M.C. Glazer, and my palm touched something solid against his lower back. When I pulled up his basketball jersey, I saw another kind of chrome gleaming, and yanked out the gun fast: A Smith & Wesson .44. My heart tumbled. He'd been going for his gun. I felt Death blow on my face like hot wind from a speeding train. I stepped away from Glaze, leveling the gun at him in case he might roll over and try to fight for it. But he was out cold, like a college kid passed out on his frat house floor. I glanced behind me, toward the living room. That stairway caught my eye again. The railings looked solid. That would be a good place to tie him.

But first, I had to strip M.C. Glazer of both his defenses and his dignity. His clothes were coming off. Everything.

I had almost finished my last knot, with Glazer slumped nude over my shoulder as I tied his hands in front of him to the banister in the living room, when I heard footsteps above me. I looked up. Chela was on the top landing staring down. Her hair was damp, hanging lifeless across her shoulders, and she was oily and red from the sun. Her bikini only showed how much growing her body still had to do. The sight of her made me feel sick to my stomach.

Slowly, Chela pulled off her headphones. Her eyes widened, focused on the gun I hadn't realized I was pointing at her. I snapped the gun toward the window instead.

"Don't worry," I said. "I'm not going to hurt you."

"You are in *so much* trouble," Chela said, twirling her curls around her finger as she took a step down the stairs. She sounded like the perfect schoolyard tattletale.

"I hope you like it in prison," Chela said.

"Quiet, please."

"But forget prison, since his guys are going to kill you. Just so you know."

"I said quiet. Please."

"You better hurry and get the hell down to Mexico. For real."

Chela stood beside me like a bystander at the scene of a car accident, and she hadn't stopped talking. Everything she said was already in my mind anyway. This was insane.

The duct tape in my hands squealed as I yanked off the last piece to tie M.C. Glazer's feet together, binding him to the legs of his dining chair while his hands were still strung above his head. He was breathing faster now, eyelids fluttering, about to wake. But with his hands firmly knotted to the staircase and his feet tied to a chair, M.C. Glazer wasn't going anywhere unless I said so. One problem solved.

"Let me explain the rules, Chela," I said, waving the .44 to get her attention. "I do the talking for both of us. The only time I want to hear *you* is when and if I ask a question. Then, all I want to hear is the answer. If you don't understand that, there's plenty of tape left for you and your mouth. Nod if you understand."

She rolled her eyes, sucked her teeth, and nodded, staring daggers.

"Mother said you didn't call on schedule. Why not?"

Chela's eyes dropped quickly. She didn't have to answer.

"Oh," I said. "So you decided you liked it here and didn't want to leave."

"She can't tell me where to go."

"*Hey*," I roared, and my anger was real. "What did I just say? You answer my questions, and that's all I hear from you."

"I'm staying here with Glaze."

I gestured toward M.C. Glazer, whose head shifted slightly as he fought for consciousness. His bloody lips twitched as he groaned softly. "Oh, I see. You'll stay here and be mistress of the manor. This is *your* house now. That right?"

"He said I can stay as long as I want."

"Forever, maybe. Is that what he said?"

"That's none of your business."

"And you believe that bull, Chela? I'm surprised at you. What happens when you're too old for him? What happens next week, when he wants somebody else?"

"He said he won't. He loves me. Get it?"

I laughed a sour laugh. "Oh, I get it. I don't think you do, sweetheart."

M.C. Glazer's groan rumbled more loudly from his throat. The harsh rasping sound became words. "Don't . . . say nothin', Chela."

"Don't worry, Glaze. I won't." She gave me a triumphant grin: *Now what?*

M.C. Glazer blinked fast, trying to clear the clouds from his eyes. "You," he said.

I pulled up a dining chair and turned it backward to sit in front of him, my arms folded across the chair back. The .44 was still in my hand. My finger was so tense on the live trigger, I didn't dare point it in his direction. "That's right, asshole. Me."

"When I saw you . . . I thought you were . . . police."

"Maybe you'll wish I was, man. Time will tell." I clocked the side of his jaw with my elbow, enough to rattle his teeth, let him know the pain wasn't over yet. I needed him talking.

"*Fuck!*" he yelled, struggling against his binds. The chair scooted on the tile as he spat stringy blood out of his mouth. The pain panicked him. M.C. Glazer was used to other people fighting for him. He also noticed that he wasn't wearing any clothes. He squeezed his thighs together, trying to hide his genitals. As for what I saw down there, let's just say that I recalled Afrodite's lyrics: *M.C. Glazer ain't no ladykilla . . . he might penetrate, but he'll never fill ya . . .*

Movement flickered in my peripheral vision, and I shot a look at Chela. She was taking snail-like steps toward the kitchen, already five yards from where she'd been. "Go over to that sofa and sit down," I said, and the look on my face made her obey.

"OK, man, you got me," M.C. Glazer said, gasping. "What do you want?"

I leaned in, nose to nose with him, and he couldn't mask the terror in his eyes. "You tell me," I said. "What do I want?"

He tried to scoot away again, but his chair was trapped against the staircase. He pressed his face against the stair, smearing blood on the paint. "If it's m-money, I got that. I pay you to keep quiet? Tell me how much, man. Just leave me alone."

"Money doesn't fix everything . . . Alphonse," I said, drawing out his name.

"Then *what?*" He sounded more scared now. If I wasn't after money, I might be a psycho, and only God knew what a psycho might do to a naked man.

"Who killed Serena Johnston?" A whisper.

M.C. Glazer's body sagged, suddenly weary. "Oh, man . . . you're back on that?"

"I never got *off* that. I was interrupted."

"What you want me to say? I'm sorry she's dead? OK, I'm sorry. She was goin' places, cut down in her prime, the very definition of tragedy. We cool now?"

"Who killed her?"

"How the fuck would I know?"

This time, I hit him in the stomach. I didn't want to leave bruises.

"You told me you killed her, Alphonse."

M.C. Glazer gasped, heaving to untangle his diaphragm. "Wait. I just said that to mess with your head, man—some cold shit to say in front of my boys, you know? I ain't never killed nobody. Why would I kill Afrodite?"

"I'm calling the police," Chela said. For the first time, she sounded nervous.

"You go on and do that," I said, not even looking back at her.

"No. Wait," M.C. Glazer said. "No need for no police, girl. Just chill."

"You heard the man, Chela," I said.

"You think I killed her 'cuz of trash-talking on her CDs? That don't mean nothing. That's just more money in everybody's pocket. Melodrama for the masses."

"Why'd you hook up with her sister?"

"What?"

"Tyra said she laid down some tracks at your studio Tuesday morning. Funny how that studio is only a couple of blocks from where Serena's body was found."

M.C. Glazer's eyes widened. "I don't know nothin' about that. I wasn't in the studio with Tyra. You know how many projects I've got popping? I use studios all over the country. Chicago, New York, Memphis . . . wherever the music is. I'm gonna put Tyra in my video, too, like a joke. Caricature? Parody? The night they say Afrodite got killed, I was at a party that went until breakfast, and a whole house full of niggas can tell you that, including two of the Lakers. Just 'cuz I hired her sister to do some voice work don't mean I killed nobody. If you've got some questions for Tyra, then you need to be talking to her."

"But I'm talking to you," I said. "You knew a lot about Serena's past. Serena's business. Maybe she knew too much about yours."

"I don't know what you—"

"How many guns are you moving, Glazer? How many rocks?"

Glaze's face hardened into a wall. "I don't know what you're talking about."

"You don't? You've got all those badges on CopKilla's payroll, so you must like cops. Especially dirty cops. Is that what Jenk does? He helps you stop *pretending* to be a thug and be one for real?"

"You're delusional, man. You need professional help."

I pulled out M.C. Glazer's cell phone, a stylish Nokia N90 that made my throwaway look like a toy from a bubble-gum dispenser: seven hundred dollars, with a top-notch camera. The first thing I saw when I flipped it open was the photo he'd posed for with Honey at Club Magique. His screensaver, just like he'd vowed.

I aimed the camera and shot a picture of M.C. Glazer bound to the stairs naked, his arms above his head. I held the camera up so he could see the shot: not the best lighting, but his features were clear. I snapped more photos, all from different angles. He turned his head away, trying to hide.

"Can't you see it on MTV News?" I said. "You know what the headline will be? 'M.C. Glazer Is a Bitch.' Will that help sales, too?"

I saved the photos and played with his touchpad, navigating my way through his menus. I sent the pictures to my email address, one by one. Even if he canceled his cell phone account, the photos would still be in my mailbox. Those photos were the only insurance policy I had, and I didn't want to lose them.

Next, I walked toward Chela and leaned over to show her the screensaver with M.C. Glazer grinning beside Honey. Chela looked away from the camera's screen, stung. "I'm sorry, Chela, but . . . shouldn't that be you? You're his best girl, right?"

"Shut up. I am."

"Is that true?" I asked, turning back to Glazer. "Is she your best girl, Alphonse?"

For the first time, Alphonse Terrell Gaines had nothing to say.

"Oh, I get it," I said. "She's your best girl, but you have to keep her a secret. The world wouldn't understand. But once she turns eighteen, it'll all be different. Maybe you two can even get married. Isn't that right?"

Chela sought out M.C. Glazer's eyes, but he was looking away from her, toward the ocean stretching across his windows. Then, Chela looked at me with accusation, as if I'd somehow turned her life against her.

"How old is she, you think?" I said. "I'd say fifteen. But even that's a little old for you, huh, Alphonse? You'd like fourteen better. Or . . . thirteen? Is that best of all?"

M.C. Glazer's lips looked sewn together. His jaw was steel.

"This man is not who you think he is," I said to Chela, gently this time. I could see that Chela didn't allow herself to shed many tears, but she was close. "Mother always calls M.C. Glazer when she has young girls. Or did you think you were special? How much money does he save if you cut Mother out?"

Again, Chela looked at Glazer, whose face was unreadable.

I leaned close to Glazer. "I know it all. I know your life story."

"You think you do." He didn't meet my eyes, still staring toward the water.

The cell phone in my hand rang. JENKINS, ROBERT, said M.C. Glazer's Caller ID. I didn't know where Jenk was calling from, but if he was still in the city, it would take him at least an hour to get here, probably much longer with traffic. I shoved the phone in my pocket.

"Maybe we're finished, maybe we're not," I said. "I still don't know who killed Serena. But I will find out. The next time you see me will be the last time."

"You got that right." For the first time, he sounded like M.C. Glazer again.

"Three things: If I start to think you've told anybody about today, *trust me*, it will be my last act on Earth to make sure the whole world sees you like this."

M.C. Glazer met my gaze, eager for an end to his nightmare. "What else?"

"You say you didn't kill Serena. Who do you think did?"

"I'm not a damn psychic—"

"Give me your best guess. Do it. Now."

M.C. Glazer sighed and shook his head, exasperated. "Man, I don't know. Tyra talks a lot of shit about her sister, but would she take it that far? I can't say that."

"Anybody else?"

"Wasn't Afrodite suing some guy in the Mob? That's what I heard. Maybe Tony Soprano did it. Maybe it was whoever killed Shareef. Hey, maybe it was Santa Claus. I didn't know then, and I don't know now. What's the third thing to get rid of you?"

I gestured toward Chela, who was sitting on her hands. She looked cold. "Look at her," I said.

M.C. Glazer glanced reluctantly, as if the sight of her would blind him. Chela gazed back at him, and something shifted in her face. One way or another, she was seeing M.C. Glazer with new eyes.

"Don't ever touch this girl again."

M.C. Glazer shrugged, his gaze with Chela unbroken. "I never touched that little bitch. She's just a fan following me around."

Chela tried not to flinch, but I saw her cheek twinge. It's hard to be denied to your face. I stayed quiet for a beat, allowing the moment to marinate.

"Touch her again, and it's over. You're done."

Glaze nodded, agreeing. "Now get the hell out of my house."

"Chela . . . go upstairs, put on some clothes, and grab your stuff. You have three minutes, starting now. I'm your ride."

Chela made a dash for the stairs, not looking back at me or Glazer. I figured she would probably call Glaze's bodyguards once she was alone, but it wouldn't matter. We would be long gone before anyone got here.

M.C. Glazer and I waited in silence. A Lakers fan to the core, Glaze's eyes went back to the television and he cursed when Kobe missed a free throw. His cell phone rang in my pocket, but I didn't even check this time. I knew it was Jenk calling. Or Kojak.

Chela came tramping back down the stairs in two minutes, carrying a heavy duffel bag. She had two coats slung over her arm, one of them leather, one thick with fox fur. I also noticed several gold chains around her neck she hadn't been wearing before.

"That little freak is robbing me!" M.C. Glazer said.

Chela gave him a slender, manicured middle finger. "You owe me," she said.

She left, slamming the front door behind her. I almost went after her to tell her to bring back anything that didn't belong to her, but ultimately didn't have the will. M.C. Glazer *did* owe her, and what he owed was far more than she could carry in two arms. My heart had been racing, and now it was slowing down. I'd come with no plan, and improvised my way through. I was tired, but I was alive. I could hardly believe it.

"Wait," M.C. Glazer called, anxious. "Somebody's gonna come looking if I don't pick up my phone. I don't want nobody to find me like this."

That was a good sign. If he didn't want his own man to see him tied up, he sure as hell wouldn't risk allowing my photos to get out. I opened my bag and pulled out my pocketknife. It would take M.C. Glazer a while to fumble his way out of my ropes with such a small blade, but he could to it. I wiped the knife down and slipped it into his bound hand. His fingers grasped it.

"Maybe you can return the favor one day," I said.

M.C. Glazer glared. "Countin' the minutes, bruh."

I shoved his bulky Smith & Wesson into my jeans. I would need it now.

Outside, Chela was waiting in my car, smacking gum. She didn't speak to me as I climbed in. As soon as the engine was running, she commandeered my radio, filling the car with angry rock music. I backed out of the sandy driveway, and M.C. Glazer's house vanished.

As I turned onto the Pacific Coast Highway, my eyes were overwhelmed by the beginnings of a sunset that had turned the sky and ocean orange, with dapples of blue and violet exactly where they should be. Chela gazed through the windows as if she was afraid she would never see the sky again. We savored it together.

"You're taking me back to Mother's?"

"I didn't say that."

"Where, then?"

"I don't know yet."

"I'll run away from state care. And I can afford a lawyer."

"I said I don't know yet."

Seagulls marched across the sky, almost close enough to touch.

Chela switched the radio station. She found Will Smith's "Summertime" and let it rest there. Then she sat back in her seat, hiding her face behind sunglasses, and we both bobbed our heads to the music. I've always liked that song, but never as much as at that moment. It sounded like happiness. Innocence.

Somehow, it was a beautiful day.

IT WAS NEARLY DARK BY THE TIME we made it back to my neighborhood, and I was so hungry that my head throbbed. I never explained to Chela where we were going, since I had never quite decided. The absence of a decision meant that I ended up pulling into my driveway. I didn't know anyone in the kid salvation business, and I couldn't chase Serena's killer with a teenager in my care. I was ready to be back at 5450 Gleason. To me, the sight of the clay-colored paint on my fortress walls and the familiar forest of cactus plants was a return to a lover's arms. There is no place like home.

"Nice house," Chela said. It was all she'd said in ninety minutes.

We trudged inside with her armful of loot from M.C. Glazer and a fragrant pizza from Barone's I'd ordered from the road. Chela planted herself in front of my TV and started blasting music videos on MTV without a word. My refrigerator was stocked almost exclusively with beer and protein shakes, but I found a hidden can of Coke. She took it without a word, mesmerized by the gyrating bodies on my television screen.

I'd left my business cell phone on my kitchen counter that morning, and the red light was flashing. Twelve messages. I hadn't checked my PO box in several days either, so I probably had a stack of mail to match. Tomorrow, I decided. I wolfed down a slice of thin-crust pepperoni and checked my voicemail.

The first message was from the production office where I'd auditioned Monday. A callback. I laughed. The part was pretty much Buppie Number Three in Bookstore, but there were six lines of snappy dialogue and it was a big-budget romantic comedy, so I dutifully scribbled down the time they wanted to see me again: noon Monday, in just a few days. *If I'm not in jail or dead, I'll be there.* Something to look forward to.

There were four anxious messages from April I ignored, but her fifth had come after I called her last. Two hours ago. She said she was on deadline and asked me to call. I wondered if she would keep her word and leave police suspicions about me out of her story. Would she tarnish Serena's legacy? I couldn't imagine enjoying a job where I might casually print things that could change people's lives for the worse.

I was about to call April back when the next message made me hold my breath. I knew who he was even though he didn't say his name. It was Jenk.

Jenk sighed into the phone. "You were asking questions about Serena . . ." His voice dropped off. During his long pause, my mind raced. His tone was calm and measured, so he couldn't be calling in response to my most recent visit to M.C. Glazer. *Could he?* "You're looking in all the wrong places, so step off for your own good. While you're getting your ass kicked, Serena is still dead and her killer is still free. Who wins? Nobody. You seem like a smart guy: Start acting like it."

His voice clicked away. I double-checked the time stamp: He had called only five minutes after April, about two hours ago. Jenk's Caller ID and number were visible, but I decided not to call back. I saved the message. Better not push my luck. Maybe I would call him tomorrow, when I'd have a better idea of how Glaze handled my visit.

It hadn't been my imagination at Club Magique: Jenk knew something, or he thought he did. Maybe he had called because I was getting too close. But if Jenk was involved in the killing, would he have called me? Not likely.

I played the message twice more, listening to the way his voice rose and fell, where he paused, how he chose his words. What I heard didn't quite match my assumptions. His sigh at the beginning of the call sounded grieved. His words could have been threatening—*step off for your own good*—but his tone was carefully neutral. More than anything, it sounded like a courtesy call. A favor. Why would Robert Jenkins want to do me a favor? I might never know. That ship had probably sailed.

My heart drummed as I went through the rest of my messages, expecting a howl of expletives from either Jenk or M.C. Glazer. Nothing. Two messages from Dad's nursing home—something about a problem with his insurance company and the last bill. One message from my cleaning lady, Elena. One hang-up.

Maybe I would live another night.

"You sound tired," April said when I called her.

"I am. Long day. Anything new from the police?"

"No. Anything new on your end?"

"No."

I hoped we weren't both lying.

"I don't know what it means yet, but there's one thing . . ." April said. "I went by that nightclub, Mackey's, where Tyra said she was Monday night."

"And?"

"Tyra's a regular. That's true. But the bartender said he hasn't seen her in a week. He asked around, and nobody else remembered seeing Tyra Monday either. I said maybe it was just too crowded, and he said Tyra's not the kind of person who blends into a crowd. When she's there, everybody knows it."

While I'd been committing a string of felonies against M.C. Glazer, April had learned something that might be important. "That's good work," I said.

April's voice turned teasing. "Now are you sorry you blew me off?"

"Very sorry."

"And, uh . . . there's something else I want to say, Tennyson."

I braced, silent. Maybe Lieutenant Nelson had given her some news after all.

"I'm not going to print what Tyra said about Afrodite's past."

I wished she was in the room, so I could hug her. "Thank you," I said.

"I can't get confirmation now, the paper's lawyers will give me a fight, and it's not worth it. If it's true, it was a long time ago. She was a kid." April sighed, and I heard Chela noisily flipping through my channels in the living room. "Besides . . . I've met a friend of Afrodite's, and he asked me not to print it. Nobody tells me how to write my stories, but . . ." She was apologizing. I don't know whether to credit the pizza or the friendly voice, but my headache was gone.

"Thanks, April," I said. "I owe you lunch."

She paused. "Make it dinner?"

I almost smiled. Almost. "You're asking a suspect out on a date?"

"Innocent until proven guilty."

I couldn't think of any good that could come to April from dating me. A girl like April would expect a first date to lead to a second, and then a third. A girl like April would want a boyfriend, someone to hold her hand on the beach, someone she could call when she was depressed and anxious in the midnight hours. I've never met a woman who wanted anything less, no matter what she pretended. That wasn't me.

"Let's talk tomorrow," I said, without a yes or no.

"I'll look forward to it." Her voice went husky in a sultry way, and I felt a shiver. I was looking forward to talking to her again, too.

I went into the living room and sat on my sofa. Chela was on the floor cradling the pizza box, not six feet from the television screen. My father would have skinned me for sitting that close to the TV, I remembered. Another painful memory to shut away.

Chela and I had to talk, but I still didn't know what to say. Deep down, I was hoping she would let me off the hook by insisting on going back to Mother's. The five thousand dollars Mother had waiting for me could make a big difference in my life. And what else could I do with a kid who had vowed to run away from foster care? Besides, she probably already had a record. She might slide straight to juvie, and no good would come from putting Chela in a cage.

I glanced at the fur coats and gleaming pile of gold Chela had left lying on my coffee table and remembered the Smith & Wesson I was still carrying. The last thing I needed was stolen property in my house. I picked up the duffel bag beneath the fur coat, which was heavy with more new acquisitions.

"That's mine now," Chela challenged me.

"We can't leave this out in the open," I said. "Come with me to the kitchen."

"The *kitchen*? For what?"

My kitchen has two entrances; one from the foyer with a bar counter near the front door, and one on the side closer to the staircase. Between the kitchen and the stairs, an elegant wooden wine rack stands against the wall with rows of wine bottles Alice left behind. The rack is taller than I am, made from maple but stained a dark mahogany, a striking contrast against the white-brick wall. It's a work of art in its own right, with fluted molding and rosette appliqués.

It's also a hidden door. It leads to what Alice always called "The Pantry."

Inside, Alice converted the original laundry room into a simple panic room; wood-paneled walls, a table and garden chair, a telephone, and two locks on the inside. Her neighbor convinced her to build it after a home invasion down the street put a documentary filmmaker and his son in the hospital. It's not a big room—more like a glorified storage space—but when I moved in, I shoved a few stacks of unpacked boxes in the corner and built a large spice rack just inside the doorway so that it really *was* my pantry. Like Alice, I rarely used the room. But it was the perfect place for M.C. Glazer's property, for now. With the police sniffing so closely, I had to take precautions.

Chela's eyes widened as I slid my fingers between the rack and the wall where a hidden groove allowed me to pull the door open with ease. To her, seeing my pantry appear was an act of magic.

"That is *sooooooo* tight!" she said, yanking on the door. Bottles clanked.

"Watch the wine."

Together, we left the gun, her two coats, four gold chains, and an unopened duffel bag on the table inside. As the door closed, they vanished behind my bottles of 1998 Gaja Barbaresco, 1999 Rex Hill Pinot Noir, and 1989 Hugel Riesling Vendange Tardive.

For the next hour, I sat with Chela and watched music videos in silence. I dozed to the sound of electronic beats and samples from music I'd grown up with, remembering images of my drab living room at Dad's house, longing to hear the original songs intact.

I opened my eyes when I heard Serena's voice.

There she was in my living room, her face bright-eyed and radiant, her ochre skin draped in flowing white that ruffled in a caressing wind. It was the same music video that had been playing in Devon Biggs's office. The director had made her look angelic, as if he had known that this video would be her last. I wished the song itself deserved the honor, but it was good to see her.

"Should I turn? You said Afrodite was a friend of yours," Chela said.

"That's okay. I don't mind."

"*You want some of this? / You better step up.*" Serena cast a special wicked glance over her shoulder just for me before the video faded away.

"Was M.C. Glazer really at a party Monday night?" I said. Chela didn't answer, and I cursed myself for pushing too hard. I decided to change the subject. "Yes, Afrodite was a good friend."

"Did you love her?" Chela said. She scooted around to give me her full attention, her arms wrapped around her folded-up knees, and I forgot any thought of sending her back to Mother's. Somebody should be sending her to school and making sure she did her homework and studied for her SAT.

"Maybe. I don't know." I was beginning to ask myself the same question.

"You always know if you're in love with somebody."

"What makes you so sure?"

"I've never been in love, and I never will," Chela said. "But you *know*."

"Maybe you're right," I said. "Maybe I never have and never will either."

"You're better off," Chela said wisely, and turned back to the television screen. I was trying to think of a way to discuss her future when she blurted: "I don't know where Glaze was Monday. I didn't see him until Tuesday. But I don't think he killed her."

"Why not?"

She shrugged, not turning around. "I dunno. I was with him when he heard Afrodite was dead. He was shocked. He was saying stuff like, *What? Oh, shit.* Like . . . he was sorry it happened."

"He didn't seem sorry to me."

"He acts different in front of you. He acts different in front of everybody." I heard sad fondness in Chela's voice. She had been brave to leave him, I realized. It must have hurt her to hear M.C. Glazer call her a *little bitch.* I wished I could erase it.

"Do you have a toothbrush?" I said.

Chela didn't answer, looking at me as if I'd asked in Zulu.

"Never mind. I have an extra," I said. "I'll get you a toothbrush, soap, and towels, and put them on your bed. The guest room is that way, on the other side of this room. The room with all the prints of Dorothy Dandridge."

"Who?"

"Never mind. There's a bathroom in there too."

"Do you get a lot of guests?"

"You're my first."

That was truer than I'd realized. If I could work things out, my guest room would belong to Dad soon. I just had to get my life together long enough to bring him here.

After I'd collected a pile of toiletries for Chela, I left her watching TV and went upstairs to hit my treadmill hard for a half-hour. Then, I sank to the carpeted floor for my nightly Hindu Squats and Hindu Pushups. One of each, then two, then three, then four . . .

I got up to twenty, a total of 420 reps in under fifteen minutes, before my lungs felt as if they'd crawl out of my throat and die. I was tired, but the sweet punishment felt brutally good. My mind slowly shifted into silence as my heart thundered, and sweat pooled beneath my exhausted body. I stretched.

I decided to unwind with some reading before bed. I have a pile of books on my nightstand, most of them read halfway through, and I usually pick one at random. Like I said, I have trouble finishing anything. I'd grab one of my mysteries by Paula J. Woods or Valerie Wilson Wesley, or maybe Barack Obama's *Dreams of My Father.*

The shower afterward felt so good that I wanted to cry. Alice had splurged on her master bathroom—marble counters, copper fixtures, and two excellent shower heads. Steaming water pelted me all over, and I felt my worries running down the drain.

The feeling was great while it lasted.

As soon as I left the bathroom, toweling off, reality slapped me again. Chela was waiting for me in my bed, posed beneath the covers. I saw her bare, pale shoulders, but I didn't look long enough to see what else was exposed. When I lunged backward, covering my eyes, I almost slipped on my bathroom tile.

"What?" Chela said, sounding hurt.

"Get the hell out of my room." My enraged voice almost shook the wall. I was the maniac from M.C. Glazer's house again. "Right *now,* Chela!"

I heard her feet pad on the carpet as she ran out. She slammed my door.

I pulled on some sweatpants and a T-shirt, cursing myself for yelling at her. I needed to explain the rules to Chela. What else was she supposed to think? In her experience, men wanted to have sex with her. Why else would I bring her to my house? In her mind, she'd been offering me an expensive gift. Sex might be the only kind of affection she could conceive of.

I sat at the edge of my bed, drained physically and emotionally.

I knew I should go downstairs and have a frank talk with her. I should tell her that I wanted to help her in a way I wished someone had helped Serena. I should tell her I wasn't going to take her back to Mother's, and that she should hang out with me until we could figure out what to do next. But I sat, unable to move except for my unsteady hands, which I planted on my kneecaps. My mind was a blizzard.

Thinking about Chela. And Serena. And Jeanine. And me. I saw a mental snapshot of my old drama teacher, remembering my visits to her backyard pool. I had been Chela's age when Ms. Jackson invited me to come over and play, and she must have been in her thirties. It was like slipping on contact lenses; for the first time, I saw the episode through clear eyes. What the hell had that woman wanted with a kid?

Before I knew it, an hour had passed. I still wanted to say something to Chela, but I was so tired my bones felt hollow. I wasn't used to feeling so exhausted, as if I had climbed a mountain with a piano on my back. It was only ten, but I forgot about reading. I turned off my lights and surrendered to my bed, where I smelled Chela's shampoo on my pillow. *I'll talk to her in the morning,* I thought. *We'll work it all out tomorrow.*

I forgot that sometimes tomorrow never comes.

The pounding on my door downstairs—and the persistent ringing of my bell—seemed to start as soon as I closed my eyes. But my clock said it was 7:00 A.M.

At first I thought Chela was playing games, but in a flash of inspiration, I knew better. I rolled out of bed and pulled back my curtain. Two police cars were parked at the curb—one black-and-white, one unmarked. Shit. Everything I had dreaded was coming to pass, and I hadn't been able to do anything to stop it.

I heard a muffled identification: "Police!" Then, more pounding.

Not too long ago, if police had showed up my door early in the morning, I would have assumed something had happened to Dad. Period. Now, I couldn't figure out *which* of my problems had brought them there: M.C. Glazer? Serena? Chela? I was in trouble that had no bottom to it. There was no end in sight.

I slipped my feet into my loafers and ran downstairs. The TV was still on, the pizza box left on the floor, but the guest room door was closed. I opened it and peeked inside. The bedsheets were rumpled, but Chela wasn't there.

"Chela?" I called, half-whispering so my voice wouldn't carry. I checked her bathroom, but that was empty except for a mound of towels on the floor.

As I passed the wine rack, I knocked on the wall. "Chela? Stay out of sight," I said, hoping she was already hiding, although a sinking part of me was sure that Chela was long gone. I hoped she hadn't somehow dragged even more trouble to my doorstep.

I dialed April's number on my throwaway cell. Her phone rang three times, then four. I gritted my teeth as the pounding at my door turned to thunder. The police would break it down if they had to.

"Hold on!" I called out from the kitchen, crossing toward the foyer.

After forever, April's voicemail picked up. I pressed "*" to bypass her greeting. "Hey, it's me," I said in a hushed tone, five feet from my door. I saw a shadow of someone on my front stoop through the smoky glass. "Cops are at my door at 7:00 A.M. See what you can find out from Lieutenant Nelson. Something's happened."

Knowing that April would hear my message soon made it easier to open the door, but my knees still felt like water.

The morning was overcast, so it was barely light outside. O'Keefe and Arnaz—the same cops who had told me about Serena's death—stood on my front stoop in a defensive stance, both of them with hands firmly on their holsters, guns unhooked. They gazed at me red-eyed: *Do not even THINK about fucking with us.* Two uniformed officers stood on the street, watching with unblinking eyes, also ready to draw.

"Can you get against the wall?" Arnaz said hoarsely. "Please."

"As soon as you tell me what this is about," I said.

Arnaz frowned, gesturing toward the wall. "Please," he said again. His eye twitched from the effort of holding so much politeness in his voice.

The two men frisked me against the front of my house while I stared up at the ceramic numbers of my street address, hoping it was too early for my neighbors to see. I'd been frisked before. I hate uninvited hands.

"Clean," O'Keefe said. A radio chattered urgent directives from a police car, too loud for the hour. The sound seemed to echo up and down my street.

Without a word, O'Keefe took my right arm and pulled it behind my back. I heard the clanking of metal, and my legs quaked. Handcuffs.

NEVER AGAIN, I had told myself. Another god damned broken promise.

"Wait—do you have an arrest warrant?" I said, as cold metal closing against the bone of my wrist told me to expect bad news. O'Keefe pulled down my other arm. A *click,* and my freedom was stolen from me. Others controlled my life now.

"Sorry, man," Arnaz said, nearly under his breath.

Four officers and handcuffs, but no Miranda?

"This is bullshit and you know it," I said as O'Keefe tugged my arm to pull me around, and not gently. Arnaz looked away from me. "Just tell me what's going on."

Nobody answered, nor would they meet my eyes. The silence made me feel like I was being kidnapped. O'Keefe pulled me to the patrol car at a brisk pace, and Arnaz guided my head as I ducked in. I didn't recognize the uniform officers, who were dead quiet. O'Keefe patted the trunk. "Right behind you," I heard him say. "Let's roll."

I grew up around cops. Bowling leagues. Beach parties. Cookouts. To me, they're just guys doing their job like anyone else. But I don't mind admitting it: I was scared. As that police car lurched away from my front curb, I wished I had learned what my father tried to teach me all those years at First AME Church.

I wished I had learned how to pray.

ELEVEN

FOR AN HOUR, I WAS LEFT ALONE in an interrogation room in the Parker Administration Building, my hands chained in front of me to an iron ring beneath the table. The room was hardly the size of a closet, so cold that my back teeth chattered. I would have paid fifty dollars for socks and a sweatshirt.

If you have never been a prisoner, trust me: There are few deeper feelings of personal shame, failure, and despair. I was left alone to experience the crushing feeling as long as possible, in the unforgiving cold.

I tried counting my breaths to calm my mind, but my mind would not be soothed. An actor's life is full of disappointment, so I always prepare for the worst. My imagination was expecting charges for anything from killing Serena to assaulting M.C. Glazer. But despite all my worst-case scenarios, it was still worse than I thought.

At nine-thirty, the door finally opened.

Two uniformed officers walked in; one white, one black. It took me a second to recognize them dressed for patrol: Kojak and his white partner, both of them circling me like I was a ham steak they wanted to carve up for breakfast. I tugged on my wrists against the handcuffs, pure instinct. Those guys looked scarier behind badges than they ever had at Club Magique. My mind suddenly foresaw how this day would end: My corpse would be laid out naked at the morgue after I was locked in a room with two of M.C. Glazer's bodyguards. It all seemed horribly clear.

Lieutenant Nelson came in behind them, followed by two older detectives I didn't recognize, and I exhaled with relief. I studied the grim collection of faces. The room was hushed, a funeral parlor.

"Well?" Nelson said. He might have been talking to me, but I only sat, frozen.

"That's him," Kojak said, hollow-eyed. He looked like he was living the worst day of his life. He also looked like he wanted to kill me bare-handed. Never had that wish been more plain on any man's face, not even M.C. Glazer's.

"Thank you," Nelson said, and gestured his head sharply. *Out.*

Kojak and the white cop slid past me, their eyes never leaving my face. The temperature in the room seemed to climb under their gazes. They were both still glaring, arms crossed, as the door fell closed behind them.

"They're the ones who should be arrested. Try assault," I said.

"We're listening," Nelson said, but his expectant face told me I'd already said something wrong. Keeping quiet hadn't helped me so far, but I pressed my lips shut.

"Why do we keep seeing the name Tennyson Hardwick?" Nelson said. "Is it because you were you an only child? Do you need a lot of attention? Need to move out from under Daddy's shadow? Congratulations. You have our attention."

The detective half-sitting on the tabletop was at least sixty, with a ruddy nose and unruly hair that grew in uneven splotches, like snowdrifts. His limbs were slender, but his stomach tugged vigorously against his shirt buttons. "Do you understand why you've been detained? Are you sick or injured? Do you have any questions or concerns?" His voice was flat as he raced through his procedural obligations. He didn't give me time to answer, and his eyes didn't give a shit anyway.

"Tell me what's going on," I said, ignoring the questions.

Nelson pulled a chair up to the table. He leaned close to me, exactly the way I'd closed in on M.C. Glazer. "We lost one of our officers last night," he said.

My throat sealed itself. I glanced at the older cops, who were listening in studied silence, waiting for my response. The weight of the world was on their minds. *We lost one of our officers.* The phrase left cool footprints across my skin. I could always tell if an officer had been killed by Dad's mood when he got home. There was a tightness brewing just beneath the surface, a hair-trigger, and I knew I better keep out of his way. When police officers died, war had been declared on civilization.

That was the official story, of course, what cops told the papers. Anyone who would kill a cop is an even greater danger to the average citizen . . . They didn't say the other part. The human part. *Anyone who killed another cop might kill me.* A cop's job is constant stress and danger. No one can do it without a certain sense of invincibility, an "I'm the baddest sonofabitch in the valley" attitude. Any cop's violent death punctured that aura, brought home to every policeman, and every criminal, that officers weren't a thin blue line. They weren't Robocops. They were mortal men heir to the same fears and failings as the rest of us. Kill a cop, and you release the fear beneath the bravado. And there is nothing more dangerous than a frightened man with a gun.

"Did you want to file a complaint against officers DeFranco and Lorenzo, Hardwick?" Nelson said. "Was there an incident involving these officers?"

I only heard Nelson's questions five seconds after his mouth moved. Fear and confusion momentarily made me deaf. "Yes," I said. "They work for M.C.—"

"Right. Security for CopKilla Records, against regs. IAG has been investigating Robert Jenkins for six months," Nelson said. "Lorenzo and DeFranco are next in the hot seat. Don't worry."

I didn't know what to say. I was sure a trap was being laid.

"But that must have pissed you off," Nelson went on.

"What?"

"Getting your ass kicked by cops. Dirty cops are trash, right?"

"LAPD should know. You tell me."

Lieutenant Nelson raised an eyebrow. Something lethal slithered across his face. He reached inside his jacket pocket and pulled out a baggie. Inside, I saw my business card. He slapped it on the table. Déjà vu.

"I already told you, I didn't kill Serena. I ran into her at Roscoe's and we—"

"This isn't the card we found on Serena," Nelson said. "This was the card in Detective Jenkins's car."

Even then, my mind fought against the knowledge. I was drowning in confusion. Then, suddenly, it hit me: *Jenk is dead.*

My stomach fisted. I felt myself try to vomit.

"So, let's go over what happened again . . ." Lieutenant Nelson said. "You confronted M.C. Glazer at Club Magique, where you assaulted him in front of witnesses. While you were being subdued, you told Detective Jenkins you were going to kill him."

"That's a lie. I got into it with Glazer—I thought he might have killed Serena—but I never said that. You can't trust anything those guys say."

"Yesterday, you assaulted M.C. Glazer again at a house in Laguna . . ."

Shit. That visit to Laguna Beach might well be my life's crowning asininity. I'd underestimated M.C. Glazer. With Chela's age and the threat of the photos, I hadn't expected Glaze to tell his bodyguards, much less go to the police. Now the photos could work against me—as evidence of the assault. I had fucked up, and badly. If I got arrested for assaulting M.C. Glazer, I would make national news, and he could spend a mountain of money to put me away. Or take my house. And I couldn't say why I had been sent there, or by whom, because that would implicate Mother.

"I need to see my lawyer," I said.

"Of course," Lieutenant Nelson said agreeably, and went on as if I hadn't spoken: "Now, when Detective Jenkins called your cell phone at 5:56 P.M. yesterday, I'm sure the conversation was lively. He said some unkind things to you, and you said some impolite things back. Bad blood, let's call it."

My ears vibrated, and I shook my head to clear them. "You're wrong. He only left a message, and I still have it. I never called back."

"You met up to settle your unfinished business. He drives his unmarked out to a parking garage in Culver City at, say . . . ten o'clock."

"I haven't seen him since that night at the club."

Lieutenant Nelson's lips were a tight line, almost a smile. "Detective Jenkins stepped out of his car. You spoke, and for some reason he turned his back. You pulled out your Nine and shot Detective Jenkins twice in the back of the head. Point-blank. You do own a nine-millimeter Glock, don't you?"

Holy Lord. Jenk had been shot with a Nine? I'd registered a Glock more than a decade ago, and it was still packed in a box in my basement. Nines are popular handguns, but I was looking more and more like a suspect.

My mind was tired of being afraid, so it shifted abruptly, and the fear evaporated. My sanity had gone around the bend and back. I was suddenly more clear-headed than I had been all morning. "I can show you my gun. It hasn't been fired in years."

"I'll know when we get our search warrant. Where were you last night?"

"At home. I went to bed early."

"Were you alone?"

Chela's name almost came to my lips. "No."

"Who can vouch for you?"

"I can't say."

One of the men observing made a chuffing sound. He had a white mustache twirled up at the ends like men used to wear in the 1920s. Nelson pursed his lips. "You may be the stupidest SOB I ever met," Nelson told me.

"There's a cell phone on my kitchen counter," I said calmly. "On that phone is a voicemail message from Robert Jenkins. Listen to it for yourself. We didn't plan to meet. His cell phone records will show you I never called him back. I haven't fired a gun. Give me a GSR." A gunshot residue test could prove there was no gunpowder on my hands, at least. I was glad I wasn't a smoker, which might give a false positive.

Nelson pulled two small paper bags from his pockets. "May I?" he said.

After I nodded, Nelson shook the paper bags open and slid one over each of my hands. That way, he could preserve any evidence on my skin before I was taken for testing at SID. "I'm sure even an academy dropout like you would wash your hands, Hardwick . . . but maybe we'll get lucky. We'd like some DNA, too."

I knew I could refuse a DNA test, but why? If I said no, Nelson would call a judge and force me anyway. Checkmate. But even with a rush, it would be at least a week before he could compare my DNA to whatever he'd found in Serena's bedroom, or any false evidence Lorenzo and DeFranco might have planted on Jenk. By then, I might find the real killers—or at least have a genuine defense lined up.

"Take all the tests you need to," I said. "I can understand how this looks."

"Oh, you can?" Lieutenant Nelson said. "This is how it looks: *The Calling Card Killer.* A killer who's so cocky, he leaves his card behind."

"You can't believe that."

"I believe what evidence tells me." Contempt leaped from Nelson's eyes. "I know you were booked for attempted murder in '99, Tennyson."

I'd wondered how long it would take him to bring *that* up.

"That charge was crap," I said.

"You broke the guy's jaw and elbow. You put his head through a window."

"He assaulted my client."

"You mean he pinched her ass?" Nelson said.

A drunken fan had been harassing my client at the bar, and I'd warned him twice to keep his distance. When he brushed past her barstool and slid his hand beneath her ass for a meaty squeeze, I pushed him away, and he came at me. What followed was brief but messy. Any bodyguard might have done the same thing, especially one who was sharing her bed. Even drunk, a guy with glass joints should have known better than to grope a movie star that way. If my client hadn't backed me to the hilt with her lawyer, I might have done real time over that.

"My charge was reduced to assault," I told Nelson. "And that arrest was expunged from my record. I assume you know that, too."

Nelson shrugged. "I know you were the captain's son."

"I'm done," said the man with the mustache. He gave me one last look askance and let himself out. The second man sighed, sharing a look with Nelson I couldn't see.

"See what the judge says," the man said, patting Nelson's back. "Keep him here."

I didn't like the sound any of it. "Am I under arrest?"

The stranger looked back at me over his shoulder, and his eyes fell away, pained. I almost recognized him then, sorting out his aging face from a collection of childhood memories. The beach, or maybe that picnic at Griffith Park. He knew my father. I was sure of it.

"You're not under arrest, son," the stranger said.

Yet. The word sat at the end of his sentence, invisible and yet impossible to ignore. The interrogation room door clicked softly closed behind him.

An hour after I was brought back to interrogation from the SID lab, no one had peeked in yet to see if I was enjoying my stay.

During my solitude, I made a list of the ways these cops had pissed all over procedure. Obviously they didn't have enough evidence for an arrest warrant. They wouldn't have had enough to bring me in, period, if not for the lies of the cops on M.C. Glazer's payroll. My house—*Alice's house*—was about to be searched without anything remotely like probable cause, and all because a judge might be feeling fevered after a police officer's murder. Jenk died at 10:00 P.M., and they rushed together their flimsy case against me by dawn. Jenk had died on the clock, and justice for cops works fast. I catalogued the names and faces I was going to crucify once I was a free citizen again.

Nelson finally came back, alone. He had taken off his jacket and loosened his shirt and tie as if he was ending his day, but it was only 11:00 A.M. Instead of looking at me, his eyes were on the floor.

"It doesn't take long, does it, Tennyson?" Nelson said. His voice was thoughtful and hushed, like a friend's.

"What?"

"Tearing down a legacy."

I didn't want that to hurt, but it did. Bad. Amazingly, I had kept Dad out of my mind most of the morning, except to take comfort in how outraged he would be on my behalf when he heard about it one day, once the trouble passed.

"Preach was my commander for twelve years," Nelson said. "My father is a retired Air Force colonel, and he and Richard A. Hardwick stand as the most courageous, conscientious, and righteous men I have ever known. Maybe you don't know what he went through. Maybe he never told you the whole story about how hard it is to be black at LAPD." *Oh, here we go,* I thought. *The brother-to-brother routine.*

"Preach helped open people's minds. He created opportunities for me, and the people behind me, that would not have existed if he hadn't worked twice as hard as the white boys—and he did that every day."

"You don't have to tell me how hard my father worked."

Dad was almost never at home. All I knew about his life away from me was what I overheard when he had a couple of beers and swapped stories with his cop friends. He never wanted to talk to me about anything except my bad grades.

"You must *not* know," Nelson said, "because you're here to shit on his name."

"I haven't seen you at the nursing home, friend," I said. I hoped my voice wasn't shaking. "I know things about my father you don't want to hear."

Nelson grimaced, but he pressed on. His voice relaxed. "Let me tell you why they sent me the Afrodite case: I'm black. She's a rapper. And the name *Hardwick* came up. Put those three things together, and that case is a shitstorm. Nobody else wanted to touch it, so I'm the go-to guy. And my luck doesn't stop there. Now Robert Jenkins, a badge under investigation for his association with CopKilla Records, is meat . . . and here we go again. More cops with gang associations. More department scandals. So these cases will get publicity. A lot of it. The only thing we can do to minimize the damage—and I mean the *only* thing—is make a swift arrest. Be on our game."

"Then I must be very convenient."

"Convenient? Hell, you're Preach Hardwick's son. Nobody who knew Preach wants to touch a hair on your chinny-chin-chin. Those two guys who were in here would rather chop off their arms than have anything to do with sending Preach Hardwick's son to prison. We're all chewing Alka-Seltzer today."

To prove it, Nelson pulled a half-empty roll of antacid out of his pocket. They weren't Alka-Seltzer—they were the Albertsons store brand—but he made his point. He pulled one out and popped the white tablet into his mouth, crushing it with his molars.

"See, I know what's coming. I've seen it before. A community that's never had a break finally finds somebody who gives a damn. He keeps his promises. He locks up the drug dealers and gangbangers, but at the same time he's helping to keep your son and grandsons from going to jail because he's listening, too. He's going to meetings. He's helping get parks built. He's at the schools. They love him for it. They name recreation centers after him. Then, something happens: His troubles at home come out in the newspaper. His son goes to jail. Yeah, it's embarrassing, but it's deeper than that: It's like your *own* son going to jail. It makes you feel hopeless. What's the point? The battles that matter have been lost. *No one* escapes."

Nelson's eyes shimmered as he gazed at me. I was startled to realize he was near tears. He must have learned well from my father, because he sounded just like him.

"That is what is at stake here. Your father's name," he said. His eyes cleared suddenly when he blinked. "But two people are dead—one of them a cop—and you're connected to both. So I'm going to take this bullet for my department. It's what Preach trained me to do, and it's my job. Is it personal? Yes, it is. *You offend me.*"

"I haven't killed anyone," I said with a tremor. "I think you know that."

Nelson sighed gently. He hushed his voice like a grandfather about to tell a reassuring bedtime story. "I need you to tell me the truth. The *whole* truth. As the great man said, 'The ultimate measure of a man is not where he stands in moments of comfort and convenience, but where he stands in times of challenge and controversy.' This is your moment, Hardwick. I'm your last chance."

I chuckled. Evoking Dr. Martin Luther King, Jr., was excessive. "We're supposed to be friends now, reverend?"

"Today, I'm your best friend, your twin brother, and the guy who paid for your first hand job. I'm all you've got, Hardwick. Start talking. Please don't make me do this the hard way."

The plea sounded genuine, and I knew a trip downtown was the least of what Nelson could do to me. I was at the center of two high-profile homicide investigations, and he needed to make something happen fast. If Nelson arrested me today, my name could be on CNN by nightfall. Nelson was right—it was time.

"I was with Serena at her house the day she died," I said.

I heard my imaginary lawyer screaming, but Nelson's face didn't change. Calmly, he pulled a microcassette recorder from his inside jacket pocket. The little red light glared up at me. "Go on."

"I ran into her at Roscoe's at eleven, like I told you. I didn't know she would be there. I just stopped by because I didn't see a line. She invited me back to her house. Years ago, I did some bodyguarding for her . . . and sometimes we went to bed."

"You mean you accepted pay for sex. You were a male prostitute."

It wasn't a question. I hadn't been charged with solicitation in '99, but rumors abounded in the tabloids, probably straight from the mouth of a cop. I'd tried to fool myself into thinking that Dad never heard the details of my previous work, but maybe everyone at Hollywood division knew. Or had Devon Biggs told Nelson?

"I prefer the term 'escort,' but yes, I was. Serena was a client," I said. The admission was difficult to force out of my mouth—it sounded like a sordid story about someone else—but I needed Nelson to know I was willing to tell the truth. "That's all I'll say about that. I've been out of that work for years, and I hadn't seen Serena since *Keepin' it Real* in 2002."

"Who cut off your business arrangement?"

"It was mutual. I quit the business, and she started a production company. She was a lot more cautious after that. We toasted our new lives, and I lost contact with my former clients, including her."

"Did you have sex with Serena Monday?"

Ooh, you're still freaky, T. Suddenly, I could smell Serena's intimate dampness inside the room's chilled air. I knew all of her smells. My stomach twisted, and I wanted to double over. "Yes. In her bedroom."

"The condom from her bedroom trash can at our lab?" Nelson said.

"That was mine."

"When did you see her last?"

"I left about two. I took a cab. She invited me to come back on Friday."

"She called Sunshine Cab at one-fifty-five. Your cab was there at two-fifteen," Nelson said.

"Then you know better than I do. That was the last time I saw her."

Nelson's face was still unreadable as he wrote notes for himself on a tiny pad. I noticed that his rhetoric and tough-ass act were gone. Now that I was talking, he'd fallen out of character. He only wanted to ask the right questions. I didn't like Nelson, but I couldn't help admiring him. Nelson was my age, in his late thirties, but he had veered right, and I had veered wrong. Every day my father saw Lieutenant Nelson at work, he'd been reminded of who I wasn't.

"Did you have an argument?" Nelson said.

"No. We were fine. She told Devon Biggs to call me about a job, and she invited me to come back on Friday. You can confirm that first part with Biggs."

Nelson nodded in a way that made me think Biggs had been telling the truth when he claimed he played Serena's message for the police. "Did she mention any trouble?"

I hadn't spoken to anyone about that day, and now I was mired in it. Serena's laugh echoed inside my ears, and fresh sadness lanced me. "She said something that stuck out: 'Someone's always trying to pull you down.' I don't know what she meant, but I try not to jump into people's business. People at Serena's level don't trust easily—everybody wants something from you—so I didn't press her. I wish I had."

"Did she have a boyfriend?"

"I don't know. She said she didn't have time for relationships. She never did."

"Did you notice anything unusual at all?"

"No," I said. "I was just glad to see her."

"What happened at Club Magique?" Nelson didn't miss a beat.

"M.C. Glazer assaulted me, aided by your three police officers: Jenkins, DeFranco, and Lorenzo. I fought back. Your officers beat me nearly unconscious, and I was rescued by bouncers. I didn't make any threats against anyone. I didn't say I wanted to kill Detective Jenkins. I could barely remember my own name. Your men are lying. They're trying to deflect attention away from their association with M.C. Glazer."

"Did you stalk M.C. Glazer at his beach house?"

Telling the unfiltered truth had been such a relief, my stomach jabbed me when I ran out of things I could say. My visit to M.C. Glazer involved several felonies, but if Mother got dragged in, the ripple effect would hurt too many people I cared about. Mother had paid my rent for years, and she would die in prison if she was arrested.

"I went to M.C. Glazer's beach house to talk to him without his body-guards. I subdued him, asked him questions, and left."

"Why would you do that?" He looked genuinely confounded.

"I thought he killed Serena."

"Based on what?"

"His own words, at Club Magique. Going to his house was a mistake. Is he pressing charges?" I had given up hope of going back home today, but if I was going to spend the night in jail, I wanted to hear someone say it.

"I'll ask the questions," Nelson said. "What did Detective Jenkins say to you after your visit to M.C. Glazer?"

"Nothing. He left a message on my phone, but we never spoke."

"How did he have your number?"

"I gave out cards at Club Magique. Maybe Jenkins was feeling me out. He knew Serena in high school—and Shareef, too. Devon Biggs thought Jenkins might have helped M.C. Glazer kill Serena and Shareef. He said Jenkins, Sha-reef, and Serena had a falling out. He said Jenkins was helping Glazer move guns and drugs."

A spark flared in Nelson's eye, then vanished. "Jenkins was a problem, yes. Why did you kill him? Was it self-defense?"

"I didn't kill him. Give me a polygraph."

Nelson clicked off his tape recorder. "You're an actor. I don't give a damn about polys," he said. He dug his key chain from his pocket and flipped through several keys, choosing a tiny one that fit into my handcuffs. The metal clicked free. "Your story stinks, Hardwick. Work on a better one, for your own good. Whatever you're not saying is missing loud and clear. Get up."

"What now?" I rubbed my wrists. When I stood up, my legs tingled.

"The judge signed the warrant," he said. "You're having company."

There was no hiding the police presence from my neighbors now.

By the time I got home, there were four unmarked police sedans parked on my street, and enough men wearing LAPD windbreakers in my driveway for a Police Benevolent Association meeting. One of the cops had a hand-held video camera.

I saw Mrs. Katz from the Spanish-style house across the road peering over as she watered her white roses. Once Mr. Katz started talking, the whole street would know by nightfall, but at least I wasn't still in handcuffs. I waved at her from the passenger side of Nelson's car. She waved back, tentatively.

"Were you robbed?" she called to me when I climbed out.

I shook my head, smiled, and gave her a politician's wave that said *Tell you later.*

My smile died as soon I began wading through a dozen cops to get to my door, snorkeling inside a school of sharks. They milled closer to me than they needed to, and stepped back only grudgingly to make way. Their eyes hammered at me. I was glad Nelson was at my flank.

Arnaz and O'Keefe were camped on the front stoop with white bags stenciled with red-lipped clown smiles. They must have been watching the house to make sure no one took anything out while I was detained. My heart raced. Where was Chela?

"Hey, man, my goddaughter was supposed to visit me this morning," I said to Arnaz. "Did she come by looking for me? About fifteen?"

Arnaz shrugged, chewing his red coffee stirrer with deliberation. To him, I was invisible, so he wasn't going to chit-chat. I sighed. At least my explanation was planted if we found Chela. But what if we didn't?

I opened the door and led the unwelcome expedition inside my house.

Even when police have a search warrant, the law says they can't just tear your place up and see what they find. That's called a general search, and it's illegal. Nelson had given me the warrant to read when he drove me back in his car, and it was very specific: They could only look for my Glock as a possible murder weapon, my clothes, my answering machine, my cell phone, and my computer, to determine if there had been email between me and Jenk. They would no doubt also search my car and trash cans. The warrant was tied to the Robert Jenkins case, but of course Nelson wouldn't be unhappy to find clues about Serena either. By law, they could search anywhere large enough to conceal a gun. Boxes. Closets. Drawers.

I thought the box where I'd packed the gun was in the basement, but suddenly I wasn't sure. Had I brought it up to the pantry instead? It was possible.

Shit. It was going to be a long day.

Inside, my house was pristine. No one had touched it. The TV was still on.

"My gun is in a box in the basement," I told Nelson. "You should start there."

Nelson didn't look at me. "We'll get to the basement," he said.

Rage surged through me, but I locked it down. I wasn't going to inflame the cops by mouthing off at their CO. I sat on my living room sofa with my hands on my kneecaps, in plain view, and forced my eyes to stare at the parade of barely dressed video dancers and instant pop stars still romping on my television set. While I sat and tried not to get pissed, Nelson sent detectives to every corner of my house: my guest room. Screening room. Office. Bedroom.

I tried not to look as a wiry, blond-haired detective crossed my living room toward the guest room, but I felt a flush of adrenaline as he went inside. I might have held my breath for thirty seconds while I waited to see if he would come out with Chela. He didn't. I closed my eyes, not sure whether to be relieved or worried. Could she have made it to the pantry in time when the police came knocking? It was possible.

Even while one part of me hoped she was in there, another hoped she wasn't. If my gun wasn't in my basement, I might have to lead them to the pantry myself. My Glock wouldn't prove I hadn't killed Jenk, but it would rule out the gun registered to me as the murder weapon. I had to help them find that gun, no matter what the other consequences.

You can make it through this. Just keep your cool.

I kept my cool for three minutes.

Then, I heard a scraping noise behind me. One of the detectives was yanking Alice's framed one-sheet poster from *A Raisin in the Sun* from my foyer wall. I turned around in time to see the cop lose his grip, and the large frame crashed to the tiled floor. Cracked glass sent spiderwebs across Sidney Poitier's face.

I still remember the first time I saw that movie on television when I was ten and up late because my father was working. Sidney's power transformed our little television set to something large and grand. Something important. Right then and there, I decided I wanted to be an actor. Sidney did that.

"Hey," I said. I was on my feet, not even thinking. That was all I had time to say. I felt one arm around my neck, and another around my waist. I was yanked from my feet, and my shoulder fell hard against the floor. Even with the inch-high living room piled carpet, I felt an electric sizzle of pain shoot from my shoulder to my neck. One of the cops, who was fifty pounds overweight, pressed his knee against my jaw while the other twisted my arm around my back as if he was warming up to break it.

Nelson had been in the kitchen, and he ran to see what the commotion was. Nelson loomed above me like Atlas.

"What?" Nelson said. I recognized my cell phone in his gloved hand.

"He made a move," said the detective on my face. He sounded sheepish. "*Let . . . him . . . up.*"

The officers backed away, and I brought myself to my feet with as much dignity as I could. Just that fast, I ached all over. I worried with my jaw, trying to rub it back into alignment. *Fat bastard.*

"That's a collectible, asshole," I said to the cop with the frame.

"Watch your mouth," Nelson said. His face was suddenly the only thing in my vision. His breathing was fast and shallow, and his pores reeked of the coffee he'd been drinking while he drove. To me, he smelled like fractured nerves.

I calmed my voice, deferring to Nelson by staring at his shining black shoes. "The warrant doesn't authorize you to—"

"I'm directing this search, so the warrant authorizes me to do whatever the hell I say it does," Nelson said. "You may have a hidden safe, so we're clearing the walls. If you can't handle it, go outside and get some air."

At first I thought it was a suggestion, but then I realized he was ordering me out. I gazed back at the cops' faces: The big one was nearly leering at me, breathing hard, and I suspected Jenk was a friend of his. The other two cops looked jumpy, especially the one with the frame. The lone, officious-looking female cop stuck her head in from the screening room to see what was going on, her face angled upward with concern.

Nelson was right. I needed to be outside.

I straightened my T-shirt, tucking it into my sweatpants. "Detective Jenkins's message is on that phone," I said to Nelson as I passed him. "Don't erase it."

"I know how to use a cell phone. Get the hell out of here."

When I opened my front door, I ran straight into Arnaz and O'Keefe. Any fantasies I might have had about running off were quelled before they were fully born. Through the door, I heard Nelson rebuke the detective inside the house: "Show some respect. The Poitier poster's almost fifty years old."

If not for O'Keefe and Arnaz watching me, I might have smiled.

I felt their eyes tracking me, so I moved slowly, cautiously, and sat on the polished stone steps to my front stoop. I'm not into fast food, but the fading scents from the McDonald's bags beside me made my stomach growl. It was lunchtime, and I'd never had breakfast. My detention hadn't included a meal plan.

"There's an extra double cheese in there," Arnaz said, and O'Keefe shot him a glare. Arnaz shrugged. "What? It's a sin to waste food."

"Yeah, whatever, go ahead and eat it, Hardwick," O'Keefe said. "The way I hear, you may never eat McDonald's again."

"Promise?" I said, but I grabbed the bag anyway. The meat was still warm, the bun not yet stiff, and McDonald's had never tasted so good.

A black-and-white cruiser appeared from around the bend on curving Gleason Street, and it slowed as it neared the house. I couldn't see who was inside as it passed, but it drove on without stopping. Onlookers, maybe. Or, maybe my neighborhood was under surveillance. Were they looking for Chela?

I was almost ready to confess to things I hadn't done just to end this day.

"You should get to Preach before somebody else does," Arnaz said quietly.

My neck didn't have the strength to turn around and look at him. "Leave Dad to me." I was still hoping for a grand reprieve—even an apology—before I would have to tell my father about it. I wanted him to hear it in past tense, not present tense. But I was only fooling myself. I was in denial, and I knew it.

Arnaz and O'Keefe resumed their earlier conversation, debating whose breasts were real and whose were fake on the Hollywood A-list. I could have enlightened them, if I'd been in the mood.

The police cruiser reappeared, and this time it coasted to a halt.

I straightened up so I could see the car better. Kojak was sitting in the driver's seat with his elbow propped in the open window, staring at me from behind sunglasses. His partner was the passenger. My heartbeat sped up again.

"Easy," O'Keefe said. "They're not going near the chain of evidence."

My lawyer would love it if they did, I thought. "They're dirty. I'm sorry about the detective who died, but he was dirty, too. This whole thing is part of a cover-up."

"Rumor and innuendo," Arnaz said, noncommittal. "Not for us to decide."

I stood up suddenly. "I want to talk to them. Alone."

"Hell, no," O'Keefe said. "Sit down and keep your mouth shut."

"They're telling lies about me, and I want to know why."

"Go knock yourself out, Hardwick," Arnaz said. O'Keefe gave him another look, and Arnaz went on: "What do we care? Just go slow. No sudden movements. And don't try to take off, because Lorenzo's king of the OIS. Don't give him an excuse."

OIS. Officer-involved shooting. I felt a chill ripple up my spinal column.

I raised my hands high, keeping them in plain view. "Five minutes," I said, and I walked toward the police car that was stalking me. The men inside seemed to smile as they watched me approach—but the smiles were tight, painful masks.

"Where you going, brother?" Kojak said. "Need a ride?" I hadn't noticed it before, but he had a slight accent almost hidden in his speech. A black Latino, maybe. Lorenzo was probably the cop I called Kojak—I thought I remembered M.C. Glazer calling him *Renzo*—and his partner was DeFranco. Acne scars on Lorenzo's face were so pronounced in the sunlight that they looked like freckles. DeFranco nodded to music in his head, chewing gum with great deliberation.

"I just came to talk," I said. I walked as close to the car as I dared, just beyond the trajectory of Kojak's door if he suddenly flung it open. "I didn't kill your friend. You probably know that, or you wouldn't have lied to jack up a case against me."

Their grins withered.

"You better watch who you call a liar," Kojak said. He took off his shades so I could see his eyes. *King of the OIS.* His dark eyes chilled me. They seemed to float like separate entities above the bridge of his nose, manic and pained.

"I didn't do it, man," I said. "I only met him that one time."

"You know what you sound like?" Kojak said. "You're whining like my three-year-old kid. '*It wadn't me, it wadn't me.*' But your business card says different, right there in Jenk's car. It was the first thing we saw when they called us to the scene."

"Why would I be stupid enough to leave my card there if I killed him?"

DeFranco spat a wad of chewing gum out of his window. "We meet a lot of stupid people," he said. "How about that guy who broke into Glaze's house?"

"*That* guy was stupid," Kojak said.

"I didn't kill your friend," I said again, struggling to hold my voice steady. "If Glaze wants to have me arrested for what happened at the beach house, fine. But I'll have to explain why I was there."

"Glaze doesn't believe in pressing charges," Kojak said dismissively. He winked. "By the way . . . how's Chela?"

My neighbors' houses blended into one as the street seemed to spin. Suddenly two facts clicked together in my mind that hadn't felt linked before: M.C. Glazer's bodyguards knew where I lived, and I hadn't seen Chela since nine o'clock last night. I felt my limbs turning leaden as new, horrible possibilities wormed into my mind. M.C. Glazer's life would get simpler if Chela disappeared.

They might have her. I forgot my morning at the police station as a new depth of helplessness held me rooted in place. I had never been responsible for a child's life. The enormity of it stunned me.

"She's just a kid," I said. "She didn't want to leave with me. If you have her, don't hurt her. Please. Seriously, she's fifteen years old, for God's sake."

Time created new rules, and the moment drew itself out. For an impossibly long interval, neither of them spoke. I couldn't see anything in their faces to tell me if the girl I had brought to my house last night was dead or alive.

Kojak's eyes narrowed, studying me. "You're good, but keep practicing," he said. "You'll be doing more of that."

"More of what, man?"

"Begging," Kojak said. His voice cracked, before it was propped up again by cold, controlled anger. "You killed our brother—that's what he was to us. I don't know how it happened, because Jenk was too sharp to go down for a *maricón* like you. But everybody fucks up sometimes. So I want to hear you begging like that when I see you again. But really play it up next time. Screaming, maybe."

"We'll help with that part," DeFranco said.

Kojak gunned the car's engine. He leaned closer, lowering his voice. "If they arrest you, we'll still get you," he said. "If they *don't* arrest you . . ." He shrugged and smiled a stomach-churning smile.

Those two men *believed* I had killed Jenk, I realized. Their accusations weren't a bluff by dirty cops trying to hide their illegal activities from LAPD brass, shielding a real suspect who might reveal criminal connections. I was under a death sentence—and not the slow, lingering sentence meted out through the justice system, with rules and warrants. The quick kind. The real kind.

I was standing within a few feet of men who had just promised to kill me. This was my chance to choose the words that might save my life, and maybe Chela's too. And I couldn't think of anything to say.

Their car squealed and was gone.

Mrs. Katz was still standing in her yard with her hose. I think she might have called out to me, but I barely heard. That time, I couldn't fake a smile.

✦ ✦ ✦

My Glock, as I'd guessed, was in its black plastic case in a box in the basement. I watched the police file out of my house as they took the automatic, my computer, a pile of clothes, my cell phones, and a few other items I wasn't worried about.

No Chela. No stolen Smith & Wesson. No stolen goods.

Police car doors slammed and engines revved along the street, a chorus.

Nelson dangled my passport out of his driver's-side window. "We'll hold on to this," he said. "Work on your story. Our people will call your people. That Hollywood enough for you?"

I stood in my yard and watched Nelson's car drive away, out of sight. I had lost seven hours of my life, but I was finally at home alone. And I was still a free man.

I could barely get my legs to work right as I ran into my house. I stumbled into my kitchen barstool. The papers and items strewn around the kitchen floor ordinarily would have upset me, but I barely noticed. My heart was shaking in my chest.

"Chela?" I called.

The wine rack was empty. All of the bottles had been lined up neatly on the floor. Had they found the pantry? Had Lorenzo and DeFranco gotten to Chela somehow?

Oh, God. Oh, God. Oh, God.

I grabbed the door by its groove and tugged. It stuck. The door was locked. "Chela!" I said, tapping on the wall. "It's me. Everybody's gone."

I pressed my ear to the wall, but I didn't hear anything. Then, the chair inside whined against the floor. I heard fumbling with the locks. The door pushed open.

Chela stood there wearing an oversized red CopKilla T-shirt that reached her knees, her hair tied in a ponytail. She'd made a pallet of fur coats on the floor, and on the table she'd opened a box of Saltines and a jar of peanut butter. The room smelled sour. "Bathroom," she said, and ran past me into the hall. I heard the door slam and stood there open-mouthed with relief as silence was followed by the sound of running water.

She returned looking about five pounds lighter, yawning. "I'm *thirsty*," she said. "And you need a CD player or something in here. Bad."

I lunged to hug her, but Chela tensed up, looking startled, so I pulled back and only squeezed her forearms tightly, at arm's length. "I was worried."

"Uhm . . . I can see that," Chela said, wary.

I could only look back nostalgically at yesterday, when I was considered a suspect only in Serena's death. Things had only gotten worse. Much worse. But at least one thing was intact, untouched. Chela. I always wondered why Alice built her panic room so close to the kitchen when most people would want it near their bedroom, but now I was glad. It had worked.

Chela didn't speak for a while, shifting her weight from leg to leg. "Are you in trouble because of me?" she said.

I shrugged. "You and a couple other things." There was a chance that the police had wired my house, I realized. I would be a fool to think otherwise. But nothing I said would prove that I had killed people I hadn't. *Let them listen.*

"Did I hear somebody say Jenk got killed last night?" Chela said.

I nodded.

She seemed interested, but not upset. "And they think you did it?"

"Not for long," I said. "There's no evidence."

"But I *know* you didn't. I watched TV all night, so I would have seen you leave."

"That's what I figured," I said.

"Then why didn't you tell them about me to save your ass?" Chela said.

"Because I haven't decided the best thing for you yet. I'm still thinking about it."

Chela considered that, but didn't object. She sighed, her voice quiet. "I thought for sure they'd find my ass. When they were moving those bottles . . ." For the first time, Chela allowed me to see some of the stress of her day on her drawn, tired face. All playfulness had vanished.

I toured my house, ignoring the misplaced or damaged items, and locked the front door, my glass sliding door, and the door to my garage. Then, I armed the alarm and stuck M.C. Glazer's gun in the band of my sweatpants. Under the circumstances, my house might be the last place Lorenzo and DeFranco would expect me to stay.

Chela was still in the kitchen when I got back, draining tap water from an upturned glass. Water dribbled down her chin. The water was running at a full gush in the sink, so I turned it off, hearing my father's lecture on wastefulness in my head.

I decided to defrost some steaks. Chela hadn't had a hot meal all day, and I would think better with something other than grease in my stomach. While the steaks were thawing in the microwave, Chela and I stacked the wine bottles again, handling them with care. Then, she sat on the barstool and watched me as I turned on my broiler. I didn't have time to marinate the steaks in Italian dressing like I usually would, but I coated them with steak rub. When they were ready, I would melt feta cheese on top for more flavor. Next, a couple of baked potatoes and a salad with Romaine lettuce, dried cranberries, cherry tomatoes, and sunflower seeds.

Chela's legs swung from the barstool. She wanted to be near me. I wondered if she had ever met anyone willing to put himself on the line for her.

"I'm from Minnesota," Chela said. "Do you think that's weird?"

"Why?"

"How many people have you met from Minnesota?"

I shrugged. "Not too many."

"That's why it's weird. Prince lives there, too, even though it's colder than frozen shit. I lived in Minneapolis with my grandmother—Nana Bessie was from Georgia a long time ago—but she died when I was eleven. My name is Chela Patrice Bryant. Patrice was my mother's name, but I never knew her."

"I never knew my mother either."

Chela went quiet, watching me work, her elbows propped on the counter. She had just repaid me with everything she had to offer—a piece of her life—and the house smelled like Sunday dinner. No wonder we were both smiling by the time the food was done.

TWELVE

ONCE I HAD A FULL STOMACH and Chela had reclaimed her spot in front of the television set, I called April from the kitchen telephone while I washed dishes. The heavy black 1940s-style phone had a rotary dial, and I don't think I'd ever lifted it from its cradle. Another one of Alice's oddities I hadn't changed.

April's relief washed over me in her breath against my ear. "What happened to you? I've been trying Lieutenant Nelson, but he hasn't called me back."

"He was busy searching my house."

I told her the whole story—well, most of it. I left out Mother, since that's not a chapter I like to share. I told April that I had heard about the underage prostitute at M.C. Glazer's house from "a source."

"They think you killed a police officer now? That's insane," April said.

"It's been that kind of week."

"I've been leaving messages on your cell phone all day," she said.

"Then you're officially a part of evidence."

"So much for my new police source," April said, sighing. "Tyra called for you. She was trying your cell, and she gave up and called me. She wants a call back."

Hope stirred, however cautiously. With the holes in Tyra's alibi and her proximity to Serena's body, Tyra gave me a queasy feeling. "About Serena?"

"She wouldn't tell me anything. But I took her number."

I grabbed a pen out of my kitchen drawer. "I'm ready."

"Can I give it to you in person? I have something else I want to show you."

Always an angle, I thought. April was a master at trading information to her best advantage. I smiled. "Tomorrow. I still owe you lunch."

"No, it can't wait. Tonight. It's important for you to see it."

I didn't bother asking her what it was, because she wouldn't give up her leverage. I peeked over at my living room, where Chela was sprawled on my floor. If not for Chela, I would have gone to see April in a heartbeat. "I'm in for the night," I said. "I feel safer looking after Chela here."

"You really think those cops will try to kill you?" She sounded intrigued.

"I believe in taking people at their word."

"Then I'll come to you, just for a few minutes. Give me your address."

I was sure of it now: April was a thrill-seeker. She'd grown up comfortably middle class in a small college town, and she craved an edgy lifestyle. She was a reporter, and but for family pressure would probably have been a cop or a soldier. Silly girl. I needed to send her on her way before she got hurt.

"You should be more careful about hanging out with double murder suspects," I said. "For your sake, I'm glad I'm not who they think I am."

"Maybe you are," she said. "Or, maybe you'll figure out who killed Afrodite while they waste time investigating you. You'll be happy to know—*Dad*—that I always tell my roommate where I'm going at night. She knows who to call if I disappear."

I felt a prick I didn't recognize. "Roommate?"

"A girl." April's voice was smiling.

My next words shocked me. "I'm at 5450 Gleason. Hollywood Hills."

Two hours later, at nine-thirty, April knocked at my door.

"You're crazy," I said. I hadn't really expected her to come. At least not consciously. To busy my mind, I'd spent the hours working out three chess puzzles, and every one of them involved the black queen. Go figure.

"I'm glad to see you, too," April said with a sarcastic grin.

I wondered why I couldn't look away from her eyes, and then I realized I had never seen her wearing mascara. Her sienna irises jumped out at me, large and bright. She had also taken care in choosing her clothes, wearing tight-fitting jeans and a lacy peach camisole that glowed just right on her gingerbread skin. Her chest size was modest enough to get away with wearing no bra, and between her freed breasts lay a necklace of large brown Hawaiian kukui nut shells, which shone beneath my porch light. She laughed as I gently pulled her into the house, as if she couldn't believe her own nerve.

April hadn't come to my house just to talk about Serena.

I gazed up and down my street for unfamiliar cars, but I didn't see any. Still, there are no streetlamps on Gleason, so it was dark except for bubbles of light from front porches and spotlights showcasing spring gardens. I locked the door behind April.

April looked like a hallucination standing beside Alice's wood-carved Ghanaian umbrella stand. Some kind of fragrant oil she was wearing made my house smell like gardenias. *Nice.* I noticed the cute bulb of her nose, her lips brushed with gloss.

"Where's the girl?" April whispered, breaking my silent appraisal.

"In the living room. She fell asleep." I gestured for her to follow me.

On a whim, I grabbed the bottle of Gaja and a corkscrew, and I handed April two wine glasses. It was a three-hundred-dollar bottle of Alice's I'd been saving, but if I didn't drink it now, I might not get another chance. I led April to the living room, where Chela was asleep on the sofa with her headphones on. She'd pulled one of my oversized terrycloth bathrobes up to her chin as a blanket, her hair still tied in a ponytail. Without her height to feed the illusion, she was just a birdlike young girl asleep on my sofa.

April covered her mouth. Her eyes flared with horror.

I held my finger up to my mouth and motioned again. We went past the stairs, toward the southeast corner of the house. My screening room. It was one of the few rooms that had been left virtually untouched during the police search.

Alice had entertained often, mostly viewing parties. She delighted in getting copies of films for private viewing before they were available in video stores—Oscar screening copies, often, since she was a member of the Academy—and she invited her actor, artist, dancer, and writer friends to her house to eat popcorn from the traditional popping cart that still stood in the corner. They watched the film du jour on her impressive screen from two rows of four movie-theater-style seats—bright crimson, each with its own cup holder. The room's walls are lined with autographed eight-by-ten smiling head shots of Alice's friends. Almost anyone you can think of is on that wall.

April admired the room only halfheartedly. Her forehead was creased with worry after seeing Chela. "You have to call child welfare, Tennyson."

"She said she'll run away."

"You can't control that. But you should give her a chance to find a family. What are you going to do? Raise her yourself?"

My face grew hot. I'm not used to answering to anyone, and the question annoyed me. I was sorry I'd told April so much. "Of course not."

April took a deep breath, realizing she sounded harsh. She pursed her lips. "Anyway . . ." she said, softening. "You've really invited a lot of chaos into your life."

"Yeah." I popped the cork and let the wine breathe. "I'm not thrilled with some of the decisions I've made these past few days. I just . . ." I sighed. Grief was closer to the surface than I'd thought. "Serena is dead. No one can change that. But they have to get caught. There has to be a . . . reckoning."

"Yes," April said matter-of-factly. "But maybe less breaking and entering?"

I laughed ruefully. "I'll keep that in mind."

"Can I get your word on that?" She offered her hand.

I smiled and shook her hand, and I didn't let go. I held on for a while. I poured two glasses of wine with my free hand, my left, and didn't spill a drop. "How much do you know about wine?" I said.

She smiled, her head inching closer. "Red with beef, white with chicken?"

"This is Italian, a legendary vintage," I said. "Flowers and berries." I raised the glass to the soft berth of her pink bottom lip so she could sip it and watched her face as she closed her eyes. Her smile relaxed. I hadn't had Gaja with anyone except Alice, who taught me everything I know about wine. I felt her ghost watching us.

"Mint?" April said.

"A little aftertaste, yes. Very good. I'm surprised you noticed."

She opened her eyes to gaze at me. "It's amazing," she said.

April swam in my eyes for a while, but she pulled her hand away just when I was trying to decide whether to kiss her, contemplating the strength and direction of the currents a kiss might sweep me into. A kiss is never just a kiss, no matter the lyrics say in the song Dooley Wilson sang in Serena's favorite old movie.

"I . . . wanted to show you something, but it might be painful for you," April said, reaching into her bag. She pulled out a DVD. "A friend of mine works at the studio . . ."

"What is it?" I took a healthy swallow of wine. Alice always scolded me for drinking wine like I was taking whiskey shots, but I was thirsty for a warm buzz.

"Excerpts. Dailies from Afrodite's last movie, the one she was shooting before she walked off and got sued. I'm writing about it in my follow-up story."

I sat up straight. "The movie with Stan Greene?"

"Exactly. He's supposed to have Mafia ties, by the way."

"I heard that rumor," I said. "Have you called him?"

"A dozen times. I don't think his office will call me back."

We traded thoughts so quickly that we might have been sharing one mind. It was a startling feeling, our unexpected partnership.

"Can you play a DVD in here?" she said.

I gave her a look. *Negro, please.*

The screen is 114 inches tall and nearly 200 inches across, so when I turned off the lights and hit *Play*, we were transported into a neighborhood movie theater. April and I sat beside each other in the front row, although I didn't take her hand this time. We sipped our Gaja and waited for Serena's face.

At first, all we saw was jumbled film splices without coherence. No Serena. "What was this called?" I asked April.

"*Uptown Moves.* Like an urban remake of *Pretty Woman.*"

I rolled my eyes. That was predictable.

An upscale hotel room set appeared. *Pretty Woman*, all right. Nicolas Cage, wearing business attire, opened a bathroom door and found Serena up to her chin in bubbles, singing while she luxuriated in the bathtub. The sound was uneven because it hadn't been mixed yet, but Serena's voice undulated with real power even when she was hardly trying. Why had she been a rapper and not a singer? Her voice was lovely.

"*So . . . now I know one of your secrets,*" he says. "*You sing like an angel.*"

Cage said what I was thinking, as if I was talking to Serena through his mouth.

She shrieks and slips down in the tub, her face disappearing beneath the bubbles. When she sits upright again, bubbles coat her face and hair. "Oh, God— don't listen to me. I'm so embarrassed. You said your meeting was until five . . ."

"*I thought you'd be out by the pool drinking mojitos with little umbrellas.*" *Cage sits at the rim of the tub in his dress slacks. He picks up a dripping sponge and squeezes it above her head. Bubbles run away with the stream, revealing more of her face.*

She smiles, but it's a hard-won smile, sour in the middle. She covers her chest beneath the mound of bubbles. "It's too hot outside for anything except a little self-reflection. Sometimes that gives me sunburn."

Cage stiffens, slowly lowers the sponge. Awkward silence.

"*I'm sorry,*" *she says.* "*I wasn't supposed to say . . .*"

"No, no," Cage says, and his face brightens. He stands up, gesticulating with sudden energy, like a flagman at a race course. "I mean, YES. Don't apologize. Yes—you should say whatever you feel. That's what I've always wanted from you. THAT."

"What?"

"Your heart. Your soul. Whatever's underneath all that smiling and politeness and businesslike, perfunctory—"

"No . . . I don't really think that's what you want. You like the mask. The mask makes you feel safe and comfortable. Makes you feel important."

"That's not me," he says. "You know it's not."

"YOU THINK YOU WANT TO KNOW ME?" she says, suddenly screaming. It's a scream so weighted with pain that it's a howl. Her face is contorted, ripped in half by pain and fear. "You don't want to know me. Believe me. YOU DON'T."

"My god," I said. I couldn't blink, watching Serena command the scene. She'd always worked hard to learn her craft, taking workshops no matter how busy she got recording and touring, but she'd started her lessons late. In her first two movies, she got by on charm, boldness, and name recognition. But this . . . She wasn't just a star; she was an artist.

April patted my knee, knowing.

Suddenly, a man's voice cut through Serena's triumph, trampling her words: "Cut!" The director's intrusion was so angry, so disrespectful, that I couldn't believe he'd witnessed the same Oscar-caliber performance. "What the fuck? How many times do we have to go through this, Afrodite? Explain to me why we can't stick to the script!"

Cage shouted something back at the director. The film sliced away with a beep, and my screen went white. Serena wasn't in the next scene, just Cage. I cut it off.

"You can see why she quit," April said. "I hear the real script was a bunch of stereotypical girlfriend banter. Nothing real like that."

My thoughts spilled: "She wasn't acting in that scene. She and Nick were talking, actor to actor. That role hit her close to home, and she felt like an imposter. Nick was helping her tap her emotions for the scene."

One scene had just taught me more about Serena than I'd known in ten years. You were trying so hard, Serena. You wanted to show your true self to the world—and the world would have recognized you no matter what.

"Well, when Afrodite pulled out, Stan Greene took a financial bath," April said. "They were coproducers, and she tried to get more control over the script. Since shooting had already started, it was a huge mess involving millions of dollars. He had to be pissed. Anyway . . . as soon as I saw it, I knew you should see it, too."

I glanced at April, almost irritated to be pulled from my thoughts. She seemed smaller than she had before. The sight of her so soon after visiting Serena had shrunken April's bones. Her cheeks were round where Serena's jaw had been vivid, and her eyes were missing Serena's smoke and fire. In that instant, Serena's absence felt so unjust that I wanted to break something.

That was when April kissed me. Her wine-sweetened tongue darted into my mouth. But I didn't kiss back.

April drew away. I saw her embarrassment in the blood brewing beneath the paper-thin skin on her face. "I'm sorry. Did I . . . ?" She didn't finish. "It's the wine."

I squeezed her hand. "It's my fault . . ."

"I'm in idiot," April said. "Obviously, you and Afrodite . . ."

"It's not that," I said. "I hadn't seen her in five years."

"But you're not risking your neck to find her killer just because the police suspect you, Tennyson," she said. Her eyes were wistful. "You loved her, right?"

How could I explain it? I'd never had a chance to love Serena. Except for the last time I saw her, the day she died, I had been an employee kept at a careful emotional distance. I knew what mask Cage was talking about, because Serena wore it all the time. She had shown a few glimpses of her true soul on Monday when she admitted to me that she was having problems—maybe she'd been asking for my help in a way I hadn't understood—but this was the first time I had seen a version of Serena I might have loved. Now, I had met her only to have to let her go all over again, and the lost promise of our chance meeting ached like a set of broken ribs.

No, I had not loved her. But maybe I was supposed to love her, and maybe she was supposed to love me, and someone hadn't given us the chance.

Ten or fifteen seconds had gone by, and I hadn't said a word. April stood up, sighing. "I'm sorry again. I'll write down Tyra's number for you. Will you tell me what she says? I'll keep chasing Greene." She hid her face from me.

"Of course," I said. Her unreturned kiss was stinging my lips, but I didn't move.

April squatted to the floor to rifle through her bag, balancing on her toes. The gossamer veil lifted from across my eyes, and I could see her in sharp focus again. She was wearing brown leather sandals with thin straps, her toenails polished copper, her heels shiny with lotion. Her legs were strong. And she had smooth, pretty toes.

I heard April whispering to herself, still embarrassed, and I couldn't stand the idea that she would leave my home feeling diminished. I also couldn't stand feeling so sad that I couldn't move. *What the hell?* I got up and knelt beside April. Gently, I tugged at a wisp of hair near her earlobe. She shivered away from me.

"I'm not a charity case," she said. "That only makes it worse."

When I gently kissed the side of her neck, I felt her arteries pounding. "I'm not civic-minded," I said. "I don't do charity."

"You need time to get over her," she said. "I was stupid to do that—I just got carried away—so let's forget it."

Instead of answering, I rested my hands on April's shoulders from behind, kneading circles with sustained pressure from end to end. Some of my clients were shy about sex with a stranger and only wanted a massage—at first. A good massage can answer a woman's remaining questions. My kisses to April's neck answered the rest.

April's head dropped back, her mouth half-open. "You know how sometimes a person is drawn to another person, and they don't know why? Sometimes a person's roommate thinks she's crazy . . . but it just . . . happens . . ." I nibbled to silence her, and it worked. A moan.

"Sometimes a person likes to live dangerously," I said between bites.

"Is it all right to be like that?" April said, squirming as she enjoyed the play of my lips and breath against her neck. I captured a sliver of skin, pinching her with the tips of my teeth. She moaned again.

"A new friend of mine is just like that," I said. "Her body makes her decisions for her. Like right here . . ." I reached around her to brush my fingertip against her nipple through the thin fabric of her top. Blood surged, and I felt her nipple bloom. I cradled the kukui shells and pulled them slowly across her breasts, tickling. "I think her body just spoke."

April closed her eyes. Her squat lost its strength, and she leaned back against me. My erection poked her back, against the knotty ridges of her spine.

April was young, twenty-five or twenty-six. If I put my mind to it, I knew I could make her feel things she had never felt before; I could give her a story to tell for years. I've always found that being kind to others takes my mind off my troubles. After a long week, I was ready to bring someone pleasure.

I stood up and quickly locked the door so Chela wouldn't surprise us. Then, once our privacy was assured, I shook off my loafers. With only the royal blue glow from the screen lighting me, I pulled my T-shirt over my head and dropped it to the floor. Next, I stepped out of my sweatpants, down to nothing.

Naked, I strode back to April, taking my time while her eyes appreciated me. April looked breathless, a child at a fireworks display. *"Damn, you are fine,"* she said. "I mean, you are straight up—"

"Shhhh."

I sat beside her on the carpet and cradled her, stroking her hair. Black women love to have their hair touched, despite all their protestations and worries about elaborate hairstyles. They're just *afraid* to have their hair touched because of the voice echoing: *There's something wrong with my hair.* I love every inch of a black woman's head; each new scalp is a discovery. My fingertips sifted through April's short-cropped, wiry strands, full of texture. No chemicals. No wig. No weave. She was a rarity.

April tensed at first, but when she realized she could relax under my touch, she closed her eyes.

"You wore glasses when you were a kid, didn't you?" I said. "High school?"

She smiled. "How'd you know that?"

I brushed my finger against her cheek. "You're a beautiful woman who's never seen herself that way," I said. "You're still getting used to the mirror. You got contact lenses, your skin cleared up . . . and your baby fat melted after college. No more late-night pizza, a high-stress job, and boom. The men all pause. Like magic."

"You're scaring me," she said, still smiling. "Is it that obvious I'm a geek?"

"Only to someone who's curious enough," I said. "Only to someone who makes it his business to notice every little thing about you."

She gave me a confused look. I could almost hear her thinking: *Is this just sex, or is it something else?* After years of getting paid for telling women exactly what they want to hear, it's hard to break the habit. A woman's ears are an erogenous zone, both inside and out. But I wasn't trying to put stars in April's eyes; I just wanted to make her body feel good. My erection had turned to stone. There's a point when a man's need for sex is so strong that it's physically uncomfortable, and I had reached that point for the first time in recent memory. Women wilt without tenderness, but they rarely need sex with the same urgency. I needed April that night, or it would hurt.

I sucked on my thumb and burrowed my hand inside her shirt to let my thumb's damp tip roam across her nipple. April's nipple swelled and marbled under my touch. The pliant, yielding flesh was a welcome change from silicone. Breasts, to me, aren't about how they look; it's how they *feel*. They fascinate me with their warm weight in my hands. Their texture in my mouth.

And they're a portal. Breasts are the keys to the queendom.

I carefully removed April's necklace, but I yanked off her shirt with enough roughness for her to notice. Her breasts popped free, pointing upward with a tantalizing invitation. Her large twin areolas were a dark chocolate. I leaned over, gently easing her down to the shag carpeting, and lathered her breasts, sucking on one and then the other, twirling circles with the fat meat of my tongue. Her scent baked off her skin, and I buried my face in a bed of gardenias. April had sweet, tasty breasts. They fit in my palms just right. They fit my mouth just right. *Mmmmm.*

I would get her first orgasm over early.

"Oh, my . . ." April sounded shocked. "My . . . Oh, Je—" She struggled not to blaspheme. Her body writhed, her legs drawing into a near-fetal position, her knees hiked close to the side of my head. She still had most of her clothes on, and she was about to come: I could smell it in her scent, feel it in the temperature of her skin and the way she squeezed her thighs. I slid my hand on the denim between her legs, my finger probing at the stitching across her crotch. Pressing and retreating. Just enough to set her free.

April gritted her teeth, quivering. "Holy . . . *shit.*"

"Can't wait to taste the main course," I whispered in her ear.

It had been a bad day, and I was going to take it out on April. I vowed to myself that I was going to put tears in this woman's eyes.

I unsnapped her fly and slid my palm lightly down April's bare back, hooking my fingers into her jeans. I pulled, and my palm met the warm plumpness of her firm, waiting cheeks. Soon she was naked, too, her body against mine. There is nothing like the feeling of new skin rubbing against your nakedness. I never get bored with skin.

I touched every corner of her, from the bones of her pelvis that made their gentle indentation above her hips, to her trembling stomach, to her waist that was so petite that I could almost reach from one end to the other when I held her between my palms. I dangled the necklace of kukui nuts on April's soft thigh, pulling them across her neatly trimmed nest of pubic hair. One by one, the hard nut casings kissed her clitoris. April squirmed, her eyes closed.

I held her shoulders, sliding our bodies together. I wished we were slick with oil or wet from the shower, but I still savored the delicious contact. Then I let the stubble on my chin tickle her chest and stomach as I leaned back on all fours, and my face sank into the heat between April's legs. I smelled baby powder and moist skin alongside her unmistakable uniqueness, seasoned by perspiration and her body's juices.

I began cautiously. I never want to douse a woman's fire, since so much female sexuality is about building and creation. Some women can't stand anyone's hands on their clit except their own. I rubbed my face against the top of April's thighs, kissing them gently. Then, I kissed her pelvic bone, and next her inner thigh. I gently massaged her labia, capturing her ultimate prize in its folds, rubbing and stimulating her without direct touch in the moist center. April moaned, my signal.

My tongue went to work.

Never underestimate the power of the tongue. Back when I was working, I did daily tongue exercises to keep up with my clients' demands. I've met women who never experienced oral sex because of selfish partners, and that curiosity led them to me. Some of my clients wanted head and nothing else, so I learned to work out my tongue like any other part of the body: in and out, up and down, poking it out as far as possible, circling.

At first, I only flicked my tongue at April. She moaned and hissed immediately, as if I'd struck a match to her. *Gentle, gentle.* I tested her with my fingertip, and she was wet. That was all I needed to know: I'm blessed with the power to roll my tongue, so I curled it into a tube, pulled her wide open, and rubbed my tongue directly against the sides of her clitoris. April shrieked as her clit surged.

"Wait," she gasped. "What about . . . ?"

"She's wearing headphones," I said. "Be loud."

I plied April with my index finger, slipping inside her. April was tight, but my second finger nudged in easily beside the first. While my rolled tongue massaged her one way, my fingers massaged her in another. I hooked my index finger upward an inch and a half, and I felt the rough, swollen sponginess I had been searching for: her G-spot.

April shrieked again, and her body bathed me with warm fluid. She stiffened from head to toe. I angled my hand so the pad of my thumb rested behind my fingers, on the puckered, sensitive spot behind the vagina most women hardly explore at all. I didn't try to insert my thumb without lubrication, but the pressure was enough to widen April's scope. She bucked, jabbering. I couldn't resist: I leaned lower and offered my tongue instead, exploring the region between her cheeks most men are afraid to taste.

I showed April no mercy.

By the time intercourse began, April was nearly hoarse and bathed in sweat. I rolled her onto her stomach, her legs pushed together, and straddled her from the rear. My legs hugged hers. I braced my arms and nudged myself slowly into her slippery vaginal walls from behind. Her skin was hot even through a lamb-skin condom. I felt her pulsing, gripping as I vanished inside her. When my pelvis pressed against her slick buttocks with no farther to go, April hissed like a tire losing its air. An animal's growl rose from her throat.

A subtle shift of angle, and I probed her G-spot for the second time.

April screamed. And screamed again. Her body flopped beneath me. Her fingers clawed at the shag carpeting, pulling fibers free. I felt her squeezing me. Milking me.

"Omigod . . . omigod . . . omigod . . . *OMIGOD* . . ."

Most women live their whole lives and never know what their bodies are capable of feeling. It's a tragic loss. "*Yes* . . ." I whispered in her ear.

She writhed again, whimpering. I gazed at April's face, which was profiled flat on the floor, slack-jawed and spent. Her eyes were open, but she didn't see me.

How could she? April's eyes were overrun with tears of pleasure.

It was eleven by the time I walked April out to her white PT Cruiser, which was parked in my driveway. She was scattered after our session, and hadn't said much. I smiled when I saw her hand trembling slightly as she fit her key into her door.

Again, I scanned up and down the street. I didn't see any cars that didn't belong, but I didn't want to linger either.

"Is that a gun?" April said, noticing the .44's bulge in my sweatpants.

"No. I'm just happy to see you," I said, and leaned over to kiss her forehead.

A surprised glint in April's eyes told me she had hoped for a different kiss. Somehow in all of the nakedness and touching, we had never finished the kiss she tried to initiate. I thought I had seen a similar fragile look when I told her I needed to go to bed—with no invitation to spend the night. Misunderstandings rarely happened on the job, but I had to be more careful in real life. The kiss to April's forehead was most honest; I didn't have room for any other kind. Like I said, a kiss is never just a kiss.

"So . . . you'll call me tomorrow or . . . whenever?" she said.

I held April's shoulders and gave her a reassuring smile. "I had a great time. I'm glad you came by. Yes, I will definitely call you tomorrow."

A wicked grin. "Oh, I'm glad I came by, too. You have gifts." April tipped upward to kiss me lightly on the lips, but she didn't push it. "Let me know if anything bad happens. If . . . you need my help with Chela, or anything else. I mean it."

"I will. That means a lot to me."

You can write me letters in jail, I thought.

Once I watched April drive away safely and locked my door, I called the number April had given me for Tyra. It was late, but something told me Serena's sister didn't live by the early-to-bed-early-to-rise credo.

Tyra answered on the first ring. "What took you so long?" she said. "I need to meet you tomorrow." I heard a man's voice near her, and she shushed him, telling him *None of your damn business.* The man grumbled back in return.

"You were a little upset the last time I saw you," I reminded Tyra.

"Look, I'm going through a hard time, a'ight? Somebody killed my sister. Sorry I slapped you. I've got more to tell you about Serena. Something you need to know."

Inwardly, I sighed. I didn't look forward to fighting off Tyra's advances, or pretending to enjoy them. "Why don't you tell me now?"

"It's more like something I have to *show* you." She gave me an address. "It's the apartment building on the corner."

My suspicions raged, since Tyra was tight with M.C. Glazer. "Why?"

"It's where me and Reenie grew up. You want to know about her past? Well, I'll walk you through it nice and slow."

I'll just bet you will, I thought. "Why do you care about helping me?" I said.

"Why do you *think*, fool? She was my sister. Blood is stronger than anything else, and cops are full of shit. At least *somebody* wants to make things right."

She sounded convincing enough, but my inner alarm bells drowned out her voice.

"I went by Mackey's," I said. "No one remembered seeing you Monday night."

"First off, you better check your tone. I don't know what you're trying to say, but I don't appreciate it. Second of all, you're a liar. You sent that reporter with her little Payless shoes and bougie attitude. Tomorrow, I'll tell you where I really was. Three o'clock. Don't be late. And be on time, or you won't see shit."

Oh, I'll be early, I thought. I would meet Tyra at the address, all right. She was my only lead now that Jenk was dead, and I couldn't afford not to. But I knew long before I hung up the phone that I wasn't going anywhere near Tyra Johnston without a gun. That was a depressing thought, but it fit right in with all the rest.

I fell asleep in my screening room, watching Serena.

THIRTEEN

THE DRIVE BETWEEN HOLLYWOOD HILLS and West Covina always seems long, but never as long as when I set out against the flow of rush-hour traffic the next morning to drive to Hope Rehabilitation Center. Arnaz was right: I had to tell Dad my troubles before someone else did. I was probably too late.

I brought Chela with me, rousing her from sleep. I had no choice. Chela insisted on a grande iced caramel macchiato from Starbucks before she would get off the sofa, but after her caffeine fix she stopped complaining. I still hadn't decided where I would stash Chela when I met Tyra later, but at least I knew she would be safe at the nursing home. Safer than the patients, anyway.

"You should call Mother. Tell her you're all right," I said as we drove.

"I already did. I called her when I was locked in your pantry all day."

I glanced at her, surprised. She was staring away from me, toward the traffic. A black-and-white speeding in the lane alongside me made my heart catch. The car passed, but I was on alert, expecting Lorenzo and DeFranco to show up and run me off the road.

"And?" I said.

"And what?"

"What did she say?"

"Who says I have to tell you?"

I ground my teeth together, silent. April was right: I couldn't control Chela, or what happened to her. I was in over my head. If Chela wanted me to drop her off at Mother's, fine. At least Lorenzo and DeFranco wouldn't get to her there.

Chela slurped the last of her macchiato. "She said your money is waiting."

"I only get that money if I bring you back."

Chela shrugged. "Then that's what you should've done."

"Maybe. But it's not what I did."

"So what's your deal, anyway? You're gonna treat me nice and cook for me and send me back out so you can get a cut instead of Mother?"

"Is that what Mother said?"

"No. Mother said you used to work for her, but you quit." Chela said *you quit* as if it made me either weak or stupid, or maybe both.

"That's true. I quit."

"Why?"

A shining moment for genuine rapport. I wished I had a profound answer ready. "Having sex for a living didn't feel good to me."

Chela chuckled. "That's your problem. Your head's all wrong."

"What do you mean?"

"With a trick, you're just fucking. It's a piece of equipment, and you're at a job. And you have to be smart, not like those skanks on the street. You find somebody like Mother, who can get you the celebrities and big money. I'm not a druggie, I never bareback, and I've got Norplant. What's the big deal?"

"Well, maybe my head is all wrong, but it seems like more than that."

"Only if you trip about it."

"I'm still tripping about things I did when I was your age I didn't know I would trip about. And I was a grown man, twenty-five, before I went to Mother. If Mother makes you happy, then wait three years. She'll still be here—Mother will outlive all of us. See if you've changed your mind. What's the difference?"

"Only a few hundred thousand dollars. What's the difference if I *don't* wait?"

"If you don't wait, you don't have a chance to change your mind. You'll be with Mother without ever knowing what else is out there."

Chela laughed a bitter laugh at me, like a cough. "Oh, I *know* what's out there."

"You know what was out there before," I said. "This is now."

"Oh, really?" Chela said. "You mean like yesterday, when I was hiding from police all day in a tiny room with nothing to eat and trying not to pee? Thanks, but no thanks."

I hardly knew Chela, but I can't remember anyone's words gutting me quite so badly, except for Dad's—and I had that to look forward to next. I blinked, but I didn't have a comeback. Chela was right. I couldn't offer her an alternative.

"Look . . . we can research . . ." I began.

"Here's what's up, Ten . . ." Chela said, as if she were the one with twenty years' more life experience. She stretched her arm across the seat, her wrist dangling behind me on my headrest. "Mother said you're a good guy. For real. She said I can trust you. But that world you live in—with that house and all that great stuff—that's not the real world. I had no mother, no father. I stopped wetting the bed when I was eight, and that's when I had to start cleaning Nana's pissy sheets. She was too poor for a doctor, or for the right medicine, and she would have died out on the street if it wasn't for me. So my life started out shitty, and I got to see how it looks at the shitty end. I knew pretty quick that foster care wasn't gonna work out for me, so I had to let that go. Then came Mother."

There, Chela paused. I glanced at her. She was blinking rapidly, but her voice was still breezy when she went on. "Now I've got a nice house. I've got my own room. And all I have to do is fuck a few guys here and there—and most of them are hotties or rich anyway—and I've got thousands of dollars in the bank. *Twenty* thousand."

She should have had more than that. Mother was taking more than her fair share. "That's a lot of money," I said anyway.

"No, see, if I told my friend Desiree back at school in Minneapolis that I had five hundred dollars in the bank, she would say, 'Hey, girl, that's a lot of money.' But I'm fourteen years old, and I have *twenty* thousand dollars."

I wanted to run Mother down with my car. "Mother said you were *fifteen*."

"Fourteen and a half," Chela clarified, which only sounded worse. "The point is, am I supposed to be happy making minimum wage working a French fryer? Which, by the way—do you know how bad that is for your skin? Or am I supposed to go live with people who get money to take care of kids nobody wants and maybe have to fuck my new daddy and brothers for free?"

My throat constricted. "I know terrible things can happen in foster care, but kids also find loving families," I said. "Things are different when you have an advocate—someone to look out for you."

"I know what an advocate is."

"I figured that. And please don't use that language around me." I couldn't help myself. Chela had an angel's face, and the word *fuck* from her mouth was sacrilege.

"What language?"

"The word that begins with F," I said. "Don't use it around me."

Chela stared at me, dumbfounded. Then, she laughed. "You are hilarious."

"You're a smart girl, Chela, but school bored you to death," I said. "I bet you were too advanced for your classes, so you thought you hated it. But what if you just never had the right classes? What if you were *good* at school? There are plenty of jobs you could get where you can earn good money. Mother isn't the only one who pays."

"Oh, you mean like in a hundred years, when I got out of college?"

"What's the rush?"

"Where the hell am I supposed to live?"

"That's the part we have to figure out."

"Yeah, no shit. That's the part *everybody* has to figure out," Chela said. Then she grinned. "Am I allowed to say 'shit'?"

"Yes. But not around my father."

"I know how to act around old people. Nana didn't raise me in the gutter."

I laughed. Chela was smart and somehow funny despite all she'd been through, and I liked her—a lot. That realization stung me so hard that my laugh faded. *I can't even take care of myself. How can I do anything for her?*

"Your dad's sick?" Chela said.

I nodded.

"Did he break his hip?" she said.

"No. Why?"

"Because I heard that when old people break their hips, they only live for six months. Not all the time, but, like a lot of them. I was trying to tell if he was . . . dying."

"He had a stroke. He has a bad heart," I said. "Yes, maybe he doesn't have much time."

Aloud, the words felt less powerful than they did when I buried them in the foggy, forbidden regions of my mind. Stripped of their mystery and intrigue, those words were just a phrase in need of special handling. It was sad and final, but I could feel some of the killing weight seeping out of the idea, my brain re-sorting it.

"When Nana broke her hip, she passed three months later, in her sleep," Chela said softly. "I was kind of glad for her. She was hurting all the time. You know?"

"I know." I imagined how pissed I would be if I was in Dad's place. He had spent his entire career upholding the law, and now his body was a prison.

Until now, I had been afraid to think the words: *Dad is dying.* I'd known since his heart attack forced him to leave his job and I started counting the minutes before he would end up lying in a bed all day. Dad needed his job to live.

I was the least of Dad's problems. I was still attaching expectations to him as his son even while his body's organs struggled to hold on. My thoughts of moving him into my house were selfish, in a way; an opportunity for me to finally demonstrate to Dad that I was a man after all. Now, I couldn't even do that.

I had no father anymore, not really. There was no more *us*, no more *we*. The man who had raised me was consumed by his own dying. We were each fighting our worst battles alone. He might die first, or I might.

One of us might die today.

"I think I might get arrested, Dad."

I'd asked Chela to wait in the lounge while I talked to my father alone in his room. Two sets of commercials passed before I finally blurted it out in the middle of *Judge Joe Brown*, right before the ruling.

Dad's eyes mooned to three times their normal size. His left arm patted the mattress beside him, searching for the remote. I would have helped him, but he only got mad when I tried to do things for him, so I stayed in my chair and waited. He finally turned off the TV. A curtain of silence swallowed us.

Dad blinked and went wide-eyed again, waiting.

"I ran into an old friend of mine Monday. A rapper and actress named Afrodite."

Dad was already nodding. He knew Afrodite's name, had to know she'd been murdered. Dad didn't miss the nightly news. If it were possible, his eyes got wider.

"Her real name was Serena Johnston, and I cared about her . . ."

Dad listened, rapt. He seemed all right through the first part of the story—even my visit to M.C. Glazer's house had no noticeable impact on him—but when I got to Jenk's death, his eyes closed tight. He looked like a funeral corpse, but one in pain, as if the mortician had decided not to sugarcoat the whole business.

I plowed through to the end. By then, my breath was scalding my throat. "So that's it, man," I said. "I'm stuck in the middle, and I'm just waiting to get locked up."

Dad opened his eyes lifted his left hand, which was trembling violently. He pointed toward his night-table. "P-p . . . pad," he said. He had to repeat it twice more before I understood. His shaking hand rattled me; seeing weeks of painstaking progress set back in an instant jammed my thoughts. I handed Dad his pad and the black marker he used to write messages. He scrawled two words, all capitals, and I had no problem reading them despite the craggy lines:

DID YOU

The two words were followed by an indecipherable squiggle that I finally recognized as my father's attempt to make a question mark.

Hurt burned my stomach, but I ignored it. He had a right to ask. I would, too.

"Dad . . ." I said. I leaned closer to him and held his bony hand, absorbing his tremors until he was still. I knew he wanted to pull his hand away—Dad wasn't one for physical displays—but I held on. "I know I'm not what you wanted me to be. I *know* that. I have messed up, I have embarrassed you, I have made you wonder where I came from because I'm not you, and I'm not the person my mother was."

Dad looked away, at the ceiling. Some widowers remarry right away because they need to be with someone, but Dad had stayed devoted to his dead wife. It was one more thing that separated us; he had known Evelyn Patricia Rutledge Hardwick—high school English teacher, church pianist, and community activist—and I had not.

"I did not kill Serena. And I did not kill Detective Jenkins. Maybe I've lied to you too many times to expect you to believe me, but it's the truth. I'm not a killer. I swear it on my mother. On her soul."

Dad's fingers suddenly tightened so hard across mine that they hurt. I tried to tug away, but couldn't. His eyes spat fire at me. "D-don't . . . you . . . *dare* . . ." For the first time in ages, I understood him with no problem.

"I would never swear on Mom's soul if I was lying, Daddy. I didn't do it." I'd been there only a half-hour, and I sounded like I was eight years old again.

Dad started breathing quickly, sucking air through his nostrils, and I was alarmed. Was he having another heart attack? I was reaching for the nurse's call button when Dad's clawlike hand stopped me. Then, he picked up his marker again. He scrawled more rapidly this time, and as a result the writing was nearly illegible. I struggled with the letters, until slowly they came into focus: SET UP.

"You're saying . . . *I* was set up?" I said, to be sure I understood. He nodded rapidly, his breathing still excited. He puffed out a breath, and I realized he was trying to speak. I leaned over him, listening. "What is it?"

"Ge-get . . . Marrrrr . . . cel . . . la . . ." he said. His tongue worked painstakingly, slowly.

"Dad, are you OK?" I reached for the call button again, but he shook his head, pointing toward the doorway instead.

"Mar . . . cel . . . la," he said. "Lunch."

He didn't want me to call the duty nurse; he wanted me to find Marcela instead.

I bolted from my chair, running to the doorway. *Please, God, don't let him be having a heart attack.* If something happened to Dad because of me, I would never forgive myself. I nearly skidded on the slick linoleum as I sped past the confab of three young nurses at the nurse's station and ran toward the cafeteria at the far end of the building. Their remote laughter followed me.

Like most institutional cafeterias, the narrow room smelled unappetizing, like sour steam and overcooked vegetables, just like at my junior high school. The smell almost gagged me, an old reflex. There were two or three patients in wheelchairs at the tables. I almost missed Marcela because she was sitting in a corner, behind a potted bird-of-paradise plant. Her face was hidden in a paperback copy of Gabriel García Marquez's *Love in the Time of Cholera* while her fork stirred a wilted Caesar's salad.

When she saw me, a shadow passed across her face. "Your father?"

I only had to nod, and Marcela was up and on my heels. She hurried to Dad's room with me, but her face was calm as she leaned over Dad's bed. He was still conscious, and he smiled when he saw her, so I relaxed.

"What is it, Captain?" Marcela said. "Your son can't turn on the TV for you?"

Dad chuckled, and I was so amazed that I almost didn't recognize the sound. Garbled whispers came from Dad's throat, and Marcela leaned so close to his mouth that her ear nearly rested against it. She listened, nodding. He spoke for a long time, in a code only Marcela could understand.

"Write this number down," Marcela said to me, and recited a string of ten digits.

Quickly, I scribbled the numbers on Dad's pad. "Whose number is this?"

Marcela didn't answer right away, concentrating on Dad's fevered whispers. She nodded. Her thick eyebrows merged with concern as she stared at me.

"It's the number of a detective, a friend of your father's. Hal . . ." She paused, and Dad whispered again. "Hal Dol . . . inski, I think." Dad nodded, smiling, and his torrent of whispers began again. Finally, Marcela straightened and picked up the phone. "I'll make this call. I'll be your father's voice. Then you can talk to the detective."

I was confused, but Marcela wasn't. Her fingers flew on the phone's keypad. In all the time Dad had been here, I'd never had any luck getting an outside line, but apparently she knew the trick. While the line rang, Marcela covered the receiver to explain: "I make calls for your father. Like with the insurance company."

"Bless you," I said. I don't use that phrase often, but it felt right. I'd gotten a message about a problem with Dad's insurance, but I never called back.

"My brother works for the L.A. County Sheriff's Office. I . . ." Marcela cut herself off, her voice snapping to businesslike precision: "Hello, this is Marcela Ruiz calling on behalf of Captain Richard Hardwick. Is this Detective Dolinski?"

A pause as the man verified who he was. "Hello, Detective. I understand there has been a problem involving Captain Hardwick's son. The captain is right here with me, and he asked me to call you. He wants you to tell his son about . . ." When she faltered, my father gestured for her again. More whispers.

"Sir, he wants you to tell his son about Richard Jenkins," she finished.

"Robert Jenkins," I corrected, and Marcela repeated Jenk's name.

"Please hold for Captain Hardwick's son," Marcela said, and gave me the phone.

The transaction had me feeling dazed, my heart pounding. I felt like part of Dorothy's entourage arriving in the Emerald City, granted an audience with the Great and Powerful Oz. "Hello?"

"You've stepped in a great big steaming pile of shit now—huh, kid?" a man said. I heard commotion in the background. A restaurant? Maybe he was on a cell phone. The voice sounded familiar, but the background noise made it hard to place.

"Do you know what's going on, Detective? I sure don't."

"Got a pretty good idea," the voice said, and I nailed him: He had been present at my interrogation, the man whose face I thought I knew. Hal. *Uncle Hal,* I'd called him, just as all of Dad's friends were Uncle this or Uncle that. I hadn't seen him since I was twelve or thirteen. He used to windsurf when Dad took me to cookouts on the beach, and I'd always thought his sunburned chest was impossibly broad. He was much smaller now. Much older. "How's Preach taking it?"

"I just told him, and the first thing he did was ask his nurse to call you."

"Figures," Hal Dolinski said, and he sighed. "How's he doing otherwise? I haven't seen him in a while . . ."

"He's good," I said, the quickest answer. "What's going on?"

"If you say you heard any of this from me, I'll call you a liar under oath."

"Go on."

The man sighed again. Despite his friendship with Dad, he *really* didn't want to talk to me. As of now, he had put his job at risk. "Robert Jenkins, aka our current Fallen Hero, was just a gangbanger with a badge. End of story. Lieutenant Nelson told you he's been under investigation for six months, but it's more like five years. Nothing sticks. I was in IAG when we first got wind of him. Every time we got close, brass intervened and tried to make it go away. Preach knows all about it. Jenkins was Hollywood division before he got run over to South Bureau."

I glanced at my father, who was watching me closely, eager to know what Dolinski was saying. His breathing had slowed to normal. I noticed a red button for the phone's speaker. "Can I put you on speakerphone? Dad's right here," I said.

"Yeah, yeah, I guess so," Dolinski said reluctantly. "Anything for Preach. Just watch who listens."

I punched the button, and the background noise on the cell phone charged into our room. "We're back," I said.

"Hey, Preach," Dolinski's voice boomed from the speaker, and my Dad smiled again but didn't speak. He still had all his teeth, and his smile was as alive as ever. My smile. "I knew I'd hear from you today. Can you believe this shit is still going on?"

Dad shook his head as if Dolinski could see him.

"Where was I? Oh, yeah: Robert Jenkins, otherwise known as a pain in my ass. Anyway, so the Hollywood streetwalkers say he's ripping them off. Dealers say he's ripping them off. Vics say he's popping innocent kids and planting guns, just like the Rampart stuff that got in the news. Jenk's questioned again and again, knows he's being tailed. Nothing fazes him. Brass bounces him around. Preach came close to getting Jenk fired, but the higher-ups wouldn't go for it. That's why Chief Randall didn't show his sorry ass at Preach's retirement, but what do you want from that prick?"

Dad mumbled something I almost understood: *Get to the damn point.*

Dolinski went on. "I guess this is what Preach wants me to tell you: There was evidence—actual physical evidence—linking Robert Jenkins to the murder of that rapper, Shareef. It was a security video from the scrapyard where the body was dumped, a DA's dream. A car, the tag number, a profile of Jenk's face. Even the body across his shoulder, wrapped in a sleeping bag. I never saw it, but that's the story. And what happens? The tape gets *stolen* out of the god-damned evidence locker. Somebody—some *cop*—walked in and took it. And what did brass do? Nothing. They don't search Jenk's car. They don't search Jenk's house. Not even a goddamned interview.

"And get this: That hands-off directive came from the chief's office. Chief Randall doesn't want to have to explain why his own *son* was a business partner with a dirty cop and suspected murderer like Robert Jenkins. Their company's closed now, but Robert Jenkins and Chief Randall's son used to have a security company called Real Deal. Their specialty was off-duty cops who were willing to play dirty. I saw a Polaroid of Robert Jenkins and the chief's son smiling over a pile of money, like in *Scarface*. Is the shit thick enough for you yet, kid?"

It was. My heart blocked my throat. "Keep going."

"And Lieutenant Nelson's a smart guy, but he's got the Disease," Dolinski went on.

"What disease?"

"Preach won't like hearing me say this, but he knows it's true: My people can do no wrong. *That* disease. It's the same with us Polacks, with everybody. If it's been us-against-them, loyalty gets tested. Chief Randall is black, and Nelson's got his back. But now *another* rapper's dead in Los Angeles? And there's an LAPD connection, like with Biggie Smalls and Shareef? The department's in a panic. So if a theory pops up linking Robert Jenkins to rappers and bangers, Nelsons's not gonna be as interested in that. Jenk's body is already cold. But *you*? Yeah, you're Preach's son—but Preach is retired. Randall's a different story, with all his reform bullshit after Rodney King and Rampart. He's a national figure. There's more at stake. You know I'm not lying, Preach."

My father sighed, dispirited. Surrendering something. I realized the magnitude of politics that must have been on my father's back as his career was ending. No *wonder* he'd had a heart attack, with a stroke on its heels three years later. Devon Biggs had warned me, and now I had confirmation from an insider.

"I need to know what happened to Shareef," I said. "It could be linked to Serena. Can you get me copies of files?"

Dolinski groaned and sighed, a windstorm on a speakerphone. "Preach, your kid is killing me," he said. "I shouldn't even be talking to him."

"From what you're saying," I said, "Jenk could have killed Serena. And then maybe he got killed in retaliation." *Whose* retaliation, I wasn't sure.

"More likely, someone got spooked and wanted to keep him quiet," Dolinski said.

Dad gestured for Marcela, who had been listening while she read Dad's prescription labels—Plavix, Aggrenox, Toprol XL, Diovan, Lipitor, the list went on—and straightened the items on his bed table. She leaned over, and he whispered in her ear.

"Captain Hardwick says to tell him about Mexico," Marcela said.

"Right," Dolinski said. "Jenk had a rep as a hired gun. In '04, I interviewed a snitch who told me Jenk drove down to Tijuana to make hits for stateside dealers, and my informant would've been willing to testify. But it never got that far. Nobody ever arrested Jenk, and my snitch got shanked at Lancaster."

"If you know all this, why don't you come forward?" I said.

My father began shaking his head. He made a sound to answer, before he remembered he couldn't trust his tongue. He only sighed, frustrated.

"Where do I start, Preach?" Dolinski said. "Look, kid, I'm two years from retirement. I'm not volunteering to be the big white elephant in a media circus. I can see it now: A white cop tries to tear down a beloved black chief? Kiss my hairy Polack ass. And most important: It's all theories. I can't prove anything. Too much evidence has been lost. Documents destroyed. There's nothing in the book linking Shareef to Robert Jenkins, believe me. RHD had its head so far up its ass on the Shareef case, the halls still stink. But I know the lead on Shareef, and he's a good detective. It's not his fault he blew the case. Chief Randall shut him down."

To me, it sounded paranoid to think that a cover-up in Shareef's death might have originated with the chief of police. But whether or not Chief Randall was involved, LAPD culture was entrenched enough to keep investigators from rocking the boat. Any version of Serena's death involving Robert Jenkins or LAPD officers would not be fully investigated—especially now that Jenk was dead. It wouldn't take a mastermind or a conspiracy; human nature would keep leading them back to me.

"Lorenzo and DeFranco came by my house during the search. Let's call it a drive-by," I told Dolinski wryly. "They promised to get to me if I'm arrested."

"That's near-fetched, kid," he said. "Lorenzo was Jenk's shadow, and his gang connections go deep. There's always bangers in lockup who could get to you, sure."

Dad nodded, agreeing, and the concern in his eyes told me how scared I should be. It's hard enough to face the specter of jail, even for a night. But if a quick demise was waiting for me inside, I had to get out of town, with or without my passport.

But I didn't say that in front of Dad. "What should I do?"

"Your best bet?" Dolinski said. "If Nelson gets his arrest warrant, call me— fast. Call this number, my mobile. I'll do what I can to get you in protective custody. But be careful. On the outside, you're on your own."

"On the outside, I can take care of myself."

Dolinski laughed in a way that was too hearty. "You hear that, Preach? He can take care of himself. I tell you, your kid really handled himself when Nelson was going at him. He didn't take any shit, just like somebody else I know. OK, I gotta fly. Preach, remember you still owe me a hundred bucks, you cheap SOB. I know you couldn't believe it, but my Seahawks really won the Super Bowl in 2005. So pay up."

Dad smiled, remembering. He looked shaken, but he was all right.

"He's smiling. I'll pay his debt when I see you," I said. "You're getting me those files on Shareef, right? And an incident report on Jenk?" Once April's voice turned up on my voicemail, Nelson would freeze her out of the information loop.

"Sorry, kid. Don't push your luck," Dolinski said.

He was gone before I could thank him for maybe saving my life.

When I hung up, Dad's face seemed more alive than usual. His eyes were dancing. *Buzzing.* I had brought something into his day he could be a part of, a true-life experience that wasn't from a television screen.

"OK, that's it," Marcela said. "No more cops and robbers, Captain Hardwick. If your son is exciting you too much, he should go. Remember your blood pressure."

"We're done today," I told her. "Promise."

Marcela scowled at me, skeptical. "I need to finish my rabbit food," she said, patting Dad's arm. She grinned. "Just like old times, eh, Captain?"

My father nodded. His eyes twirled again.

"I owe you a drink," I told Marcela, kissing her cheek.

"My boyfriend wouldn't like that," she said. "The fantasy is nice, *gracias*, but you don't owe me. Captain Hardwick knows I would do anything for him."

Dad mumbled for her again, and she listened with her ear to his mouth, laughing girlishly. This time, Marcela only smiled to herself and turned to leave without a translation. That moment was theirs.

That old dog, I thought, staring at my father with new admiration. Dad still had his own life. Everything wasn't gone. Dad stared at me, too, equally amazed to have learned something about me. I wondered what he had learned, and what he thought.

Stripped of our buffers, our silence was back. But I felt more at ease beside him than I had in longer than I could remember. And one thing was sparkling clear: My father and I needed to talk more.

"I was scared to death to tell you before," I said. "Now I wish I had, man."

Dad nodded and shrugged. *It's done now,* his shrug said.

"I'm going to fix this. Somehow."

Dad grabbed his marker and started to scribble something on the paper, but he got frustrated and gave up. Instead, he looked back up at me and nodded. *Come here.*

I walked to the side of the bed and leaned close, mirroring Marcela. I was so close, I smelled the soap on my father's face. I smelled his breakfast on his breath. I smelled his hair tonic, and the coconut oil scent reminded me of his bathroom medicine cabinet in the old house. Our house.

"Kayyyy . . . fooool . . ." Dad said.

I didn't understand. He repeated it, more loudly. My eardrum vibrated, but I couldn't make it out, except that it sounded like he was calling me a fool. I felt like one.

"Kaye? Is that someone's name?" I said, desperate to understand.

"He said 'careful.' "

Chela's voice startled me. How long had she been standing in the doorway?

"As in *be careful*. Nana had trouble talking, too," Chela said, walking to the opposite side of the bed. She gripped the bed's metal railing, rocking on her heels with a sudden bout of shyness. Why could everyone hear my father except me?

"Dad, this is my friend Chela," I said. "I told you about her."

"Hello, Mr. Hardwick. Pleased to meet you," she said.

Chela was right; Nana had raised her with good manners even if their time together had been cut short. Dad assessed Chela with a smile, impressed by her. He had never been a hands-on father, but Dad adored young people from a distance. That was why he had visited so many schools over his career, why he cared about building parks. Making a safer world for girls like Chela had been a part of his calling.

"You . . . too," my father said.

At long last, I had brought a girl to meet my father.

Chela, I learned, kept a regimented schedule—breakfast by eleven o'clock, coffee refill by midday, and lunch no later than two—so I spent the early part of my day shuttling her from one drive-thru window to the next.

Between feedings, I had time to learn more about Shareef's murder. I couldn't expect Dolinski to come through with more detailed information, so I got myself started at Wired on Vineland, my favorite internet café. Good food, easy chairs, reasonable rates. Chela sat at the computer beside me and disappeared into My-Space. I checked over her shoulder once in a while and saw photo signatures of other teenagers on her screen, mostly girls. Harmless enough, I hoped.

I checked my email account, too. I have an encrypted account—one I established years ago, when I was working for Mother—and signed on without a problem. I smiled when I found the emailed photos of M.C. Glazer were waiting for me, in full color. I printed six copies, hiding them from Chela, and deleted the files. Someone who was determined enough could retrieve the files, but I wasn't going to make it easy for the police to charge me for assaulting Glaze. Unless someone planted evidence against me, the cases involving Serena and Robert Jenkins would fall apart—so Nelson would be eager to pin anything on me he could find.

Next, I searched for details on the death of Shareef Pinkney.

I was traveling with Alice in South Africa when Shareef died—our farewell journey, because I was about to quit the business and Alice was sicker than I knew. But news of his death trickled to us in Cape Town, which is a testament to the international appeal of hip-hop. Street vendors in the sprawling Cross Roads township were selling T-shirts memorializing Shareef's face within forty-eight hours of his death. *Has Serena's face reached the Cross Roads yet?*

I tried to call Serena from overseas but never heard back, and I was sad for a day on her behalf. But as a result of my distance and a daily schedule of wine tours and safaris with Alice, I didn't hear much about how Shareef died. All I knew was that he'd had a concert at the Staples Center earlier that night. At the café, I pieced together a timeline from the internet, including what seemed like a well-researched story from the *L.A. Times* written by another reporter while April was probably still in college.

Shareef finished his set at the Staples Center and left the venue at 12:30 A.M. He and his entourage arrived at the Hollywood nightclub Concorde by 1:00 A.M. He reportedly drank heavily and made out publicly with at least three different women during a brief contractual appearance at the club. All three women were invited to ride in a limousine back to his house, but only one took the offer; she said she never saw Shareef the rest of the night. Outside of Concorde at 2:15 A.M., Shareef exchanged words with two men police suspected were tied to local gangs, but despite a lot of shouting, no one saw any violence. Shareef's bodyguards confirmed that Shareef was driven back to his house, where several party guests—including Serena—remembered seeing him.

But no one saw Shareef after 4:00 A.M. And his car wasn't in his driveway.

Six hours later, his corpse turned up wrapped in a sleeping bag at a local dump. He had been shot twice in the chest with a .32 that was registered to him. But the gun was never found. None of Shareef's bodyguards were charged, but police complained that they were tight-lipped and unhelpful—probably embarrassed about losing their employer on their watch, I figured. But they did finally admit that Shareef kept that gun in his car even though he didn't have a concealed-weapons permit. There was no evidence that the shooting had taken place at the party. Forty-five guests were questioned, but none were arrested. There was a quotation from Devon Biggs, something stunned and pain-filled. Biggs had been negotiating tour details in London when he got the news, and it sounded as if a reporter had thrust a microphone in his face without warning him of the question to come.

With the facts laid out before me, I was amazed at one major similarity between Shareef's death and Serena's: both had vanished overnight and been found *wrapped up* several hours later. Serena had been found in a garbage bag, Shareef in a sleeping bag. First Shareef, then his protégée. Did someone think they were disposing of a little trash?

Shareef had been killed before April was working in Los Angeles, or she would have noticed the link sooner. But what excuse did the police have? There were signs that the killings might be the work of the same person, or related somehow—but I had been out of the country when Shareef died, not to mention that I'd never met him. And Hal Dolinski said a security video might have shown Jenk disposing of the body!

What if evidence existed proving Jenk was involved in Serena's death, too? What if it really was a cover-up to protect the chief and his son? Maybe another cop had killed Jenk to cover the trail, with orders from on high. And now there was only me.

I went to the men's room and dry-heaved over the pristine toilet, bracing myself against the stall's narrow lime-green walls. I hadn't had enough food to throw up, but my stomach tried anyway. Afterward, I washed my face in the sink, my heart drumming. No wonder Devon Biggs was wearing Kevlar to his office. I was glad I had Glazer's Smith & Wesson in my Beemer; but I'd better hope my car wasn't searched.

It was two o'clock when I found a working pay phone outside Wired and called April. I could tell from the sound of her voice that something had happened on her end, too. She was distant. I summarized what I had learned about Robert Jenkins and Shareef, but her responses were bland, almost uninterested.

Maybe the unreturned kiss was nagging her, I thought. Women can feel very different in the light of day after sex; I once had a client who told me that she wiped away all evidence of my presence late at night so that, by morning light, there would be nothing to remind her of her sinful indulgences.

"Are you okay?" I said finally. I almost ignored the difference in her, considering my more pressing problems. But I missed her.

"Lieutenant Nelson called me," she admitted.

Ah, I thought. I heard doubt in her voice, for the first time.

"And?" I said.

She paused. "He said an arrest is imminent. He feels good about his evidence."

"What evidence?"

"He didn't say." I didn't believe her.

"He's bluffing, April," I said. I hoped he was, anyway. "What else?"

During her silence, I remembered what Nelson had told me during my questioning: *Whatever you're not saying is loud and clear.* The silence, as they say, was deafening.

I sighed, glancing inside the Wired window to keep an eye on Chela. She had struck up a conversation with a man at the computer beside her who was at least fifty, disguising his age with a shaved head and extra hours on weight machines. Well-dressed, designer shades, nice watch. Chela slipped a flirtatious pinky finger into her mouth. Sex workers know how to spot a mark.

"I'll be more than happy to answer to anything Nelson said about me," I said to April, my eyes still trained through the window. "I just can't have that conversation now. I have an appointment with Tyra."

April didn't press me; in fact, her tone brightened, as if she was happy I was letting her go. She didn't ask if she could tag along—not that I would have invited her—and the sudden, stinging chasm between us didn't just hurt because I was losing an important ally. I grasped the sun-warmed receiver for a long time, trying to think of what to say. I was sick of trying to convince people I wasn't a killer, and April needed more from me anyway. But what?

April broke the silence. "Remember how I told you that Lieuteanant Nelson was my dad's student at FAMU?"

I was glad she was talking to me again. "Yeah. Go, Rattlers."

She went on. "Well . . . sometimes teachers and students keep in touch."

"He said something to your father?"

"Not yet, maybe—but I think he might. Looking out for his prof's kid." April's discomfort made her sound like she was Chela's age. She was a Daddy's girl.

My chest tightened. Through the window, I saw Chela laughing at something the man beside her said, far too loudly. I could hear her through the glass. "Would you feel more comfortable if . . . we cut off contact?" I said. Those were the last words I had expected to hear out of my mouth when I called April.

"I don't know, Tennyson. Like you said, you have to go. We'll talk later."

The click of the telephone felt like a physical blow. She had been craving reassurances, and instead I'd given her a chance to cut loose.

"*Fuck*," I said. The meeting with my father had gone so well that I'd never considered a bad turn with April. But I couldn't blame her. I couldn't even blame Nelson. The only person to blame was staring back at me in the reflection of the café's window with a silent telephone receiver pressed to his ear as if a voice would magically appear to grant him a wish.

And *wasn't* it better for April if she kept away from me?

By the time I got back inside Wired, the man beside Chela had abandoned his computer, leaning toward her with his legs spread wide, his hands dangling between his knees. I could see his hunger for Chela in his eyes as he talked to her.

"This girl is fourteen years old," I said, loudly enough to turn heads. "Move on."

The man's face and neck shot full of blood. He raised his hands as if I'd leveled a pump-action shotgun at him, leaping from his seat. He nearly stumbled into the door as he left the café, and I heard the clerk snicker. Chela gave me a look that rivaled Lorenzo's death stare in front of my house.

I could have been more tactful with the guy, maybe. But I was in a bad mood.

"Let's go," I told Chela.

"We were *TALKING* about his *movie*," Chela said. "You have control issues. Take me to Mother's—*RIGHT NOW*." She screamed the last words, a full-blown temper tantrum. Observers looked away uncomfortably, assuming we were father and daughter; oblivious to the magnitude of the custody battle between Mother and me.

I had to get Chela quiet. If someone called the police, I was done.

"Chela? I don't need a scene right now," I said softly, with emphasized eye contact. "Can we . . . ?" I nodded toward the hallway leading to the café's restrooms.

She raised her eyebrows. "Get me a nonfat latte, and we'll talk. Double shot."

With Chela, nothing came for free.

While Chela listened with folded arms, I assured her I would take her back to Mother's if she wanted me to—but I didn't have time right now. It was part stalling, maybe part inevitability. I might be taking her back home the long way, in the end. After a melodramatic sigh, Chela slung on her Gucci purse. "So where *are* we going?"

I still wasn't sure. My appointment with Tyra was in less than an hour, across town, and I wanted Chela near Tyra even less than I wanted her near Mother. Tyra scared me, and all my instincts told me that it wouldn't be safe to let Chela wait in the car. I made a mental map of the area, and suddenly I had my answer:

"Somewhere you can catch up on your reading."

✦✦✦

As usual, James was in the rear storeroom when I got to Eso Won bookstore in Leimert Park. Booksellers are some of the hardest-working people I know. I'm an *actor,* and I feel sorry for booksellers trying to squeeze out a living. In the long shadow of Amazon and the chain stores, selling books looks more like a mission than a business.

I've been going to Eso Won for years. My tastes are for expensive art and photography books for my coffee table, but since my income dropped I've been browsing more than buying until they go on sale. I never like to leave empty-handed, so I'm quick to pick up black DVDs: 1943's *Cabin in the Sky* with Ethel Waters, Eddie "Rochester" Anderson, Lena Horne, Butterfly McQueen, and Louis Armstrong; *Carmen* with Dorothy Dandridge; Carl Franklin's *One False Move;* and documentaries like the History Channel's *Save Our History: Voices of Civil Rights.* My father always said you can't know where you're going until you know where you've been.

Eso Won also isn't a bad place to network. A couple of years ago, I spent forty-five minutes talking craft with a black actor on a hit series who happened to be there with his wife, and that conversation led to a guest spot. The work didn't come a minute too soon, either—which is the case any time I can get work. Eso Won has always felt lucky to me.

The store was nearly empty when I got there with Chela on a weekday afternoon. Oversized posters featuring book covers from Cornel West, Walter Mosley, Octavia E. Butler, and Terry McMillan loomed above us on the walls. The tables near the cash register were empty, so I pointed them out to her.

"What am I supposed to do *here?*" she said. Every sentence had an accented word to drive home her complaints. Now I understood why Dad used to tell me to stop whining or go get him his belt.

"They're called books," I said. "Pick a couple from the shelves, start reading, and I'll buy them for you when I come back."

"You're shitting me," she said. "How long am I supposed to sit here?"

"I shouldn't be more than a couple hours." I didn't know what Tyra had in mind, but I would have to let her know I couldn't hang out with her all day.

"Two hours? Then you should've taken me over the Magic Johnson Theater, because I am *not* going to—"

I didn't have to say another word. My eyes hushed Chela. She sucked her teeth.

"Whassup, Ten?" said Terrell, the new part-timer behind the register. He was white-haired although he probably wasn't older than forty-five, a former schoolteacher who could talk about black science fiction all day and all night. He was deep.

I asked Terrell to keep an eye on Chela, privately handing him April's telephone number in case Chela took off or I wasn't back by closing time. April might not be able to do anything, but it was either April's number or Mother's. I had run out of resources.

Terrell winked at Chela, ignoring her puckered face. "Come on back with me, kiddo. I guarantee you I can find you something you'll like."

"I doubt that," Chela muttered, but she followed him anyway. Chela looked back at me over her shoulder, looking small and nervous. She was more shy than I would have guessed, considering her affiliation with Mother. But then again, Mother's gigs were just an act, a persona for the clients. In real life, Chela wasn't comfortable around strangers.

"I'll get back as soon as I can," I called after her, and she waved dismissively.

Then, I left the sanctuary of Eso Won to face whatever was waiting for me next. When I turned onto Crenshaw, the million-dollar-plus homes gleamed like treasure on high in Baldwin Hills, but I wouldn't be climbing up that far to get to The Jungle.

It took four minutes for my car's GPS to find the address Tyra had given me, so I pulled up in front of the building nearly a half-hour early. I didn't stop, but I drove slowly as I scanned the territory. The street had a schizophrenic quality: simple but well-kept 1950s-era homes on one side, complete shambles on the other.

The two-story apartment complex where Tyra wanted to meet was half a block deep, squat and bullied into submission. The building's paint was literally gray, or else it was so weatherworn and sun-bleached that all color had bled away. The structure was horseshoe-shaped, but with sharp corners, and I could see the long courtyard hidden behind rusting wrought-iron gates. The grass grew so high in the courtyard—and in all of the crevices where enough time, persistence, and neglect had allowed weeds to muscle through—that the complex looked like it was being swallowed into the ground. The building also looked bombed-out, since the units on the top second floor on the north side had already been stripped of their rooftop, replaced with unsightly tarp, and there was so much razor wire around the perimeter that the site could have doubled for a concentration camp. Signs against trespassing plastered the fences like concert posters.

But I understood the security measures: An abandoned building this big could be a crack palace, drawing consumers from miles around. I felt sorry for the homeowners across the street whose living rooms and front porches stared straight into the whole insult. I guessed neighborhood outrage was responsible for the site's only bright spot: a jubilant billboard picturing full-color condominiums beneath a promise that the Newly Refurbished Baldwin Chateau Villas would be open by last month.

So much for promises.

I kept driving, my heart pummeling my throat. If I'd ever had any question that Tyra had sent me out here to set me up, it was answered. I hoped the building had looked much better when Serena lived there.

I thought about heading straight back to Eso Won, but instead I took a drive around the block, scanning for both police cars and anyone who looked unfriendly. A well-preserved older black woman pulling weeds from the base of her mature magnolia tree eyed me carefully as I drove, and she didn't return my smile. She knew I didn't belong. Maybe she thought I was a developer or a politician, and neither would be welcome in her sight.

I was surprised by the absence of police. In the areas bordering the apartment building, I'd seen a police car at almost every turn, as if they were touring on a timer. But the street Tyra had chosen was quiet; almost serene. Maybe the street had some hard-won peace, even in sight of the ultimate monument to the neighborhood's decline.

I finally parked across the street from the abandoned apartments, in front of a blue Craftsman with an empty driveway and the lights turned off behind the burglar bars. Stragglers from the knots of high school kids walking home from school made it as far as my car, most of them ignoring me as they passed my window. The girls wore bare midriffs and too-tight jeans, and the boys were dressed like an NBA All-Star team, laughing as they tested their newly deepened voices. The kids walked with the same carefree meander I remember from that age; nowhere to go and nothing to do, enjoying their last stop before adulthood. A strategically timed ice cream truck appeared around the corner, tinkling atonal music as it crawled with the promise of sweet and cold on a hot after-noon. *How can I find this for Chela somewhere?*

It was twenty to three. After looking around to make sure I wasn't being watched, I reached under my seat for Glaze's Smith & Wesson. As I grabbed the butt of the gun, my fingertips pulsed. Another look around, and I slipped the gun into the front of my pants, where the cold metal sank into my stomach. It was bulky, so I had worn a loose-fitting shirt to keep the weapon out of sight. The Beemer's AC was blowing lukecool air on me, but now I was sweating.

Movement in my rearview mirror caught my eye. I tensed until I saw three high school boys rounding the corner behind me, hunched over what looked like a box of CDs. The tallest of them whooped, excited by what he found.

I glanced away from them, back across the street toward the apartment building to see if anyone else had driven up while I wasn't looking.

The rap on my driver's-side window almost made me jump out of my skin.

My hand made it to the gun in my pants, grasping tight, even before my head fully turned. When I looked up, I saw one of the high school kids standing over me, his free hand outstretched to say *What's up?* In his other, he held the box of CDs.

It was Devon Biggs.

POW.

I heard a gunshot so loud that I didn't realize it was only in my imagination. When I saw the face at my window, I expected to die with the last flash of knowledge that Tyra and Devon Biggs had set me up somehow.

But I blinked, and the sound faded. Just impatient knocking on my win-dow. "Hey, man—you deaf?" he said. "What the hell are you doing here?'"

He didn't look any happier to see me than I was to see him.

FOURTEEN

IN A WHITE NIKE BASEBALL CAP, low-hanging baggy jeans, and Lakers jersey, Devon Biggs blended with the kids in a way that seemed deliberate, and my hand hugged the butt of the gun beneath my shirt. I wasn't ready to let go, but I wasn't ready to pull it out either. I didn't move, except to roll my window down. Slowly.

The boys Biggs was walking with loped on without him, calling out *Thanks, D* over their shoulders. He waved back to the kids, but Biggs's eyes didn't leave me.

"Tyra asked me to meet her here," I said.

He cocked his head, skeptical. "Three o'clock?" he said.

I nodded. Tyra had called *both* of us to meet her?

Biggs's stance was cautious as he checked my face for lies. Then he cursed and threw the box of CDs to the ground. "That bitch is always playing games. She begged me to come over here and meet her, talking about how much she misses Reenie, so let's walk through the old building. Blah, blah, blah. Three o'clock, she says. I should have known she was up to some shit. And I brought her a gift!"

I peered inside the box and noticed Serena's face on a stack of CD covers. I didn't recognize the photo or the title, *Songs from the Chariot,* so it wasn't out yet. The black-and-white photo was a striking shot of Serena's profile at a close angle, styled after the Egyptian Queen Nefertiti; much more artistic and self-reflective than her other CDs. Once Serena became a film star, she only had to record music she cared about, so she hadn't released a CD in at least three years. "That new?" I said.

"It was supposed to drop next month, but the label's rushing it. Funeral's not till tomorrow, and the CDs are here today." Biggs said it with both resentment and humor, almost chuckling. "White boys don't waste time when it comes to printin' green."

After glancing around the street again—and I studied the half-dozen strolling kids more closely this time—I finally decided it was safe to get out of my car. Biggs noticed the movement of my right hand, the straightening of my shirt.

"You strapped?" he said.

I didn't answer, but I didn't deny it. Let him be cautious.

"Now I wish I was," Biggs said. "I left my piece at home."

Neither one of us trusted Tyra, or so it appeared. We didn't trust each other, either. Biggs's eyes flinched as he glanced down toward my belt.

"Afraid I'm going to shoot you?"

"I wasn't, but now that you mention it, maybe I've got you all wrong."

"If you mean that you thought I was the kind of brother who rolls over while he gets fucked," I said, "then, yeah—you've got me all wrong." This was my first opportunity to talk to Biggs outside his powerful domain, and since he knew I was armed, he might treat me with some respect for a change.

Fear flitted in his eyes. "Who said you're getting fucked?"

"What did you tell Lieutenant Nelson about me?"

"I didn't tell Nelson shit about you, but he won't let you go. My assistant says I got another message from him right after I left today. Questions about Tennyson Hardwick. But I took off early to see Tyra, so fuck him." He was already playing it as if we were old friends who had each other's backs.

Maybe Devon Biggs was an actor, too. Maybe he was a good one.

"Jenk got killed," I said.

Biggs only blinked, nodding. No news to him. "Yeah. That's some sad shit. I guess the pushers and hos got tired of getting ripped off. Some people ain't meant to be cops." He tugged on his cap's brim, cutting the sun from his eyes.

"Nelson thinks I did it."

Biggs stared at me, waiting for a punchline. He laughed. "*You?* Yeah, when I piss gasoline. What does Jenk have to do with you?"

"Nothing," I said. "But LAPD politics have plenty to do with me."

Biggs turned away from me, suddenly looking down the street, as if he'd heard a dog whistle. "Shit."

My hand crept toward my gun. "What?" *Here it comes,* I thought. Somebody was about to come out blasting, conveniently giving Biggs enough time to duck.

"My mama's calling me," Biggs said.

"What?" I thought I'd heard him wrong.

He gestured his thumb down the street, toward the homes I had cruised by when I first arrived. A block and a half from us, the woman who had watched me drive past was on her feet, waving a towel from the sidewalk. I finally heard a thin voice in the wind: *"Deeeeevvvvvvvv-onnnnn!"*

Devon waved back. "Figures she'd be out in the yard," he said through the gritted teeth of his phony smile. "Shit. I was gonna do a quick dodge and dash after I saw Tyra. That's why I parked around the corner. But I guess she's seen me now. I gotta go run over there real fast."

I looked at my watch. Twelve minutes. "We need to talk before Tyra gets here."

"Come on and walk with me. But you can't go near my mama with a gun."

I shrugged. *Yeah, right.* "I won't tell if you won't."

"I'm serious, man." Biggs sounded nervous, almost petulant. Just like me in my father's presence, he was already regressing.

"Don't worry, I won't get you in trouble with your mom. Let's walk."

I began ambling toward the house down the street, my eyes jumping to anything that moved. Grudgingly, Biggs jogged to catch up with me. "This shit right here is messed up," he said. "You and Tyra can both fuck off."

"You kiss your mother with that mouth?"

"I've never needed to roll with a bodyguard, but I'm gonna hook myself up after today. I don't know you, man. This is definitely messed up."

"I happen to be a bodyguard," I said. "So unless you're trying to play me, you just lucked out."

"A bodyguard?" He scanned me, seemed to notice the thick upper arms, flat chest, and narrow waist for the first time. "No shit. I thought you were just Reenie's dick for cash."

I squeezed back my anger, and a pinch of pain. My eyes were on autopilot, sweeping from side to side, watching everything. Two male mongrels chased a female dog in heat, her teats still flopping from her last litter. Except for the four kids still in sight, the street was empty. The ice cream truck was gone. A fading Pinto sped by, but the gray-haired driver never slowed. The bumper sticker warned me to ACCEPT JESUS.

"Who do you think killed Jenk?" I said.

"How much time you got? Could be anybody."

"Like?"

"Any of the dealers he was shaking down. Somebody he ripped off in a deal. Gang turf shit. Hell, knowing Jenk, he could've pissed off somebody at a club feeling up the wrong hoochie. Glaze could've done it, trying to clean up his trail."

I'd thought of that, too. M.C. Glazer had plenty more guns at his disposal. And so did other LAPD officers, rogue or otherwise, who considered Jenk a liability.

We walked slowly alongside a five-foot wall of blooming hibiscus hedges that shielded a neighbor's house from the street. My eyes never left the hedges; they were a perfect hiding place. A Chihuahua yapped at us from the window of the cream-colored bungalow. My shoulders flexed, hard.

"Could it be retaliation for Serena?" I said, looking at Biggs sidelong so he wouldn't miss my point. It was hard to imagine someone as nervous as Biggs taking down Jenk, but he could have hired it out. Tyra was Serena's only family, so who would want retaliation more than Biggs?

But he only shrugged. "You mean me? If I was gonna kill Jenk, it would've been after Shareef died—just in *case*," he said, his voice fracturing. "But as much as I loved Reenie, I'm not crazy enough to jack a cop. Casanegra doesn't have bangers on the payroll like Glaze. Nobody's killing cops in Reenie's name . . . unless it was you."

I ignored his probing. "Why did you think he killed Shareef?"

Biggs didn't answer right away, glancing toward his house ahead. Biggs's mother's house was twenty yards from us, almost within earshot, so he lowered his voice.

"Glaze hated Shareef 'cuz of the shit Shareef said on his CDs, trying to be gangsta. I told him it was playing with fire, but Shareef was going after those sales. If Glaze wanted Shareef gone, Jenk would've had a price—fuck how long we knew each other. Even when we invited that brother to parties, we felt like we had to look over our shoulders 'cuz you never knew who Jenk was working for. Jenk would know how to do a job fast, how to dispose of the body, how to make the gun disappear. A professional. And it had to be somebody Shareef knew."

"Why?"

"Shareef wasn't a banger, but he belonged to the Beverly Hills Gun Club, man. That shit might sound funny, but the brother could *shoot*. Nobody was gonna cap him with his own piece unless they got close. *Real* close."

"Was Jenk at the party at Shareef's house the night he died?"

"I was eight time zones east, man, so I didn't see shit," Biggs said. "But that don't mean he wasn't there."

Biggs's face suddenly transformed in his mother's shadow. A boyish grin wiped away our conversation, and I understood how I hadn't recognized him at first glance. His cheeks dimpled, his teeth radiating in the sun. He wrapped his arms around the woman and swung her from side to side, rocking with her.

"Mama . . . hey," he said gently, burying his face against her neck. He kissed her and let go, clasping her hand. Watching them, I felt the sting of envy I always feel when I see people with their mothers, starting in kindergarten.

Dorothea Walton Biggs was a fit, coffee-skinned woman smartly dressed in a skirt and blouse from a job behind a desk—except that she wore faded slippers on her stocking feet. Her hair was dyed black to cover the gray, but her skin was so vibrant that she didn't even look fifty-five.

"You look like Ole Miz Susie out here in your house shoes, Mama," Biggs teased.

"I couldn't keep looking at those weeds," she said. "What were you doing?"

"Business. But we were just on our way over," Biggs said, a glib liar. "This is a buddy of mine, Tennyson Hardwick. A friend of Reenie's."

"Oh!" That credential brought a sad smile to her face. She reached over to hug me, and I'd barely shifted away my gun side before she squeezed me tight. "You must be hurting." *You must be hurting, too,* she meant. Our grief made me family.

"Yes, ma'am," I said, and hugged her back. My chin rested naturally on her shoulder, and I smelled talcum powder at the nape of her neck. Hers was a mother's hug, tight and warm, without expectation. From the time I was thirteen, women old enough to be my mother rarely hugged me maternally. It was a nice change.

"I saw you drive by before. I'm sorry if I gave you the evil eye, sugar," she said. "I didn't know if you were a reporter or what. They've been a nuisance. But this was Reenie's old street, so they want their footage, or B-roll, or whatever they call it."

"I wish you would move on out of here," Biggs said. "I got you that house—"

"Just stop it, Dev," she said. "*This* is my house."

Biggs sighed, irritation pressed between his lips. I tried to imagine being a multimillionaire trying to convince his mother to move into a bigger house in a more scenic neighborhood. I drew a blank. Devon Biggs and I had very different problems.

Biggs opened his box and showed his mother one of Serena's CDs. She examined the photo of Serena with a heartsick smile, tracing her finger lightly across the jewel case. Then her smile fell, and tears flooded her eyes. She gave the CD back to Biggs and patted his hand. *Not now.*

She looked up at me, as if her tears needed defending. "She used to come over here after school. Her and Shareef. I'm having hard talks with God over this one. I don't understand it. What's wrong with this music? Why is it killing our children?"

"I don't know, ma'am," I said. "I wish I did."

"Mama . . ." Biggs said impatiently, talking to her like a remedial schoolteacher. "Music doesn't kill people."

"This music does," she said. "The Temptations never shot at the Four Tops."

I chuckled despite myself.

"True, Mama," Devon said, smiling a little. "True."

Dorothea Biggs walked toward the front porch past a shiny, cream-colored Audi in her driveway that I guessed was a gift from her son. She waited for us to follow.

Devon hesitated, looked at his watch. He waved me in, and together we climbed the porch steps to Devon Biggs's childhood home. A girl's loud laughter from down the street reminded me that if I had walked through these doors twenty years sooner, I might have bumped into Serena.

People who visit my house don't learn much about me, even after thorough searching. I had noticed the same detachment at Serena's house, her absence in Casanegra's décor. Tyra's place, too. We lived as if we didn't expect to stay anywhere long, were on our way somewhere else. But Dorothea Biggs lived on her walls, plain as day. Her home was her family's shrine.

The walls were so crammed with photographs, certificates, and framed newspaper stories that there was hardly space between them to show the stained wood planks. While Devon and his mother spoke in low tones about Serena's funeral, I looked around.

The living room was stuffed without looking cluttered. A regal chesterfield with African mudcloth-styled upholstery was draped with a rug picturing the solemn faces of Martin Luther King, Jr., John F. Kennedy, and Robert Kennedy side by side. That was the sofa for show; a plainer beige couch sat in a corner of the living room near a small television set mounted alongside rows of hardcover novels in an entertainment center. The King James Bible was most prominent on the shelves, but I scanned the other titles: *Encyclopedia Africana. Middle Passage* by Charles Johnson. Alex Haley's *Roots.*

Against the wall, a black-and-white stereo console stretched at least four feet across, a relic from the seventies. Remarkably, an eight-track was playing softly from the stereo's mouth. Al Green's "Let's Stay Together." I noticed a stack of eight-tracks and LPs: Aretha Franklin. Mississippi Mass Choir. Roberta Flack. This stereo had been here back in Serena's day, probably playing the same songs.

My impression of a cultured, education-oriented family was confirmed by the certificates bearing various Biggs names on the wall: Dorothea's Bachelor of Science degree in sociology from Pepperdine. Devon Biggs's law degree from UCLA. Even Devon's high school diploma from Dorsey High was framed on the wall. A business license for Legacy Insurance.

Photographs filled another wall, leading toward the hallway. The first photo I noticed was almost too high to be in my line of sight, but I couldn't miss Serena's face. Dressed in a halter top and shorts, her hair was pulled into Afro-puffs, sitting between Devon and Shareef on the house's front porch. All three of them lifted Popsicles to the camera in a toast.

I peered closely, urging the photo to come to life and talk to me. The porch outside was identical, down to the white wicker rocking chair, as though I might open the door and find them all still waiting.

In the photo, Serena, Devon, and Shareef were about thirteen or fourteen—after the trouble started in Serena's house. The photo in Devon's office with her old Impala was from earlier days; unless it was my imagination, I could see an unspoken life in Serena's eyes as she grinned for the camera. Maybe it was because I knew too much about how they spent their time after school, but

Serena's lips were curled as if she had a grand, ugly secret. Her eyes weren't smiling nearly as much as the rest of her face. Devon's picture had captured the three of them at play, but in this one, they had grown up, only playing a child-like role.

"Am I riding with you to West Angeles, then?" Devon's mother asked Biggs.

"Of course! I'm swinging by to get you. But I have to come by ten, 'cuz that church is gonna be a madhouse. I just heard from Will and Jada. Stevie. Nick Cage," Devon said, sounding distracted while he messaged someone on his Blackberry.

"Is there room for one more at the church?" I said, trying to sound casual.

Biggs nearly glared at me, since his mother's back was turned, but he caught himself and faked a pleasant expression. "It's pretty tight, man. Remember, I told you I was working on it . . ." In other words, *fuck off.*

"Well, that hardly seems right, Devon," his mother said, giving her son a withering look. "He can't get a seat to his own friend's funeral? Half those people you mentioned hardly knew her."

"He'll handle it, Mrs. Biggs," I said. "Besides, I'm saying good-bye to Serena in my own private way." *I'm going to find out who killed her—the kind of tribute that actually means a damn.*

Biggs tugged on his mother's arm, eager to change the subject: "What's up in the kitchen? I thought you already had somebody look at that microwave . . ."

His tactic worked. While his mother began a litany of complaints against the company he had contracted to fix her household appliances, I studied a large Sears-style family portrait taken when Devon Biggs was eight or nine, with only a missing front tooth to mar his angel's face. Dorothea Biggs had been maybe fifteen pounds heavier, but had a professional makeup job that made her look like a model. On the other side of Devon sat a light-skinned black man in a United States Navy dress uniform. The Eagle and two stripes told me he was a petty officer first class. Devon's father was slightly built and smooth-faced, like his son, with large, kind eyes. They were a striking family.

If Devon Biggs had grown up with both parents in the house, he was one of the few.

But I felt a sense that Biggs's father wasn't around anymore, and I was right: Beneath the portrait sat a small table that looked like a smaller shrine: a framed wedding photo taken on a beach when Dorothea and her lanky groom were still teenagers, and a funeral program dated August 12, 1987.

Devon Biggs's father had died when Devon was about fifteen. *Ouch.*

"Wallace would've been fifty-five last Saturday," Devon's mother said, noticing my attention. "So this has been a hell of a week. He retired from the navy, then we started Legacy Insurance with our savings. Now Legacy's been in the neighborhood twenty years." She was almost talking to herself, amazed at how time had escaped her. Suddenly, she turned to Devon. "What have you heard about Robbie?"

"Nothing, Mama," Devon said. "Just what's on the news. Nobody knows."

Dorothea Biggs shook her head viciously, and her face clouded with rage. "Wallace's birthday, and then Serena and Robbie in the same week. They say the Lord won't put more on you than you can bear, but this is a test."

Robbie. Robert Jenkins.

"You knew Detective Jenkins?" I said to Mrs. Biggs.

"Goodness, yes. He was one of our regulars. Those kids loved Wallace, you see. Robbie never knew his father, and neither did Shareef or Serena, so Wallace was the neighborhood stand-in. 'Keep the kids busy, keep the gangs away,' that's what he'd say. So he'd fire up the grill, and the boys played pickup on the street while I braided Serena's hair on the front porch. And Shareef always did a talent show right out in the yard."

"With that little cheap-ass microphone—remember, Mama?" Biggs said, smiling.

"Oh, it was cheap, all right. You could hear him better without it. We all knew he had talent. Now, Serena . . ." She sighed.

"What?" I said.

"I worried about her. So withdrawn, she would hardly open her mouth. It's hard to believe she ended up such a public person. She jumped at her own shadow."

"It wasn't like that, Mama," Biggs said. "But see, you're right: Serena owed Shareef everything. He really made her what she was."

"Well, you, too," Mrs. Biggs said in a way that sounded almost obligatory.

"Were Shareef and Serena dating?" I said.

The question surprised her, as if I should have known better than to ask. "Of course not. The three of them were like cousins. Siblings. Wallace and I wanted to move her in with us, when her mother was struggling to keep the lights on. I even asked Serena's mother once, but she got insulted." Dorothea Biggs sighed. "It was plain she couldn't take care of those girls by herself. Children are always hard. There wouldn't have been any shame in letting Serena live with us for a time."

Dorothea Biggs's voice wavered. Her moist eyes said she was convinced that if she had only broached it the right way—or if Serena's mother had been more reasonable—that shy, pretty girl wouldn't have died. Maybe that was true and maybe it wasn't, but if Devon's mother knew more about her son's enterprise with Serena, I was sure she would relinquish one painful regret and replace it with one that might hurt even more.

"The Three Musketeers. That's what we used to say," Devon said, flicking a tear from his eye. "But you can't change that, Mama. Come on and show me what's up in the kitchen. We've got a meeting in five minutes."

"Well, Dev, if you're busy, then I'll call back and—"

"No way. You're my mama, and your things should work right." Biggs probably was more concerned about his name's weight than his mother's comfort, but she gave him such a grateful smile that it didn't bother me.

Because no one asked me not to, I strolled a few paces behind them in the narrow hall to try to hear more of their conversation and check out the house. The scent of last night's dinner still clung to the walls; roasted chicken and cornbread. My mouth watered. I wished Tyra had asked us to meet her closer to dinnertime.

The kitchen was large enough for a table and four chairs, with a matching sea green-colored gas stove and refrigerator. Dorothea Biggs loved strawberries, because strawberries covered the wallpaper, refrigerator magnets, and neatly folded dish towels. Only the crisply tied white lace curtains over the large window were free of strawberries. While Devon and his mother fussed over the microwave, I pulled the curtains aside and took a quick peek into the backyard.

What I saw made my blood crawl: A large wooden shed, painted barnyard red with white trim, sat against the back fence, ringed by blooming rosebushes. Was this the shed where Serena, Devon, and Shareef used to sneak her customers for ten-dollar sessions while his parents were at work? The thought put a bad taste in my mouth.

Devon caught me looking outside, and his face snapped to rigidity. "Hey, man, wait in the living room. I'll just be a minute."

Dorothea Biggs took my hand, ready to usher me away. Her quick appearance beside me at the window made me wonder if she knew something about the shed, too. Her eyes avoided mine. "Devon doesn't like people watching him try to be a handyman," she said. "It embarrasses him."

"Everybody's entitled to their secrets," I said, giving Devon a long look as I allowed his mother to lead me back into the hallway. His eyes sparked at me.

Dorothea Biggs walked at a deliberately slow pace, and I matched her halting steps. I was about to ask her if she was feeling well, but her face told me she was trying to work out her thoughts, so I stayed quiet. Once we were back in the living room, she led me to the photograph of Serena I'd been admiring on the wall.

"So pretty," she said sadly. "And sweet as she could be. If she was walking over to the Handi Mart, she'd come knock on the door and ask what she could bring me. Every time, I mean. And it really was such a help. Serena was the way I always pictured a daughter might be, if I'd ever had a girl." Devon's mother had yet to mention Tyra, so her affection apparently didn't extend to Serena's half-sister. I wasn't surprised.

I wished I had more time to talk to her. Devon might not let me near her again.

"You'd never know all she was going through from the way she's smiling," I said.

Devon's mother searched my face, as if to ask *How much do you know?* Then she looked away from me again, her eyes back on the photograph. "Lord, that's the truth." She breathed in a long, shuddering inhalation and exhaled, shaking her head. Weary. It reminded me of the way my father had sounded in his sickbed.

"I wanted to come to this street and walk in Serena's shoes for a while," I said. "All I keep wondering is, 'Where did it go wrong? How could it have been different?'"

I felt Devon's mother stiffen against me. I heard moisture on her lips as they opened. "Tell you the truth, sugar, I was right here and I don't know myself. Serena's family was a mess before I met her. But I will say this . . . Do you have children?"

"No, ma'am," I said. "Not yet."

"Well, when you do, just remember a lesson: Wallace and I both grew up without anything, so we thought a nice house and nice clothes and a good education would be enough for Dev. But it's not. We were working ten-, twelve-hour days trying to keep that insurance business going. But maybe we should have let it go, because when you have kids, you have to *be there*. You have to watch them. Do you understand?"

My heart pounded. Maybe she and her husband had heard more than I'd thought. Her words made me think of Chela. Was she still at Eso Won, or had she called herself a cab as soon as I was out of sight? "Yes, ma'am, I hear you," I said.

Dorothea Biggs went on quickly, unburdening herself. "Pull them apart, they were ordinary kids. But together?" She shook her head to let go of the thought. When she went on, she sounded energized. "Shareef just *knew* he was going to be somebody—so funny and smart and fearless, really. Devon lit up like a bulb around Shareef, and their friendship pushed Dev to try to be somebody, too. All his life we'd told him about going to college, but he didn't show a flea's speck of interest until Shareef told him to go learn about business so they could work together."

"Really?"

"Oh, yes. Shareef made Dev aspire to higher heights. And Serena, too, of course." Her face soured. "But it was different with Serena. With her, it was more like she thought Shareef *was* her Way and Light. If you ever asked her about the future, all she said was Shareef this and Shareef that. Not a boyfriend-girlfriend thing like you were saying, but she just followed him, followed him, *followed* him.

"I was so glad when she broke out on her own. You just heard Devon even now talking about how much Serena owed to Shareef. That may be true, but he owed her, too. Those boys loved Serena—they really did—but I never thought they gave her proper credit. Young people are selfish by nature. You never see everything all at once. Sometimes it takes a long time. A different perspective."

"Yes, ma'am?" A subtle inflection to encourage her to keep talking. Gently.

Her voice took on a faraway quality again, as if she were speaking to herself. "If I'm honest, Robbie was the only one who treated her the way she deserved. Like a queen. It was all Robbie's idea, you know."

My heart thundered so loudly when she said *Robbie*, I almost missed everything she said afterward. "What was his idea?" My voice was hoarse.

"To record her own CD. To become Afrodite. He was always pushing her for that, even in high school. Serena could rap *and* sing, but she was too shy in front of people. Robbie always said she should step more out front. I wish she had stayed with him, but they only dated a few months in high school. Robbie would have kept Serena out of a lot of trouble she didn't need to be carrying. And now look—they're both dead only a few days apart. Like the Lord planned to bring them home together."

My mind was doing cartwheels. Jenk had been much more important in Serena's life than I thought. "Did they keep in touch?" I asked.

"Here and there. They both stopped by the house to see me after Shareef's funeral. The girl was so distraught, you would have thought she just buried the rest of her own life over at Forest Lawn. She *worshiped* Shareef. And like always, Robbie was here holding her hand, cheering her up. I asked Serena if she was back with Robbie . . . but she said they were just friends—"

"Robbie?" Devon said, cutting her off from where he was eavesdropping in the hallway. "Mama, how many times I gotta tell you he doesn't deserve that pedestal you're always trying to put him on? He wasn't the Robbie you used to know. Reenie was too polite to say it, but he turned cold-blooded, Mama. She was scared of him. Shareef wouldn't be dead now if not for Robbie. *Bet.*" His fists were clenched, and anger had flushed his face nearly crimson. "Don't be surprised if he killed Reenie, too."

"How can you say that?" his mother said, shaking her head and swatting at the air as if she had walked into a nest of flies. "He was a police detective, Devon. It makes you sound so spiteful and ugly when you say that."

Devon met my eyes—*Keep out of it*—so I knew my line of questioning was over. If Devon told his mother about my visit to Robbery-Homicide, she would be quick to blame me for Serena's death rather than her beloved "Robbie." Had Serena and Jenk loved each other once? Love can curdle into hate . . . but enough hate for him to kill her?

Devon hugged his mother. She almost wrenched herself away from him, but she relented, accepting his tight embrace. He kissed her cheek. "Mama . . . I wish I lived in your world. You only see what you want to see."

"I've seen plenty in this world, Dev. *Plenty.*" Then, almost despite herself, her voice broke. The sound was choked and heartbroken, laden with history. The horrible sound pricked my eyes, too.

I wanted to hear more about Serena and Jenk, but I recognized a private moment when I saw one. I excused myself and waited outside on the front porch.

The ghost of Serena sat beside me, offering me her Popsicle with a smile.

✦✦✦

"Can you believe that shit?" Biggs said as we left his yard and walked back toward the abandoned apartment building at a brisk pace, nearly a jog. It was five after three, so we were late. "I built a multi-million-dollar empire, and she's still talking about Lap Dog Jenk. To her, I'm not my daddy, that's all. Never wore a uniform."

Dorothea Biggs *was* right about one thing: Her son was self-absorbed. "Serena had a little something to do with Casanegra," I reminded him.

"I know that, fool. Reenie *was* Casanegra. Man, we were gonna storm Hollywood like the Marines at Normandy." His voice gave a tremor, and I wondered if he was sorrier to lose Serena or his helm at the Casanegra landing boat.

"Why doesn't your mom talk about Tyra?"

"Tyra pisses on everybody around her, and Mama knows that. People don't change. That's a fact."

"So why did you agree to meet her today?" I said. "You're a busy man."

"Yeah, that's a good damn question," Biggs said, gazing toward the shattered building waiting at other end of the block. "Maybe for Serena's sake. Tyra seemed all broken up, like she needed somebody to talk to. Reenie never gave up on her, so . . ." He shrugged. "It's funny about history. It cuts deep, like family. The good and the bad."

Under the circumstances, I figured I owed Biggs a more complete rundown of everything I'd learned about Tyra. While the Chihuahua yapped and I kept my eyes on those tall hedges, I told him how Tyra's alibi didn't hold up. And how Tyra had been sighted at the grocery store on Sunset, half a block from where Serena was found.

Biggs listened, bug-eyed, walking faster and faster. "You weren't straight with me about what you had on Tyra," he complained.

"We're even, since you forgot to mention how tight Jenk and Serena were. Is it true Jenk talked her into becoming Afrodite?"

"Jenk didn't talk her into shit. We all planned for Reenie to bust out. Jenk whispered a few things in her ear way back, but *Shareef* made Afrodite." Devon's mother had said Serena had worshiped Shareef, and I could see that worship shining from Devon's eyes, too. Shareef must have been highly charismatic at a young age.

A white van squealed around the corner from the street behind us, and I shifted 180 degrees, remembering my gun. ELDER SERVICES TRANSPORTATION was painted in script on the door of the van, which was empty except for a young female driver. It never slowed. We both watched the van until it was gone.

"You still want to meet Tyra?" I said.

"Hell, yes," Biggs said. "Maybe she wants to confess. I mean, Reenie was her *sister*—there's no coming back from that. That's Cain and Abel shit, Old Testament: *And now art thou cursed from the earth, which hath opened her mouth to receive thy brother's blood from thy hand.*" Biggs's face had gone flat while he recited the biblical passage, as if he was being washed in an emotionally cleansing pool. Then, his jaw sharpened with pained rage. "Crazy bitch."

"It's just a theory," I said. "Don't do anything stupid."

My car was still parked where I'd left it. I glanced through my windows at the front and back seats. No one hiding. I scanned the street for creeping cars. Clear.

"You really are a bodyguard, huh?" Biggs said. "How does that work? You go to school, or what?"

"There's training. Defensive driving, awareness, weapons skills . . ." I shrugged. "Most of us are former cops. I dropped out of the Academy, but . . . let's just say friends hooked me up after I dealt with a problem or two for them."

He would have known the names instantly, but keeping my mouth shut is one of the things I'm paid for. I didn't talk about that part of my life with strangers, but I didn't mind talking to Biggs.

"So you like know karate and shit?" He chopped the air with his hands.

"And shit."

"So . . . how does a brother with skills end up selling his ass? Enlighten me on that one."

"My only clients were women," I said, and immediately regretted falling for his goading. Why did he get under my skin so much? From the moment he'd first met me on Serena's arm, he looked at me as if he could see straight through to my core.

"Men, women, whatever. Selling ass is selling ass."

"I'd rather sell my ass than suck out somebody's soul for a free ride. Isn't that what the pimp game is all about? Your mom's shed is nice, by the way. You and Shareef had a tight little operation. Did you sneak in the johns through the back fence? Enlighten me on that one."

Devon winced, his eyes churning. *Bull's-eye.* "Fuck off, man," he said in a hollow voice. "We were kids who didn't know any better. And yeah, in case you're wondering, Tyra ran her big mouth, so my parents found out about the shed a week before my dad died in a crash on the 10—which is still the worst week of my life. So skills or not, you best not bring up this particular subject again." He was nearly whispering, his eyes straight ahead.

I let it go. At least Tyra had told me the truth about Serena's childhood. Maybe Tyra really did know something more about how and why Serena had died, especially if Tyra was connected to her sister's death.

We crossed the street to the ramshackle Baldwin Chateau Villas. The front curb was empty except for a fire hydrant. There was no sign of Tyra, and I laughed at myself for assuming she would show up on time—or at all. The building loomed in front of us, a forgotten dream full of trash and shadows. Beyond the gate, I saw an empty swimming pool and a vending machine tilted on its side, but nothing else.

"How long has this been like this?" I asked Biggs.

"Two, three years. My mother's worn out her phone calling to bitch about it. Developers couldn't get their act together. But don't think this was Club Med when Reenie lived here. Only time there was water in that pool was when it rained."

Beyond the crumbling walkway, the wrought-iron front gate was unchained, and the door hung open slightly in invitation. The gate was dull and rusty, but the chain was brand new, with a new Master padlock. I was almost sure it had been chained when I got here. Or could it have just *looked* chained from across the street?

"Is that usually locked?" I asked Biggs.

"Hadn't noticed. It's been a while," Biggs said. "Maybe she went in already."

"Where would she go?"

"Second floor. Apartment 12B. That's where they used to live."

My hindbrain's bullshit detector went on full alert, sirens wailing. If I was looking for places to ambush someone, Chateau Villas would have topped the list.

"Feel free to go check it out," I said with a sarcastic grin. "I'll wait here."

Biggs was gazing beyond the gate to the shambled, shadowed courtyard, littered with debris from a parade of uninvited visitors.

"I'm hanging here with you, man," Biggs said. "Your company ain't shit, but at least you're strapped." He cupped his hands to his mouth, shouting toward the courtyard: "Hey, Ty-RRRAAAAAAA." His voice echoed endlessly inside the building's shell.

Otherwise, silence.

Biggs got on his Blackberry, waiting a long time with it pressed to his ear. "Hey, Ty, we're here," he said, leaving her a message. "Where are you?"

It was twelve after three. We were late, so maybe she went inside. She could have thought Biggs would go to 12B. It was possible. She had told him she wanted to walk through the old building.

"Screw it," I said, against my better judgment. "Let's go in."

I hope several more lifetimes pass before I ignore my better judgment again.

FIFTEEN

SOMETIMES A PLACE LOOKS SO WRONG that it makes the fine hairs on the nape of your neck start dancing. That was how Serena's old apartment building looked as we forced open the gate's screaming hinge. Biggs walked so closely beside me, I had to nudge him back to leave half a foot between us. He was making me nervous, but I couldn't afford to think about Biggs; my eyes had too much work to do.

The building was a nightmare warren of places to hide—the drained swimming pool ahead, the toppled vending machine to my left, the stacks of crates everywhere, a Dumpster to my right, sheets of leaning cardboard. Not to mention at least three dozen apartments that lined the walls on two floors all around us, more than half of them missing their doors and some of them missing their walls altogether. From where we stood at the mouth of the courtyard, the building looked like a mouth full of broken teeth.

Forty yards separated us from the other end of the courtyard, where the gate was closed and chained. There might be only one way out—the front gate. The elevator to my right was useless with its doors propped open, stuck midway between floors.

The neglected swimming pool about fifteen yards inside the gate could have been a bomb crater. I reached the pool a few seconds before I smelled it, or I would have kept clear altogether. The pool was empty except for a large puddle of brown-black muck six feet down that smelled bad in so many ways that I couldn't catalogue all the odors. Human waste. Decomposing rats, maybe. You get the idea. We pinched our noses.

As we walked, we tried to keep our feet clear of the debris: food wrappers, a diaper soiled green, discarded condoms full of DNA, broken hypodermics, empty baggies that had once carried weed or cocaine rocks, toys broken beyond recognition, vomit. I didn't want any souvenirs from Baldwin Chateau Villas on the soles of my Bruno Maglis, but I stepped on a few unpleasant items because I couldn't keep my eyes down. It was better not to look anyway. Behind me, Biggs cursed to himself after stepping on something that crunched.

I held my finger to my lips: *Shhhhh.* I pointed up: *How do we get upstairs?*

He peeled off left and motioned for me to follow. I pulled out my gun, wondering why I hadn't thought of that sooner. By instinct, I tried to shadow him the way I would if he were a client, keeping my own body between Biggs and the overturned vending machine beneath the second-floor overhang. As we passed the machine, I was relieved to see only a pile of newspapers—a vagrant's bedding, maybe—but nothing else behind it.

A stairwell appeared, just out of sight from the entrance. Biggs began climbing the gum-blackened concrete steps, but I grabbed his shirt and pulled him back. I held up a finger: *Wait.* Then, I crept around to peek inside the darkened shaft beneath the stairwell. A movement and a flash of white.

I snapped my gun's nozzle up, ready to fire, but my brain stayed calm and told me it was only a small animal. When I blinked, I saw a dingy white alley cat scamper away. I thought I heard a scraping sound—a sound more like a sole on concrete, not a cat—but after twenty seconds, I didn't hear it again. I pointed the gun down, took one more glance around for movement, and motioned for Biggs to follow me up the stairs.

He did, smirking like he thought I was paranoid.

More trash on the steps, and an unmistakable cat piss smell.

Nearing the top landing, I held out my arm to keep Biggs back and scanned left and right. The apartment closest to the stairs was missing most of its front wall and part of its roof. Inside the darkened space I saw piles of concrete, debris, tarps, and more endless places to hide. If this was an ambush, we were screwed.

Biggs peered around, disoriented. "Damn," he said, stunned by the chaos.

So far, there was no movement except for the end of a tarp flapping from a wind tunnel inside the demolished apartment. I looked around twice more. Three times.

"Which way?" I said.

He pointed right. "The end. Corner unit."

"You hear anything you don't like, be ready to duck," I told him.

"You're a trip, man," Biggs said, chuckling. "Secret Service. Who knew?"

We walked as carefully as I knew how, never venturing too far from the concrete wall that stretched around the length of the building, overlooking the courtyard. Every open doorway and hole in a wall was a danger zone, so thirty yards felt like a mile. My armpits were sopping. From above, the pool looked like an open sore.

"This one," Biggs said.

Apartment 12B was the only one nearby that still had a door, and it was closed. I motioned for Biggs to step back and pressed my ear to the door. No sound or sign of movement. Two feet from the door, a picture window was still intact, so I crouched to take a look. The window was bare, without curtains. I was surprised to find a normal living room bathed in light from a dining area window at the other end of the room. The light-colored carpet was filthy. Lumber and debris were piled against the wall, but at least the walls were intact. This looked like a place someone could have lived.

"How big is it?" I asked Biggs. The softest whisper.

"Two bedrooms. This side." Biggs pointed away from the door and window to the other side. "She in there?"

"Maybe not."

I touched the doorknob and tested it, expecting it to be locked. The door clicked itself free and fell open so fast that the knob nearly got away from my hand. Inside, there was a tiny foyer with the same filthy shade of carpeting. Living room and kitchen right, bedrooms left. I mapped the apartment in my mind.

I ducked back out of the doorway, toward Biggs. "Tyra?" I called.

More silence. Either we had beaten Tyra, or she hadn't planned to come. It was possible she was waiting outside, but it felt more like a game.

I scouted the rooms with Biggs hanging behind me, checking the closets and hidden corners. The bathrooms and the kitchen were stripped, the fixtures exposed. But aside from peeling walls, ravaged carpeting, and an unidentifiable rankness always close to my nostrils, Serena's apartment had fared better than most.

"Man . . ." Biggs said, once we were in the foyer again.

"What?"

"I didn't know it would look the same like this. See this?" He pointed to a large hole in the foyer wall, the drywall flaking around it. "That's where their mama used to keep a big picture of Jesus." He looked awestruck.

"Which room was Serena's?"

Biggs led me to the bigger of the two shoeboxes at the end of a dark hall-way; Serena's mother sacrificed the larger bedroom so her daughters would have more space, but it was hard to imagine two twin beds fitting inside, never mind a desk. The window was large, though, overlooking rooftops from houses and duplexes on the next street.

Biggs opened the closet door and cackled. "Oh, shit," he said, grinning.

"What?"

"They've still got—"

But I cut Biggs off suddenly, raising my hand. It had been faint, but I'd heard something from outside. Downstairs. A high-pitched sound. The cat? I stood still and listened. Nothing.

I followed Biggs to the closet to see what had caught his eye. He was gaz-ing at an elaborate carving inside the closet door, painted over but so deeply grooved that I could still make it the large lettering: SHAREEF #1, it said.

Ice-water tickled my skin as the realization came: *Serena really lived here.*

"Sure seems like love," I said. "You sure they never hooked up?"

"You'll never understand it, man," Biggs said. "Shareef was the sun in her universe. He was God to her. You don't hook up with God."

Biggs would have punched me for what I was thinking: He could be talk-ing about himself as much as Serena. Shareef Pinkney had cast a spell on his two friends.

"I'm gonna send somebody here to get this door," Biggs said, stroking the splintered wood. "I'm gonna keep this to remember them."

Biggs should have been worrying about how *we* would be remembered.

No mistaking the noise I heard this time, because it was much closer—maybe a few feet outside the apartment door: Footsteps. Creeping, but *running*. Heavy. Male?

My finger snapped to my lips: *Shhhhh.*

Biggs went quiet and listened, too. I wondered if the front door was the only way out. No time. Too late. At the pace I'd heard, someone might come bursting into our closet-sized room in about twenty seconds. *Somebody's here,* I mouthed, moving toward the doorway for a better position. I motioned for Biggs to flank me, where we would be out of sight from the doorway.

Maybe Biggs panicked. Maybe he expected to run into Tyra. For whatever reason, Biggs ran straight past me to the open doorway. He was so quick, my fingers missed when I tried to snatch him back by the shirt. Biggs was only halfway out of the room when—*POWPOWPOW*—three quick explosions contorted him into a wild dance before he fell back against the wall, screaming.

My heartbeat thundered. My skin turned hot and taut, every cell in me ready to fight for my life. I could hear the gunman's heavy breathing, probably behind a mask. He was running toward me.

Your life doesn't always flash before your eyes right before you die. Sometimes there are no visions. No faces. No memories. No regrets. I know, because I should have died in Serena's bedroom that day.

I lunged into the hallway like a baseball player trying to steal third, angling my shoulder so I could hope for decent aim when I hit the carpet. The gunman wouldn't expect me to come at him from so low to the ground, which might give me a half-second's advantage. In gunplay, half a second is all you need.

Biggs's shrieks stabbed my eardrum as I landed nearly on top of him, my elbows locked. I squeezed the trigger twice at the blurry image running toward me in the hall.

The blur stopped running and tripped. *"Fuck!"* A man fell.

A gun flew free and hit the wall. A nine-millimeter. The Glock landed two feet from me on the floor, and I dived just as the gunman reached for it. One quick sweep of my arm was the difference between living and dying.

I stomped the gunman's ribs hard, hitting him with my heel. And again. He groaned behind his black ski mask, rolling over in a fetal position. I saw a singed hole in the middle of his chest, but Biggs wasn't the only one wearing Kevlar. The gunman was holding his lower abdomen, just below the vest. Blood spattered the carpet beneath him. That second wound could kill him, but not before I asked him some questions. I didn't want to take off his mask to see his face yet. I might have to shoot him again.

"You OK?" I asked Biggs. I didn't dare look behind me, on one knee as I cautiously jabbed at the gunman's legs and waist, searching for another weapon while I kept one eye on the foyer. The gunman made a move toward me, so I leaped back.

"H-he *shot* me!" Biggs gasped. He sounded as if he was going into shock.

The gunman rolled into the wall and wailed, agonized. Convinced he was unarmed and wasn't going anywhere, I backed up and knelt beside Biggs, stealing quick glances to see how badly he'd been hit.

Biggs was doing better than the gunman. Of the three shots fired, two had hit him in the vest and one had lodged into the meat of his upper right thigh, near the femoral artery. A little higher, and he would have been a soprano. He was bleeding, not spurting.

"Congratulations," I said. "He missed your balls."

Biggs blinked petrified tears from his eyes. "F-for real?"

I gave Biggs the Smith & Wesson, which he aimed toward the gunman with a shaky hand, his chest heaving as he breathed.

"Chill," I said to the cold rage in Biggs's eyes. "We need him. Cover the door."

It takes self-control not to kill someone who has just tried to kill you, if only out of fear. Once I was convinced Biggs wasn't going to blow his attacker away on principle, I checked the Glock's clip. He'd fired three times, so he still had fourteen shots left. The Smith & Wesson only had three.

"You still got your phone? Call 911," I told Biggs.

"You're in The Jungle, man. You can time 911 with a calendar. I know who to call," Biggs gasped, fumbling for the phone in his pocket. He moaned from a wave of pain, but he dialed.

Now, the gunman.

"Man, I'm dyin' . . ." the man whimpered as I walked cautiously toward him. From the puddle of blood on his clothes and the sharp smell in the hallway, I didn't think he was exaggerating.

"How many more?" I said. "Answer me, and you go to the ER."

"Two, two," he said. "Get me a *doctor*, man!"

I had to see his face. More than I wanted to know who had tried to kill me, I wanted to know who I had just shot. "Take off the mask. *Do it.*"

Behind me, Biggs was shouting excitedly on his phone, half in expletives.

The gunman groaned and yanked off his ski mask, leaving a smear of blood across his cheek. He was my complexion and square-jawed, about thirty, with three days' worth of facial hair. His hair was in cornrows. I didn't know him. I was glad he wasn't a kid. The teardrop-shaped prison tat on his cheek told me he was proud to be a killer.

"Where are the other two?" I said.

"Shit, I don't know. Trey was outside, was gonna lock the gate. Billy might be anywhere."

Suddenly, I realized what distant sound I'd heard while Biggs was talking to me in the bedroom: *the rusty gate being closed.* We were locked in the complex, and two more gunmen named Trey and Billy were hunting for us.

Biggs was right. We didn't have time for 911.

"Who hired you?" I asked the gunman.

"Who the fuck you *think*?" he said. "I ain't sayin' no names, so go on and shoot me. I'll be dead now or dead later."

"M.C. Glazer?" I said.

He wrenched his face away without answering—but of course it was Glazer. Like Lorenzo had told me, M.C. Glazer didn't believe in pressing charges. I humiliated Glaze—and he probably thought I'd killed his man, Jenk—so I'd won myself an execution. Tyra might not have even known why Glaze asked her to make the call. It was easy to understand why the rapper might want me dead, but why Devon Biggs?

"Devon, can you stand up?" I said.

"—and I mean *RIGHT FUCKING NOW,*" Biggs was saying on the phone, his eyes wild. He tried to stand, leaning against the wall with a bloody palmprint. He yelled out in pain.

"I know it hurts, man, but we gotta get out of sight," I said, rushing to support him. He hopped on one leg and yelled again, holding me as if he would fall five stories if I let him go. "Cops on the way?"

Biggs nodded, in too much agony for conversation. Not only was his leg injured, but two bullets had slammed into his chest at close range. The Kevlar had saved his life—it stops penetration—but the energy load is non-negotiable. Biggs might have broken ribs, and one of those ribs might have pierced his lung. Should I take Biggs back into Serena's bedroom to hide, maybe the closet?

Crash. A change of plans flew through the living room window.

A dull *BOOM* rattled the apartment, dwarfing the gunfire. I dropped Biggs to crouch and aim, expecting the team of shooters to appear. Instead, I smelled acrid smoke and sickly sweet gasoline. A blast of heat snaked its way from the living room.

Molotov cocktail, I realized. The hired killers were trying to draw us out, or burn us to death. Either way was probably fine with them.

Biggs panicked, firing twice at the empty foyer before I pinned his arm to the wall so he wouldn't shoot me by mistake. I thought my left eardrum had burst from the sound. The gunman was yelling, his face terrified, but all I heard was buzzing in my head.

"Is there another way out?" I shouted into Biggs's ear. Pale smoke had already crept to us in the back of the hall, with more on the way.

Biggs's eyes were blank, and he went limp. His phone was on the floor, and he nearly dropped his gun. "Wh-what?" he said. Biggs was fading, and I understood: We had walked into a war. Three more seconds, the smoke in the hall was as thick as fog.

The front door twenty feet ahead of me was still closed, reflecting shimmering patterns from flames in the living room. No one had stormed in to pick us off. Had they thrown the bomb and run?

I leaped over the writhing gunman. After plugging my nose and mouth with my forearm, I crouched and took a look around the corner at the living room. Heat baked my face. Orange-white flames gobbled at the carpeting and walls. The way the gas stuck to the walls in lumps told me it wasn't simple petrol: This was "foo-foo gas," homemade napalm. Gasoline and detergent. I had hoped there would be little to burn in an unfurnished room, but the pile of debris had provided plenty of food already, and the smoke needed even less. The roiling clouds were already so clotted that I couldn't see the kitchen, or even as far as the back wall.

I had to test the front door. I turned the knob.

Gunfire chopped a zig-zag of four holes through the wood. Bullets pinged in a chorus around me. I collapsed to the floor with a yell, ducking by pure instinct. Fear cramped my muscles, so I didn't know at first that I hadn't been hit. Four bullet holes in the foyer wall behind me were the testament to my luck.

I could forget about the front door.

Two more shots chipped away at whatever glass remained in the living room window, a reminder that the living room was a gauntlet, too. We were pinned. The wounded gunman was still yelling, begging his crew to let him out. He knew as well as I did that we were all about to be killed by bullets or the smoke.

I went back to Biggs, who was a blinking, wide-eyed mess. I shook his shoulders, hard. "*Is there another way out?*" I yelled again.

Biggs pointed to Serena's room, so I grabbed him and helped him hop inside. This room still had its door, which I closed and locked, although the lock was old and flimsy. The air in Serena's room was less smoky than the hall, so it felt a lot less like sudden death. I pulled off our shirts to stuff under the door and stave off the smoke.

I thanked God for the large window, which was already hanging halfway off its track and only needed a hard shove to fall out, shattering two stories below. Suddenly, we had ventilation; the smoke in Serena's room thinned. I peered outside, ready to duck, but I didn't see anyone. All that waited thirty feet below was broken glass, slabs of concrete, and an empty Dumpster. I could make it, but Devon sure as hell couldn't.

Please let there be a fire escape, I thought. But the only thing remotely like an escape route was a rusting storm pipe hugging the corner of the building from the rooftop, not quite at arm's reach. The pipe might have reached the ground floor once, but it was broken off four feet below Serena's window. Even if I wanted to take a chance on being ambushed once I got down, jumping from the pipe was the same as jumping out of the window. Not an option for Devon, and I couldn't leave a wounded man.

"What's the way out?" I asked Biggs.

Biggs was barely on his feet, leaning against the closet door. Blood from his gunshot had left an ominous stain on his pants; he needed a doctor, too. Biggs's lips moved, but the buzzing in my ears roared over it. Then I felt a *pop,* and suddenly I could hear again. "—climb down that pipe to get past her mama," Biggs was wheezing. "It's strong, and it's got grips all the way down. I did it when I was sixteen."

"The pipe's broken," I said.

"*FUCK!*" Biggs said. He dragged himself to the window, losing his balance. He collapsed against the window frame, gazed out at the storm pipe, and cursed again. I craned my ears for sirens, but there was a surreal silence in my head. All I could hear was my breathing. And my heart thumping.

"Where's the *cops?*" Biggs said. "I called ten minutes ago!"

"It just seems that way," I said, wiping sweat from my eyes. It felt like three minutes, but it might only be one. I was losing track of time.

In the hallway outside, the gunman was screaming and hacking in the smoke. I would have done more for him if I could have.

Biggs's eyes went blank again. "We're gonna' die here, man. *Right here.* Oh, God, please, not a fire . . . Not on my mama's street . . ."

While Biggs tried to negotiate his terms with God, I sifted through the options and picked one: Couldn't I use the pipe to climb *up* to the rooftop and find a way down from there? But I couldn't take Biggs with me. He was in no condition for climbing, and I would be lucky if the pipe would support me alone.

I put my hand on Biggs's shoulder, looked into his eyes, and told him my plan.

"Keep the gun. Hide in the closet. Close the door. Then . . ." I answered his anxious eyes with a shrug. "I'll come back for you." It sounded like a fairy tale.

Biggs blinked. He got it: His life depended on me, and my life was on shaky ground. If I hadn't been so scared myself, I would have felt sorry for him.

"Save my ass, Hardwick, and I'll pay you anything," Biggs said. He reached to shake on the deal, and I clasped his hand. He probably needed to touch someone.

"My weekly rate is three grand, plus hazard pay."

"Five bills," he said, so earnestly he might have been asking for my hand in marriage.

"That'll work." I wasn't going to throw my life away for Devon, but I would fight like hell to avoid facing Dorothea Biggs. I couldn't send people she'd never met to bring her the news that her only child was dead. If Devon died, I would have to tell her myself.

"You want the vest, Ten?" Biggs said suddenly. The offer surprised us both.

I thought about it. Shook my head. "Just weight. You keep it, D." Shit, we were Ten and D now. Just two old friends at a barbecue.

He drew in a labored breath. "Get your ass back here quick."

Biggs suddenly clung to my hand. Tears crept from his eyes as he spoke between hitching breaths. "No matter what you think . . . all I wanted was the best for Reenie. Shareef and me both . . . would have done anything for her. All I *ever* wanted . . . was to take care of her." His eyes were desperate to be understood. Forgiven.

"Like you said, man, you were kids," I said.

I hooked my arms beneath Biggs's armpits and dragged him to the closet. He crawled inside, where Serena's childhood tribute to Shareef would keep him company. I hoped Biggs was a praying man, because I wasn't sure God would recognize my voice.

"Keep out of sight," I told Biggs. "You've got one shot now. Don't waste it."

"I'm saving one for sure," Biggs said, gulping at the air. He shivered in the corner, shirtless and bleeding. "I ain't dying in no fire."

Lucky for him, then. The smoke would get him first.

"It won't come to that," I said, even though it just might.

I closed the closet door, shutting Devon Biggs into the dark.

✦✦✦

A single step. That was all that stood between me and freedom.

When I balanced at the edge of the window frame, holding the wall for support, the storm pipe's first support brace was a three-foot reach to the corner of the building. That would be the strongest part, least likely to crumble under my hands and send me cartwheeling down to the alley below. I would have to jump off the window frame, or leave myself flailing. It was one long, hard step to freedom.

I kept my mind on the plan: Jump. Grab the pipe, hope that all that daily exercise had put enough juice in my biceps and fingers and lats. It wouldn't be a comfortable climb, but it was only about fifteen feet to the top, close enough to touch. I'd burned enough calories on my gym's climbing wall to know I could do it—but would the pipe hold?

My palms were wet, and I rubbed them on my pants. If I slipped, or if the pipe broke off, I wouldn't have another chance to get it right. I might be able to grab the window ledge on the way down, but there were no guarantees.

We might have to jump. We might not have a choice.

My mind tried to break it to me gently, but I pushed the thought away.

My heart jackhammered my ribs. With my gun in my jeans, I closed my eyes and prayed—to Dad, I think, or at least I saw Dad's face. I balanced myself on the window ledge, kept my eyes on the rung . . . and jumped.

My right hand caught pipe, and my left scrabbled for the support brace. For a second I had it, and my feet swung wide then set against the stucco wall. I was hanging like a monkey on a tree—then my grip slid. I lost skin on my right hand as the rusted pipe ripped at me, but my left hand held. Squeezed. Stopped the slide.

Breathing hard, I steadied myself and started to climb. The pipe shook and groaned. The world swayed beneath me.

If you fall, grab the window . . . If you miss the window, bend your damned knees, and get ready to hurt.

My face was pressed against the pipe, and the rusty smell pricked my nose. For what seemed like forever, I didn't move. I don't think I could have moved at gunpoint. I was sure the pipe would fall free. Then, quietly, a thought released my limbs: *You did it.*

My heartbeat slowed, but my breathing sped up. Now I was in a race.

The rest of the climb was like scaling a skinny, rectangular tree trunk. I dug my toes into the braces, kept my eyes on the edge of the roof, kept my belly tight. One pull, hand over hand, and a moment's rest. Hang by one hand and tensed toes as the other one reaches high, grasps, arms tense, pull again. The awkward angles never let me relax, and my left foot slipped on a brace once, but I don't think it took thirty seconds before I was hoisting myself onto the rooftop.

I'd made it out of Serena's apartment. Now I had to get back in.

I stood up on the flat gravel roof ringed with a foot-high cement barrier. The view of the homes and squat apartment buildings around me was dizzying. I still didn't hear any sirens, even with my recovering eardrum. In the smoggy horizon a couple of miles off, I saw a procession of five or six police cars with their flashers on, but traffic patterns told me it might take them four minutes to get here. And if the gates were locked, even longer. The smoke from Serena's living room was already a thick haze on the rooftop, floating from the other side. Not good news for Biggs.

Dorothea Biggs was a speck standing on the sidewalk in front of her yard, pointing a neighbor our way. Even if I'd planned to ditch Biggs and split, seeing his mother would have convinced me to go back for him.

I crouched and ran toward the smoke.

As soon as I had a birds' eye view of the courtyard, I saw a masked man running toward the stairs Biggs and I had climbed to Serena's floor, nearly tripping in his baggy pants. Trey or Billy? He would see me if he turned his head. He was too far for a clear shot, so I fell flat and crawled to the edge of the rooftop to wait him out behind the barrier. If he didn't know I was waiting for him, I might get a shot.

But who had thrown the bomb? Where was the other bastard?

The instant after I saw the man in the baggy pants raise a walkie-talkie to his lips, I heard loud feedback from below, right underneath me. A voice crackled on the radio: "We'll blast in and get the fuck out."

I wished to God he was on my side.

Baggy Pants reached Serena's floor, running toward me, and I tracked him with my Glock. I trusted my accuracy with a handgun up to fifteen yards, and he wasn't there yet. I couldn't afford to give away my position with wild shots. And he wouldn't stay in my range long once he got there; as soon as he made it to the corner, he'd be sheltered by the ledge. He would only be in my range for about five paces, when he reached the broken wall of the apartments near Serena's.

Even now, he was almost out of my sight, as if he knew I was waiting for him. Every few seconds, his white sneaker appeared from beneath the ledge's shadow, then gone. No target. He wasn't running close enough to the edge.

Shit. If I didn't get this guy, Biggs was dead.

Baggy Pants hit my range. The white sneaker landed, and this time I saw a flash of his jeans. But he was gone, and I missed the shot. *Shit, shit, shit.*

I shifted aim, anticipating, and suddenly his lower torso materialized in full view, almost running in slow motion. I squeezed the trigger twice, aiming for the biggest hunk of flesh I could find.

When I didn't hear a yell, I was afraid I'd missed. But after a last clumsy stride, the man fell over, long limbs tangling in his baggy pants. "I'm *hit!*"

I squeezed off two more, aiming higher, and I saw the back of his shirt stain crimson above his right shoulder. This time, his scream was strangled, wordless. He pulled himself out of sight, hiding in the ledge's shadows before I could shoot him again.

Random gunfire sprayed from beneath me, but the remaining gunman was only guessing my position. Then I heard him answer my prayer: "Fuck this! I'm gone."

I heard frantic footsteps as he ran *away* from where the other man lay, toward the western side of the building. The crew M.C. Glazer had hired wasn't sentimental, lucky for me. When the shit hit the fan, it was every man for himself.

I didn't hear the gunman inside Serena's apartment yelling anymore.

I didn't know if Baggy Pants still had his gun, or if he would get a bead on me as soon as I came down from the rooftop, but I had to take the chance. I saw what looked like a red fire ladder on the far western end of the rooftop, about twenty-five yards from me, so I decided not to risk a dead drop from the rooftop. I was sure I could swing myself onto the balcony with arm strength alone, but why take the chance?

The ladder was intact, and it was a quick descent. A flat queen-sized mattress met me when I touched solid ground; it was a rainbow of stains and smelled like it looked, but I was glad to see it. I propped it up and dragged it with me. The plumes of smoke from Serena's apartment told me I didn't have time for a more cautious approach.

I felt the heat before I got to the picture window that had been shot out, and the smoke brought tears to my eyes. What I saw inside stunned me: The living room's walls were charred black, and smoke choked the air. The biggest fireball was about eight yards inside, climbing the eastern wall.

Where was Baggy Pants?

I spotted him to about twenty yards from me, past the L-shaped corner. I saw his legs splayed out after he'd halfway dragged himself through the broken wall of an apartment. He was panting, so he wasn't dead, but he seemed to have more than me on his mind. I aimed at his head. "Hey, asshole!" My voice was deadly calm. "Look at me, or I will shoot you."

A pause, and then he dragged his body around until his strained, pain-widened eyes were locked with mine through his mask.

"Throw your gun over the edge," I said.

He didn't ask if I was bluffing. He didn't try to aim. The wounded man made a soft grunting sound and pushed his pistol across the walkway and under the rail. It fell, bounced, landed in the bottom of the pool.

"Stay," I said.

Holding the mattress in front of me, I held my breath and charged through the doorway into the burning living room. Heat blasted my fingers, which were curled around the mattress. The floor was as hot, and my shoes seemed to vanish. I hurried, taking the next step just as the pain spiked on the soles of my feet. Flames near the wall licked at my pants, and I scooted away, nearly losing balance. I got as close as I could as heat seared my face, and I flung my mattress toward the fire's heart. Sparks flew, stinging my eyes. Choking smoke invaded my nose. I coughed, and more smoke charged into my lungs, scorching my throat. Like trying to breathe tar.

Blinded, I tried to get outside to the air, and I backed into a broiling, sooty wall. The door was only two feet from me; the smell of clean air led me back out to the ledge.

Outside, I gasped, trying to make amends to my lungs.

Finally, I heard sirens. Across the courtyard, I saw three police officers shaking the front gate, realizing it was locked. They wouldn't get here soon enough.

My lungs still weren't speaking to me when I ran back inside. It didn't seem as hot; maybe the mattress *had* smothered some of the fire. The smoke in the hall was so thick now that I couldn't see. I stumbled over the fallen gunman, but I didn't stop to check his pulse. I ran to the end of the hall. Serena's room.

The door was locked, of course. I shook the wobbly knob. "Biggs? It's me!"

I didn't hear an answer, but it was hard to hear over my rasping breathing.

I rammed my shoulder and hip against the plywood. The wood splintered around the doorknob cracked, and the door opened. "Biggs!" I called again. The door caught against our bundled shirts halfway. I peered inside. Smoke was a white fog in here, too, but I was glad it wasn't worse. Biggs might not have been overcome yet.

I squeezed inside and knocked on the closet door. "Biggs! It's Ten!"

Did he shoot himself already?

I heard Biggs say something, but his voice was muffled.

When I opened the closet door, Biggs was stripped to his boxers. He'd taken off his jeans and balled them up to shield his nose and mouth from smoke. The bullet had left an ugly, bloody gash in his leg.

Biggs only stared at me wide-eyed at first, not moving. I don't think he could believe I had come back for him.

"Gotta go," I said, and grabbed him.

I used a fireman's carry: sat Biggs up, hooked my arms under his armpits, tucked my butt under to protect my back, then pulled him almost upright. Hoisted him across my shoulders then turned and plunged him into the furnace toward the front door. The living room was hotter already; it felt like hell's front porch. My lungs felt afire, too, but I forced myself to take one step, then another, holding my breath.

My thighs and calves were trembling by the time I deposited Biggs near the fire ladder twenty yards west of Serena's apartment. Downstairs, I saw a fire engine pull up to the curb. The police were just getting through the lock, and eight officers swarmed into the front gate.

Again, they wouldn't get here in time.

I was staggering when I went back into the apartment and checked the pulse of the first man I'd shot. My hand was unsteady at first from the adrenaline, but I concentrated and held my fingertips across his carotid. If there was a pulse, it was so weak that that it was hard to tell it from mine—but something *was there*. I grabbed his legs and pulled while the heat lashed against my back. The smoke tried to make me forget all about air.

Outside, I put my ear against his chest. The man was breathing. His heart was hanging on. I had given him more than he deserved, but I didn't do it for his sake; I just didn't look forward to being someone who had killed a man. My father had been proud to retire without that notation on his conscience, no matter how justified.

I dragged myself back over to Devon Biggs, who was sitting against the wall, hacking toward the ground. We both took grateful sips of air beside that fire ladder, watching the first cops climbing the stairs to the second floor. Biggs's hand rested on my shoulder in unspoken thanks.

I knew the cops had found Baggy Pants when shouts went up and they formed a half-circle, guns all aiming toward someone we couldn't see. It would still take them at least a minute or two to get to us, especially if Baggy Pants didn't know how to act.

I tossed my gun out several yards ahead of us. I held out my hand for Biggs's gun and tossed that, too. I wasn't about to go out like the brother on *Night of the Living Dead,* cut down by friendly fire after the battle had been won. Biggs and I both raised our hands above our heads, waiting for the police to rescue us.

Downstairs, more cops were coming through the gate. Maybe twenty.

"Who'd you call to get all these cops here so fast?" I wheezed.

Biggs dropped his head back against the wall and chuckled. "Arnold," he said. His voice was unrecognizable, but I suppose mine was, too.

"Who's Arnold?"

Biggs shook his head with a weary laugh. "*Ah*-nuld," he grinned.

"The governator?" I said.

Biggs just laughed louder, before he doubled over in a coughing fit. "Don't ask," he said, catching his breath. "You want a job, man? I need a bodyguard."

"Yeah, maybe." It might be nice to have a steady paycheck waiting when the madness ended.

The concrete beneath us shook from the approaching officers' running footsteps. That sound reminded me of what imminent death feels like: sudden, matter-of-fact, always around the corner. I might have been shot through the front door. I might have been shot instead of Biggs. I might have been suffocated, or burned to death.

I really was going to die, one day.

Up until then, I don't think I really believed it.

SIXTEEN

TRAFFIC WAS A NIGHTMARE, so it was seven by the time I made it back to Eso Won. Almost too late. Chela was walking up to a yellow cab parked outside the store when I honked. At first, she just glared and opened the cab door, ready to jump in.

When I screeched beside her, she saw my face and closed the cab door again.

"Sorry I'm late," I said.

"Oh, my *God*. What happened?"

"Someone just tried to kill me," I told Chela. "Let's get dinner."

I slipped the cabbie five dollars from the wad of cash Devon Biggs had insisted on shoving in my pocket. He'd had about five hundred dollars of loose change in his car, and he promised to give me my full week's fee at Serena's funeral. I didn't refuse the money, just as I didn't refuse the invitation to sit with his family at the church. I had to promise Dorothea Biggs after she painted my face in lipstick with grateful kisses. She might have said something about seeing me for Christmas and Kwanzaa, too.

I told Chela the story while I drove toward Bamboo Cuisine for Chinese takeout on the way home. At a stop light, I noticed myself in the rearview mirror for the first time: My face and chest were covered with sooty sweat, and my eyes were so red that I looked strung out. The car stank from the smoke on my skin and clothes. My left eardrum was still vibrating, and I would be tasting ash in my mouth for days.

"I told you Glaze would kill you." She might have been discussing last week's dinner menu. "You didn't listen."

Her casual tone irritated me. "Next time, maybe I will."

"But he's a jerk, anyway," she said quickly. It was the closest she had come to thanking me, and yet another layer of tension rolled off my back. I was glad I had gotten to Chela before she'd climbed into that cab.

"Do you think he'll try again?" she said.

"Not soon. Not if he's smart."

I might still have to answer for the illegal possession of M.C. Glazer's gun, but I hadn't been arrested because Biggs backed up my version of the attack. The gunman who threw the Molotov cocktail got away, apparently, and neither of us had gotten a look at him. But police arrested the two injured gunmen, whom they recognized as Bloods with long rap sheets. Antwan Evans, age thirty-six, was in critical condition after being shot in the abdomen and nearly succumbing to smoke inhalation; and Trey DuPree, age twenty-nine, was in stable condition after being shot in the buttocks and the shoulder. Neither of them had admitted they'd been hired by M.C. Glazer or anyone associated with Glaze, but one of them might talk.

Tyra, not surprisingly, was nowhere to be found. I hoped she would attend her sister's funeral tomorrow. Tyra and I had seriously unfinished business.

"Whoa!" Chela said, suddenly picking up the CD on my floor. "A new one by Afrodite? Is it okay if I put it on?"

"Yeah, go ahead." I had already forgotten that Devon gave me the CD. Somehow, my tired heart glowed. Maybe I would learn something from Serena's words from beyond the grave—and even if I didn't, it would be good to hear her voice.

As I'd expected, the new CD sounded different from her older music. Instead of rapping about her sexual exploits—or about men doing her wrong; most of whom, she had confided to me, were only imaginary—this CD sounded more like Lauryn Hill. In the first track, "The Island," Serena said she felt like she lived between worlds, quoting Tupac's lament that he lived on an island. Her voice was backed up by exotic worldbeat, reggae, and salsa riffs. Serena didn't rap at all on the second track, instead singing "My Funny Valentine" in an earthy tremolo that sounded so much like Billie Holiday that I got goosebumps. Impressive.

Chela pumped up the volume when the third track started, a mellow but steady beat with a bass drum, shakers, and record-scratching, sampling vocals from "Ooh Child" by the Five Stairsteps. I liked the sound. Serena's impassioned voice began rapping in a sing-song style that would have fit a poetry slam:

If a girl called Reenie could future-see,
The sight of my height would have traumatized me.
She went from ashy knees and plaited hair
To ten times over a millionaire.

La la-la-la la-la la laaaaa

You saw a goddess and showed her to me;
You said to call the deity "Afrodite."
And you kept my secret underground,
Even when I dumped your heart in the Lost and Found.

La la-la-la la-la la laaaaa

But blood in your eyes is reflecting at me
Like pools from the Dead Emcee Sea.
Who says forgive and forget are synonymous?
I'm taking twelve steps to Life Anonymous.

"What's that called?" I asked suddenly.

Chela studied the liner notes. "Just 'Life Anonymous.' "

My brain tried to snatch a morsel of insight, even as tired as I was. The lines about *blood in your eyes reflecting at me* and *the Dead Emcee Sea* definitely sounded like Serena was talking about Shareef's murder. Dorothea Biggs said Jenk was the one who suggested that Serena call herself Afrodite, and Jenk had definitely known her secret. Was that song her way of telling Jenk good-bye?

"I called that lady, by the way," Chela said suddenly. "That reporter?"

"April?" I said, surprised. Chela had waited fifteen minutes to bring it up. I glanced at her, but she was staring at Serena's photo on the CD.

"Yeah, I told her I didn't know where the hell you were, and she said I could hang out at the newspaper with her. She's working late."

"Is that where you were going in the cab?"

"Maybe. I dunno," Chela shrugged. "Is she your girl?"

This time, she was looking at me expectantly. The ring in her voice was part curiosity, part territoriality. I would be a fool not to realize Chela might have a crush on me. The only men in her life were sexual partners.

"She could be something like that," I said. *If we're still speaking.* "I'm not sure."

A small pout, and a pause. "And she doesn't care about us hanging out?"

"She knows I want to help you. She does, too."

"Don't act like I'm some orphan charity case," Chela said. "I have money."

Chela talked about having twenty thousand dollars, but I hadn't seen her spend a cent. She might not even have an ATM card. "Does Mother let you make withdrawals?"

"She gets me whatever I want. Gucci, Louis Vuitton, whatever."

Nope. Chela didn't have direct access to her own money. When I got the chance, I was going to have to talk to Mother about her business practices. Apparently, a lot of Mother's rules were different for Chela.

M.C. Glazer's voice suddenly growled from Chela's purse, rapping "Ain't This Where the Party At?" A ring tone from her cell phone.

"It's that April lady," Chela said, reading her phone's Caller ID.

Chela handed me the phone, so I stared at April's name while it rang. A few hours ago, I had leaped for my life from a window, and in some ways that hadn't felt much scarier. "Hey, April, it's Ten."

"Oh," April said. She didn't sound happy. "I thought . . ."

"I made it back. Thanks for looking out for Chela."

"I said I would. I keep my promises," April snapped. I hadn't made any promises to her I could break, not verbally—but in her mind, I must have.

"April . . . I'm sorry you're not happy with me," I said. "I'd like to start fixing that the first chance I get, if you'll let me. This has been a bad day: Devon Biggs and I were just ambushed when we went to Serena's old apartment to meet Tyra. Both of us could have been killed. We think Tyra set us up, but Glaze was probably behind it. You won't have any trouble finding the police report to verify my story."

"Oh, my—"

"I'll tell you more about it when I'm not so brain-dead. But I just wanted to say . . ." I sighed. I'd forgotten in midsentence. "Look, if you need to hear me say again that I didn't kill Serena or Detective Jenkins—I didn't. If you don't believe me, there's nothing I can do. And if you think I'm a killer, I'd rather we didn't talk anymore. You have to want to talk to *me*, not a source or a story. But if you are still talking to me . . . I'd like to ask you to be my escort tomorrow."

Beside me, Chela rolled her eyes. During the long silence, the phone hissed loudly enough that I was afraid we'd been disconnected. Finally, April said, "You're asking for a lot of trust, Tennyson."

"I guess I am. But I promise not to give you a reason to regret it."

More silence. Chela waved to me frantically when we passed Bamboo Cuisine on Ventura, and I scooted over a lane to make a U-turn.

"You want me to escort you where?"

"Serena's funeral at West Angeles Church."

"I have a press pass," she said. "I don't need an escort."

"But I do," I said softly. My voice shook. "I'd really . . . like you to be with me." I couldn't say what I was thinking: *I'm tired, April, and I don't think I can climb the church steps without you holding my hand . . .* I wasn't used to thoughts like that.

April exhaled, and I could almost see her cheeks dimple in a grin. "Okay, I'll meet you," she said. "But I'm writing about the funeral, so I'll be working."

"That's okay. I'll be working, too."

This time I felt better, not worse, when I hung up with April. After I'd ordered the takeout—lemon scallops for me, and sweet and sour pork for Chela—I asked Chela to put on track three from Serena's album while I drove the rest of the way home. The steady, soothing drumbeat started, and after the familiar trumpet peal, the Five Stairsteps promised that things were going to get easier. Things were going to get brighter.

"*If a girl called Reenie could future-see . . .*" Serena's husky voice began, still full of breath and life. "*. . . The sight of the height would have traumatized me . . .*"

Tomorrow, it was time to bury Serena.

Alice used to say that celebrities are our society's royals. Alice was so secretive about her illness that her death was hardly noticed—but Serena's funeral was fit for a queen. Traffic was closed as two jet-black majestic stallions pulled an antique glass carriage down Crenshaw while onlookers lined the street with signs and placards proclaiming their love for Afrodite. Inside the carriage, Serena's coffin gleamed in gold.

When the carriage pulled up in front of the West Angeles Church of God in Christ, five hundred people who couldn't get a seat were waiting outside. The pallbearers pulled the casket from its carriage, and flashbulbs glittered throughout the waiting crowd as if Serena were arriving at a movie premiere.

Devon Biggs was a symbolic pallbearer, limping with a wooden crutch as he walked with his free hand balancing part of the front of Serena's casket. His face was sweating from the effort already, but his teeth were gritted with determination. Devon glanced at me as he walked into the church with the casket. Yesterday's trauma haunted his eyes, just as it probably haunted mine.

I almost didn't recognize the picture of myself standing there in the church entryway: I had April on one side and Chela on the other. I was wearing a white linen suit; April nearly matched me in a cream-colored chiffon dress. Chela was a typical L.A. teenager in black leather jeans and an AFRODITE FOREVER T-shirt we bought from a vendor outside. Anyone would have thought we were a handsome family.

April held my hand and squeezed as the casket passed us.

Inside the church, a sea of spring hats turned to see the casket's arrival. The chapel could seat about two thousand, and it was full. The organist pounded out "Precious Lord, Take My Hand" underneath the swell of the mass choir dressed all in white. That was my father's favorite gospel song. After his heart attack, Dad casually told me from his hospital bed that he wanted it played at his funeral. At the time, all I could do was pretend I hadn't heard him.

I hate funerals.

We walked along the left side of the church so we could find our seats in the first row beside Dorothea Biggs. All the while, I searched for Tyra. No burgundy weave in sight. To get to Devon's mother, we had to excuse ourselves past Usher, Tyrese, Nicolas Cage, and Missy Elliott, who all nodded politely. There were so many celebrities crowding the front rows, I wondered if Dorothea Biggs was the closest family Serena had at her own funeral. Chela's face glowed brighter with every famous face. When we sat down, Chela nearly bounced in her seat while she snapped photos with her camera phone. I put a firm hand on her shoulder to remind her where she was, and why she was there.

When Dorothea Biggs saw me, she smiled through her black veil. "He has no business trying to carry that casket," she whispered while I hugged her. "The doctor said to stay off his feet, but he won't listen."

"He'll be all right, ma'am," I said.

Even while I embraced Devon's mother, my eyes were roaming the room for Tyra. It was hard to tell with all the hats, but I didn't see her.

The funeral was part concert, part remembrances. Beyoncé and Usher sang "His Eye Is on the Sparrow" with the mass choir and brought everyone to their feet, including me. A line of speakers followed; a record company executive, an actor, a singer. Show business friends, not real friends. They talked about Serena's humor, her determination, her drive. Devon Biggs didn't speak on the program, instead squirming in discomfort beside his mother while he whispered to his assistants to make sure the service stayed on schedule.

The speaker who moved me most—a national civil rights leader—admitted he had never met Serena Johnston. But he said he had flown from New York to attend her funeral because her death so filled him with sadness.

"A culture that eats its young is a culture that cannot survive," he said in a vibrato preacher's voice. "What has happened to our young people? What has happened to our music? We're so lucky nobody killed Paul Robeson and Billie Holiday. I praise God nobody gunned down Aretha, Diana, and Smokey. Stevie's still with us. Amen. Prince wasn't shot in a drive-by. We must, we must, we *must*, stop this violence in our music.

"As Robert Kennedy said after the assassination of Martin Luther King, Jr., only sixty days before another assassin's bullet would take him, too: 'No one, no matter where he lives or what he does, can be certain who next will suffer from some senseless act of bloodshed. And yet it goes on . . . and on . . . and on . . . in this country of ours. *Why?*' "

His question hung in the hushed church as he took his seat. I heard Chela sob.

Like most funerals, it was beautiful but excruciating. All I could think about was Tyra and what she might know. I needed to understand why Serena was in that casket. Like the man said—*Why?*

After the service, April kissed my cheek and excused herself to conduct interviews. I hated to let her go, and I watched her slender form slide past the mourners. We hadn't had a moment alone yet, so I knew I still owed her a conversation. Maybe I would invite her home with me for the night. Maybe I should have done that before.

Haltingly, a stocky white man in a gray pinstriped suit and an old-fashioned gold pocket watch made his way up to Devon Biggs. His graying red-brown hair was cut as short as a Marine's, with a build to match; the expensive suit looked like an ill-fitted costume on him. The man watched at a respectful distance while Biggs relied on his mother and his crutch to bring him to his feet.

"Mr. Biggs?" the man said. "Sorry to disturb you . . ."

"We're on the way to the cemetery," Biggs said, hardly looking at him.

The man produced an envelope and held it out to Biggs. He pursed his lips, sheepish. "I'm sorry this will seem crass, but Serena and I had some business related to her Stan Greene lawsuit. I thought it would be better if I saw you in person . . ."

The man won Biggs's undivided attention, and mine.

"What kind of business?" Biggs said.

The man lowered his voice, but I could still hear him over the church's din. He had a pronounced New Jersey accent. "I'm Jim Marino, an attorney with Marino, McGruder, & Stein. Serena retained me . . ."

"Retained you for what?" Biggs said. "I was Serena's lawyer."

The man paused. "Yes," he said. His voice seemed condescending. "But Serena and I conferred several times on the Greene case, and I've written you a letter to explain these expenses. She asked me not to bill Casanegra directly, but now . . ."

Biggs snatched the envelope from the man. "Get the fuck out of my sight," Biggs said. I was ready to intervene if I had to, mentally charting a course in the narrow space past Dorothea Biggs to get to Marino.

"The nerve of you!" Dorothea Biggs told the stranger, wrapping her arm around her son as if he'd been threatened with physical harm. "This is a *funeral.*"

The man didn't lose composure, smiling slightly as he lowered his eyes and gave a genteel half-bow before excusing himself. I watched him weave his way toward the rear exit, a pale neck in a mostly black crowd. I couldn't let him get away.

"Chela, stay right here," I told her. "I'll be right back."

Chela's eyes were glued to Usher, who was having an impassioned conversation with Missy Elliott at the end of our row. "Yeah, okay," Chela said, hardly hearing me.

After telling Dorothea Biggs that I was going to find a restroom, I took off after the lawyer. I finally caught him right outside the chapel doors, in the crowded lobby.

"Mr. Marino?" I called.

He turned, surprised to hear his name. "Oh." He recognized me from the pew.

"Yeah, sorry about that back there," I said, shaking his hand. "I'm Mr. Biggs's financial director, Lenny Jackson. He asked me to catch you and apologize for that reception. This is a hard day for us. He's not himself."

"Say no more," Jim Marino said. "I feel like a moron for doing it that way. I came to the funeral because I liked Serena, and I just thought . . ." He sighed. "Well, that's the problem—I wasn't thinking. There's a time and a place . . ."

As his voice trailed off, I pulled the small notebook from my pocket. "Mr. Biggs won't have time to read your letter before the interment, but he asked me to jot down a few details. Or if you have a copy, I'll make sure it gets processed right away."

Marino hesitated, eyeing me with the first glimmer of suspicion. "No . . . I just had the one copy. But there's no rush."

"Actually, Mr. Marino, you'd be doing *us* a favor. This Stan Greene case has been a real cross to bear. He's been calling since Serena's death, demanding money." I remembered a call from Greene when I visited Biggs's office.

"You're fucking kidding me," Marino said. If he was a lawyer, he hadn't gotten his degree in the Ivy League. His face compressed in anger, Marino ran his fingers through his short-cropped hair as if he wanted to go beat the hell out of Greene.

"No, I'm not kidding. So you can see our dilemma. He's very persistent. And with Serena gone, any information about additional expenses is very helpful to us. I hope you understand."

"Listen, the numbers are in the letter, and that's just business," Marino said. He folded his arms, leaning closer to me, and I smelled a midmorning martini on his breath. "But on a personal note . . . I would appreciate it if you would tell Mr. Biggs that Serena came to our firm because she wanted to protect him. Greene is known for violent tactics, and our firm has more experience with his type. No offense to Biggs, but he was in over his head. I understand he and Serena were childhood friends . . ."

"Did Stan Greene have Serena killed?" I said.

I saw a hard glint in Marino's dark eyes, but he shrugged. "Truthfully, I gotta tell you, if Stan Greene had ordered the hit, her body would never have been found. But who knows? If he did it, I wish I could prove it." He tipped an imaginary hat. "Gotta run. Tell Biggs sorry again. When he's ready to call me, my number's in the letter."

"We've been trying to reach Mr. Greene . . ." I said, just as he was turning away.

"Join the club," Marino said. "Try Palm Springs."

Before I could ask where in Palm Springs, the thickly built lawyer had slipped into the herd at the church doors. He didn't look like a guy who tolerated harassment, so I didn't follow him. I wrote *Palm Springs* in my notebook.

But I wouldn't have to wait long to track down Stan Greene.

When I got back to my seat, the church had emptied out halfway. Biggs was talking to one female and two male assistants, and his mother was putting on her wrap to go to the cemetery. Chela was still waiting, even though Usher and Missy were gone.

I slipped into the huddle around Biggs to eavesdrop, but he grabbed my arm and motioned for the others to go. His assistants looked like they ranged in age from twelve to sixteen, almost literally. Biggs pulled me out of his mother's earshot, closer to the pulpit, where we were nearly hidden behind a giant floral display.

"I got a lead on Tyra," Biggs said.

"Where is she?"

"A promoter told me she's shooting a video in Palm Springs with M.C. Glazer. And guess who's directing it."

"Stan Greene?"

"Can you believe that shit?" Biggs said. "The Axis of Evil for real. Her sister's getting buried, and Tyra's shaking her ass with Glaze."

Tyra had nerve, all right. It wasn't necessarily evidence of a guilty conscience, but it was far from sisterly. I showed Biggs my notebook. "That lawyer, Marino, just told me where Greene is."

Biggs's face changed again, from an almost exuberant rage to something harder to identify. The lawyer's name wiped all expression away, deflating him. "Just another motherfucker with his hand out," he said casually, but meeting that lawyer had not been casual for him. When Biggs leaned forward slightly, adjusting his crutch, I saw the letter in his inside jacket pocket. The envelope was ripped; Biggs had opened it.

"For what it's worth, he said Serena wanted to protect you," I said.

Biggs blinked, peering at me the same way he had when he saw me sitting in my car across from Serena's apartment. Shocked incredulity. "Protect me from *what*?"

"Greene's hard guys, is what Marino said. She didn't want you to get hurt."

Biggs forced himself to laugh, an effort that made him sway. "Don't believe a word that guy says," Biggs said, his voice hoarse. "He could sell shit to a toilet."

"Let's hope he was right about Palm Springs," I said.

"Tell Nelson," Biggs said. "Let him do some police work for a change. If he can't nail their asses for Serena, he can nail them for yesterday."

"No," I said, thinking aloud. Approaching the police now felt wrong. M.C. Glazer would erect a wall of lawyers around him if he got a whiff that he was a suspect in yesterday's attack. "It'll be hard to make it stick to Glaze unless one of the shooters talks. I should go to Palm Springs first. I'll talk to Tyra alone, and I'll try to get to Greene. Maybe I'll get something more solid to take back to Nelson."

Biggs shook his head. "You live dangerously, man," he said. "Me, I'm through with all this shit. I ain't meeting nobody for nothing. Let Five-O handle it."

"I know what you mean," I said. "But the police aren't my friends right now."

"Well, hang tight," Biggs said, sliding a new silver-colored cell phone from his pants pocket. I wish I'd thought to buy another one, too. "I'm gonna get you a room in Palm Springs so you can find out where they're at. It's the least I can do."

"Make it two rooms?" I said.

Biggs raised his eyebrows, but didn't question me. It's hard to quibble with a man who just pulled you out of a burning building.

Now, I had to negotiate the rest of my travel plans.

I peered beyond the flowers to check on Chela, and was surprised to see April standing beside her. Both of them were waiting for me.

The *Los Angeles Times* building at the corner of First and Spring was like a city of paper, with endless desks stacked with newspapers, notepads, books, and more newspapers. The reporters looked like college professors to me; smart people who didn't have time to fuss in the mirror each morning and couldn't afford designer suits, a bland corporate culture that seemed misplaced in the bosom of Hollywood. *No wonder April dresses down so much*, I thought. At the office, she stood out in her stylish funeral attire.

Hell, she would have stood out in a Glad bag.

Chela sat at a neighboring reporter's empty desk to chat on MySpace while April and I sat in front of her monitor and researched Marino, McGruder, & Stein, L.L.P., headquartered on Wilshire with a second address on New York's Upper East Side. James Marino III was a founding partner, and his photo on the *Meet Our Firm* page matched the man I'd met at the funeral. His biography said he'd been born in Hackensack, New Jersey, and received his law degree from USC. Not the Ivies, but a good school.

James Marino's name came up on endless pages of Google as the attorney for high-profile clients with names ending in vowels. He successfully defended developer Louis Carbonella in a racketeering case, politician Harold Esposito in his bribery trial, and Jesus Rivera in a jury-tampering civil lawsuit. But Marino was probably best known for his role in defending a comedian, Rocco Conti, who killed his ex-wife in an alcoholic rage. All acquitted. The firm also cropped up in a story where a witness claimed he had been roughed up by affiliates of Marino, McGruder, & Stein.

Don Corleone would have loved these guys.

"This firm is the guilty man's paradise," April said. "I don't get it. Serena got sued in civil court, so she hired a criminal lawyer?"

"It looks like Serena wanted to fight fire with fire. That's what Marino said."

"Yeah, if you can believe anything a guy like Marino tells you."

"True. But he was good for the Palm Springs lead on Greene."

Oops. I'd brought up Palm Springs again. I had promised April we wouldn't talk about Palm Springs again until after her deadline. Maybe over dinner.

Two hours east of Los Angeles, with its rustic luxury in the cradle of smog-free Mount San Jacinto, Palm Springs is a popular getaway for the celebrity set. I still knew a few hotel managers and security personnel from my traveling days, so in two calls, I learned that M.C. Glazer, Stan Greene, and his crew were staying at the Le Parker Palm Springs Resort, where they were filming a video through the weekend. As promised, Biggs had secured me two rooms at the nearby Palm Springs Hilton, in addition to handing me forty-five hundred dollars in cash.

As soon as I mentioned Palm Springs, April smiled and wagged her finger at me.

"Sorry," I said. "Forget I said it."

"I feel weird about it, Ten."

"We could ask for two beds in the room."

"That's not it," April said softly. "I feel weird going with you and Chela."

I glanced toward Chela, who was still absorbed in a cyber world full of friends. By the speed of her tapping, I guessed Chela was telling everyone she knew that she had seen Usher up close. But Chela hadn't said much to me since the funeral. Chela kept herself at more of a distance when April was with us.

"Chela has her own room. And she's a big girl," I said. "I know it feels awkward, but I don't have anywhere to put her and we can't let that stop us. We'll figure out a way to get to Greene, and you'll keep me out of trouble."

"Oh, so if you say, 'Hey, I think I'm gonna go pop by M.C. Glazer's room,' and I tell you, 'Hell, no,' you'll actually listen?"

"Promise," I said. "I hope he never even sees me."

"As soon as you talk to Tyra, she'll go running to him."

"And we'll plan to be on the road before she can do that. I won't be reckless, because I can't put you and Chela at risk. I'll treat you as if you're my clients."

April gave me a knowing look: *Your clients?* Suddenly, I remembered that Lieutenant Nelson had probably told April about my sex work. But I couldn't have that conversation with Chela sitting nearby. For the first time I could remember, I felt my earlobes sizzle with embarrassment. My eyes begged April to keep quiet, for now.

"My security clients," I clarified.

"I've seen how you treat your clients," April said, nearly under her breath. Her eyes crackled at me; part anger, part something else.

I took April's hand and slowly ran my fingertip across her smooth, tiny knuckles. She had a doll's skin. "Is that a yes or a no?"

Heat filled the space between us. Attraction is a physical thing I can almost touch in the air. April wrapped herself around me without moving a muscle.

Her only answer was a smile.

SEVENTEEN

EAST OF LOS ANGELES, after the traffic thins out past the suburban sprawl of strip-mall bedroom communities in the easternmost refuges from Southern California's monstrous real estate market, the 10 interstate finally turns friendly. Hospitable, even. Palm Springs isn't there in your face: You have to look for it. If you haven't found the 111 after the stretch of the 10 renamed Sonny Bono Memorial Freeway, you'll miss the town in the desert altogether.

Funeral clothes discarded, April was wearing mirrored shades, a black tank top, shorts, and a black baseball cap stitched with the word "Writer" in white, in old-fashioned typeface. She was the perfect hybrid of female grace and tomboy, so cute that I found myself stealing glances at her profile, hoping to see that dimple again. Out of the corner of my eye, I saw her checking me out up close, too.

The cash in my pocket had lightened my stress, so in addition to buying myself a new throwaway Nokia cell phone, I also rented a red Lexus convertible for our bizarre family trip. I didn't want anyone to be able to track my car. On a spring night, before it gets too hot, it's nice to drive out in the desert with the top down; once you know that, it's a shame to do it any other way. A forest of gargantuan white windmills sprang up on both sides of us like redwoods, as if we were driving into an alien world. The desert wind chopped their stretch-limo-sized blades into slowly whirring circles.

Drives are good for talking, and April and I had plenty to talk about.

Chela was in her own world in the backseat, her earphones implanted. The mousy vocals and hissing percussion told me her music was loud, so April and I might as well be alone. I had planned to save the meatier conversations with

April for the hotel, but I knew I could think of other things to do once we were in our room.

"I'm sure Nelson told you an earful about me," I said, just to get it out.

"You could say that." April held her baseball cap in place in the wind, staring straight ahead. She was going to make me do the work.

"I've changed my life in the past five years," I said. "I make my living as an actor. I may do some more security work, too." The burning apartment had taught me I was a better bodyguard than I remembered. If I could handle my acting career as well as I handled myself under fire, I would have been Denzel by now. Or at least Vin.

"Sure took an interesting detour, though," April said.

"That's what it was—a detour," I said. "In ten years, you'll be glad to have a few chapters of your life behind you, too."

"Thanks, Grandpa." That dimple again, magnified in passing headlights. The last of the daylight was just being snuffed out over the edge of the western horizon, painting everything in the lilac, orange, and purple haze you always see at dusk in the desert.

"Ask me questions. I don't have anything to hide."

"At least I know you were good at your job. A real pro."

"It wasn't about work with you, April. I just wanted to please you. I wanted to teach you things about yourself." I noticed she wasn't wearing a bra again. "Your body."

"Don't they all just seem the same after a while?" she said. "Women's bodies?"

"Never."

"So you need an endless variety."

"I didn't say that."

April's opening questions were fired so quickly, she could have been at a press conference. Now she softened her tone, sober. "Were you with men, too? Be honest."

"Nope. Had offers, but just not wired up that way." I knew male escorts who had regular male clients—Gay-for-Pay—all the while claiming to be straight. They were fooling themselves.

"Do you have a long list of girls?"

"No," I said. "Just you, I hope."

April sighed, staring at the dashboard. "I guess you think I have nerve asking about your private life after I came to your house acting like a ho."

"I didn't say that either. You were acting like a woman who knows what she wants. I like that about you."

April was quiet for a while, staring out at the cracked, rocky desert yielding less and less to anything green. "When you knew Serena . . ."

She didn't finish the question, but I felt as tense as I had in the interrogation room with Lieutenant Nelson. It's hard for me to betray a client's confidence. "She hired me for sex," I said. "I saw her a couple dozen times over five years. She was a regular."

"And it was all business?"

"Until I saw her this week." I almost said *last week*. So much had changed, but it hadn't even been a week since Serena died.

"She never told you about her past?"

"No." I wish she had, but my list of wishes was already overflowing. My biggest regret was letting Serena out of my sight. I shouldn't have let her push me away. I should have stayed with her. Protected her.

"No offense, Ten, but you fell for her pretty hard." April spied on my thoughts.

A sudden image of Serena's gleaming gold casket almost clouded my eyes. I wasn't sure what to say, until I decided to say what I was thinking. "With Serena . . . it's more like I got *stuck* to her. I ran into her, she died, and I got pulled into her life. I just need a little time to get through it."

"Can I just say one thing, and then I'll drop it?" April said.

"Sure."

April pulled against her chest harness to turn and look at me more fully, so her face was in my periphery as I stared at the road. She pulled off her sunglasses to show me the earnestness in her eyes. "You're obsessed with Serena right now, and I totally understand. If I were you, I'd be obsessed, too.

"But you should think about letting her go. Getting *unstuck*. And if this lead in Palm Springs doesn't work out, instead of chasing Serena's killer, you might want to concentrate on hiring a lawyer like Marino to get the police off your back. Maybe you're trying to solve this murder—putting your life in very real danger—because you're so sad she's gone. Maybe it's because you couldn't help her, and you think you should have. But you couldn't, Ten. She didn't ask for help."

April hit an emotional well in my psyche; I had to tighten my fingers on the steering wheel to keep them steady. I was used to casually analyzing other people, but I felt singed by April's laser microscope. "Okay," I said. My tone was flat so I wouldn't sound as violated as I felt. As always, the worst part was that she was probably right.

April sighed. "Well . . . I just know how it works in my job . . ." she said, leaning back for the ride. "Sometimes you can't see what's right in front of you."

That night, all that lay in front of me was the road to Palm Springs. A night in a hotel room with a woman I was really starting to like, and who seemed to like me despite seeing me at my worst.

Tomorrow, Tyra. Stan Greene.

Palm Springs felt like the answer to everything.

Our suite had a living room, a modest dining table for five, and a glass sliding door leading directly to the hotel's cabana-dotted pool. The room's conservative décor looked best suited for business travelers, but the sight of the giant pool outside reminded us that we were on vacation. We ordered room service, found a movie on pay-per-view we could agree on—no easy task—and sat at the table as if we'd been eating together for years. I don't remember what I ordered, but it was one of the best meals I'd ever had.

Next, dessert.

Chela was glad to return to her matching suite down the hall with her iPod and a bounce in her step. I was sure she had visited more luxurious hotel rooms, but the power of having a room to herself brought out Chela's childishness, as if she were having an adventure. Chela had her evening all planned out: Super Mario Brothers. Hot wings. HBO. Jacuzzi bath. I walked her to her room, just to make sure she got there.

Back in my room, I turned off all the lights except the tamed fire of flickering candles from the bedroom. I found April on my king-sized mattress, nude. She was on her stomach, facing the doorway with one foot daintily raised and waiting. The twin mounds of her ass rose from the bed, a different kind of mountain view. A movie agent would tell April to slim her ass down, but that would be a sin against nature. Its smooth, curving expanse was so beautiful, she made my mouth water.

She smiled, watching me appreciate the gift of her nakedness. April patted the mattress beside her. "Come here," she said.

"Yes, ma'am."

It was a familiar setting: a romantic encounter in a hotel room. But something about it was completely different already. My heart skittered, an eager acceleration.

I sat at the edge of the bed, fully clothed. Awaiting instructions.

"The last time you were with me, you wanted to rock my world," April said, curling herself around me from behind. "To take me into outer space. And I have to admit—*damn*. You certainly did that." I started to speak, but she shushed me with a gentle finger to my lips. "Well, now it's my turn. Lie down."

April began with tender kisses.

As she kissed me, she caressed my face with both palms, trying to see me even while her eyes were closed. My jaw. My cheeks. My temples. My bruised lip. She ran her fingers over my whole face, mapping it with her hands. Feathery, quenching touch.

April rested her index finger across my collarbone, then dribbled it down my chest, across my shirt buttons; I hadn't changed my formal white guayabera since the funeral. April started at the lowest button as she freed me of my shirt, the heel of her hand gently brushing my lower stomach. She traveled upward, kissing my navel. My ribs. My nipples. She recognized my sensitivity and lingered, licking me. Sucking. I was mesmerized by the sight of her mouth tasting me.

My legs dangled over the edge of the bed, and April tugged my pants down to my ankles, binding my legs. She studied me up close, appreciating me the way I had appreciated her. Her fingernails skated across the tip of my pubic hair, then her mouth dove around my taut skin, wet and eager. My toes flinched tight, still helpless, my ankles wrapped with cotton. The lack of control heightened the sensations of her wet lips and curious, active tongue. April was earnest, taking her time. She didn't rush; she liked the taste of me. She teased me by resting my head at the edge of her lips, and then she guided me all the way through her mouth's tunnel to the softness of her throat.

I have something close to absolute control, and she tested me time and again, making a game of it. I grabbed a handful of the bed's plump comforter in my fist and squeezed, hard. Gritted teeth. Just when I felt myself surge toward release, she would change direction, shift the pressure, lick a new spot on my flesh, and a different delicious pleasure was built from its foundation again. Her slippery hand massaged me while her mouth worked in intoxicating counter-turns.

I started to pull her away, but her eyes met mine and their message was clear: *No. I want it like this.* As if that single shared glance gave me permission to fall deep into the feeling, I suddenly sensed a fire that had been banked deep, down at the core, expanding rapidly now, as if it had merely awaited my acknowledgment. The deep muscles in my stomach spasmed and suddenly my control was nothing at all, the fire spiraling up and up as my back arched helplessly and I made a sound halfway between "God" and "yes," words in no language, and in every language a man had ever spoken.

The world went away.

Perhaps a minute passed before I could remember my name.

I pulled April's face toward me to kiss her, and I tasted myself on her lips. April's eyes were shining, but I saw her unspoken question; she wanted to make love to me. I guided her hand downward. A part of me was spent, but a reserve was already building. She squeezed, smiling when her fingers curled around a stone made out of flesh.

"I keep going," I said. "I'm blessed."

"How many times?"

"That's one."

April grinned, and those dimples made me want to feel her insides against me. We popped open a little foil package, and April slid the lambskin ring into her mouth, then swallowed me again, her tongue more agile than most women's fingers. She climbed astride me. Her ass slid across my stomach, her breasts tickling my chest. Her thighs swallowed me, and then she was warmer still. Tighter. Her body grasped me inside her with hardly room to breathe. I held her waist and raised my torso upward slightly, probing, but she shook her head and smiled.

"Like I said . . . it's my turn," she said.

While I lay flat and still, April slowly worked her pelvis in tiny motions— up and down, back and forth—releasing her juices. Soon, she was tight *and* slick. Her hot insides tensed and released, well trained. I helped guide her to an angle that shuts my brain down, and once she learned it, she never strayed, kneading me with her body's steady bobbing. I held two handfuls of her ass just to touch her and savor her skin against mine, but she controlled her movements. April controlled everything.

"Thank you . . ." I gasped, feeling my next orgasm swelling, stronger and deeper than the first. What I meant was, *Thank you for believing in me.* I don't usually talk during sex, but I had to. April trusted me, and her trust was something to treasure.

April's only response was a rolling motion with her hips and an exotic tug that made my mouth fall open, mute.

After we made love, I let myself rest inside April Forrest, as deep as I could go. Our hearts pulsed to one rhythm as we fell into sleep.

After breakfast on our terrace, April and I left a note under Chela's door asking her not to leave the hotel. I could only hope she wouldn't.

"Are you clear on the rules?" I said to April while I drove toward Le Parker hotel.

"What rules, Dad?" April's eyes were smug and full of sex, and her smile was an aphrodisiac. I felt my mind try to wander.

"This isn't a joke, April," I said. "Tyra just tried to have me killed, and M.C. Glazer is probably behind it—but he may not be. Assume that both of them are dangerous. We can play our game with Greene, but I talk to Tyra alone—and we don't talk to Glaze at all. I won't bring you if I don't trust you to follow the rules."

"Nobody gives me rules when I'm on a story," April said.

Shit. My foot eased up on the accelerator. My next chance, I was going to turn the car around and take her back to the hotel. I wasn't about to end up with April weighing on my conscience, too. Maybe she noticed that the car was slowing, so April quickly went on: "But in this case, I'll make an exception."

"You sure?"

"I won't give you any crap, Ten. Promise."

I glanced at her to make sure she had a sober expression on her face. She did. "I'll use a code, as a precaution," I said. "If I say, 'It's time to check on the kids,' that means I want you to get out of there fast, take the car, and go to the room."

"Got it. But how will I know if something's happened to you?"

"Give me a half-hour to call or show up in a cab. If I don't, take off for L.A. On your way, feel free to call the police—but get on the road first."

"I will, Ten," April said softly, resting her palm on my cheek. Her touch was a distraction, and I almost pulled away from her. It was hard enough to consider the prospect of running into M.C. Glazer, but I didn't know what I would do if April got caught up in it. Caring about April meant I might do something stupid.

Slowly, April pulled her palm down, her fingertips grazing my chin before her touch was gone. "You know I want this story. And we both want justice. So let's just be a team, period. I can't afford for you to be nervous over me, and neither can you. I don't need a black knight in shining armor—I just need you to be on your game."

As usual, April seemed to be able to read my thoughts. I glanced at her beside me, looking officious in a gray Gloria Vanderbilt skirt and jacket her mother bought after she graduated from college, a hint that she should go to law school. To make Mrs. Forrest happy, April and I had decided to be lawyers for the day. We were posing as a married couple who were also business partners. I was dressed for my part in my only three-piece, a blue Armani, and a Ben Nye stage beard applied with prosthetic adhesive—not the cheap spirit gum stage actors can get away with, but the kind of glue that tolerates closeups on an IMAX screen.

We looked good together. Maybe that was part of it. April made me uneasy, but I didn't want to take her back to the room. I wanted to see how we worked together.

"As long as you understand the stakes, I'd rather have you with me," I said.

"No more jokes until we get back to our room," she promised.

"When we get back to our room, I don't think I'll want to hear jokes." I smiled, indulging myself with one last peek at April's bright, active eyes. "Remember: We're not Ten and April. We're not actors playing roles. We're *tourists*. My name is Richard." After my father, of course. My typical alias.

"That flight from Tokyo last night was awful, wasn't it, Richard?" April said. Her face was deadpan, already playing her part. A natural.

Most of Palm Springs looks like a movie set, with midcentury architecture, but the Le Parker unfolded in front of us like our own mountainside country estate. Palm trees and expansive grounds made it feel like the most private place on Earth.

"Wow," April said. "I can see why Greene is shooting the video here."

It was too bad we were on such serious business—such dangerous business—because the Le Parker was the ideal backdrop for the beginning of whatever April and I were doing together. The Le Parker is one of Palm Springs' trendiest hotels, a weekend retreat for famous faces. It's also literally a work of art designed by Jonathan Adler, so no other hotel looks quite like it. Even tourists who can't afford the high season prices sometimes visit just to see what they're missing.

But I couldn't take time to admire the décor. As I always do, I let myself sink into my character. From the time we deposited our car with the valet at the curb, my facial expression and manner were someone else's. Impatient. Wealthy. Distracted.

"Ten!" a man's voice called from behind me. "What's up, man?"

A Latino accent. My spinal cord locked into place. It sounded like Lorenzo.

But when I turned around, I saw a portly younger man with close-cropped hair in a hotel uniform. Not Lorenzo. It was Enrique. So much for the stealth approach.

The last time I saw Enrique Gonzalez, he'd been a scrawny kid fresh from Nicaragua studiously making the most of his new job at the reception desk at Le Parker. Five years later, he was thirty pounds heavier, married with a baby, and the five-star hotel's head of security. I almost didn't recognize him. He hugged me warmly, whipping out baby photos.

A few years back, an irate guest who'd spent too much time in the bar confronted Enrique at the front desk, and he was grateful when I stepped in with soothing tones and commanding body language, enabling Enrique to broker peace and look good in front of his boss. That was how our friendship started. It pays to be kind; it's not only good policy, but you never know where people will land.

I glanced around to make sure his effusive greeting hadn't caught the wrong attention, but the lobby was nearly deserted before nine on a Sunday morning.

"Haven't seen you lately," Enrique said, grinning. "What's going on, Ten?"

I hate to lie to a friend, so I told Enrique as much truth as I could: April was a reporter (he studied her press pass), and we were investigating Afrodite's murder. Afrodite's sister, M.C. Glazer, and a Mr. Stan Greene were people we wanted to observe without being noticed. No bugs. No wiretaps. No trouble.

Enrique hesitated, worried. "So you need to book a room?"

"We don't need to stay," I said, and he looked relieved I didn't expect to be comped for the night. The rooms at the Parker don't come cheap. "But if you're expecting a late check-in . . . maybe a poolside/garden view? We could watch the shoot without drawing attention. We only need it a few hours."

"*Perfecto.* I'm almost sure that's no problem," he said, brightening. "But I must tell you: The guests are already irate about the video, so if I get a single complaint . . ."

"Then we'll be gone. I wouldn't burn you, man." *Not on purpose, anyway.*

Our temporary headquarters was a dream, of course: colorful, eclectic décor and a featherbed with a sheepskin rug folded across the foot. Plantation shutters led out to the balcony, where the pool was easily in view.

Downstairs, shooting for the day had not yet begun, although crewmen were setting up their cameras and equipment. The hotel has four pools, but I could understand why guests were complaining: One of the outdoor pools had been commandeered for the shoot, restricted only to extras. The pool area was overrun with curvy brown and black women in string bikinis; I counted thirty. There probably hadn't been this many black folks by the pool in the hotel's history, and between them they weren't wearing enough clothing to cover a nun. The pool was Flesh Central. I knew M.C. Glazer must have paid a small fortune to make his intrusion in the peaceful retreat worth the trouble.

M.C. Glazer gets what he wants. If he wants me dead, I'm a dead man, I thought. What made me think a thirteen-acre resort would be big enough to keep us apart? Glaze had probably brought an army of bodyguards, including Lorenzo and DeFranco. The only thing I had going in my favor was that M.C. Glazer wouldn't expect me to be crazy enough to go near him. Suddenly, I wished I wasn't.

I squatted on the balcony, staring down through the rails. While my mind frantically tried to make a case for driving back to Los Angeles, I whipped out my Pentax DB100 digital camera/binoculars to gaze down at the pool. Amplified images appeared: blurry champagne glasses, someone's nose. I adjusted the binoculars, pulling back, and suddenly I saw whole faces as clearly as if I was standing beside them.

"Any sign of Greene?" April said, sitting beside me.

"Not yet." I'd seen Greene's picture on the internet; he was swarthy and olive-skinned, probably about two hundred pounds.

Suddenly, I did see M.C. Glazer. He sat in a lounge chair, bare-chested except for his obligatory gold chains and medallions, wearing loose-fitting polo pants. He was holding a meeting with two squatting white men whose faces I did not recognize. The men looked like part of the film crew, not the crew that wanted to stomp me into extinction. M.C. Glazer was up early taking care of business.

Then, I spotted Serena by the pool. She was five yards from M.C. Glazer, dressed in the flowing white from her "You Want Some?" music video. I blinked, sure I had to be hallucinating. It was only Tyra, of course. But through binoculars, her face was indistinguishable from her sister's. Even once I knew better, my heart still sped up as I stared at Serena's ghost. I forced myself to look away.

"There's Tyra," I said, pointing her out to April and giving her a look. "With M.C. Glazer right behind her."

April gasped softly. "She looks just like—"

"Glaze told me he was hiring Tyra to parody Afrodite," I said.

"Even now that she's dead? That's so tasteless!"

"You sound surprised." A thought suddenly into my mind: *What if Serena hadn't been the target at all? What if Tyra pissed off the wrong person, and look-alike Serena just ended up in the line of fire—*

Whatever way it had happened, Tyra had no business playing with Serena's ghost. Now I was really pissed off.

"I think we have Greene, too," April said, excited. She gave the binoculars back to me, pointing the way. I still saw M.C. Glazer lounging, but the squatting men had stood up to make room for another. He was wearing sunglasses, but I recognized his profile and his dark, wavy hair. Greene.

"It's him," I said. "But if these three don't separate, it's going to be a long day."

"We may have to wait until after the shoot."

"Lunch break," I said, at the same time she did. I noticed her arm against mine, and my skin was prickled, hot, despite the fabric that separated us. I made myself keep my eyes away from her, though. I tried to forget the feathered in the other room.

Greene leaned over to say something to Glaze privately, then he walked a few feet away with the three crewmen to point out the mountain range, which sat practically at the pool's doorstep. It was just part of the long list of minutiae Greene would have to think about before shooting began. Some actors yearn to direct, but I don't have the patience.

I sighed. "Maybe we'll get—" *Lucky,* I was going to say. Greene suddenly gave a quick wave, and he walked away from his crewmen. Past Glaze, after a deferential salute to him. Toward the lobby.

"Watch Greene," I told April, and grabbed the phone. I dialed the extension Enrique had given me, and a woman picked up on the first ring. When I asked for Enrique, she put me on hold.

"He's almost at the lobby," April reported.

Enrique picked up, lightning-quick. "It's Ten," I said, before he could finish his hello. "Stan Greene just left the patio for the lobby. White golf shirt, black khakis, sunglasses. I need a tail to tell me where he goes."

Long silence.

"You there?" I said.

"You're trying to get me fired, aren't you?" Enrique said.

"Man, you can help us get out of here a lot faster."

Enrique cursed in Spanish and hung up. I took that as a *yes*.

"I lost him," April said, still peering down.

"Not for long."

Not two minutes later, the room phone rang. It was Enrique in a hushed voice, breathless. "I found him. He was going into Norma's."

"Still there?"

"Just got seated. Terrace. He's alone with a Sunday *New York Times*."

"You're beautiful, man."

"Don't make me escort your ass out of my hotel." Enrique hung up. He wouldn't want any more calls from me, but if I did this right, I wouldn't need him again.

"We're on," I said to April. "Another breakfast?"

She grinned. "Most important meal of the day."

Even outside on the terrace, Norma smelled like sweets and coffee. The terrace woke up my eyes with its bright orange foam seats, upscale white garden chairs adorned with orange and green cushions, freshly cut flowers—and an open view of the ripe spring greenery defying the desert air around us. Norma's wasn't nearly as bustling as I expected, maybe because of the midmorning hour, so Stan Greene had a corner of the terrace to himself. We had gotten to him in three minutes flat, and Greene already had his coffee. Just as Enrique said, he was absorbed by his *New York Times*, reading the paper folded vertically the way New York subway riders do. Old habits die hard.

With the perky host's blessing, we took a table two removed from Stan Greene, where he could see us if he looked up but not close enough to crowd him. Greene could hear us if we wanted him to, and that was all that mattered. Every word out of our mouths was in character, part of our chosen scenario. If we played it right, we wouldn't have to go to Stan Greene—he'd come to us.

Action.

"But she's *dead* now, darling," April said, as soon as we'd ordered our French toast and red-berry risotto oatmeal. She pushed the blueblood bit a little far, I thought, but most of acting is selling it, and she was committed. "Instead of getting tied up in litigation, we should cut our losses. We can move forward with the Beyoncé project."

"We can't walk away from losses like that, babe," I said. "You must still be on Tokyo time: You're not thinking straight. A quarter mil? And Biggs knows he owes us. Biggs was the one who said to go ahead and hire a screenwriter before we went to the studios. It's easy for him to spend *our* money.

"But we'll look like vultures if we go after Afrodite's estate."

"Sentimentality doesn't put our kids through Harvard."

"Yale," I said.

"Over my fabulous dead body."

And so on. We were so convincing, I almost believed us. By the time Greene's entrée arrived, we were in a full-blown debate, in polite tones. It reminded me of improvisation exercises in acting workshop classes. April was good at role-playing.

I only dared look at Greene from the corner of my eye; April had a better view.

I wrote a note to her in my notepad: IS HE LISTENING?

After a glance at Greene, she only shrugged. Our elaborate scenario might be wasted on him, I realized. A busy man like Greene had to learn how to tune out background noise. If he didn't show a sign of interest soon, we would have to approach him more directly. That was riskier, and he was more likely to be guarded.

I raised my voice slightly, throwing out bait I hoped he couldn't resist: "I hear that funeral was a spectacle—a church full of people she owed money, I bet. I'd like to bring Afrodite back just to have one last chance to call her on her bullshit."

April raised her eyebrows. "Remember your blood pressure, Richard," she said. "You can't—" She stopped, eyes wide. I followed her gaze.

Stan Greene was on his feet, nearly at our table. I closed my notepad.

"Excuse me," he said. "I happened to overhear: Are you talking about Afrodite?"

I gave him a wary look, and April followed my example.

"You are . . . ?" April began.

"Stan Greene," I said, as if I'd suddenly recognized him. "Of course. The director." I rose to my feet and shook his hand. "What a pleasure. You did *Twisted*. And all your videos are so fresh."

"I'm still more a producer than a director, but thanks," Greene said, smiling. No one in Hollywood can resist a compliment, and I was probably one of only a dozen people who'd said anything nice about *Twisted*, Greene's trite feature film debut. Greene was about fifty-five, but his hair looked thirty, full and richly hued. "No need to stand. I was finishing my breakfast, I heard you talking . . ."

"Join us?" April said quickly, pointing out an empty chair.

Good girl. An invitation from a pretty woman is hard to resist, too.

He smiled at her, considering. "Maybe I will. Let me grab my coffee . . ."

April and I had a half-second to share a gaze. Her eyes were dancing, and I tried to warn her to keep cool. I pointed at my chest: *Let me do the talking.*

"I relate to you on that Afrodite problem," Greene said with a sigh, collapsing into the seat at our table. He held up his mug, motioning the waiter for a refill. "I'm caught up in that, too. I was shooting a movie with her, then she pulls out . . ." He sounded tired.

I nudged. "I might have heard something about that. You'd already commenced principal photography . . . ?"

"We were in the *middle of the fucking shoot*," Greene said, now animated, leaning toward me with both elbows on the table. He wanted to unload. "You talk about blood pressure? Every time I think about it . . ." He shook his head, sighing so hard that my napkin billowed. "Then she goes and dies. *Millions* up in smoke."

"You don't have any recourse? We're thinking about suing."

"You gotta do it. You gotta do the lawyers and the paperwork and the bullshit, but in the end, what's the difference? Dead is dead. The movie's gone. Do what you can, but kiss it good-bye."

So far, Stan Greene wasn't talking like a man who had killed Serena Johnston. If I'd been Serena's killer, I would have ignored the conversation at the neighboring table. Or I would have been afraid we were cops and gotten up to leave.

"Can you recommend a good lawyer?" I said.

Greene grinned, reached into his wallet and pulled out his business card. "What the hell? Call me next week. We'll do a class-action suit against that fucking company." He winked. "No, seriously, I'll send you some names."

"Afrodite's lawyer is a prick. Jim Marino?" I said.

"A Grade-A prick," Greene agreed. "Biggs is a prick, too, but at least he was a prick who didn't know what the fuck he was doing. Casanegra was always a bunch of monkeys running the zoo. What a fucking headache, trying to work with those people. I could tell you stories . . ."

I almost flinched at the *monkeys running the zoo* and *those people* comments. April was only lucky Greene wasn't looking in her direction when her eyebrows shot up. I nudged her foot under the table, gently. She snapped back into character.

"I'd love to hear a story," April said, her eyes eager and dewy.

Good girl again. Greene glanced at his watch. His knee was bouncing up and down beneath the table. He knew he should go, but he wanted to share. We had him.

"You want a story? On the set, she starts making up her own shit," Greene said. "She's not telling the screenwriter, 'Hey, let's do it this way,' like most divas who can't act worth a fuck anyway. No, instead she's making shit up out of thin air. Then *I'm* the bad guy when I ask her what the fuck she's doing. She turns the cast against me, so I've got a full-blown mutiny. Not only that, I'm like scared for my life."

My heart skipped. "What do you mean?" I said.

Greene shrugged. "Listen, I'm no pussy. I grew up in Brooklyn, so I'm not shy. But have you ever worked with these rappers? M.C. Glazer's a classic example: He shows up like he's king of the jungle with this entourage. So when Afrodite comes to the set, it's not just her—it's her crazy sister, it's her maniac bodyguard . . ."

"Her sister?"

"Yeah, yeah. Looks just like Afrodite, except out of her mind. Crazy temper. She's in my face asking for a part every five minutes—forget that she's never had an acting lesson. She's just a body double, and damn lucky to be that, but she's delaying the shoot with her bitching. She's relentless."

Tyra told me she hadn't seen Serena in four months, and Serena had been shooting *Uptown Moves* sixty days ago. Another lie. Serena had thrown her sister a mighty big bone by getting her work as a body double on a feature film— so why hadn't Tyra mentioned that when we talked to her? Tyra definitely knew how to use her resemblance to her famous sister to every advantage.

"How was her bodyguard a maniac?" I said.

"He threatened me," Greene said. The rage in Greene's bouncing leg flashed in his eyes. "On my own fucking set, he's got me up against the wall like I'm his jailhouse bitch, trying to tell me how to run my movie. And *I'm* supposed to be a gangster because of how I did business in Vegas? This shit he's pulling is right out of a rap video."

Greene lowered his voice. "One day this guy flashes a fucking piece at me, like *Hey, you better do what Afrodite says*—and when I tell him I'll call the police, he laughs and shows me his badge. He's a *cop*. M.C. Glazer waved a big check under my nose to do this video, but I'm done after this. I'm too old for this hip-hop bullshit."

April and I both made sounds to show him how shocked we were, and I don't think either of us was acting. It hadn't occurred to me that Jenk had been on Serena's set. Could that be why Tyra hadn't mentioned the shoot?

"Wait—I think I met that guy," I said. "Glasses? Named . . . Jenk?"

"That's the asshole. I should get his full name and report him."

I decided not to mention that Jenk was dead. If we were just back from Tokyo, we wouldn't have heard about his death. Greene hadn't either, apparently. Or he wanted me to *think* he hadn't.

"Did Afrodite threaten you, too?" I said.

"Afrodite? That's not her style," Greene said, and I felt relieved to hear a depiction of Serena I recognized. "Her spiel is how she's so embarrassed, apologizing for their behavior, yada yada. Then why bring them on the set? And after I'm threatened and harassed by Afrodite's fucking entourage, she has the balls to start screaming about creative differences and quit. She's as big a nutcase as her sister. Not only that, but when she turns up dead, Biggs goes around saying I did it. Fucking *prick*. Now I've got fucking newspaper reporters calling me like I'm a suspect."

"That's regrettable," I said, my mind spinning. April, thankfully, stayed quiet.

"Sorry to talk your ear off, but I've had it," Greene said, scooting his chair back. He held up his check to the waiter. "Who's the first person I see this morning? Afrodite's sister. A daily reminder of my living nightmare. Take my advice: Go after what they owe you—business is business. If people look at you cockeyed and call you names, fuck 'em. But after it's over, stay away from rappers. I'm gonna go do my job and get this piece of tits-and-ass in the can, but then I'm gonna kick M.C. Glazer out of my beach house and move on with my life."

"How did M.C. Glazer end up in your beach house?" I said casually.

"I've got a great place in Laguna Beach I never have time for, so I said he could hang out for a while. Guess how long he's been there? A fucking *month*. I just heard Afrodite's sister tell somebody there's a party at the beach house next week. I'll need a fucking SWAT team to get him out."

I knew it then and there: Greene didn't kill Serena. And if M.C. Glazer had anything to do with it, Greene probably didn't know. Greene wasn't a part of M.C. Glazer's inner circle; he was only a hired hand. Greene might have been mad enough to kill Jenk after their confrontation, but instinct told me it wasn't likely. Greene would never function in the business world if he had a habit of killing everyone who threatened or pissed him off. But Serena and Jenk were both dead, and Tyra knew something about it. I was sure of it.

"Welcome to Hollywood. Hell of a town, ain't it?" Greene said.

As the waitress signed his bill, we thanked him for his advice, gushing about how generous he was with his time. After Greene excused himself, April and I held hands under the table, silently congratulating ourselves. The restaurant had filled up around us, but we'd hardly noticed.

Breakfast with Stan Greene would be the best part of what was very nearly my last day on Earth.

EIGHTEEN

BY TWO O'CLOCK, APRIL AND I had almost lost hope of a lunch break for the video cast and crew, and Tyra had never been out of M.C. Glazer's sight. If I had to listen to the thumping bassline for "Pimpin' Paradise" another minute, I was afraid I would storm the set and bitch-slap all of them, just so I wouldn't have to hear that song again.

Tyra's role in the video was a major coup for her: She shadowed Glazer's every move, throwing herself at him only to be cast aside again and again. At one point, Tyra was on her knees as if performing fellatio, but her face was far enough from his zipper that it might actually fly on MTV. Tyra was an uncoordinated dancer, stumbling through the shots, but all Glaze needed was her face.

In every conceivable way, it was torture to watch.

Finally, the music went silent.

"Damn. That was just starting to grow on me," April muttered. She was halfway through a Sudoku puzzle she'd found in one of the room's tourist magazines.

I found Greene with my binoculars, and he was signaling for a break. Quickly, I looked for Tyra: She was slipping into a terrycloth robe, talking to one of the other girls. Having the time of her life.

M.C. Glazer was walking back into the hotel, flanked by a flock of assistants and two large security guards I didn't recognize. Glaze never paid any attention to Tyra when the cameras weren't rolling, not even for polite conversation. So far, I hadn't seen Lorenzo and DeFranco, and I was glad. I watched Glaze until he was out of sight.

Tyra stayed by the pool, giving a harried waitress her drink order. It must have been ninety degrees outside and she didn't need a tan, but Tyra Johnston wanted to stay outside and be the center of attention. Other hotel guests were staring from their patios, too; mostly teenagers. *That looks just like Afrodite!*

"Glaze is finally gone," I told April. I'd packed up my suit in favor of a faded T-shirt and surfing shorts so I wouldn't stand out any more than I needed to. "I have to go down and talk to her somehow."

April looked disappointed. "Maybe we can use Greene to—"

"No, I have to do this alone. Sorry. If you don't hear from me within a couple of hours, call the police. And thanks, April. You did great this morning." As I kissed her lightly, a thought emerged: *You may never see this woman again.* It felt like a premonition. "We make a good team."

"Yeah, we do," she said, smiling. Then, her smile faded. "Be careful, Ten."

"I will. Go to our spa or something. Get a massage for me."

"I might have to, or I'll sit in the room and worry."

I sent April out of the room with our bag first, so no one would see us together if Glaze happened to be in my wing. After two minutes, I slipped out, too.

No hotel stay is complete without a visit to the pool.

Tyra had reclined in a lounge chair since I'd seen her last, surrounded by envious dancers hanging on her every word about how to make it in show business. I watched her from the wings twenty yards away, beneath the cover of a palm tree.

"I'm sorry, sir, but this pool is closed." A woman's voice.

When I turned around to look at the blond-haired waitress, she seemed startled, as if she knew me. The Face, I realized. A *Malibu High* fan, maybe; a favorite show during her formative years. Everything helps.

The waitress's name tag said her name was DONNA. She was about twenty-one, with bobbed hair and a lightly freckled nose on a sun-browned face. She was cute, but I was more inspired by the mimosas on her drink tray. I didn't want to go near Tyra out in the open, but perhaps I could lure Tyra closer to me.

"Donna, where's the nearest ladies room?" I asked, ultrapolite.

Donna smiled when I called her by name, but she gave me a puzzled look. "The restrooms are right behind you." She pointed. "That way and to the right."

I glanced back at Tyra again; I was in the middle of her path to the bathroom.

"You see that woman in white over there?" I said, nodding toward Tyra.

Donna tried not to show too much, but her jaw clenched. "What about her?"

"She's my sister, and I want to play a joke on her. But I need your help, and it'll definitely cost you your tip. How does fifty bucks sound?"

Donna smiled. "It sounds hilarious already. Let's hear it."

"A waitress walks by and 'accidentally' spills a drink on the woman in question. Ha, ha. Get it?"

Donna frowned. "That's not as funny as I thought."

I found two more fifties. "Funnier now?"

Donna sighed, but she took the money. "Hysterical. But I'm not getting chewed out by my boss for you—I'm doing this for me," she said. "No offense, but your sister is the biggest bitch I've ever met."

"Makes two of us. Just do it fast, before the cameras start rolling."

Donna's smile turned flirtatious; we shared a secret now. "Now I'm glad I never had a brother," she said.

"I'm just glad I never had you for a sister," I said, my eyes roaming across her compact, well-toned body. I gave Donna my signature grin and wink, and blood colored her cheeks. Donna would do a good job.

Although I was hiding in shadows, I don't think it occurred to her that I might not be Tyra's brother. People have a hard time believing that someone they find attractive is capable of doing wrong.

I knew Donna's mission was accomplished when I heard a shriek from the patio. The hurricane of expletives began as Tyra leaped to her feet. I winced, feeling for Donna. I wished I had told her to duck.

"*. . . Oh, HELL NO, BITCH, you did NOT just spill that shit on ME!*"

Onlookers gasped as Serena's look-alike took a wild swing at Donna, but Donna was alert and quick, sidestepping the blow with her empty tray raised as a shield. Donna's reflexes made me wonder if she had karate training. Maybe Tae Bo. Two male hosts ran up to intervene, and it started to look like my plan would end up with Tyra getting arrested instead.

"*. . . Get your GODDAMNED HANDS OFF ME, or I will SUE YOUR ASS!*"

Soon the bar manager was there, and three or four others in crisp white shirts. Everyone tried to speak to Tyra in calming tones, assuring her they would pay for the dry cleaning, insisting that Donna apologize. Tyra was offered everything from free drinks to a free dinner to a comped room, and soon her tantrum quieted. I looked at Donna, who could barely hide a smirk even as she hung her head and tried to look contrite.

"The ladies room is right that way," I heard a man say, pointing in my direction. I ducked quickly behind the plant. "If you want, someone can escort you—"

Tyra broke out of the middle of the huddle, racing toward me. "Leave me the fuck alone," she said over her shoulder.

Tyra was so angry and focused on brushing the spilled drink from her clothes that she practically ran straight into my chest before she saw me. My beard didn't fool her: Her mouth opened, and her eyes widened with surprise and fear. Smiling for the sake of onlookers, I grabbed her arm, tucked her elbow inside mine and twisted her wrist into the classic, painful come-along.

"Motherfu—"

"Make one more sound," I whispered. "I dream about nothing but breaking your bones."

It's all in the delivery. It was in my eyes. She damned well knew what she'd done. Tyra's lips were sewn together, quiet. She was breathing hard.

"Let's walk," I said, and I yanked her farther into the lobby, looking for privacy. She whimpered, and I tightened my grip to shut her up. I wished I could hustle her to the elevators, but we would be too exposed there. Instead, I peeled off toward a corner where two luggage carts had been left, piled with designer bags and golf clubs. Enrique saw us and gave me a disdainful look, but he turned away, shaking his head.

A service elevator appeared around the corner from the carts, out of guests' sight. Relieved, I pushed the button for the second floor. The door opened immediately.

"Missed you at Serena's funeral," I said, shoving Tyra inside.

She stumbled and nearly lost her balance, but my wrist-lock kept her close to me. "You know cops are lookin' for me," Tyra said. "And I didn't know what was gonna happen at the apartment. I swear, I didn't know they was gonna try to shoot nobody. I didn't know nothin' about no fire."

"What did you think was going to happen?"

"Maybe you'd get a beat-down, that's all. He was . . ."

I tightened my wrist-lock, and Tyra yelped. "You're gonna *break* it!"

"That's the idea. Who's 'he'?"

"I'll tell you, but nobody else. It was Glaze. You already know that."

There was a pause in our conversation after the elevator reached the second floor. With my free hand, I fished the room key Enrique had given me out of my pocket. I hustled Tyra down the hallway to the room April had just left.

The key still worked, a relief. I was afraid Enrique had frozen me out.

Tyra wriggled to free herself. Her wrist must hurt like hell, but she probably thought I was going to kill her. I shoved her face into the wall, leaning hard. "Chill out," I said. "We're just talking. Then you can go finish pimping your sister's corpse."

Tears filmed Tyra's eyes. "Fuck you," she said. "You don't know shit." But she stopped resisting. I closed the door behind us, and we were finally alone. I yanked Tyra away from the door, where it was less likely someone would hear her.

The room had a CD player. Still holding tight to Tyra, I turned it on and rested my finger on the volume button. Fleetwood Mac's "Don't Stop Believing" suddenly blared in the room, loud enough to drown out a woman's screams.

I sat Tyra in a chair and pinned her with my knee, still holding her wrist in a lock. I was right on top of her, and I could see the contours in her face that mimicked Serena's perfectly, the uncanny sameness of their noses and cheeks. I could also see where she and her sister were nothing alike—their eyes.

"You're right. I don't know shit—so you're going to fill me in," I said. "Why did Glaze try to set me up?"

"Man, I don't know. Glaze don't tell me his business." My gut told me she was lying. Her forehead fluttered, creasing, and I almost grinned, knowing I'd spotted a nervous tic, what poker players call a *tell*.

"You know what? You're full of shit. This is what happens when you lie."

I squeezed just enough to feel the tendons and ligaments stretching. Tyra yelled out, and Christine McVie and Lindsey Buckingham screamed back at her in harmony. I'd rarely subdued a woman—most notably the time a drunk woman tried to get too close to a client—and I was so uncomfortable about the size differential that I went too easy on her and nearly got hit in the head with a beer bottle. This time, I was afraid I might really hurt Tyra just because I wanted to.

"*You SONOFABITCH!*" Tyra shrieked. More tears flooded her red-rimmed eyes.

I eased up. "Try the truth this time. Why did Glaze tell you to call me?"

"What the hell you think? You broke into his damn house and stole his girl. Glaze ain't gonna stand for that shit. You must've been out your damn mind, fool. And they're saying you killed Jenk, too."

"What about Biggs? Why did Glaze go after him?"

I saw it again: the forehead flutter, completely unconscious. "He figured Biggs must've told you where his beach house was," Tyra said. "Payback."

That lie was so flimsy, Tyra sounded like she didn't believe it herself.

"Bullshit. Why would he have Biggs killed for that?"

"You better ask Glaze. I told you, he don't tell me all his business. Shit, when M.C. Glazer calls you up *personally* to ask you to do some shit, you do it. What planet you living on, asshole?"

"And it had nothing to do with Serena? Like Biggs helping me figure out Glaze was the one who had her killed?"

"Glaze didn't kill Serena," Tyra said. Her forehead was still, this time; either she was telling the truth, or she thought she was. "He didn't give enough shit about Serena to waste time on her. Why's he gonna kill her?"

Jenk had said the same thing on my voicemail the day he died. So had Glaze.

"But what about you, Tyra?" I said. "It must have eaten you alive to see the whole world paying attention to Serena—and nobody noticing you."

"Fuck you. You don't know me."

"You weren't at Mackey's when Serena died, so where were you?"

For the first time, Tyra didn't answer right away. She was still breathing hard, but she took an effort to slow down, stopping to think. Tyra took a deep breath. "OK," she said. "I'll tell you. But like I said, nobody else."

"Go on."

"I was getting high. I've got this friend, and sometimes we smoke out."

Tyra wasn't talking about smoking weed; she was smoking crack when Serena died. That was why she lied about being at the nightclub. She'd probably told the police the same story she tried to sell me. If Lieutenant Nelson hadn't been so obsessed with nailing me for Serena's death, he would have discovered the lie himself.

"What else?" I said. There had to be more.

"And . . ." Tyra shook her head, as if trying to block out the memory. "She called me that night. That same night she died."

No forehead tic. I almost held my breath.

"What did she say?"

"Like I said, I was high—I don't remember. But she was all pumped up. She talked about this new track she had coming out, something Anonymous."

" 'Life Anonymous'?" I said.

"Yeah. She was saying how she wanted to start her life over again, like a twelve-step program. She said she wanted to start out fresh. She said she was gonna finally take her bronze man home."

My heart leaped. "What bronze man?" *Was she talking about me?*

Tyra paused, and I thought I saw the forehead flutter again. "I don't know. She figured out I was high, and we got in a fight. She told me to go to hell and hung up. She said she didn't know why she kept wasting her time with me."

"What time did she call?"

"I don't know. Maybe eight. Maybe nine."

Serena had called Tyra within two hours of her death. Maybe less than that.

"Why didn't you tell the police she called?"

" 'Cause I was at a friend's house, that's why. I don't tell police my business."

"That might've helped them solve your sister's murder, if you give a shit about that," I said. I resisted the urge to slap her face. "Was Serena sleeping with Jenk?"

Tyra's lips soured. "He wanted to be. She cut him loose."

"When?"

"High school. She said he was too wild, running the streets. But he never stopped sniffing her ass like a damn puppy. Sometimes he hooked up with me so he could feel like he was getting the real thing." It was a painful admission; her voice softened. Her forehead was smooth. Those last words were probably the truest Tyra had spoken all day.

"Did Serena mention Jenk when she called you?"

"No. It was all about her and her life."

"Could Jenk be the bronze man?"

Tyra squinted, confusion pinching her expression. She shook her head. "I don't know."

I tried to remember what I could from the lyrics to "Life Anonymous" again: *But blood in your eyes is reflecting at me / Like pools from the Dead Emcee Sea.*

"Did Jenk kill Shareef?"

Tyra shrugged, turning her face away from me. "I guess we'll never know now. Jenk's dead. You killed him, remember?" I saw it again: Her forehead was waving like a flag on Independence Day.

"You know I didn't kill Jenk," I said. "And you know I didn't kill Serena. My guess? The only reason you know I didn't is that you know who *did*. And everywhere I go, it all points back at you."

Tyra's eyes spat acid at me, taunting. "Like I said . . . you don't know shit. The cops said somebody dumped her body in that alley, and I can't see good enough to drive at night, fool. It's on my license."

"Jenk could drive."

"I wasn't with him. I was with my friend all night, both of us fucked up, and then I caught a bus over to Sunset in the morning to get the studio time. We don't want to mess up my friend's parole, but she'll back me up if she has to." Tyra's forehead was still, so she might have been telling the truth again. Twice in one day. I was surprised she hadn't sprained her tongue.

I was frustrated, and I knew I was running out of time. Tyra was a harridan of the lowest breed. Even if she hadn't killed her sister, whoever killed Serena couldn't possibly be more evil than the woman who had stolen Serena's face. But there is no law against being vile. I could try to have her arrested in connection with the apartment fire and shooting, but that wouldn't get me closer to Glaze. It wouldn't take me any closer to the truth about how Serena died.

Our conversation was interrupted by banging on the hotel room door.

"Keep quiet," I warned Tyra, my heart pounding. "If not, you'll be talking to Palm Springs police about a fire in your old neighborhood."

My grip loosened, so Tyra yanked her wrist away from me. By the way she smiled to herself, she was probably thinking that she'd rather face the cops in Palm Springs than I would M.C. Glazer's bodyguards, who might be at the door.

On my way to the door, I turned the music down. The room was silent.

I peeked through the peephole: It was Enrique, with two other uniformed hotel employees with him. He no longer looked like my friend, but I was glad to see him.

After I opened the door, Enrique stared at me a moment before he spoke. "Your music's too loud, sir," he said, glancing over my shoulder to see inside the room. Tyra was barely visible, rubbing her wrist near the bed. "We're getting complaints."

"Yeah, I'm so sorry about that. We love Fleetwood Mac, and we got carried away. It won't happen again."

Enrique could feel something wrong vibrating in the room, and he was scared. He looked at me—really *looked* at me. I tried to assure him with my eyes. If I'd known him longer, or if we'd shared more history, he could have trusted my word. But he didn't.

"It's time for you to leave this room, sir," he said.

I nodded toward the balcony. "Can I . . . ?"

Enrique sighed and followed me to the balcony, and I closed the glass door behind us. M.C. Glazer was back at the pool in conference with Stan Greene. I couldn't hear what they were saying, but it wasn't hard to imagine: *Where's Tyra?*

"One last thing, man . . ." I breathed to Enrique.

"We're all paid up now," Enrique said. "In fact, now you owe *me*. Get out."

"You're right. I do. But that woman is dead center of a murder investigation. The minute you let her loose, she's going to run to M.C. Glazer and tell him I was here, and he will try to kill me. All I need is time to get off the grounds before that happens."

Enrique gazed through the glass door at Tyra, his face as pained as if I'd asked him to cut off a toe. Tyra was complaining to the other two security men about the drink Donna had spilled on her clothes. Loudly.

"I thought gangsta music was just an act," Enrique said. "Like Mafia movies."

"It is, for some rappers. Not for M.C. Glazer. He's the real thing, man."

Enrique closed his eyes, probably begging the heavens to get me out of his life. Then he sighed, glancing at his watch. "You ask a lot of your friends, Ten," he said. "You've got ten minutes. *Largate.*" In other words, *Get Lost.*

My limbs loosened with relief. I shook Enrique's hand, clasping it. "Thanks, man. I owe you, and I always pay. Kiss that pretty baby for me."

While Enrique and his two men dutifully took notes from Tyra about the accident poolside, I slipped out of the room without another glance at her. By the time the door closed behind me, I could hear her voice ringing through the hall. "Motherfucker, *WHAT* did I just say? That bitch was giving me attitude *ALL DAY* . . ." I realized I hadn't paid Donna nearly enough for what I had asked her to do.

Enrique was right. I was asking a lot of everyone I knew, expecting them to carry my burdens. And why? I still didn't know how or why Serena died.

I hardly breathed until I was out of the hotel, and the valet summoned me a cab. Tyra didn't want to see the police any more than I wanted to see M.C. Glazer, or I never would have made it that far.

After the cab pulled away from the palatial hotel's curb, I looked through the rear window to make sure no one was following me. The only people I saw were two women dressed for tennis and a set of middle-aged parents and two teenage girls piling out of their Mercedes minivan, excited to begin their vacation.

As the resort's idyllic green grounds rolled behind me, there was no one chasing me, or even noticing me. That peaceful, lovely appearance hiding the presence of a creature like Tyra Johnston was the biggest lie I had ever seen.

When I got to my room, April wrapped her arms around my neck and kissed me as if I was a soldier just home from Baghdad. Everything else in my head went away as I sank into that kiss. I felt bruised from my time with Tyra, torn by the contradiction between the cruel trick of her face and what I saw in her heart, but April had no contradictions. I cherished her soft body and lips against mine.

"Where's Chela?" I said, finally coming up for air.

"She was at the pool when I got here. Should we get her?"

"Yeah, in a minute," I said, and kissed her again.

While April and I made sure we'd packed everything, I told her about my conversation with Tyra. She was as surprised and disgusted as I was to learn that Tyra had talked to Serena the night of her sister's death and never mentioned a word about it.

"It was a sick little ménage à trois," April said. My thoughts exactly. "The 'bronze man' is Jenk. He wanted Serena—but Tyra wanted Jenk. Maybe things got cozy between Jenk and Serena on the movie shoot, so Serena called Tyra to give her sister notice that she was going to take Jenk for herself. Tyra freaked out and killed her before she could steal him."

"Then Tyra killed Jenk . . ." I said, mulling it over.

"Maybe Jenk figured out what happened. Or she was afraid he would."

April liked to think aloud, but I liked to confine my thoughts to my head. The police said Jenk had been shot in the *back* of the head—so either he had been taken by surprise, or he was killed by someone he had trusted enough to turn his back to. Someone he knew well enough to underestimate.

Someone like Tyra.

"That could be why Jenk called me," I said. "He *knew* M.C. Glazer hadn't killed Serena. He wanted to warn me off before I got hurt."

Tyra was the nexus. Tyra had a connection to every event this week, from her sister's death to the attack in the apartment building. Either she was the mastermind or she was a gamepiece, but she knew much more than she had told me. I could be underestimating Tyra, just like Jenk probably had.

But it still didn't fit together neatly. Tyra had *told* me about the phone call from Serena. She *told* me about Serena and her Bronze Man. Why would she incriminate herself? Out of guilt?

Nothing made sense. Maybe it never would.

"Let's see if that's enough to get Lieutenant Nelson off my back," I said, holding April's shoulders. "I got some good advice from someone about dealing with Serena's death."

"Really?"

"Yes. She said I might be trying to solve this for all the wrong reasons."

April gave a sad smile, kissing my chin lightly. "Not *all* the wrong reasons, Ten. It just hurts when people die, especially when it's a murder. Pain shows up in different ways." She sighed. "And I hate to say it, but you already have your hands full."

"What do you mean?"

"Chela. She's one very confused kid, and she's got a thing for you."

"She said that?"

April pursed her lips. "Come on, Ten. She didn't have to. You can see it. She barely looked at me when I tried to talk to her at the pool."

It seemed like ages ago when Chela had presented herself to me, naked in my bed. I'd shoved the whole episode away in my mind just to banish the image, but then I'd behaved as if it had never happened. That hadn't been smart.

The room phone rang. "Speak of the devil?" I said, and picked it up.

"You're back, finally." It was Chela, and I could tell she was straining not to sound upset. In her mind, I'd been ignoring her. Hell, I *had* been ignoring her.

"Yeah, Chela, sorry we ran out before you got up, but—"

Chela snapped off my words. "Come to my room right now. I want to talk to you. And don't bring *her*."

"I'll be right there, hon." I hung up and looked at April, wincing. I had just dodged one minefield with Tyra, and now I had another with Chela. I'd been so intent on planning our family vacation, I had forgotten that April, Chela, and I weren't a family.

"This trip always felt weird to me," April said. "I'm sure it does for her, too. Maybe she should sit up front with you while we're driving back."

I nodded. Right. I hadn't even thought about how Chela might have felt being exiled to the backseat while April sat up front with me. *Shit.* I had no business trying to take care of this child on my own. I didn't know anything about children, much less a child carrying as much damage as Chela.

"I'll start making some calls later today," I told April. The thought made me sad.

"A friend of mine did a big piece on foster care a few months ago, all these success stories, and she has great contacts. We'll find Chela a good home."

As I stood in front of Chela's hotel room door, it was like walking into a cloud of gloom, almost exactly the way it had felt to cross the threshold into Serena's old apartment building. I felt anxious and sad and even scared. I blamed my dread on not wanting to let go of Chela, maybe because it felt like letting go of Serena. I was so busy overanalyzing my feelings that I ignored the obvious: *Something was wrong.*

Chela's voice had been wrong. Something outside of that door felt wrong. Room 138 was all wrong.

I knocked anyway.

"Come in. Don't speak. Show me your hands."

Lorenzo's voice was calm, disciplined. The first thing I saw when he opened the door was the shiny black Glock in his hand. Pointed right at my chest.

Where's Chela? My two breakfasts bloated in my stomach, and my mouth filled with a sickly acid taste while my heart rattled my ribcage. I prayed that if I did everything Lorenzo said, I was the only one who would get hurt.

I'm a dead man. I might not die here at the Palm Springs Hilton, but my body would be dumped somewhere by nightfall. Just like Serena and Shareef. Had Lorenzo and DeFranco been Serena's killers all along? M.C. Glazer's elite personal hit squad?

Slowly, I raised my hands. Lorenzo stepped back with a smirk in his eyes— *I got you, motherfucker.* Two steps brought me into the room. He closed the door behind me. I expected an immediate taser jolt, or an arm around my neck choking me into unconsciousness. No violence came.

"Where's Chela?" I said. My voice was soft. I didn't want to piss him off.

"Yeah, that's a good question," Lorenzo said. "Come on out here, Chela!" Lorenzo knew better than to take his eyes off me while he called over his shoulder. He was five feet away, too far to risk any kind of disarm motion.

I saw movement from the bedroom, and my heart withered.

Chela was wearing nothing but a pathetic string bikini, and even that was askew, as if she'd donned it in the dark. She was hugging herself, her face all scarlet shame and terror. "They made me call," she whispered. She couldn't look at me.

DeFranco appeared next from the bedroom, fully dressed but zipping up his fly. He offered me a grin, chewing his gum as he wrapped his arm around Chela. I saw how pink her bottom lip was; swollen. A tendril of blood crept from its corner.

An enraged scream welled up from my throat. Miraculously, I stuffed it back, but the sound still exploded in my head. I panted from the effort of not pouncing on DeFranco and beating that grin from his face as he hugged Chela beside him. It might have felt worse if she was my daughter, but I don't see how.

"That's not too nice, you keeping her all to yourself," DeFranco said.

"T-Ten . . . I'm s-sor-ry . . ." Chela said. Her teeth were chattering.

"My grandmother would say you're all balls, no brains," DeFranco said. His gun waved casually in his free hand as he spoke. He could shoot Chela without a thought. Cops can always shoot you, if they come up with a good story.

DeFranco went on: "There we are sitting at Norma's, and we see you and your lady friend. We decide to see what you're up to. We follow her back here—and who's by the pool but Chela? We've been talking about his lady friend, haven't we, Chela? Turns out, Chela doesn't like her too much."

Chela's eyes darted away again.

"Funny story, really," DeFranco went on. "Chela here, she always had a little crush on me. Didn't you, girl? You know you did." He pinched her cheek, hard.

"Let her go," I said.

"Shut up and let me finish," DeFranco said, all mirth drained from his tone. His eyes dared me to move or speak, and I didn't defy him. "I mean, she was a little scared when she saw me at first, thinking Glaze was mad at her. I had to set her straight and tell her Glaze ain't pissed at all. Fact is, he's still waiting for her. He wants to move her into his beach house with him, just like he told her."

Chela stared me in the eye at last, her bottom lip trembling. Like a schoolgirl in the worst trouble of her life. I'll never forget that look.

"So she's out at the pool looking hot as hell, and I said I'd buy her a drink. You figured out yet this girl's crazy for rum and Coke? I said, 'Hey, let's chill out in your room, raid the minibar, and then Glaze will rescue you from this shithole and put you up in real style.' And by the way, since Glaze was busy doing his video, we finally had a little private time to get to know each other like she always wanted. But I guess that part goes without saying." He leaned over and held Chela's face to kiss her on the mouth, his gun carelessly against her head. Chela gagged, pushing at his chin.

Every muscle in my body wanted to knock him off Chela. Pound him through the wall. I was trembling. I thought my legs would collapse.

"*Tranquilo*," Lorenzo whispered to me, raising his gun to aim at my head. He had a madman's eyes. "Don't have an accident."

He *wanted* me to spring. It was Lorenzo's deepest desire.

DeFranco finally moved his hairy lips away from Chela. For the first time since I had known her, there were tears in her eyes. "So now we're all gonna go pay Glaze a visit," DeFranco said, winking at me. "He wants to see *you* especially. Whaddya say, Ten? We heard a rumor you like to do it for money. Kinda like Chela here, huh? If Glaze shoves a twenty down your throat, will you bend over and take it up the ass?"

I barely heard him. I couldn't think about anything except Chela standing in front of me. Every man wonders what his breaking point is, and that day I came closer than I ever want to come again. For all I knew, I was about to watch Chela get raped and killed. She might have been raped already.

DeFranco pushed Chela into a chair and circled behind me. I felt a sudden sharp pain as he kicked the back of my right knee, driving me to the carpet. I braced my hands to stop my face from smacking into the rug, and looked up at Lorenzo.

"You got me, man," I said. "But this is between us. Leave Chela out of it. You wanted me to beg? I'm begging. She's only fourteen, man."

DeFranco laughed. "*Fourteen?* In dog years, maybe."

I ignored him, focusing on Lorenzo. DeFranco was the big talker today, but Lorenzo was the Alpha. And somewhere inside all that rage and madness, I thought I saw a man I could talk to. "Man, she's a *kid*. You said your kid is three years old. You wouldn't want your kid to end up like this. Let her go. Let her find a family."

Time skidded, then iced over. In some ways, time has never moved on. I still have nightmares about it: I'm being held at gunpoint, and Chela, helpless, is wide-eyed in that plush chair. The dream ends ugly. Always. And I had brought Chela here. This was the worst moment of my life; the first time I was willing to die to fix something.

"You want to kill me? Maybe I earned that. But leave her out of it. You don't want to do this to a kid. *Please.*" Yes, I have spoken those words. Chela looked at me in horrified confusion.

"If we leave her, she'll call the cops," Lorenzo said, shrugging. If they were afraid Chela would talk to the police, she would never leave M.C. Glazer alive.

"Cops? No way," I said. "Her record would send her to juvie. Tell them, Chela."

"I hate cops," Chela said. She sounded like she was three inches high.

"Chela has money," I said. "She can jump on a bus and you'll never see her again. Man, please—let her go."

"No way," DeFranco said to Lorenzo. "Glaze wants her back, and now I know why. Let Glaze figure it out."

Lorenzo blinked once. Twice. He made up his mind.

"The kid stays," he said. Almost as if he'd been planning to leave her all along. *Thank you, God. Thank you, Jesus.*

Lorenzo leered at me, seeing the relief on my face. Maybe I had made the mistake of smiling for Chela's sake. "You feeling good about yourself, asshole?" Lorenzo said. "You feel all warm and fuzzy inside 'cause you think you saved a soul?"

"I didn't kill your friend." My voice cracked midway through.

But I knew what was coming next—the real reason Lorenzo and DeFranco tracked me to my hotel—and there's nothing you can say to your executioner.

Lorenzo strode to where I knelt, swung his leg, and buried his foot in my gut, just below the place where the ribs come together. My diaphragm spasmed, and all air rushed from my lungs in a fear-soured cloud. Like a piston, he kicked me again. Harder.

I hurt too much to make a sound. I crumpled on the carpet, craving the womb. I might have heard Chela cry out, but I hardly had awareness of anything except how desperate I was for even a spoonful of air. Without breath, any pretense to composure was gone. It felt like he had taken a hatchet and sliced off everything below my ribs, leaving me to bleed to death on the hotel floor.

"There's only one soul you need to worry about today, *puta*."

I managed to gulp in a half-breath, and then wasted it trying to explain. "I didn't kill your—"

The back of my head seemed to shatter to pieces.

And then everything was gone.

I opened my eyes in time to see a blinding burst of white afternoon light.

Then, a *whump*, and complete darkness. I was in a sweltering, airless tomb.

My hands were chained behind me. Metal handcuffs, by the sound and feel. Other than that, I was lying in a fetal position on a flat surface with my face pushed against wiry carpet fibers that tickled my nostrils. I tried to sit up and slammed my head into a low ceiling. I'm limber enough to work handcuffs around from behind my back—but there was no room: My back was pressed against something hard and grooved. I smelled gasoline and air freshener, but I couldn't think straight because of my throbbing head and the raging pain in my gut.

Where am I?

The sound of a car engine and a sudden rocking motion told me I was in the trunk of a car. The object behind me, then, was the spare tire.

On my way to die. That's where I was.

The horror of the realization made the air in the trunk thinner, compressing it like a plastic bag over my face. *How much oxygen is in here?* I blinked into the dark, trying to find enough light to see by. The only thing worse than the heat was the darkness.

If it was 90 degrees outside, it felt like 150 in the trunk. All they had to do was park somewhere secluded, and I'd be dead by dark. But I'd known that from the moment I'd stared down the barrel of a Glock in Chela's doorway.

My heart tried to squeeze into my throat. Trying to escape my doomed body. *Think. Think. Think. Think.*

Panic was ready to take over as soon as I ran out of logic. Believing in a solution was the only thing that kept me from screaming in that trunk, even if I should have been screaming a long time ago.

Muffled thumping resonated from inside the car. Music. M.C. Glazer's "Pimpin' Paradise" vibrated against my back.

I knew it then: I was in hell, or it was just around the bend. To this day, the sound of that song makes me sick to my stomach. The bassline nearly smothered my thoughts. Sweat drowned my eyes in the salty sting. It was torture to breathe, to fight the impulse to gasp at the air. But somehow, I had to . . .

Think. Think. Think. Think.

Forget about the fantasy they'd spun for Chela about taking me to M.C. Glazer: They thought I had killed their friend. They were going to drive me out into the desert. If they let me out of the trunk at all, they would pump me full of bullets. If I was lucky.

My only chance: to convince them I hadn't killed Jenk. The only way to do that—and even that was a long shot—was to tell them who *had* killed Jenk and make them believe it. It would be the acting job of my life.

I quieted my head. I beat back my panic, searching for stillness.

Think. Think. Think.

In the darkness of that trunk, I hallucinated that I could see a faintly glowing outline floating in my vision; a man's face. He was the Murderer. Could be a She, but I had to forget about Tyra. I already knew she didn't fit, and these two cops would, too. If I started spouting off a theory they knew was bullshit, I would be dead.

Who had killed Jenk? Why had he died?

Because he killed Serena, my mind suggested.

That was possible, I thought, gulping at the air, trying not to pant, because I wouldn't be able to stop. *The high school flame never stopped burning. Serena decided to break things off with Jenk for good and remake her life—Life Anonymous—and he wasn't ready to let her go.*

But that wouldn't help me. It would look like I killed Jenk for vengeance. Besides, Jenk wouldn't have called me if he had killed Serena. What sense did that make? He would have stayed as far away from me as possible.

Another possibility burrowed up from my unconscious:

Maybe Jenk died because he KNEW who killed Serena.

The heat in the trunk was cooking my face, chafing my lungs. I realized I wouldn't last an hour, never mind a day.

Still, I struggled not to lose my train of thought: *Jenk called me the day he died because he knew M.C. Glazer hadn't killed Serena—and he knew who had.*

I could hear it in his voicemail message, the strange inflections that had intrigued me at the time. And the way he'd stared at me when I started asking about Serena at Club Magique. *He knew.*

If Lorenzo and DeFranco did it, why else except at M.C. Glazer's bidding? And if not Glazer or Tyra, then who else could have done it?

The car jounced wildly, turning off the paved road at a high speed. My head slammed against the top of the trunk, waking up the old pain. White spots filled my vision. For a while, my mind was only soup, thoughtless.

I'm going to get my Bronze Man, Serena whispered in my ear.

Think. Think. Think. Think.

"Who killed you?" I said aloud, to anchor my thoughts to my own voice. "If I can say who killed you . . . I can figure out who killed Jenk."

Who benefited from Serena's death?

Not M.C. Glazer. He had his own empire, and Serena wasn't even competition: She'd been more an actress than a rapper for years, ever since Shareef died.

Not Tyra. Her only livelihood, as far as I could see, was pretending to be her sister. Now that Afrodite was dead, work would dry up. And as stormy as the sisters' relationship had been, Tyra couldn't bet on inheriting much from Serena. Tyra was nothing without her sister.

Not Devon Biggs, whose investment in Serena had bottomed the moment she stopped breathing. Even if Biggs turned out to be the big winner from Serena's estate, wouldn't she have been worth more to him alive than dead? Unless . . .

What about JENK? You have to tell them who killed JENK.

The car jounced again, and my body was assaulted by pain. The back of my scalp felt damp and heavy, and I didn't know if it was blood or perspiration. The throbbing started at the back of my head and traveled through all my nerves to my gut, which answered with a sour throbbing of its own. I was racked in the cycle of pain.

That time, I couldn't pull myself out of it.

Think. Think. Think. Thi—

In that last second before I passed out again, I realized how wrong I had been.

At last, I knew.

✦✦✦

Ice-cold liquid on my face woke me up with a yell.

Sour beer dribbled into my mouth. I couldn't see anything for all the light.

"Wake up, Sleeping Beauty," Lorenzo said in that same measured monotone, dousing me with another swing from his beer can. My whole body jumped at the shock. "We're not finished with you just yet. Not by a long fucking way."

Finally, I saw Lorenzo above me, bathed in light. A crowbar on his shoulder.

He had promised me a painful death. I remembered that. Just my luck to finally meet someone in Hollywood who keeps his promises.

"Man, *I didn't kill your friend!*" I said. "I can prove it. Just let me—"

"Time to be quiet now," Lorenzo said. He sounded bored.

My body braced for a blow from the crowbar. When Lorenzo grabbed a handful of my hair, I tried to thrash my head away. The next thing I saw was a leather gag with a red plastic ball, something from a sex shop.

My words were my last chance.

I struggled, kicking in the trunk. "*I know who—*"

My tongue was stilled by the weight of the gag, my mouth pulled wide and useless by the two-inch rubber ball. Lorenzo yanked the strap hard. My mouth was so taut it hurt. My lips and tongue felt like they were being ripped apart.

Lorenzo held his hand up to his ear, leaning over. "You were saying?"

Domination. Humiliation. Lorenzo wouldn't just kill me: He would enjoy it.

Where was I? I tried to see around me, but the sun and beer attacked my eyes. I was half-blind. I was running out of reasons not to panic. All I had left was my dignity.

Lorenzo and DeFranco grabbed me, and I bucked and flailed as they pulled me out of the trunk and tossed me on the ground. The left side of my face skidded into rubble. I tasted bitter dirt in my mouth. I coughed, and my tongue's paralysis made me feel like I was choking. I writhed on the ground, gasping for air.

Panic always comes, in the end.

"Oh, yeah, it's gonna be a long day for you," Lorenzo said. He swung his leg around again, and it sank into my abdomen.

I could forget about breathing. I bit into the ball, my gasps muffled.

"I knew Jenk since I was nineteen, you piece of shit," Lorenzo said. I heard him walking around me, out of my spotty vision. I tried to crawl away from him. "He was the best man at my wedding. I'm married to his stepsister. Did you know that?"

"Stupid fuck," DeFranco said.

Two armed men, my hands behind me, and I was already disoriented. But even if you die, you have a choice of dying fighting and scheming and trying to take the bastards with you . . . or you can cry and beg and plead. I had hoped words might mean something, that I might live if they knew I hadn't killed Jenk. But that option was gone. There was no option except death, now. But I wasn't going out like a punk.

They were going to remember Tennyson Hardwick.

As Lorenzo raised the crowbar, I arched my back, bucked up, braced my shoulders and cuffed hands on the ground, and thrust my right heel squarely into his balls. I felt the contact, didn't need to see the reaction, because I was already pivoting, tearing the flesh on my hands, kicking at DeFranco. He could have shot me, but instinct forced him to drop his free hand to cover his groin. Unfortunately for him, it was a feint. My left foot hit his right knee, skidding that leg back so that he pitched forward. My right foot, fresh from Lorenzo's groin, caught him squarely, beautifully, on the side of the head. It was the kick of a lifetime, and his eyes crossed, the switchboard in his brain momentarily short-circuited.

Now Lorenzo was dropping to his knees, gagging. DeFranco reeled, looking for balance. This was the only moment I was going to have.

I rolled to my knees and sprang forward, head-butting Lorenzo in the face hard enough for my vision to explode with stars. He tumbled over backward, sprawling in the sand, his split lips a gory mess. Tightening my stomach muscles, I exhaled all the air I could, making my midsection as tiny as possible as I slid my cuffed wrists down over my hips, then over my heels . . .

Bound or not, my hands were in front of me now. Despite the pain, I felt the corners of my mouth bend up into a feral, humorless grin. Any chance is better than none.

I rolled back to my knees and looked up in time to see DeFranco swinging his gun at my head like a club. But the game had changed now. I rolled with the blow, caught his wrist with the chain between my wrists, and twisted out and down. DeFranco screamed as his arm torqued at the shoulder, and he drove face-first into the ground.

And now, we were both holding that damned gun, our fingers tangled together. I knew five ways to wrest it away from him. Another second, and I'd have the gun. I could see the moves in my mind: I would tear it from his hands and pivot, shooting Lorenzo. *Back to DeFranco, and drop him. Find the cuff key, the car key—*

Lorenzo rose, dazed. I watched the sick shock in his face as he realized that despite the fact that he and his partner had held all the cards, he was too late. I had him, was dragging DeFranco's arm and pistol up to aim—

And that was as far as I got. The very chain that had ensnared DeFranco's wrist kept him tangled to me, his dead weight slowing my turn. I cursed into my gag, yanking at him, but some barely conscious part of his cop mind understood the implications of a perp disarming an officer, and he clawed and clung at me. I pulled DeFranco in and smashed his face with my knee, then turned—

Or tried to. I heard a *thwump* sound, and my back exploded in pain, a gash ripping across my shoulder blades. I yelled and rolled away. My hearing faded. I only heard my heaving breaths, struggling past the gag. My nostrils pinched shut.

Lorenzo was a shadow over me, and I saw the crowbar raised high. I thrust out to try to scissor his legs with my own, and missed. He was still reeling, but he snarled.

"I'm gonna take my time with you, asshole," Lorenzo said.

Thwump. The crowbar caught my ribs this time. I felt bones break.

The gag swallowed my cry. All the strength, all the adrenal desperation, all training, discipline, and hope drained away. I thrashed on the rocky ground like a beached fish, digging my shoulders into the dirt to try to move away from Lorenzo before he could beat me to death. My ribcage screamed, nearly paralyzing me with each stabbing breath. Someone kicked me in the groin, and it was almost a relief not to be struck in the ribs again. Almost.

My vision cleared, and I thought I was hallucinating again: Above me, I saw mammoth towers with rotating propellers, as if we were on a space station on alien terrain. The blades were spinning as if we could all take off in flight. Was I staring at the final fantasies of a cooling brain?

We were at the windmills.

Thwump. The crowbar took a bite out of my leg, just above the knee. I grunted into the gag. My mind spun with lines from my mother's favorite poem: *When will the wind be aweary of blowing Over the sky? / When will the clouds be aweary of fleeting? / When will the heart be aweary of beating?* Alfred Lord Tennyson, of course.

I'm sorry, Dad.

Now I know what my last thoughts might have been.

Another kick to my abdomen. Everything melted away. Black.

Then, another shock of cold. More beer in my face.

Laughter and an idling car, a roaring dragon in my ear.

"Oh, *shit*," I heard M.C. Glazer say. He hooted. "I don't *believe* it."

"Told you we'd put a smile on your face." Lorenzo.

"Hey, man—we knew you wouldn't want to miss a minute of *this* party." That was DeFranco.

The pain was dizzying. I needed a doctor. But that was the least of my problems.

I blinked, trying to see past the stinging beer and the light. Grinning teeth. M.C. Glazer's face slowly emerged above me, leaning over to get a good look. He smelled like rum. He was fascinated.

"Man, what happened here? Ya'll look fucked *up*!"

"So he knows some Jackie Chan," DeFranco said, breathing heavily and wiping blood from his face. "Didn't mean much, did it?"

"This looks like some hardcore S&M shit," Glazer said. "You tied him like Zed in *Pulp Fiction*, man. Ya'll been taking turns? Just so you don't get it twisted—the only bitches I fuck are bitches."

Glaze howled with mirth, and after another moment of steadying themselves, Lorenzo and DeFranco laughed along. Two other men laughed from the silver Hummer I saw parked on the other side of me, although the laughter sounded nervous.

An audience for the execution.

"What I tell you? They're cold-blooded," Glaze bragged to the men in the Hummer. "They got badges, but they still step up. Just like Jenk."

"He killed a cop," Lorenzo said, planting his foot on my chest. "Got to be this way. Otherwise, you know what happens. Lawyers. Trial. Fuck that. He killed Jenk."

"Always wanted to get my hands on a cop killer," DeFranco said.

I thrashed, moaning against my gag. *I DIDN'T KILL HIM. LET ME TELL YOU WHO DID IT.* I was not going gently into that good night.

"How y'all know he killed Jenk?" one of the men in the Hummer called out. Was he just curious, or did I suddenly have an advocate?

Glaze looked at me again, and I tried to claw into his eyes for his attention. "What's he saying?" Glaze said.

" 'Hail Mary, full of grace,' " Lorenzo said. More laughter.

Call it instinct or hysteria, but I had an inspiration: I laughed, too. I tried to pull my lips into a smile. I laughed again, more loudly; a real laugh this time, an invitation to insanity. When Glazer looked at me, I mumbled against my gag. Then, I laughed again.

M.C. Glazer couldn't resist. "You want to talk to me, fool?" he said.

I bucked. *TAKE THIS THING OFF ME.*

Maybe Glazer was curious. Maybe he just wanted to hear me beg.

"Man, take that shit out his mouth," Glaze said. "Nobody's gonna hear him way out here." He kneeled above me. "You like it out here in the windmill forest? You see where cops with badges can take you? Cops are the *shit*, man. You gotta pull over if they tell you. They walk around strapped. They're gods among men. They're my army. Afrodite didn't have no army. Afrodite wasn't nothing. Afrodite didn't have no Grammys. She never had nothin' except a Black Music Award, punk. You're about to die over some bullshit trick." His rant sounded almost frantic; he was high on adrenaline. Or something.

I felt yanking behind my head, and suddenly the ball was out of my mouth. I spat, sucked air, thought I'd never tasted anything so delicious in my life. Lorenzo slapped my face with the leather harness, reminding me where I was. I might have cracked one of his front teeth. God, I hoped so. I fervently wished him a long, slow root canal.

I steadied myself: the next words out of my mouth might very well be the last. *"YOU DIDN'T KILL AFRODITE,"* I choked.

"Tell me some shit I don't already know," Glaze said. "Where Chela at?"

I saw Lorenzo and DeFranco exchange a look, but neither of them spoke. DeFranco shoved his hands in his pockets, impatient, but Lorenzo didn't move.

I ignored Glaze this time, looking for Lorenzo's eyes. It almost hurt to look at him, but my instincts told me to forget about Glaze: Lorenzo was the one to negotiate with. My mind ran away from me with thoughts so quicksilver I could barely grab them.

I have to get my Bronze Man. Take him where he belongs.

"Devon Biggs killed Afrodite," I told Lorenzo. "Your man Jenk, too."

I was no longer as certain as I'd been in the trunk, but Biggs was my best shot.

"Who the hell is Devon Biggs?" Lorenzo said. At least he was listening.

Glaze stood over me and spat down on my face. I hardly felt it land on the river of sweat on my cheek. "Tell me where that little bitch is, or my boys will shoot your balls off one at a time."

The cops were covering for Chela. If I could drive a deeper wedge between the cops and Glaze, I *might* have a chance. Jenk was the key.

"Biggs told me Glaze killed Afrodite," I gasped to Lorenzo. "He told me to go to the club that night. Jenk knew something. I could tell as soon as I said Afrodite's name. That's why Jenk called me the day he died. That's why my card was in his car. He warned me I was after the wrong guy. He told me to back off, or I'd get hurt."

"The man was a prophet," M.C. Glazer said.

"He was trying to help me," I said. *"He knew who killed her, and he died for it."*

Glaze kicked me in the face, catching me just beneath my jaw. "Where's Chela?"

I'd rolled with it, but still bitten my tongue, enough to bleed. With my hands now in front, I might have blocked, maybe even gotten my hands on his ankle. But fighting wasn't going to get me out of this—talking might. I had to go on; the pain was only going to get worse, not better. Again, I looked for Lorenzo, praying he would hear me. His eyes were riveted. His crowbar was on his shoulder again, not waving above me.

"Jenk and Afrodite had a high school thing," I gasped. "He loved her. He boosted her up when she was just starting out. He told her to go out on her own."

"That triflin' ho dissed Jenk day and night," Glazer said.

Go on, Lorenzo's eyes said.

"But Jenk didn't kill her," I said. "It was Biggs. Afrodite was leaving Biggs behind, and he wouldn't let her go . . ." The shadowy figure I'd hallucinated in the trunk seemed to appear again, this time with Biggs's face. I tried to see through his eyes.

There's a story that during the filming of *Marathon Man*, Dustin Hoffman showed up on-set disheveled and unshaved. "Dear boy! What's the matter?" Laurence Olivier said, distressed. Hoffman explained that he had been up all night, really working to get into the mental state of his tortured, tormented character. Olivier stared at him. "Haven't you ever heard of *acting?*"

Well, what Hoffman was doing, the Konstantin Stanislavsky or Lee Strasberg school of "Method" acting, has influenced generations of actors, including Paul Newman and Marilyn Monroe. And me. I'd taken lessons at the Strasberg Institute, where they hammered at my ego, seeking to drive me deep enough to release the spiritual essence of acting. Seemed a little woo-woo to me, but there had been times I felt so close to a character that his trials and suffering became my own. I could feel myself being swallowed by the fiction.

In the desert north of Palm Springs, I slipped into that space again, allowing everything I knew about Devon Biggs to collapse together into a critical mass, and to my vast surprise, it exploded back out into clarity, light, and hope.

I'll be damned.

"Stuff that gag back," Glaze said. "He talks too damn much."

I lunged away, my knees scrambling in the gravel. *"B-Biggs was her pimp, and she wanted to be free."* Suddenly, I remembered visiting Biggs's office, seeing Afrodite's music awards on display. Was the statue I'd seen bronze? It was possible. It might be a bronze figure of a man; it had looked like an Oscar. What had Biggs's alibi been? He was working late at his office, making calls.

Serena had called Tyra after business hours to say she was going to get her Bronze Man. *Was that why Tyra seemed to be toying with me? Did she know all along that Serena went back to the office to get that statue?*

"Afrodite went to her office to get her Black Music Award. Biggs was there, but he lied and told me he didn't see her that night. But Tyra knows he did. He hit Serena on the head. She died of blunt force trauma." The scene played itself in my mind like a memory. Biggs on the phone, Serena surprising him in his office. A fight.

Lorenzo straddled me with the gag, but he was listening. His eyes were all I had.

"He killed her, and Tyra knew all along," he said. "Ask her. Serena called Tyra right before she died. She told me."

"What the *fuck* does that have to do with Jenk?" Lorenzo snapped the leather.

The story and scenes in my mind, so real before, faded. Facts scattered. In my nanosecond of silence, Lorenzo reached around my head with the gag.

I bobbed my head away. *"Tyra was sleeping with Jenk!"* I blurted.

"True that," called one of the men in the Hummer. They sniggered. Lorenzo wavered above me. "So?"

"Tyra told him what Biggs did. She knew as soon as her sister was dead." *But she didn't go to the police. And Jenk didn't go after Biggs. But Biggs was wearing Kevlar. He knew he was in danger, and not from M.C. Glazer. He was afraid of Jenk. You saw it in his eyes when you mentioned Jenk's name.*

But why didn't they go to the police? What did they gain by keeping quiet?

"It was a shakedown!" I said. "Tyra knew if Biggs died—or if they went to the cops—there's no money. She could fight for her sister's estate, but why fight? Jenk could help her intimidate Biggs into paying big money to keep quiet."

DeFranco searched out Lorenzo's gaze. DeFranco could *see* it.

I was talking so fast, spittle and blood flew out of my mouth. "Biggs didn't want to pay. I say he brought a satchel of bills, and Jenk turned his back to count. Biggs shot him, and Jenk never saw it coming. Jenk didn't think Biggs would have the balls—they'd known each other since they were kids." I held Lorenzo's eyes with my own. "Biggs shot your friend, man. Tyra knows, but she's not talking because she still wants a payoff. *It wasn't me.* I've never killed anybody, much less a cop. My *dad* was a cop. I was at the wrong place at the wrong time, trying to get payback for Serena. *Biggs killed both of them.*"

At the end, I was so breathless that my voice was a hoarse whisper. I felt like I hadn't tasted water in a year.

"Could be that guy shot Shareef, too, huh?" one of the men in the truck mused, and my heart danced. I'd sold him. Had I sold anyone else?

A gasp, and I went on. "When Afrodite started to blow up in movies, maybe Biggs got rid of Shareef so he could have her all to himse—"

"Put the gag *back*," Glazer said, cutting me off.

Lorenzo yanked my head back, against my struggles. *"I DIDN'T KILL JENK—"*

And my mouth was gone again. I bit into the rubber ball, yelling to be heard. Otherwise, I could barely move. All strength had flown.

M.C. Glazer laughed. Doubled over, his hand pressed to his mouth. He pointed at me. "Aw, shit . . . You know what? I gotta hand it to him, man—he nailed that shit. I'm listening to him saying, 'Damn. He's got that bitch Tyra *figured out.*' "

My heart stopped in midflight. What was he saying?

Lorenzo wiped blood from his mouth, his eyes suddenly sharp and focused on Glaze. "What do you mean?" Lorenzo said, in the measured tone he reserved for me.

M.C. Glazer held his hands out, a *You got me* pose. "This fool didn't kill Jenk."

"Say *what?*" DeFranco said, cocking his head and rubbing his ear.

"*My diffen ill Ink!*" I screamed around the ball. They couldn't understand me, but they got the gist.

"Naw, man, he's right," Glaze said. "Tyra was pissed off and crying after Jenk got shot. She told me Biggs did it, the shakedown, all this shit. I decided to take care of Biggs myself, but Biggs and this fool here both got nine lives. Dead men walking. Tyra says now that I got his attention, I should lay off Biggs until she gets paid—which is why he's breathing to this day. But not for long."

I could barely register the words. Holy shit. I was *right?*

"And you knew who killed Jenk. She told you," Lorenzo said, standing up straight. His spine unfolded one vertebra at a time, snakelike. "But you kept this shit to yourself."

Glaze pointed at me, his face tight with rage. "This motherfucker broke in my house, *tied me up*, and stole my girl."

"Yeah. Your fourteen-year-old girl." Lorenzo's voice was low, mild.

Glazer started almost as if Lorenzo had slapped him. "Shit," he said, changing tactics. "He stole my *phone!* You don't get to live after fucking with M.C. Glazer."

DeFranco's face, already puffy from my efforts to escape, swelled with anger. "Oh, I get it. You're pissed off at this guy, so you take us along for the ride. We'll find him faster if we think he killed Jenk."

The windmills whirred on as usual, but the wind was changing direction. Gusts of tension stirred around me, in everything and everyone, including the two guys sitting quietly in the Hummer. This was a secluded place. Guilty or innocent, bad things happened where people couldn't see.

Glaze shrugged, sounding apologetic. Like me, he knew he needed to talk to Lorenzo. "Nothing personal, man. Y'all can still take Biggs down. Fuck Tyra and her money. You think I was gonna let Jenk go down without payback? Shit, I tried to take him myself. That's what you don't understand about me: I think outside the box. But now that you got *this* fool . . ."

Glaze swung his leg around, and this time his sneaker landed at the hinge of my jaw. I couldn't roll my head back fast enough: If he'd been wearing boots, he'd have taken my head off. The world tried to melt into blackness, but I blinked to hang on. ". . . I'm gonna get Chela back. And he's gonna learn why you don't fuck with M.C. Glazer."

Lorenzo took two steps away from me. I watched him, praying fervently, and God answered me right away: He dropped his crowbar.

"No." It was a simple word, but it seemed to part the skies, a non-negotiable declaration strong enough to power the windmills whirring above us.

"No, *what?*" Glaze said.

"I'm here for Jenk. *Punto.* I'm not a hitman."

"Yeah, it's not like that, Glaze," DeFranco said, sounding sheepish.

Glaze blinked. "Jenk would have done it."

Lorenzo's face flexed. The taunt had hurt, but not necessarily in the way Glazer had intended. "I ain't Jenk," he said. "I got kids."

"Internal Affairs is already on our asses," DeFranco said. "It's one thing if we got the fuck-face who killed Jenk, but . . ."

Glaze didn't know what to say. He glanced toward his Hummer, seeking counsel from his boys. Not a word. No sound except the mills harnessing the wind. Five men alone in the desert, voting on whether I would live or die.

"So, wait," Glaze said to Lorenzo. "You think you're just gonna walk away and he won't say shit about you dragging his ass out here?"

Lorenzo squatted above me. His eyes crushed me beneath their weight. "I think he'd be smart, that's what I think. His word against ours. He broke into your house, held you at gunpoint. That's assault and unlawful detention. That's a lot of time."

I nodded, blinking to let him know I heard him. *I can't even SPELL trouble, man.*

"I can't believe you've gone pussy like that on me," Glaze said.

My prayers of thanks were cut short when Glaze reached around and pulled out his own gun. Another Smith & Wesson. The nickel flashed Morse code in the sun.

Glaze aimed at me, turning the gun sideways the way actors do in ghetto Godfather epics. *He doesn't know anything about guns. Maybe he's never shot anyone.* Even as my life spiraled down the drain, my mind wouldn't give up hope.

Glaze cocked his head so he could stare down the barrel, fixing his gaze at the center of my head while he bit his lip. He could taste it now. I felt his heartbeat's acceleration as he sat at the edge of the Thing that had fascinated a certain type of man since the beginning of time: *How does it feel to kill someone?*

Lorenzo and DeFranco stared at Glazer. Neither of them moved or spoke.

"Kiss my foot, fool," Glazer barked at me.

My eyes were locked with his. He could kill me. Beat me. He could take my life, but only I could give him my dignity. I tried to find Lorenzo's eyes again, but he wouldn't look at me.

A shot boomed, and for an instant I thought I was dead. The bullet kicked up a dust cloud three feet to my left. The smell of sulfur clogged my nostrils.

"Bitch, you better do it."

M.C. Glazer's trigger finger itched, trembling. I heard a tiny voice in my head: *Do it. It's just kissing leather. And then they'll laugh, and you will live . . .*

I just couldn't. Everything swayed as dizziness rocked me. My ribs were on fire. Gagged and bleeding, I stared at my killer. I looked at his eyes, not his feet.

M.C. Glazer smiled at me with a kind of faraway rapture. He was ready.

I closed my eyes then. The panic was gone. I was empty.

I heard the steady, beating wind. The wind massaged my face and ears. They say the windmills near Palm Springs provide electricity to a hundred thousand homes, and I was glad to be in a powerful place. I could feel the world's heart beating above me. Beneath me. Inside me.

I remembered the way my father's eyes shone the last time I saw him, when he knew his son needed him. I thought about Chela and April, somewhere safe. Alive.

And I heard Serena's voice, one last time:

Come on, Ten. I'm taking my Bronze Man home.

It's all right to die. It really is.

A time comes when there's nothing more you can do. Just close your eyes. Say good-bye.

NINETEEN

"PUT THE FUCKING GUN DOWN, GLAZE."

At first, I didn't believe I'd really heard Lorenzo's voice anywhere except my mind, but his order triggered a flurry of motion. When I opened my eyes, Lorenzo and DeFranco both had their guns drawn, trained on M.C. Glazer. The doors to the Hummer flew open, and Glazer's two men fell out, one of them leveling a shotgun at DeFranco. Lorenzo had moved smoothly, placing Glazer between him and the buckshot. His right arm was straight as a rifle stock, his left cupping the weapon, elbow bent in a modified Weaver stance. No matter what went down, M.C. Glazer was an obit.

Glazer stood frozen, as stunned as I was. But he didn't drop his gun.

Lorenzo balanced his gun with both arms for accuracy. Glazer whipped the gun at Lorenzo, and a shotgun cartridge jacked into place from the Hummer. DeFranco spun, aiming his sidearm at the guy with the sawed-off.

It was a miracle no one was dead yet.

"Get away from Glaze, man," the shotgunner said in a husky voice, trying hard not to sound as scared as he had to be. The stock shook against his shoulder.

Lorenzo never took his eyes off Glazer. Neither Lorenzo nor Glazer made a move to lower his gun. Aiming to kill each other, and neither flinched. "Mo?" Lorenzo called to the man with the shotgun, almost casually. "This shit's got nothing to do with you. I'm LAPD, and you do *not* want to shoot me."

"You better have a magic bullet, Mo," DeFranco said to Shotgun, crouching. Aimed and ready to fire.

"I never thought I would live to see *this* shit," M.C. Glazer said. But I was still staring down the barrel of his S&W.

Lorenzo took a single, deliberate step toward Glaze. "You want to live another minute? Put that fucking gun down. There is no part of me bullshitting you."

Glazer sneered. "You're fired, man. No more VIP pussy for your broke ass."

"I'm counting to three, Glaze," Lorenzo said. "One . . ."

Glazer didn't wait for *two*. He threw his gun to the ground, where it skittered behind a dry, ragged bush that looked as tired as I felt.

"You too, Mo," DeFranco said. "Don't throw it. Lay it on the hood."

Lorenzo and DeFranco sounded like cops again.

"What's this?" Glaze said. "Some kind of entrapment bullshit?"

Lorenzo shook his head. He lowered his gun, but didn't holster it. "You're cool, Glaze, and you've been good to me. But I'm not gonna piss my life away over a whore and a phone. No disrespect intended. We came out here for Jenk."

"We still love the pussy, man," DeFranco said, as if he hoped to negotiate.

Glaze gave them a contemptuous look. "I miss Jenk already."

"Not like I do," Lorenzo said. His voice was raw.

Glazer walked past me and gave me one last shot, a solid punch to the face that whipped my head around and sprayed blood on the sand. I was already hurting so much that the pain didn't bother me, but it pissed me off. I hate getting hit in the face.

"Used to be pretty, didn't you, motherfucker?" Glaze said.

And he walked to his Hummer.

As Glazer drove off with his music blaring, a cloud of dust climbed over me in the Hummer's wake. Lorenzo yanked the gag out of my mouth and held my hair so my head would be steady enough to meet him at eye level. Maybe I was about to pass out.

"What happened to you, sir?" His eyes told me not to say anything stupid.

"I walked into a hotel room, and somebody hit me over the head."

"What did you see?"

I swallowed blood. Coughed. "I didn't see shit. I think a couple of heroes saved my ass, though."

"We were never here."

"Never got a good look. S-sorry about your friend."

Lorenzo searched my face for a while. His lips were puffy, and blood filmed his teeth. He sucked at one of them, winced . . . and smiled, nodding. Our business was finished. "He looks like he needs a doctor, huh, DeFranco?"

"He's jacked up," DeFranco agreed.

Lorenzo grabbed me beneath my armpits, pulling me to my feet as if I were weightless. He was used to carrying heavy loads. "While we're riding over to the hospital, I want to hear more about Devon Biggs . . ."

Biggs killed Serena. Biggs killed Jenk.

It wasn't just a story in my head.

Arguing for my life, I'd wondered if my story was more fantasy or reality— but it felt so real now that I didn't know how I hadn't seen it before. It was impossible to tell one piece of misery from another that day—I was in agony, yet numb—but I felt more grief than anger. I had a concussion, two broken ribs, probably a broken nose, and severe dehydration, but my mind kept looping back to Dorothea Biggs.

First chance I got, I was going to call my father's friend, Hal Dolinski.

Dorothea's son would need protective custody when he went to jail.

I spent three days in the hospital, and I could have stayed three weeks. April was good enough to keep Chela with her—and Chela was grateful enough to do anything I asked of her—so for three days I didn't have anything to think about except how much I hurt from one end of my body to the next.

I'd almost died over nothing. I'd treated my life carelessly. And like anyone who's tasted what dying feels like, I vowed never to play peek-a-boo with death again.

Madness.

And I'd done it for Serena; to put her to rest. To put *me* to rest.

I was still sorry I never had my Friday night date with Serena. She'd been ready to make changes in her life, and I'd been ready to make changes in mine. It's the stuff of Hollywood: right place, right time.

Sometimes, you meet too soon. Or too late. Or both.

After my first one, Lieutenant Nelson never returned my phone calls. When he heard my theory about Devon Biggs, even as I urged him to interrogate Tyra, he'd sounded noncommittal and hung up before I thought he'd gotten my point.

But my last night in the hospital, I got a visitor I wasn't expecting. It was after visiting hours, but like M.C. Glazer said, you can go anywhere with a badge.

Detective Hal Dolinski stood at the foot of my bed, wearing a classic desk-jockey rumpled shirt and slacks that don't fit quite right. He looked like a man who wished he'd retired five years ago, fifty pounds overweight and walking with a slouch he probably hadn't noticed. I remembered how big he'd seemed when I was young, and felt jarred. When it came to ass-kicking, Lorenzo and DeFranco were nothing compared with Father Time.

"You're lucky to be alive, kid," Dolinski said. The look on his face told me I wouldn't want to use a mirror for a long time.

"I got a pretty bad bump on my head," I said. The bandages across my nose made me sound muffled. Gagged.

Dolinski laughed. "Yeah, right. Some kind of bump. Bumped *off*, you mean."

A part of me almost laughed, but I couldn't. Funny wasn't in my vocabulary yet.

Dolinski waited for me to fill in the blanks during the silence. When I didn't, he finally said, "If you file charges, we'll get you protection."

My insides cinched. "I was hoping this was a social visit."

Dolinski shrugged. "We've been after these guys for a while, Ten."

I resented being leaned on in a hospital bed, but cops are cops.

"What guys?" I said. I said it like I meant it.

Dolinski sighed and nodded. He knocked the pile of fast-food wrappers off the chair at my bedside and took a seat, pulling the chair close. "That's the way it always is, Ten," he said. "Nobody wants to talk. I'm not saying I'd do it any different . . ."

"I'm not sure I catch what you're talking about, Detective."

"But there are bad people out there. Preach knows. Cops have to carry that around, and it's hard on the body. It sucks years out of you. But you're trying to do something good in the world. If you're not, you've got no business with a badge."

His speech was moving, but the man had no idea how deaf my ears were to any conversation that involved trying to prosecute Carlos Lorenzo and Paul DeFranco. They had almost killed me; I had almost killed them. Then they had saved my life, their every Palm Springs action motivated by the same thing: a strange sense of honor that had nothing at all to do with what was legal or even what was right.

Even if there was no come-back, I just wouldn't rat them out. Some of my loyalties are . . . complicated.

"What goes around comes around, Ten," Dolinski said.

"I'm less and less clear on your meaning, Detective."

"People ask me all the time about these rap murders. Tupac, Shareef. Everybody says, 'How come nobody got arrested?' " The detective's frustration splotched his ears. "It's easy as pie: Nobody will talk, that's why."

"Or nobody listens when they try."

Dolinski pinched the bridge of his nose. He nodded again, stiffly, as if his neck hurt. "You know I had to ask."

"That's what a good cop does."

Dolinski gave me another few seconds to have a change of heart. Then he clapped his hands, grinning. Our social visit began. "We've got him," he said.

"Who?"

"Devon Biggs. He surrendered yesterday. Press conference will be in time for the nightly news cycle. Not even a week, and it's closed. We owe you, Ten."

I wished I had heard it from Lieutenant Nelson, but it was nice to hear gratitude from someone at LAPD.

"What's the evidence?"

Dolinski laid it out for me: Blood in Biggs's office. A strand of hair caught at the base of the bronze statuette. Blood on Biggs's phone. *Looks like the sonofabitch kept making calls even after she was dead, probably so he could seal his alibi.* Detergent residue on Serena's skin. Blood on a laundry cart from Biggs's building. *They figure he rolled her out of the office in the cart, to the parking garage.* Blood in Biggs's car.

Once the police knew where to look, the truth was impossible to ignore.

"He killed her, no question," Dolinski said. "It looks like what you said— they were fighting over the damn statue. They were alone, things got out of hand. Doesn't feel like premeditation. It was a dumb-ass move to kill her in his office."

"He didn't know she was coming." I was sure of that.

How could Biggs keep going to work day after day, knowing what he had done? That was one cold, tightly wrapped little man.

Dolinski went on: "They haven't been so lucky pulling together a case on Jenk, but they will. For now, closing Afrodite is a huge boost. We needed some good damn news. All the talking heads get to powder up and go on CNN." He slapped my shoulder harder, his eyes twinkling. Good old Uncle Hal.

"What's the surprise?" he said. "Like father like son, right?"

It was the nicest thing anyone had ever said to me.

While the name *Devon Biggs* raced over the national news, claiming its place in music history, I tried to pull my life together a piece at a time. In the process, I was buried in paperwork.

April found me a family law attorney.

Marcela found me a practical nurse.

I was building a home.

Devon Biggs tried to call me at least once a day. His messages were always frantic but polite, but I never picked up or listened to what he had to say. The sound of his voice awoke rage I didn't have time for. Devon Biggs was buried in a hole that went straight through the center of me. I wanted to forget he existed.

But like I told Serena the last time I saw her, you don't get to do what you want.

A week and four days after I ran into Serena at Roscoe's, I finally checked my mail at my rented mailbox. Just as I had expected, it had piled up. Mr. Niyogi walked out with me to my car to help me carry a box of letters and bills, since I was on crutches. I wasn't supposed to walk at all, but I've never been good at lying around the house.

Most of the mail was junk; I'd been pegged a sucker for every course, every seminar, every miracle "insider" tip sheet on How to Make It in Hollywood.

I pawed through, looking for checks and bills, the only mail I care about. Everything was due at once, but two residual checks from *Malibu High* made me smile. Six thousand dollars was a good haul for work I'd done ten years ago. I had decided to chuck the rest of the mail when an envelope marked CASANE-GRA PRODUCTIONS caught my eye, buried at the bottom.

Only curiosity made me open it. I still had one question for Devon Biggs: *How could you?*

The letter was on plain typing paper. Handwriting filled the page; careful and elaborate, with flourishes on the Ys unmistakably feminine. And familiar.

The letter electrocuted me. I was sitting at my kitchen table, but I felt like I had lost my mind in the desert after all.

It's from Serena.

Serena hadn't dated it, but there was only one day the letter could have been sent.

Dear T—

What a trip seeing you again after all this time! You were a sight for sore eyes—and I mean that in every way. They say God sends angels in many forms—ha, ha. I am writing the "old-fashioned" way because I don't trust email. Remember people can read your email without you knowing. I know I don't have to say it, but this letter is just for me and you. I am shocked at myself for writing to you, but I guess it boils down to how you have always treated me like a lady. I know that was an act before, but I don't think it was an act today—and I am looking forward to some more of that jerked goat or whatever you made for me that time in Negril.

Ten, you're the only man who's never raised his voice at me. Isn't that sad? If it's not an act and you are someone I can trust, maybe we will see each other again soon. But you may not want to see me after what I'm about to tell you. You might be the only one I can trust my secrets to.

After half a glass of water, I read on.

A long time ago a girl named Reenie started out her life the wrong way. She didn't speak up for herself and she put herself down. She believed she only had one thing to offer, and that the only way she could find any great-ness in the world was through the greatness of others. And she went along with things she shouldn't have, afraid to make a change.

Five years ago, I made a change, and someone I knew didn't like it. I guess I always knew deep down, but he was playing an act with me, trying to be what he thought I wanted, but underneath he was like a vampire. Charming and sweet, but always sucking until one day there's nothing left. I started talking to my pastor, and I was seeing through his games. I was not the same person I was when I met him. I had grown up.

I started Casanegra Productions so I could have something of my own. 'Pac and I talked about movies and the Hollywood thing. He understood the importance of being freed from bad influences, and even then, he knew it was going to cost him.

When I was ready to start Casanegra, this person I knew acted like he was fine with it, but he had jealousy in his heart, so he had too much to drink one night and got violent. He had never been physically violent before—only with his words. Ten, he tried to rape me. It was the most confusing moment of my life. I can't tell you how much that hurt my heart. But when you are attacked you act on instinct and I had to fight him. I felt blessed when I saw the gun he'd put on the counter before he pulled his pants down.

I have killed a man. I shouldn't even write those words on paper.

My sadness gave way to shock. I had thought Serena was describing her complex relationship with Devon Biggs. *Five years ago?*

Shareef.

Serena had killed *Shareef?* The world spun. The three children posing by the Impala in the photo in Devon Biggs's office had been blown to bloody pieces. That car might as well have been wired with a bomb on a timer.

I hope God will forgive me, but I got scared and only made it worse so no one would ever know what happened. I was more worried about Afrodite than Reenie, so I went the selfish route. I used a friend to help me with details, and I know that took him farther from his salvation after I'd tried to help him walk a straighter path for years. I feel so bad most of all because the man who died was like family to me.

It was the beginning of a nightmare. I confided in someone else I thought was a friend, and in his heart I don't think he ever could forgive me. He changed toward me. He used the secret over me, and I made decisions concerning my career that I would not have made otherwise. When we argued, he said he would tell what I did and tear my name down, so I always shut up. I knew I was paying the price for what I had done.

But I can't live with the lie anymore. And I can't be a prisoner. You are right when you say we have to do what we have to do. I have to stop being Reenie and stop being Afrodite and be Serena for once. Once this secret is out in the world, no one will have power over me but me. So now you can see there is a reason I ran into you today. You always knew how to make me see only the best in myself.

You will probably hear some things about me on the news. If you are wondering if the story is true, well, now you know what happened. I will have a legal fight to stay out of jail, but it is in God's hands now.

If you still want to talk to me, call me any time. I will need a friend.

S.

TWENTY

I WENT TO SEE DEVON BIGGS the same day I got Serena's letter.

Biggs had been denied bond. The judge considered him a flight risk; maybe because he was a multimillionaire, but probably because he had killed a cop. Even a bad cop is still a cop. Dolinski arranged to have Biggs sent to a solitary cell away from anyone Lorenzo and DeFranco could hire or bribe.

I looked everywhere except Biggs's eyes. Orange wasn't Biggs's color. His jailhouse jumpsuit was too big on him. His hair was growing out around his bald spot, uneven and uncombed. His hands played nervously with the fabric of his clothes.

Biggs was lucky I'd taken his beating for him. And he was lucky there was glass between us to prevent me from passing it on to its rightful owner.

"Shit," Biggs said when he saw me. "I didn't know they would come down on you, Hardwick. Sorry, man."

If he had asked me here for apologies, this visit would take more time than I had; my painkillers wore off in three hours, and I might be civil until then. Devon Biggs couldn't make up for what he had done. He couldn't even begin to undo it.

"Watch what you say to me," I said. "I'll tell every word in court."

"You just remember what I told you in Reenie's apartment. Remember?"

"Some bullshit about doing what's best for Serena?"

"I loved her," Biggs said. "She was my sister."

"I should have let you burn in that fire." My civility ran out.

Biggs didn't blink. "I should have pulled the trigger in that closet. I almost did."

"What stopped you?"

"I couldn't do it."

"A fuckup to the end."

Biggs sighed. "I'm worried about my mama. I'm worried somebody's gonna drive by and hurt her to get to me. Mama's so stubborn."

"What's that got to do with me?"

"You're a bodyguard, aren't you?"

"Try the Yellow Pages."

"Man, she likes you," Biggs said, glassy-eyed. "She'll trust you."

I shook my head. Even if I wanted the work, I was in no condition for it. I needed time to heal. "I'll talk to her," I said, staring Biggs in the eye. "I'll tell her there are dangerous people where you least expect to find them."

"I loved Reenie, man."

The painkiller was wearing off early. I had a monstrous headache, and my ribs, leg, and back were competing for my attention, too. I found Serena's letter in my back pocket, unfolded it, and pressed it to the glass where Biggs could see it. He leaned forward. His eyes dashed across the lines as he read faster and faster. He kept leaning closer, until his nose nearly pressed against the glass.

"I see how you loved Serena," I said.

Biggs sat back, assessing me. I might as well have had a gun in my hand. "Where'd that come from?"

"My mailbox. She mailed it after she saw me. Before she went back to the office to get the Black Music Award you were too greedy to share with her."

"It wasn't like that," Biggs said. "She was trying to take my shit. She was gonna fire me and lock me out of my own office so I couldn't get in. *My* office!"

"That happens sometimes," I said.

"I didn't mean to . . ."

"Bullshitting on the phone while she was lying dead in your office. I know."

"Nobody in their right mind wants to go to jail, Hardwick. No matter what."

"Some of us want to go less than others."

I was ready to leave. If Biggs didn't have sense enough not to talk to me, I would have the sense not to waste my time with him. I stood, and Biggs bolted to his feet, panicked. "Wait," Biggs said. "How much?"

"What?"

"The letter," he said. "How much for it? A million? Five. I'll set you up."

"Like you set up Jenk?"

"You think that sociopath would have let me live?" If Jenk was anything like his friends—and he might have been worse—Biggs was right. "How much? Don't be a fool. You'll be a millionaire by the end of the day, man. All your hopes and dreams."

I don't mind admitting it: I thought about it. I've always wondered what six zeros would look like in my bank account. I could add on a wing to my house, put Chela through college, and travel again. Money makes life go down smoother.

"Destroying the letter won't clear you," I told Biggs.

"Fuck that. I got lawyers working on that."

"Then why do you want it?"

Biggs pushed his palm up against the glass, a pleading gesture. "Don't go out trashing Reenie, man. Don't tell anybody about Shareef." He whispered the last word.

"She thought you would tell."

"I couldn't have done that. Shareef fucked up that night." Biggs's eyes said we shared one mind.

Shit. Shareef Pinkney, Serena Johnston, Devon Biggs: three children posing by an Impala, and with their summer Popsicles on Dorothea Biggs's porch. Two dead in body, one in soul. It had happened for nothing. Someone could have defused the bomb before it disintegrated their world. I didn't know everything, but I knew that.

I folded the letter again and put it back in my pocket. "What's past is past," I said. "You're the only person I'm showing Serena's letter to."

I didn't buy that Biggs was only worried about Serena's legacy, but his face seemed to melt with relief.

"They looked at the tape," Biggs said suddenly. A sick smile crawled across his face. "Serena's videotaped will?"

"So are you set for life now?" I said. "Or is that thirty to life?"

Biggs blinked. His eyes shone with a manic light. "Reenie gave me a lil' bit, just a token. She left the rest of it to only one person. Everything. Almost thirty million."

This was the part where I was supposed to guess who.

"Tyra?" I said. I don't know how I knew. I just did.

Biggs shook his head. "Fucking bitch. There's no justice in this world."

At least that was one thing we could agree on. Without another word, I left Devon Biggs to contemplate injustice on his own. I couldn't stand the sight of him.

I've often wondered what it felt like to be Tyra Johnston the day she stared into her sister's eyes as the probate court played that damned tape. Tyra had no way to thank Serena. No way to take back the past. Even thirty million wouldn't soothe that sting.

I hope she chokes on every penny.

I keep Serena's letter somewhere safe. From time to time, I read her words again and remember what almost happened between us.

As for Shareef, I don't feel bad about the speculation and conspiracy theories; some of the theories are crazy, and some of them are standing right on top of the truth. I read somewhere that a college in New York offers a course called "The Music and Murder of Shareef." But Devon Biggs and I are the only two people who know. He won't talk, and neither will I.

Murders go unsolved every day.

Dad's first day at my house was rocky. He felt too confined in the guest room, where I'd made the preparations for him, so his bulky hospital bed ended up in the living room, in front of the sofa. Chela would have to watch TV in her room upstairs, which used to be my gym. I had already given up possession of my bedroom TV to her. I didn't recognize my own home anymore.

I felt crowded and overwhelmed. I was still hobbling around on a codeine diet, and now I was responsible for two other people in my house. Even with help from April and the new nurse, who left at six, I was exhausted by the end of the day.

While April and Chela made a racket cooking something that didn't smell very promising in the kitchen, I sat on my sofa beside Dad's bed and stared at the TV.

The People's Court, of course. He was waiting for the ruling.

I looked at Dad's face, trying to decide if he would get better or worse. His color was good; his cheeks seemed a little fuller than the week before. And even though he didn't talk to me much, I'd overheard him talking to Chela—and his speech seemed better, too.

Maybe those two would be good for each other. Chela had already offered to bathe him for me—if I paid her, of course. But it was money well spent. The thought of bathing him was too much to bear, for now. But I would soon. I knew that already.

And it would be OK.

The commercial came on. "You want something to drink, Dad?" I said.

To my surprise, my father wasn't paying attention to the television set; just as I'd been looking at him, he was examining me, too. I could see my injuries in his eyes.

"It's not as bad as it looks," I said.

Without a word, he reached out his knobby hand toward me. I froze at first, not sure what he wanted. "Your pen?"

My father shook his head.

I understood. I slipped my hand into his, where it nestled, a perfect fit. We clung to each other's fingers for a long time, maybe the longest I can remember. From his bed, Dad was peering down the same tunnel I'd glimpsed in the desert. We understood something most people didn't. One day, life just stops.

But we were still here, for now. Both of us.

"Welcome home, Dad," I said.

My father smiled.

Dad didn't mind when I excused myself to eat at the table with Chela and April. The television was better company now that he wasn't alone.

Dinner was Hamburger Helper and an iceburg lettuce salad drowned in Thousand Island dressing. I ate to be polite, but I didn't have an appetite even if the food had been more inspired. I could see I was going to have to do the cooking.

"How was school?" I asked Chela.

For two days, Chela had been attending the nearest public school—which, it turns out, is one of the best in the county. Based on her Minnesota test scores and transcripts, she placed in tenth grade, so I sent her to the ninth-grade classes for the last few weeks just so she could get back in the habit. There was nothing else for her to do.

"It was retarded," Chela said. "The school year's almost over."

"You said you liked your drama class."

"Yeah, and that's like one hour out of *six*."

It was good to hear her talking, even if she only opened her mouth to complain. Chela was much quieter since Palm Springs, and she'd never been a big talker. She said she hadn't been raped—DeFranco had only been taunting me—but I knew there was more to the story. Her eyes tuned me out every time I tried to bring up that day, and she refused to go to a hospital to put my worries to rest. She didn't know it yet, but I'd made her an appointment for an AIDS test. I wanted that worry put to rest, too.

After that, a child therapist. Hell, maybe a family counselor. I didn't know who, but I knew I would find one. We both needed all the help we could get, if we were going to live together.

"I'm done," Chela said, leaping from her chair, which scraped on the floor. She'd hardly touched her plate either, no better than my effort.

Across the room, Dad called out loudly: "*May . . . I . . . be . . . excuuuuused?*"

Chela rolled her eyes. Her sneakers squeaked on my Mexican tile as she turned back to me, her eyes on the ceiling and her hand on her hip. "May I be excused . . . please?"

"Don't do your homework with the TV on," I said. Chela complained that I was always telling her what to do, but I couldn't help it; especially with Dad so close by.

Chela gave me a look that said *Don't push your luck*. Then the expression shifted, deep and soft. I always knew when Chela was remembering how I offered my life for hers. Her eyes fell away from mine. "G'night, April," she said over her shoulder.

April smiled, glad to be included. Chela still sometimes seemed to forget that April was in the room. "Thanks for helping with dinner, hon," April said.

Chela shrugged. Instead of going past the wine rack or my stairs, she walked around to the living room. I saw her lean over Dad's bed and kiss his forehead. "G'night, Captain," she said.

"*Good . . . night.*"

Because my leg was still hurting, April did the dishes. The nursing tendency I'd first seen when we met at the alley on Sunset hadn't let up since Palm Springs; April was definitely making it her business to take care of me.

But she wouldn't start sleeping over. Not yet. We had both agreed on that. The reasons were many, but let's just say that April and I both understood there would be more harmony in the house all around if she wasn't sharing my bed at night.

More than half the bottle of Gaja had been sitting on my kitchen counter for a week, with a silver stopper to plug it. The flavor wouldn't be as fresh, but Gaja was Gaja. As April finished the dishes, I picked up the bottle of wine and two glasses.

Dad was still watching TV. Silently, I motioned April.

Toward the screening room.

April smirked and tiptoed behind me. We were sneaking around my father. Apparently, I was back in high school, too.

This time, we didn't look at the footage of Serena. We just sat on the carpet in the near darkness, lighted by the blue movie screen, and enjoyed each other's company. It was a challenge to carve out time in the day for April, even when she was right there.

"I can't stop thinking about it," April said. I didn't have to ask what *it* was. No matter how hard we tried, Serena was still just beneath the surface. Serena had brought us together, and we hadn't yet broken free; April and I talked about Serena and Devon Biggs a little every day. "Childhood friends. It just seems so sad."

It was sadder than April knew, but a secret was a secret.

April sank her hand against my cheek, one of the few spots free of pain. "I can go get my mirror out of my purse, if you're ready," she said.

"I'm in no hurry." Maybe I would face a mirror in a week, but not before then. I might need plastic surgery for my nose. I wouldn't be the first.

"You're still beautiful, you know." April's voice wasn't teasing.

"Not like you," I said.

"Scars show what we've been through, Ten. You've lived through a lot."

"Why don't you kiss me and make it better?"

April and I sat on the floor and kissed. She didn't hug me—too much contact with my ribs—but my mouth was happy to take any punishment April Forrest had to offer. I couldn't do anything except sit up against the wall, but that was enough to receive the gift of her sweet, soft lips and tongue.

April's tank top came off. She closed her eyes while my fingers played across her breasts. Her breasts filled my hands, warm and waiting. She still tasted like gardenias.

My groin throbbed, and not in a good way. I'd been badly bruised in the desert, and I hissed when pleasure gave way to pain. I groaned, pulling away. April kissed my forehead. "It's all right, Ten," she said. "We'll take it slow."

I didn't know if I could ever recapture the elation I felt leaving Serena's house the day she died, expecting to see her again soon. I hoped my heart hadn't buried itself somewhere I wouldn't find it again, the way it probably had since my mother died.

But it was an extraordinary thought, enough to keep my spirit from drowning in the awfulness of Serena's death: *Am I ready for April?* I might be. Like she said, we should take it slow; wait for the pain to subside. Pain ebbs and flows. Who knows?

This might be the beginning of a beautiful friendship.

ACKNOWLEDGMENTS

To God; though many will choose not to understand why this book was written, I thank YOU for granting me the understanding that we are all flawed, damaged, and fall short of your Glory. Like Tennyson Hardwick, our central figure, many have drifted from their true calling and yearn to find themselves. Often, the journey is not as politically correct as some would like and sometimes the journey is sordid, dark, and even erotic. Nonetheless, the odyssey must be embarked upon for one to discover and embrace the peace that lies within each of us.

Tananarive Due and Steven Barnes, your genius runs deep and wide. You are inherently decent and profoundly gifted, and it has been my extreme honor to collaborate with you on this, our first installment on the life and times of Tennyson Hardwick. *Casanegra* has become a dream realized because of you both. I learn from you and am perpetually inspired by your abilities to delve into the infinite depths of your imagination.

Several years ago, while sitting in the Simon & Schuster office of Judith Curr, our publisher, I gazed up at her bookshelves that stretched toward the ceiling and noticed two authors that I admired and respected, Tananarive Due and Zane. I admired Zane because, through her astounding success in the erotic fiction world, she had completely shattered the misconception that African Americans would never be interested in romance novels, much less purchase them in record numbers. Zane, I will forever owe you a debt of gratitude.

While pondering the insatiable appetite of the audience that is constantly searching for characters and worlds that embody the genuine desires and aspirations of black folk, I was reminded of a character that I was initially meant to portray on the silver screen. Though that project has been relegated to the graveyard of neglected dreams, I've never forgotten the fascinating complexities and contradictions of a character who aspires to moral correctness yet sells his body—eventually his soul—and ultimately languishes in moral ambiguity.

I thought: Who better to collaborate with than the eloquent and brilliant team of Tananarive Due and Steven Barnes? You are both accomplished, exciting, and celebrated novelists. Because of you, Tennyson Hardwick is a living, breathing human being who leaps from the pages into the hearts, minds, and, yes, souls of our readers.

To my wife, Desiree, your contribution to this erotic, murder mystery is more than I can or should put into writing. Thank you, girl, for so much, well, inspiration . . . enough said.

To my family, Col. Frank and Marilyn Underwood; Frank Jr.; Marlo; Jackson; Mellisa; my little miracles, Paris, Brielle, Blake; my cousin Lynne Andrews, who keeps things flowing; all of my nieces, nephews, and friends, too many to name, thank you for always encouraging me to dream. By consistently grabbing life by the horns and embracing the joys of the world around us, every one of you stimulate and motivate me daily.

Ron West, my manager, thank you for never saying, "you can't." We started as such, years ago, and we remain on the same page today.

Lydia Wills, your insight and expertise are absolutely invaluable and I am honored to have you on the team. In addition, you simply redefine the word "cool."

To everyone at The Paradigm Talent Agency, many thanks for taking the reigns and for taking the ride with me on my many endeavors.

Mark J. Wetzstein; Eric Suddleson; Patti Felker and the gang at Nelson, Felker, Toczek and Davis: thank you for always going the distance for me.

Lee Wallman, what can I say, "you're priceless." Thank you for always being ready to roll and for going down the path with me, even when it may lead to White Castle.

Malaika Adero, I cannot thank you enough for shepherding, now, our second book together. You are an incredible editor to work with and I hope to continue this partnership for many years to come.

Judith Curr, heartfelt thanks to you for, once again, believing in my vision and for seeing the extraordinary potential in such a novel as this. Every author should be blessed with as much support and encouragement from his publisher as you have given us.

And to the team and staff at Atria Books at Simon & Schuster, God bless you and thank you for all of your hard work on *Casanegra: A Tennyson Hardwick Story*.

We've only just begun!

—Blair Underwood

Thanks, first, to our readers, for taking a chance on something new. We are so excited to offer our first novel-length collaboration, a process that is almost worthy of a book unto itself. Writing *Casanegra* lived up to all of the clichés about peak moments: It was sometimes frustrating, always challenging, and never boring. In the end, it not only brought us closer together as a married couple, it also helped us become better writers. What a blessing!

Thanks to Blair Underwood, a friend who called one day back when we were living in Longview, Washington, and first planted the seed of what would later become this collaboration. Aside from his talents as an actor and producer, Blair is one of those few rare souls who is exactly what he seems to be at first glance: gracious, smart, and kind. It has been a joy working with you, Blair.

At Atria Books, thanks to Malaika Adero, for believing so earnestly in both the potential and the vision of *Casanegra*. Also, thanks to Judith Curr and Krishan Trotman.

Thanks to our literary agents, John Hawkins and Moses Cardona of John Hawkins & Associates, and Eleanor Wood of Spectrum Literary Agency. Thanks, too, to our film agents, Michael Prevett of the Gotham Group, and Jonathan Westover of the Gage Group. And many thanks to our attorney, Richard Solomon.

For advice and assistance, thanks to Darryl Miller, reader and editor extraordinaire. Thanks also to L. A. Banks, for those lovely conversations in Antigua. For his insights into L.A.P.D., thanks to retired Lieutenant George Johnson for his time and memories. Readers who are curious about the purported L.A.P.D. connection to the murders of rappers Tupac Shakur and Biggie Smalls should read *LAbyrinth* by Randall Sullivan.

Many thanks to Guru Cliff Stewart for his insights into the bodyguard profession, as well as his masterful knowledge of an incredible range of martial arts disciplines. We would also like to thank M.O., J.C., H.R., and the others who gave us a working understanding of sex workers: the call girl/male escort professions. We omit their names not from lack of appreciation, but from a desire to protect their privacy.

Eternal love and gratitude to Tananarive's parents, John Due and Patricia Stephens Due.

Thanks most of all to Jason and Nicki, for tolerating a household headed by two writers.

—Tananarive Due and Steven Barnes